CATRIONA

CATRIONA

*Being memoirs of
the further adventures of
David Balfour
at home and abroad
in which are set forth his misfortunes anent the Appin murder,
his troubles with Lord Advocate
Grant: captivity on the Bass Rock,
journey into Holland and France,
and singular relations with James
More Drummond or Macgregor, a
son of the notorious Rob Roy, and
his daughter Catriona: written by
himself, and now set forth by*

ROBERT LOUIS STEVENSON

KÖNEMANN

🐌 Notes (on pp. 289 to 314)
   are keyed thus in the margin

© 1996 for this edition
Könemann Verlagsgesellschaft mbH
Bonner Straße 126, D–50968 Köln

Series editor: Michael Hulse
Volume editor: Iain Galbraith
Cover design: Peter Feierabend
Layout and typesetting: Birgit Beyer
Printed in Hungary
ISBN 3-89508-258-9

CONTENTS

DEDICATION

TO CHARLES BAXTER
Writer to the Signet

My dear Charles,

It is the fate of sequels to disappoint those who have waited for them; and my David, having been left to kick his heels for more than a lustre in the British Linen Company's office, must expect his late re-appearance to be greeted with hoots, if not with missiles. Yet, when I remember the days of our explorations, I am not without hope. There should be left in our native city some seed of the elect; some long-legged, hot-headed youth must repeat today our dreams and wanderings of so many years ago; he will relish the pleasure, which should have been ours, to follow among named streets and numbered houses the country walks of David Balfour, to identify Dean, and Silvermills, and Broughton, and Hope Park, and Pilrig, and poor old Lochend—if it still be standing, and the Figgate Whins—if there be any of them left; or to push (on a long holiday) so far afield as Gillane or the Bass. So, perhaps, his eye shall be opened to behold the series of the generations, and he shall weigh with surprise his momentous and nugatory gift of life.

You are still—as when first I saw, as when I last addressed you—in the venerable city which I must always think of as my home. And I have come so far; and the sights and thoughts of my youth pursue me; and I see like a vision the youth of my father, and of his father, and the whole stream of lives flowing down there far in the north, with the sound of laughter and tears, to cast me out in the end, as by a sudden freshet, on these ultimate islands. And I admire and bow my head before the romance of destiny.

R. L. S.

Vailima, Upolu,
Samoa, 1892.

PART I

THE LORD ADVOCATE

CHAPTER I

A Beggar on Horseback

The 25th day of August, 1751, about two in the afternoon, I, David Balfour, came forth of the British Linen Company, a porter attending me with a bag of money, and some of the chief of these merchants bowing me from their doors. Two days before, and even so late as yestermorning, I was like a beggarman by the wayside, clad in rags, brought down to my last shillings, my companion a condemned traitor, a price set on my own head for a crime with the news of which the country rang. Today I was served heir to my position in life, a landed laird, a bank-porter by me carrying my gold, recommendations in my pocket, and (in the words of the saying) the ball directly at my foot.

There were two circumstances that served me as ballast to so much sail. The first was the very difficult and deadly business I had still to handle; the second, the place that I was in. The tall, black city, and the numbers and movement and noise of so many folk, made a new world for me, after the moorland braes, the sea-sands, and the still countrysides that I had frequented up to then. The throng of the citizens in particular abashed me. Rankeillor's son was short and small in the girth; his clothes scarce held on me; and it was plain I was ill qualified to strut in the front of a bank-porter. It was plain, if I did so, I should but set folk laughing, and (what was worse in my case) set them asking questions. So that I behoved to come by some clothes of my own, and in the meanwhile to walk by the porter's side, and put my hand on his arm as though we were a pair of friends.

At a merchant's in the Luckenbooths I had myself fitted out: none too fine, for I had no idea to appear like a beggar on horseback; but comely and responsible, so that servants should respect me. Thence to an armourer's, where I got a plain sword, to suit with my degree in life. I felt safer with the weapon, though (for one so ignorant of defence) it might be called an added danger. The porter, who was naturally a man of some experience, judged my accoutrement to be well chosen.

"Naething kenspeckle," said he; "plain, dacent claes. As for the rapier, nae doubt it sits wi' your degree; but an I had been you, I would hae waired my siller better gates than that." And he proposed I should buy winter hosen from a wife in the Cowgate-back, that was a cousin of his own, and made them "extraordinar endurable."

But I had other matters on my hand more pressing. Here I was in this old, black city, which was for all the world like a rabbit-warren, not only by the number of its indwellers, but the complication of its passages and holes. It was indeed a place where no stranger had a chance to find a friend, let be another stranger. Suppose him even to hit on the right close, people dwelt so thronged in these tall houses, he might very well seek a day before he chanced on the right door. The ordinary course was to hire a lad they called a , who was like a guide or pilot, led you where you had occasion, and (your errands being done) brought you again where you were lodging. But these caddies, being always employed in the same sort of services, and having it for obligation to be well informed of every house and person in the city, had grown to form a brotherhood of spies; and I knew from tales of Mr. Campbell's how they communicated one with another, what a rage of curiosity they conceived as to their employer's business, and how they were like eyes and fingers to the police. It would be a piece of little wisdom, the way I was now placed, to tack such a ferret to my tails. I had three visits to make, all immediately needful: to my kinsman Mr. Balfour of Pilrig, to Stewart the Writer that was Appin's agent, and to William Grant, Esquire of Prestongrange, Lord Advocate of Scotland. Mr. Balfour's was a non-committal visit; and besides (Pilrig being in the country) I made bold to find the way to it myself, with the help of my two legs and a Scots tongue. But the rest were in a different case. Not only was the visit to Appin's agent, in the midst of the cry about the Appin murder, dangerous in itself, but it was highly inconsistent with the other. I was like to have a bad enough time of it with my Lord Advocate Grant, the best of ways; but to go to him hot-foot from Appin's agent was little likely to mend my own affairs, and might prove the mere ruin of friend Alan's. The whole thing, besides, gave me a look of running with the hare and hunting with the hounds that was little to my fancy. I determined, therefore, to be done at once with Mr. Stewart and the whole Jacobitical side of my business, and to profit for that purpose by the guidance of the porter at my side. But it chanced I had scarce given him the address, when there came a sprinkle of rain—nothing to hurt, only for my new clothes— and we took shelter under a pend at the head of a close or alley.

Being strange to what I saw, I stepped a little farther in. The narrow paved way descended swiftly. Prodigious tall houses sprang up on each side and bulged out, one storey beyond another, as they rose. At the top only a ribbon of sky showed in. By what I could spy in the windows, and by the respectable persons that passed out and in, I saw the houses to be very well occupied; and the whole appearance of the place interested me like a tale.

I was still gazing, when there came a sudden brisk tramp of feet in time and clash of steel behind me. Turning quickly, I was aware of a party of armed soldiers, and, in their midst, a tall man in a great-coat. He walked with a stoop that was like a piece of courtesy, genteel and insinuating: he waved his hands plausibly as he went, and his face was sly and handsome. I thought his eye took me in, but could not meet it. This procession went by to a door in the close, which a serving-man in a fine livery set open; and two of the soldier-lads carried the prisoner within, the rest lingering with their firelocks by the door.

There can nothing pass in the streets of a city without some following of idle folk and children. It was so now; but the more part melted away incontinent until but three were left. One was a girl; she was dressed like a lady, and had a screen of the Drummond colours on her head; but her comrades or (I should say) followers were ragged gillies, such as I had seen the matches of by the dozen in my Highland journey. They all spoke together earnestly in Gaelic, the sound of which was pleasant in my ears for the sake of Alan; and though the rain was by again, and my porter plucked at me to be going, I even drew nearer where they were, to listen. The lady scolded sharply, the others making apologies and cringing before her, so that I made sure she was come of a chief's house. All the while the three of them sought in their pockets, and by what I could make out, they had the matter of half a farthing among the party; which made me smile a little to see all Highland folk alike for fine obeisances and empty sporrans.

It chanced the girl turned suddenly about, so that I saw her face for the first time. There is no greater wonder than the way the face of a young woman fits in a man's mind, and stays there, and he could never tell you why; it just seems it was the thing he wanted. She had wonderful bright eyes like stars, and I daresay the eyes had a part in it; but what I remember the most clearly was the way her lips were a trifle open as she turned. And whatever was the cause, I stood there staring like a fool. On her side, as she had not known there was any one so near, she looked at me a little longer, and perhaps with more surprise, than was entirely civil.

It went through my country head she might be wondering at my new clothes; with that I blushed to my hair, and at the sight of my colouring it is to be supposed she drew her own conclusions, for she moved her gillies farther down the close, and they fell again to this dispute where I could hear no more of it.

I had often admired a lassie before then, if scarce so sudden and strong; and it was rather my disposition to withdraw than to come forward, for I was much in fear of mockery from the womenkind. You would have thought I had now all the more reason to pursue my common practice, since I had met this young lady in the city street, seemingly following a prisoner, and accompanied with two very ragged indecent-like Highlandmen. But there was here a different ingredient; it was plain the girl thought I had been prying in her secrets; and with my new clothes and sword, and at the top of my new fortunes, this was more than I could swallow. The beggar on horseback could not bear to be thrust down so low, or, at the least of it, not by this young lady. I followed, accordingly, and took off my new hat to her, the best that I was able.

"Madam," said I, "I think it only fair to myself to let you understand I have no Gaelic. It is true I was listening, for I have friends of my own across the Highland line, and the sound of that tongue comes friendly; but, for your private affairs, if you had spoken Greek, I might have had more guess at them."

She made me a little, distant curtsey. "There is no harm done," she said, with a pretty accent, most like the English (but more agreeable). "A cat may look at a king,"

"I do not mean to offend," said I. "I have no skill of city manners; I never before this day set foot inside the doors of Edinburgh. Take me for a country lad—it's what I am; and I would rather I told you than you found it out."

"Indeed, it will be a very unusual thing for strangers to be speaking to each other on the causeway," she replied. "But if you are landward bred it will be different. I am as landward as yourself; I am Highland, as you see, and think myself the farther from my home."

"It is not yet a week since I passed the line," said I. "Less than a week ago I was on the braes of Balquhidder."

"Balwhither?" she cries. "Come ye from Balwhither? The name of it makes all there is of me rejoice. You will not have been long there, and not known some of our friends or family?"

"I lived with a very honest, kind man called Duncan Dhu Maclaren," I replied.

"Well, I know Duncan, and you give him the true name!" she said; "and if he is an honest man, his wife is honest indeed."

"Ay," said I, "they are fine people, and the place is a bonny place."

"Where in the great world is such another?" she cries; "I am loving the smell of that place and the roots that grow there."

I was infinitely taken with the spirit of the maid. "I could be wishing I had brought you a spray of that heather," says I. "And though I did ill to speak with you at the first, now it seems we have common acquaintance, I make it my petition you will not forget me. David Balfour is the name I am known by. This is my lucky day, when I have just come into a landed estate, and am not very long out of a deadly peril. I wish you would keep my name in mind for the sake of Balquhidder," said I, "and I will yours for the sake of my lucky day."

"My name is not spoken," she replied, with a great deal of haughtiness. "More than a hundred years it has not gone upon men's tongues, save for a blink. I am nameless, like the Folk of Peace. Catriona Drummond is the one I use."

Now indeed I knew where I was standing. In all broad Scotland there was but the one name proscribed, and that was the name of the Macgregors. Yet so far from fleeing this undesirable acquaintancy, I plunged the deeper in.

"I have been sitting with one who was in the same case with yourself," said I, "and I think he will be one of your friends. They called him Robin Oig."

"Did ye so?" cries she. "Ye met Rob?"

"I passed the night with him," said I.

"He is a fowl of the night," said she.

"There was a set of pipes there," I went on, "so you may judge if the time passed."

"You should be no enemy, at all events," said she. "That was his brother there a moment since, with the red soldiers round him. It is him that I call father."

"Is it so?" cried I. "Are you a daughter of James More's?"

"All the daughter that he has," says she: "the daughter of a prisoner; that I should forget it so, even for one hour, to talk with strangers!"

16

Here one of the gillies addressed her in what he had of English, to know what "she" (meaning by that himself) was to do about "ta sneeshin." I took some note of him for a short, bandy-legged, red-haired, big-headed man, that I was to know more of, to my cost.

"There can be none the day, Neil," she replied. "How will you get 'sneeshin' wanting siller? It will teach you another time to be more careful; and I think James More will not be very well pleased with Neil of the Tom."

"Miss Drummond," I said, "I told you I was in my lucky day. Here I am, and a bank-porter at my tail. And remember I have had the hospitality of your own country of Balquhidder."

"It was not one of my people gave it," said she.

"Ah, well," said I, "but I am owing your uncle at least for some springs upon the pipes. Besides which, I have offered myself to be your friend, and you have been so forgetful that you did not refuse me in the proper time."

"If it had been a great sum, it might have done you honour," said she; "but I will tell you what this is. James More lies shackled in prison; but this time past, they will be bringing him down here daily to the Advocate's..."

"The Advocate's?" I cried. "Is that...?"

"It is the house of the Lord Advocate Grant of Preston-grange," said she. "There they bring my father one time and another, for what purpose I have no thought in my mind; but it seems there is some hope dawned for him. All this same time they will not let me be seeing him, nor yet him write; and we wait upon the King's street to catch him; and now we give him his snuff as he goes by, and now something else. And here is this son of trouble, Neil, son of Duncan, has lost my fourpenny-piece that was to buy that snuff, and James More must go wanting, and will think his daughter has forgotten him."

I took sixpence from my pocket, gave it to Neil, and bade him go about his errand. Then to her, "That sixpence came with me by Balquhidder," said I.

"Ah!" she said, "you are a friend to the Gregara!"

"I would not like to deceive you either," said I. "I know very little of the Gregara and less of James More and his doings, but since the while I have been standing in this close, I seem to know something of yourself; and if you will just say 'a friend to Miss Catriona' I will see you are the less cheated."

"The one cannot be without the other," said she.

"I will even try," said I.

"And what will you be thinking of myself?" she cried, "to be holding my hand to the first stranger!"

"I am thinking nothing but that you are a good daughter," said I.

"I must not be without repaying it," she said. "Where is it you stop?"

"To tell the truth, I am stopping nowhere yet," said I, "being not full three hours in the city; but if you will give me your direction, I will be so bold as come seeking my sixpence for myself."

"Will I can trust you for that?" she asked.

"You need have little fear," said I.

"James More could not bear it else," said she. "I stop beyond the village of Dean, on the north side of the water, with Mrs. Drummond-Ogilvy of Allardyce, who is my near friend and will be glad to thank you."

"You are to see me then, so soon as what I have to do permits," said I; and, the remembrance of Alan rolling in again upon my mind, I made haste to say farewell.

I could not but think, even as I did so, that we had made extraordinary free upon short acquaintance, and that a really wise young lady would have shown herself more backward. I think it was the bank-porter that put me from this ungallant train of thought.

"I thoucht ye had been a lad of some kind o' sense," he began, shooting out his lips. "Ye're no' likely to gang far this gate. A fule and his siller's shune parted. Eh, but ye're a green callant!" he cried, "an' a veecious, tae! Cleikin' up wi' baubee-joes!"

"If you dare to speak of the young lady..." I began.

"Leddy!" he cried. "Haud us and safe us, whatten leddy? Ca' a leddy? The toun's fu' o' them. Leddies! Man, it's weel seen ye're no very acquaint in Embro!"

A clap of anger took me.

"Here," said I, "lead me where I told you, and keep your foul mouth shut!"

He did not wholly obey me, for though he no more addressed me directly, he sang at me as he went in a very impudent manner of innuendo, and with an exceedingly ill voice and ear—

"As Mally Lee cam doun the street, her capuchin did flee,   ♪
She cuist a look ahint her to see her negligee.
And we're a' gaun east and wast, we're a' gaun ajee,   ♪
We're a' gaun east and wast courtin' Mally Lee."

CHAPTER II

The Highland Writer

Mr. Charles Stewart the Writer dwelt at the top of the longest stair that ever mason set a hand to; fifteen flights of it, no less; and when I had come to his door, and a clerk had opened it, and told me his master was within, I had scarce breath enough to send my porter packing.

"Awa' east and wast wi' ye!" said I, took the moneybag out of his hands, and followed the clerk in.

The outer room was an office with the clerk's chair at a table spread with law-papers. In the inner chamber, which opened from it, a little brisk man sat poring on a deed, from which he scarce raised his eyes upon my entrance; indeed, he still kept his finger in the place, as though prepared to show me out and fall again to his studies. This pleased me little enough; and, what pleased me less, I thought the clerk was in a good posture to overhear what should pass between us.

I asked if he was Mr. Charles Stewart the Writer.

"The same," says he; "and if the question is equally fair, who may you be yourself?"

"You never heard tell of my name nor of me either," said I, "but I bring you a token from a friend that you know well. That you know well," I repeated, lowering my voice, "but maybe are not just so keen to hear from at this present being. And the bits of business that I have to propone to you are rather in the nature of being confidential. In short, I would like to think we were quite private."

He rose without more words, casting down his paper like a man ill-pleased, sent forth his clerk of an errand, and shut-to the house-door behind him.

"Now, sir," said he, returning, "speak out your mind and fear nothing; though before you begin," he cries out, "I tell you mine misgives me! I tell you beforehand, ye're either a Stewart or a Stewart sent ye. A good name it is, and one it would ill become my father's son to lightly. But I begin to grue at the sound of it."

"My name is called Balfour," said I, "David Balfour of Shaws. As for him that sent me, I will let his token speak." And I showed the silver button.

"Put it in your pocket, sir!" cries he. "Ye need name no names. The deevil's buckie, I ken the button of him! And deil hae't! Where is he now?"

I told him I knew not where Alan was, but he had some sure place (or thought he had) about the north side, where he was to lie until a ship was found for him; and how and where he had appointed to be spoken with.

"It's been always my opinion that I would hang in a tow for this family of mine," he cried, "and, dod! I believe the day's come now! Get a ship for him, quot' he! And who's to pay for it? The man's daft!"

"That is my part of the affair, Mr. Stewart," said I. "Here is a bag of good money, and if more be wanted, more is to be had where it came from."

"I needn't ask your politics," said he.

"Ye need not," said I, smiling, "for I am as big a Whig as grows."

"Stop a bit, stop a bit," says Mr. Stewart. "What's all this? A Whig? Then why are you here with Alan's button? and what kind of a black-foot traffic is this that I find ye out in, Mr. Whig? Here is a forfeited rebel and an accused murderer, with two hundred pounds on his life, and ye ask me to meddle in his business, and then tell me ye're a Whig! I have no mind of any such Whigs before, though I've kennt plenty of them."

"He's a forfeited rebel, and more's the pity," said I, "for the man's my friend. I can only wish he had been better guided. And an accused murderer, that he is too, for his misfortune; but wrongfully accused."

"I hear you say so," said Stewart.

"More than you are to hear me say so, before long," said I. "Alan Breck is innocent, and so is James."

"Oh!" says he, "the two cases hang together. If Alan is out,

James can never be in."

Hereupon I told him briefly of my acquaintance with Alan, of the accident that brought me present at the Appin murder, and the various passages of our escape among the heather, and my recovery of my estate.

"So, sir, you have now the whole train of these events," I went on, "and can see for yourself how I come to be so much mingled up with the affairs of your family and friends, which (for all of our sakes) I wish had been plainer and less bloody. You can see for yourself, too, that I have certain pieces of business depending, which were scarcely fit to lay before a lawyer chosen at random. No more remains, but to ask if you will undertake my service?"

"I have no great mind to it; but coming as you do with Alan's button, the choice is scarcely left me," said he. "What are your instructions?" he added, and took up his pen.

"The first point is to smuggle Alan forth of this country," said I, "but I need not be repeating that."

"I am little likely to forget it," said Stewart.

"The next thing is the bit money I am owing to Cluny," I went on. "It would be ill for me to find a conveyance, but that should be no stick to you. It was two pounds five shillings and three-halfpence farthing sterling."

He noted it.

"Then," said I, "there's a Mr. Henderland, a licensed preacher and missionary in Ardgour, that I would like well to get some snuff into the hands of; and as I daresay you keep touch with your friends in Appin (so near by), it's a job you could doubtless overtake with the other."

"How much snuff are we to say?" he asked.

"I was thinking of two pounds," said I.

"Two," said he.

"Then there's the lass Alison Hastie, in Limekilns," said I. "Her that helped Alan and me across the Forth. I was thinking if I could get her a good Sunday gown, such as she could wear with decency in her degree, it would be an ease to my conscience; for the mere truth is, we owe her our two lives."

"I am glad to see you are thrifty, Mr. Balfour," says he, making his notes.

"I would think shame to be otherwise the first day of my fortune," said I. "And now, if you will compute the outlay and your own proper charges, I would be glad to know if I could get some spending-money back. It's not that I grudge the whole of it to get Alan safe; it's not that I lack more; but having drawn so much the one day, I think it would have a very ill appearance if I was back again seeking the next. Only be sure you have enough," I added, "for I am very undesirous to meet with you again."

"Well, and I'm pleased to see you're cautious too," said the Writer. "But I think ye take a risk to lay so considerable a sum at my discretion."

He said this with a plain sneer.

"I'll have to run the hazard," I replied.—"O, and there's another service I would ask, and that's to direct me to a lodging, for I have no roof to my head. But it must be a lodging I may seem to have hit upon by accident, for it would never do if the Lord Advocate were to get any jealousy of our acquaintance."

"Ye may set your weary spirit at rest, " said he. "I will never name your name, sir; and it's my belief the Advocate is still so much to be sympathised with that he doesna ken of your existence."

I saw I had got to the wrong side of the man.

"There's a braw day coming for him, then," said I, "for he'll have to learn of it on the deaf side of his head no later than tomorrow, when I call on him."

"When ye on him!" repeated Mr. Stewart. "Am I daft, or are you? What takes ye near the Advocate?"

"O, just to give myself up," said I.

"Mr. Balfour," he cried, "are ye making a mock of me?"

"No, sir," said I, "though I think you have allowed yourself some such freedom with myself. But I give you to understand once and for all that I am in no jesting spirit."

"Nor yet me," says Stewart. "And I give you to understand (if that's to be the word) that I like the looks of your behaviour less and less. You come here to me with all sorts of propositions, which will put me in a train of very doubtful acts, and bring me among very undesirable persons this many a day to come. And then you tell me you're going straight out of my office to make your peace with the Advocate! Alan's button here or Alan's button there, the four quarters of Alan wouldna bribe me further in."

"I would take it with a little more temper," said I, "and perhaps we can avoid what you object to. I can see no way for it but to give myself up, but perhaps you can see another; and if you could, I could never deny but what I would be rather relieved. For I think my traffic with his lordship is little likely to agree with my health. There's just the one thing clear, that I have to give my evidence; for I hope it'll save Alan's character (what's left of it), and James's neck, which is the more immediate."

He was silent for a breathing-space, and then, "My man," said he, "you'll never be allowed to give such evidence."

"We'll have to see about that," said I; "I'm stiffnecked when I like."

"Ye muckle ass!" cried Stewart, "it's James they want; James has got to hang—Alan too, if they could catch him—but James whatever! Go near the Advocate with any such business, and you'll see! he'll find a way to muzzle ye."

"I think better of the Advocate than that," said I.

"The Advocate be damned!" cries he. "It's the Campbells, man! You'll have the whole clanjamfry of them on your back; and so will the Advocate too, poor body! It's extraordinar ye cannot see where ye stand! If there's no fair way to stop your gab, there's a foul one gaping. They can put ye in the dock, do ye no' see that?" he cried, and stabbed me with one finger in the leg.

"Ay," said I, "I was told that same no further back than this morning by another lawyer."

"And who was he?" asked Stewart. "He spoke sense at least."

I told him I must be excused from naming him, for he was a decent stout old Whig, and had little mind to be mixed up in such affairs.

"I think all the world seems to be mixed up in it!" cries Stewart. "But what said you?"

I told him what had passed between Rankeillor and myself before the house of Shaws.

"Well, and so ye will hang!" said he. "Ye'll hang beside James Stewart. There's your fortune told."

"I hope better of it yet than that," said I; "but I could never deny there was a risk."

"Risk!" says he, and then sat silent again. "I ought to thank you for your staunchness to my friends, to whom you show a very good spirit," he says, "if you have the strength to stand by it. But I warn you that you're wading deep. I wouldn't put myself in your place (me that's a Stewart born!) for all the Stewarts that ever there were since Noah. Risk? ay, I take over-many: but to be tried in court before a Campbell jury and a Campbell judge, and that in a Campbell country, and upon a Campbell quarrel—think what you like of me, Balfour, it's beyond me."

"It's a different way of thinking, I suppose," said I; "I was brought up to this one by my father before me."

"Glory to his bones! he has left a decent son to his name," says he. "Yet I would not have you judge me over-sorely. My case is dooms hard. See, sir, ye tell me ye're a Whig: I wonder what I am. No Whig, to be sure; I couldna be just that. But—laigh in your ear, man—I'm maybe no' very keen on the other side."

"Is that a fact?" cried I. "It's what I would think of a man of your intelligence."

"Hoot! none of your whillywhas!" cries he. "There's intelligence upon both sides. But for my private part I have no particular desire to harm King George; and as for King James,

God bless him! he does very well for me across the water. I'm a lawyer, ye see: fond of my books and my bottle, a good plea, a well-drawn deed, a crack in the Parliament House with other lawyer bodies, and perhaps a turn at the golf on a Saturday at e'en. Where do ye come in with your Hieland plaids and claymores?"

"Well," said I, "it's a fact ye have little of the wild Highlandman."

"Little?" quoth he. "Nothing, man! And yet I'm Hieland born, and when the clan pipes, who but me has to dance? The clan and the name, that goes by all. It's just what you said yourself; my father learned it to me, and a bonny trade I have of it. Treason and traitors, and the smuggling of them out and in; and the French recruiting, weary fall it! and the smuggling through of the recruits; and their pleas—a sorrow of their pleas! Here have I been moving one for young Ardshiel, my cousin; claimed the estate under the marriage contract—a forfeited estate! I told them it was nonsense; muckle they cared! And there was I cocking behind a yadvocate that liked the business as little as myself, for it was fair ruin to the pair of us—a black mark, branded on our hurdies like folk's names upon their kye! And what can I do? I'm a Stewart, ye see, and must fend for my clan and family. Then no later by than yesterday there was one of our Stewart lads carried to the Castle. What for? I ken fine: Act of 1736: recruiting for King Lewie. And you'll see, he'll whistle me in to be his lawyer, and there'll be another black mark on my chara'ter! I tell you fair: if I but kennt the heid of a Hebrew word from the hurdies of it, be damned but I would fling the whole thing up and turn minister!"

"It's rather a hard position," said I.

"Dooms hard!" cries he. "And that's what makes me think so much of ye—you that's no Stewart—to stick your head so deep in Stewart business. And for what, I do not know: unless it was the sense of duty."

"I hope it will be that," said I.

"Well," says he, "it's a grand quality.—But here is my clerk

26

back; and, by your leave, we'll pick a bit of dinner, all the three of us. When that's done, I'll give you the direction of a very decent man, that'll be very fain to have you for a lodger. And I'll fill your pockets to ye, forbye, out of your ain bag. For this business'll not be near as dear as ye suppose—not even the ship part of it."

I made him a sign that his clerk was within hearing.

"Hoot, ye needna mind for Robbie," cries he. "A Stewart too, puir deevil! and has smuggled out more French recruits and trafficking Papists than what he has hairs upon his face. Why, it's Robin that manages that branch of my affairs.—Who will we have now, Rob, for across the water?"

"There'll be Andie Scougal, in the *Thristle*," replied Rob. "I saw Hoseason the other day, but it seems he's wanting the ship. Then there'll be Tam Stobo; but I'm none so sure of Tam. I've seen him colloguing with some gey queer acquaintances; and if it was anybody important, I would give Tam the go-by."

"The head's worth two hundred pounds, Robin," said Stewart.

"Gosh, that'll no' be Alan Breck?" cried the clerk.

"Just Alan," said his master.

"Weary winds! that's sayrious," cried Robin. "I'll try Andie, then; Andie'll be the best."

"It seems it's quite a big business," I observed.

"Mr. Balfour, there's no end to it," said Stewart.

"There was a name your clerk mentioned," I went on: "Hoseason. That must be my man, I think: Hoseason, of the brig. Would you set your trust on him?"

"He didna behave very well to you and Alan," said Mr. Stewart; "but my mind of the man in general is rather otherwise.

If he had taken Alan on board his ship on an agreement, it's my notion he would have proved a just dealer.—How say ye, Rob?"

"No more honest skipper in the trade than Eli," said the clerk. "I would lippen to Eli's word—ay, if it was the Chevalier, or

27

Appin himsel',” he added.

"And it was him that brought the doctor, wasna't?" asked the master.

"He was the very man," said the clerk.

"And I think he took the doctor back?" says Stewart.

"Ay, with his sporran full!" cried Robin. "And Eli kennt of that!"

"Well, it seems it's hard to ken folk rightly," said I.

"That was just what I forgot when ye came in, Mr. Balfour!" says the Writer.

CHAPTER III

I go to Pilrig

The next morning I was no sooner awake in my new lodging than I was up and into my new clothes; and no sooner the breakfast swallowed, than I was forth on my adventures. Alan, I could hope, was fended for; James was like to be a more difficult affair, and I could not but think that enterprise might cost me dear, even as everybody said to whom I had opened my opinion. It seemed I was come to the top of the mountain only to cast myself down; that I had clambered up, through so many and hard trials, to be rich, to be recognised, to wear city clothes and a sword to my side, all to commit mere suicide at the last end of it, and the worst kind of suicide besides, which is to get hanged at the King's charges.

What was I doing it for? I asked, as I went down the High Street and out north by Leith Wynd. First I said it was to save James Stewart; and no doubt the memory of his distress and his wife's cries, and a word or so I had let drop on that occasion worked upon me strongly. At the same time I reflected that it was (or ought to be) the most indifferent matter to my father's son, whether James died in his bed or from a scaffold. He was Alan's cousin, to be sure; but, so far as regarded Alan, the best thing would be to lie low, and let the King, and his Grace of Argyle, and the corbie-crows, pick the bones of his kinsman their own way. Nor could I forget that, while we were all in the pot together, James had shown no such particular anxiety whether for Alan or me.

Next it came upon me I was acting for the sake of justice: and I thought that a fine word, and reasoned it out that (since we dwelt in polities, at some discomfort to each one of us) the main thing of all must still be justice, and the death of any innocent man a wound upon the whole community. Next, again, it was the Accuser of the Brethren that gave me a turn of his argument; bade me think shame for pretending myself concerned in these high matters, and told me I was but a prating vain child, who had spoken big words to Rankeillor and to Stewart, and held myself bound upon my vanity to make good that boastfulness. Nay, and he hit me with the other end of the stick; for he accused me of a kind of artful cowardice, going about at the expense of a little risk to purchase greater safety. No doubt, until I had declared and cleared myself, I might any day encounter Mungo Campbell or the sheriff's officer, and be recognised, and dragged into the Appin murder by the heels; and, no doubt, in case I could manage my declaration with success, I should breathe more free for ever after. But when I looked this argument full in the face I could see nothing to be ashamed of. As for the rest, "Here are the two roads," I thought, "and both go to the same place. It's unjust that James should hang if I can save him; and it would be ridiculous in me to have talked so much and then do nothing. It's lucky for James of the Glens that I have boasted beforehand; and none so unlucky for myself, because now I'm committed to do right. I have the name of a gentleman and the means of one; it would be a poor discovery that I was wanting in the essence." And then I thought this was a Pagan spirit, and said a prayer in to myself, asking for what courage I might lack, and that I might go straight to my duty like a soldier to battle, and come off again scatheless, as so many do.

This train of reasoning brought me to a more resolved complexion; though it was far from closing up my sense of the dangers that surrounded me, nor of how very apt I was (if I went on) to stumble on the ladder of the gallows. It was a plain fair morning, but the wind in the east. The little chill of it sang in my blood, and gave me a feeling of the autumn, and the dead leaves, and dead folk's bodies in their graves. It seemed the devil was in it, if I was to die in that tide of my fortunes and for other folk's affairs. On the top of the Calton Hill, though it was not the customary time of year for that diversion, some children were crying and running with their kites. These toys appeared very plain against the sky; I remarked a great one soar on the wind to a high altitude and then plump among the whins; and I thought to myself at sight of it, "There goes Davie."

My way lay over Mouter's Hill, and through an end of a clachan on the braeside among fields. There was a whir of looms in it went from house to house; bees bummed in the gardens; the neighbours that I saw at the doorsteps talked in a strange tongue; and I found out later that this was Picardy, a village where the French weavers wrought for the Linen Company. Here I got a fresh direction for Pilrig, my destination; and a little beyond, on the wayside, came by a gibbet and two men hanged in chains. They were dipped in tar, as the manner is; the wind span them, the chains clattered, and the birds hung about the uncanny jumping-jacks and cried. The sight coming on me suddenly, like an illustration of my fears, I could scarce be done with examining it and drinking in discomfort. And as I thus turned and turned about the gibbet, what should I strike on, but a weird old wife, that sat behind a leg of it, and nodded, and talked aloud to herself, with becks and courtesies.

"Who are these two, mother?" I asked, and pointed to the corpses.

"A blessing on your precious face!" she cried. "Twa joes o' mine: just twa o' my old joes, my hinny dear."

"What did they suffer for?" I asked.

"Ou, just for the guid cause," said she. "Aften I spaed to them the way that it would end. Twa shillin' Scots: no pickle mair; and there are twa bonny callants hingin' for't! They took it frae a wean belanged to Brouchton."

"Ay!" said I to myself, and not to the daft limmer, "and did they come to such a figure for so poor a business? This is to lose all indeed."

"Gie's your loof, hinny," says she, "and let me spae your weird to ye."

"No, mother," said I, "I see far enough the way I am. It's an unco thing to see too far in front."

"I read it in your bree," she said. "There's a bonny lassie that has bricht een, and there's a wee man in a braw coat, and a big man in a pouthered wig, and there's the shadow of the wuddy, joe, that lies braid across your path. Gie's your loof, hinny, and let Auld Merren spae it to ye bonny."

The two chance shots that seemed to point at Alan and the daughter of James More, struck me hard; and I fled from the eldritch creature, casting her a bawbee, which she continued to sit and play with under the moving shadows of the hanged.

My way down the causeway of Leith Walk would have been more pleasant to me but for this encounter. The old rampart ran among fields, the like of them I had never seen for artfulness of agriculture; I was pleased, besides, to be so far in the still countryside; but the shackles of the gibbet clattered in my head; and the mops and mows of the old witch, and the thought of the dead men, hag-rode my spirits. To hang on a gallows, that seemed a hard case; and whether a man came to hang there for two shillings Scots, or (as Mr. Stewart had it) from the sense of duty, once he was tarred and shackled and hung up, the difference seemed small. There might David Balfour hang, and other lads pass on their errands and think light of him; and old daft limmers sit at a leg-foot and spae their fortunes; and the clean genty maids go by, and look to the other side, and hold a nose. I saw them plain, and they had grey eyes, and their screens upon their heads were of the Drummond colours.

I was thus in the poorest of spirits, though still pretty resolved, when I came in view of Pilrig, a pleasant gabled house set by the Walk-side among some brave young woods. The laird's horse was standing saddled at the door as I came up, but himself was in the study, where he received me in the midst of learned works and musical instruments, for he was not only a deep philosopher but much of a musician. He greeted me at first pretty well, and, when he had read Rankeillor's letter, placed himself obligingly at my disposal.

"And what is it, cousin David?" says he—"since it appears that we are cousins—what is this that I can do for you? A word to Prestongrange? Doubtless that is easily given. But what should be the word?"

"Mr. Balfour," said I, "if I were to tell you my whole story the way it fell out, it's my opinion (and it was Rankeillor's before me) that you would be very little made up with it."

"I am sorry to hear this of you, kinsman," says he.

"I must not take that at your hands, Mr. Balfour," said I; "I have nothing to my charge to make me sorry, or you for me, but just the common infirmities of mankind. 'The guilt of Adam's first sin, the want of original righteousness, and the corruption of my whole nature,' so much I must answer for, and I hope I have been taught where to look for help," I said; for I judged from the look of the man he would think the better of me if I knew my Questions. "But in the way of worldly honour I have no great stumble to reproach myself with; and my difficulties have befallen me very much against my will and (by all that I can see) without my fault. My trouble is, to have become dipped in a political complication, which it is judged you would be blithe to avoid a knowledge of."

"Why, very well, Mr. David," he replied, "I am pleased to see you are all that Rankeillor represented. And for what you say of political complications, you do me no more than justice. It is my study to be beyond suspicion, and indeed outside the field of it. The question is," says he, "how, if I am to know nothing of the matter, I can very well assist you?"

"Why, sir," said I, "I propose you should write to his lordship, that I am a young man of reasonable good family and of good means: both of which I believe to be the case."

"I have Rankeillor's word for it," said Mr. Balfour, "and I count that a warrandice against all deadly."

"To which you might add (if you will take my word for so much) that I am a good churchman, loyal to King George, and so brought up," I went on.

"None of which will do you any harm," said Mr. Balfour.

"Then you might go on to say that I sought his lordship on a matter of great moment, connected with his Majesty's service and the administration of justice," I suggested.

"As I am not to hear the matter," says the laird, "I will not take upon myself to qualify its weight. 'Great moment' therefore falls, and 'moment' along with it. For the rest, I might express myself much as you propose."

"And then, sir," said I, and rubbed my neck a little with my thumb, "then I would be very desirous if you could slip in a word that might perhaps tell for my protection."

"Protection?" says he, "for your protection? Here is a phrase that somewhat dampens me. If the matter be so dangerous, I own I would be a little loath to move in it blindfold."

"I believe I could indicate in two words where the thing sticks," said I.

"Perhaps that would be the best," said he.

"Well, it's the Appin murder," said I.

He held up both his hands. "Sirs! sirs!" cried he.

I thought by the expression of his face and voice that I had lost my helper.

"Let me explain..." I began.

"I thank you kindly, I will hear no more of it," says he. "I decline to hear more of it. For your name's sake and Rankeillor's, and perhaps a little for your own, I will do what I can to help you; but I will hear no more upon the facts. And it is my first clear duty to warn you. These are deep waters, Mr. David, and you are a young man. Be cautious and think twice."

"It is to be supposed I will have thought oftener than that, Mr. Balfour," said I, "and I will direct your attention again to Rankeillor's letter, where (I hope and believe) he has registered his approval of that which I design."

"Well, well," said he; and then again, "Well, well! I will do what I can for you." Therewith he took a pen and paper, sat a while in thought, and began to write with much consideration. "I understand that Rankeillor approves of what you have in mind?" he asked presently.

"After some discussion, sir, he bade me to go forward in God's name," said I.

"That is the name to go in," said Mr. Balfour, and resumed his writing. Presently, he signed, re-read what he had written, and addressed me again. "Now here, Mr. David," said he, "is a letter of introduction, which I will seal without closing, and give into your hands open, as the form requires. But since I am acting in the dark, I will just read it to you, so that you may see if it will secure your end:—

"Pilrig, August 26th, 1751.

"My Lord,—This is to bring to your notice my namesake and cousin, David Balfour, Esquire of Shaws, a young gentleman of unblemished descent and good estate. He has enjoyed besides the more valuable advantages of a godly training, and his political principles are all that your lordship can desire. I am not in Mr. Balfour's confidence, but I understand him to have a matter to declare, touching his Majesty's service and the administration of justice: purposes for which your lordship's zeal is known. I should add that the young gentleman's intention is known to and approved by some of his friends, who will watch with hopeful anxiety the event of his success or failure."

"Whereupon," continued Mr. Balfour, "I have subscribed myself with the usual compliments. You observe I have said 'some of your friends'; I hope you can justify my plural?"

"Perfectly, sir; my purpose is known and approved by more than one," said I. "And your letter, which I take a pleasure to thank you for, is all I could have hoped."

"It was all I could squeeze out," said he; "and from what I know of the matter you design to meddle in, I can only pray God that it may prove sufficient."

CHAPTER IV

Lord Advocate Prestongrange

My kinsman kept me to a meal, "for the honour of the roof," he said; and I believe I made the better speed on my return. I had no thought but to be done with the next stage, and have myself fully committed; to a person circumstanced as I was, the appearance of closing a door on hesitation and temptation was itself extremely tempting; and I was the more disappointed, when I came to Prestongrange's house, to be informed he was abroad. I believe it was true at the moment, and for some hours after; and then I have no doubt the Advocate came home again, and enjoyed himself in a neighbouring chamber among friends, while perhaps the very fact of my arrival was forgotten.

I would have gone away a dozen times, only for this strong drawing to have done with my declaration out of hand, and be able to lay me down to sleep with a free conscience. At first I read, for the little cabinet where I was left contained a variety of books. But I fear I read with little profit; and the weather falling cloudy, the dusk coming up earlier than usual, and my cabinet being lighted with but a loophole of a window, I was at last obliged to desist from this diversion (such as it was), and pass the rest of my time of waiting in a very burthensome vacuity.

The sound of people talking in a near chamber, the pleasant note of a harpsichord, and once the voice of a lady singing, bore me a kind of company.

I do not know the hour, but the darkness was long come, when the door of the cabinet opened, and I was aware, by the light behind him, of a tall figure of a man upon the threshold. I rose at once.

"Is anybody there?" he asked. "Who is that?"

"I am bearer of a letter from the laird of Pilrig to the Lord Advocate," said I.

"Have you been here long?" he asked.

"I would not like to hazard an estimate of how many hours," said I.

"It is the first I hear of it," he replied, with a chuckle. "The lads must have forgotten you. But you are in the bit at last, for I am Prestongrange."

So saying, he passed before me into the next room, whither (upon his sign) I followed him, and where he lit a candle and took his place before a business table. It was a long room, of a good proportion, wholly lined with books. That small spark of light in a corner struck out the man's handsome person and strong face. He was flushed, his eye watered and sparkled, and before he sat down I observed him to sway back and forth. No doubt he had been supping liberally; but his mind and tongue were under full control.

"Well, sir, sit ye down," said he, "and let us see Pilrig's letter."

He glanced it through in the beginning carelessly, looking up and bowing when he came to my name; but at the last words I thought I observed his attention to redouble, and I made sure he read them twice. All this while you are to suppose my heart was beating, for I had now crossed my Rubicon and was come fairly on the field of battle.

"I am pleased to make your acquaintance, Mr. Balfour," he said, when he had done. "Let me offer you a glass of claret."

"Under your favour, my lord, I think it would scarce be fair on me," said I. "I have come here, as the letter will have mentioned, on a business of some gravity to myself; and as I am little used with wine, I might be the sooner affected."

"You shall be the judge," said he. "But if you will permit, I believe I will even have the bottle in myself."

He touched a bell, and a footman came, as at a signal, bringing wine and glasses.

"You are sure you will not join me?" asked the Advocate. "Well, here is to our better acquaintance!—In what way can I serve you?"

"I should perhaps begin by telling you, my lord, that I am here at your own pressing invitation," said I.

"You have the advantage of me somewhere," said he, "for I profess I think I never heard of you before this evening."

"Right, my lord, the name is indeed new to you," said I. "And yet you have been for some time extremely wishful to make my acquaintance, and have declared the same in public."

"I wish you would afford me a clue," says he. "I am no Daniel."

"It will perhaps serve for such," said I, "that if I was in a jesting humour—which is far from the case—I believe I might lay a claim on your lordship for two hundred pounds."

"In what sense?" he inquired.

"In the sense of rewards offered for my person," said I.

He thrust away his glass once and for all, and sat straight up in the chair where he had been previously lolling. "What am I to understand?" said he.

"'A tall strong lad of about eighteen,'" I quoted; "'speaks like a Lowlander and has no beard.'"

"I recognise those words," said he, "which, if you have come here with any ill-judged intention of amusing yourself, are like to prove extremely prejudicial to your safety."

"My purpose in this," I replied, "is just entirely as serious as life and death, and you have understood me perfectly. I am the boy who was speaking with Glenure when he was shot."

"I can only suppose (seeing you here) that you claim to be innocent," said he.

"The inference is clear," said I. "I am a very loyal subject to King George, but if I had anything to reproach myself with, I would have had more discretion than to walk into your den."

"I am glad of that," said he. "This horrid crime, Mr. Balfour, is of a dye which cannot permit any clemency. Blood has been barbarously shed. It has been shed in direct opposition to his Majesty and our whole frame of laws, by those who are their known and public oppugnants. I take a very high sense of this. I will not deny that I consider the crime as directly personal to his Majesty."

"And unfortunately, my lord," I added, a little drily, "directly personal to another great personage who may be nameless."

"If you mean anything by those words, I must tell you I consider them unfit for a good subject; and were they spoke publicly I should make it my business to take note of them," said he. "You do not appear to me to recognise the gravity of your situation, or you would be more careful not to pejorate the same by words which glance upon the purity of justice. Justice, in this country, and in my poor hands, is no respecter of persons."

"You give me too great a share in my own speech, my lord," said I. "I did but repeat the common talk of the country, which I have heard everywhere, and from men of all opinions, as I came along."

"When you are come to more discretion you will understand such talk is not to be listened to, how much less repeated," says the Advocate. "But I acquit you of an ill intention. That nobleman, whom we all honour, and who has indeed been wounded in a near place by the late barbarity, sits too high to be reached by these aspersions. The Duke of Argyle—you see that I deal plainly with you—takes it to heart as I do, and as we are both bound to do by our judicial functions and the service of his Majesty; and I could wish that all hands, in this ill age, were equally clean of family rancour. But from the accident that this is a Campbell who has fallen martyr to his duty—as who else but the Campbells have ever put themselves foremost on that path?—I may say it, who am no Campbell—and that the chief of that great house happens (for all our advantages) to be the present head of the College of Justice, small minds and disaffected tongues are set agog in every change-house in the country; and I find a young gentleman like Mr. Balfour so ill-advised as to make himself their echo." So much he spoke with a very oratorical delivery, as if in Court, and then declined again upon the manner of a gentleman. "All this apart," said he. "It now remains that I should learn what I am to do with you."

"I had thought it was rather I that should learn the same from your lordship," said I.

"Ay, true," says the Advocate. "But, you see, you come to me well recommended. There is a good honest Whig name to this letter," says he, picking it up a moment from the table. "And– extra-judicially, Mr. Balfour–there is always the possibility of some arrangement. I tell you, and I tell you beforehand that you may be the more upon your guard, your fate lies with me singly. In such a matter (be it said with reverence) I am more powerful than the King's Majesty; and should you please me– and of course satisfy my conscience–in what remains to be held of our interview, I tell you it may remain between ourselves."

"Meaning how?" I asked.

"Why, I mean it thus, Mr. Balfour," said he, "that if you give satisfaction, no soul need know so much as that you visited my house; and you may observe that I do not even call my clerk."

I saw what way he was driving. "I suppose it is needless any one should be informed upon my visit," said I, "though the precise nature of my gains by that I cannot see. I am not at all ashamed of coming here."

"And have no cause to be," says he encouragingly. "Nor yet (if you are careful) to fear the consequences."

"My lord," said I, "speaking under your correction, I am not very easy to be frightened."

"And I am sure I do not seek to frighten you," says he. "But to the interrogation; and let me warn you to volunteer nothing beyond the questions I shall ask you. It may consist very immediately with your safety. I have a great discretion, it is true, but there are bounds to it."

"I shall try to follow your lordship's advice," said I.

He spread a sheet of paper on the table and wrote a heading. "It appears you were present, by the way, in the wood of Lettermore at the moment of the fatal shot," he began. "Was this by accident?"

"By accident," said I.

"How came you in speech with Colin Campbell?" he asked.

"I was inquiring my way of him to Aucharn," I replied.

40

I observed he did not write this answer down.

"H'm, true," said he, "I had forgotten that. And do you know, Mr. Balfour, I would dwell, if I were you, as little as might be on your relations with these Stewarts. It might be found to complicate our business. I am not yet inclined to regard these matters as essential."

"I had thought, my lord, that all points of fact were equally material in such a case," said I.

"You forget we are now trying these Stewarts," he replied, with great significance. "If we should ever come to be trying you, it will be very different; and I shall press these very questions that I am now willing to glide upon. But to resume: I have it here in Mr. Mungo Campbell's precognition that you ran immediately up the brae. How came that?"

"Not immediately, my lord, and the cause was my seeing of the murderer."

"You saw him, then?"

"As plain as I see your lordship, though not so near hand."

"You know him?"

"I should know him again."

"In your pursuit you were not so fortunate, then, as to overtake him?"

"I was not."

"Was he alone?"

"He was alone."

"There was no one else in that neighbourhood?"

"Alan Breck Stewart was not far off, in a piece of a wood."

The Advocate laid his pen down. "I think we are playing at cross-purposes," said he, "which you will find to prove a very ill amusement for yourself."

"I content myself with following your lordship's advice, and answering what I am asked," said I.

"Be so wise as to bethink yourself in time," said he. "I use you with the most anxious tenderness, which you scarce seem to appreciate, and which (unless you be more careful) may prove to be in vain."

"I do appreciate your tenderness, but conceive it to be mistaken," I replied, with something of a falter, for I saw we were come to grips at last. "I am here to lay before you certain information, by which I shall convince you Alan had no hand whatever in the killing of Glenure."

The Advocate appeared for a moment at a stick, sitting with pursed lips, and blinking his eyes upon me like an angry cat. "Mr. Balfour," he said at last, "I tell you pointedly you go an ill way for your own interests."

"My lord," I said, "I am as free of the charge of considering my own interests in this matter as your lordship. As God judges me, I have but the one design, and that is to see justice executed and the innocent go clear. If in pursuit of that I come to fall under your lordship's displeasure, I must bear it as I may."

At this he rose from his chair, lit a second candle, and for a while gazed upon me steadily. I was surprised to see a great change of gravity fallen upon his face, and I could have almost thought he was a little pale.

"You are either very simple, or extremely the reverse, and I see that I must deal with you more confidentially," says he. "This is a political case—ah, yes, Mr. Balfour! whether we like it or no, the case is political—and I tremble when I think what issues may depend from it. To a political case, I need scarce tell a young man of young education, we approach with very different thoughts from one which is criminal only. *Salus populi suprema lex* is a maxim susceptible of great abuse, but it has that force which we find elsewhere only in the laws of nature: I mean it has the force of necessity. I will open this out to you, if you will allow me, at more length. You would have me believe——"

"Under your pardon, my lord, I would have you to believe nothing but that which I can prove," said I.

"Tut! tut! young gentleman," says he, "be not so pragmatical, and suffer a man who might be your father (if it was nothing more) to employ his own imperfect language, and express his own poor thoughts, even when they have the misfortune not to coincide with Mr. Balfour's. You would have me to believe Breck innocent. I would think this of little account, the more so as we cannot catch our man. But the matter of Breck's innocence shoots beyond itself. Once admitted, it would destroy the whole presumptions of our case against another and a very different criminal; a man grown old in treason, already twice in arms against his king, and already twice forgiven; a fomenter of discontent, and (whoever may have fired the shot) the unmistakable original of the deed in question. I need not tell you that I mean James Stewart."

"And I can just say plainly that the innocence of Alan and of James is what I am here to declare in private to your lordship, and what I am prepared to establish at the trial by my testimony," said I.

"To which I can only answer by an equal plainness, Mr. Balfour," said he, "that (in that case) your testimony will not be called by me, and I desire you to withhold it altogether."

"You are at the head of Justice in this country," I cried, "and you propose to me a crime!"

"I am a man nursing with both hands the interests of this country," he replied, "and I press on you a political necessity. Patriotism is not always moral in the formal sense. You might be glad of it, I think: it is your own protection; the facts are heavy against you; and if I am still trying to except you from a very dangerous place, it is in part of course because I am not insensible to your honesty in coming here; in part because of Pilrig's letter; but in part, and in chief part, because I regard in this matter my political duty first and my judicial duty only second. For the same reason—I repeat it to you in the same frank words—I do not want your testimony."

"I desire not to be thought to make a repartee, when I express only the plain sense of our position," said I. "But if your lordship has no need of my testimony, I believe the other side would be extremely blithe to get it."

Prestongrange arose and began to pace to and fro in the

room. "You are not so young," he said, "but what you must remember very clearly the year 'Forty-five and the shock that went about the country. I read in Pilrig's letter that you are sound in Kirk and State. Who saved them in that fatal year? I do not refer to his Royal Highness and his ramrods, which were extremely useful in their day; but the country had been saved and the field won before ever Cumberland came upon Drummossie. Who saved it? I repeat; who saved the Protestant religion and the whole frame of our civil institutions? The late Lord President Culloden, for one; he played a man's part, and small thanks he got for it—even as I, whom you see before you, straining every nerve in the same service, look for no reward beyond the conscience of my duties done. After the President, who else? You know the answer as well as I do; 'tis partly a scandal, and you glanced at it yourself, and I reproved you for it, when you first came in. It was the Duke and the great clan of Campbell. Now here is a Campbell foully murdered, and that in the King's service. The Duke and I are Highlanders. But we are Highlanders civilised, and it is not so with the great mass of our clans and families. They have still savage virtues and defects. They are still barbarians, like these Stewarts; only the Campbells were barbarians on the right side, and the Stewarts were barbarians on the wrong. Now be you the judge. The Campbells expect vengeance. If they do not get it—if this man James escape—there will be trouble with the Campbells. That means disturbance in the Highlands, which are uneasy and very far from being disarmed: the disarming is a farce . ."

"I can bear you out in that," said I.

"Disturbance in the Highlands makes the hour of our old watchful enemy," pursued his lordship, holding out a finger as he paced; "and I give you my word we may have a 'Forty-five again with the Campbells on the other side. To protect the life of this man Stewart—which is forfeit already on half a dozen different counts if not on this—do you propose to plunge your country in war, to jeopardise the faith of your fathers, and to expose the lives and fortunes of how many thousand innocent persons?...These are considerations that weigh with me, and that I hope will weigh no less with yourself, Mr. Balfour, as a lover of your country, good government, and religious truth."

"You deal with me very frankly, and I thank you for it," said I. "I will try on my side to be no less honest. I believe your policy to be sound. I believe these deep duties may lie upon your lordship; I believe you may have laid them on your conscience when you took the oaths of the high office which you hold. But for me, who am just a plain man—or scarce a man yet—the plain duties must suffice. I can think but of two things: of a poor soul in the immediate and unjust danger of a shameful death, and of the cries and tears of his wife, that still tingle in my head. I cannot see beyond, my lord. It's the way that I am made. If the country has to fall, it has to fall. And I pray God, if this be wilful blindness, that He may enlighten me before too late."

He had heard me motionless, and stood so a while longer.

"This is an unexpected obstacle," says he, aloud, but to himself.

"And how is your lordship to dispose of me?" I asked.

"If I wished," said he, "you know that you might sleep in gaol."

"My lord," said I, "I have slept in worse places."

"Well, my boy," said he, "there is one thing appears very plainly from our interview, that I may rely on your pledged word. Give me your honour that you will be wholly secret, not only on what has passed tonight, but in the matter of the Appin case, and I let you go free."

"I will give it till tomorrow or any other near day that you may please to set," said I. "I would not be thought too wily; but if I gave the promise without qualification your lordship would have attained his end."

"I had no thought to entrap you," said he.

"I am sure of that," said I.

"Let me see," he continued. "Tomorrow is the Sabbath. Come to me on Monday by eight in the morning, and give me your promise until then."

"Freely given, my lord," said I. "And with regard to what has fallen from yourself, I will give it for as long as it shall please God to spare your days."

"You will observe," he said next, "that I have made no employment of menaces."

"It was like your lordship's nobility," said I. "Yet I am not altogether so dull but what I can perceive the nature of those you have not uttered."

"Well," said he, "good-night to you. May you sleep well, for I think it is more than I am like to do."

With that he sighed, took up a candle, and gave me his conveyance as far as the street door.

CHAPTER V

In the Advocate's House

The next day, Sabbath, August 27th, I had the occasion I had long looked forward to, to hear some of the famous Edinburgh preachers, all well known to me already by the report of Mr. Campbell. Alas! and I might just as well have been at Essendean, and sitting under Mr. Campbell's worthy self! the turmoil of my thoughts, which dwelt continually on the interview with Prestongrange, inhibiting me from all attention. I was indeed much less impressed by the reasoning of the divines than by the spectacle of the thronged congregation in the churches, like what I imagined of a theatre or (in my then disposition) of an assize of trial; above all at the West Kirk, with its three tiers of galleries, where I went in the vain hope that I might see Miss Drummond.

On the Monday I betook me for the first time to a barber's, and was very well pleased with the result. Thence to the Advocate's, where the red coats of the soldiers showed again about his door, making a bright place in the close. I looked about for the young lady and her gillies: there was never a sign of them. But I was no sooner shown into the cabinet or antechamber where I had spent so weariful a time upon the Saturday, than I was aware of the tall figure of James More in a corner. He seemed a prey to a painful uneasiness, reaching forth his feet and hands, and his eyes speeding here and there without rest about the walls of the small chamber, which recalled to me with a sense of pity the man's wretched situation. I suppose it was partly this, and partly me strong continuing interest in his daughter, that moved me to accost him.

"Give you a good-morning, sir," said I.

"And a good-morning to you, sir," said he.

"You bide tryst with Prestongrange?" I asked.

"I do, sir, and I pray your business with that gentleman be more agreeable than mine," was his reply.

"I hope at least that yours will be brief, for I suppose you pass before me," said I.

"All pass before me," he said, with a shrug and a gesture upward of the open hands. "It was not always so, sir, but times change. It was not so when the sword was in the scale, young gentleman, and the virtues of the soldier might sustain themselves."

There came a kind of Highland snuffle out of the man that raised my dander strangely.

"Well, Mr. Macgregor," said I, "I understand the main thing for a soldier is to be silent, and the first of his virtues never to complain."

"You have my name, I perceive"—he bowed to me with his arms crossed—"though it's one I must not use myself. Well, there is a publicity—I have shown my face and told my name too often in the beards of my enemies. I must not wonder if both should be known to many that I know not."

"That you know not in the least, sir," said I, "nor yet anybody else; but the name I am called, if you care to hear it, is Balfour."

"It is a good name," he replied civilly; "there are many decent folk that use it. And now that I call to mind, there was a young gentleman, your namesake, that marched surgeon in the year 'Forty-five with my battalion."

"I believe that would be a brother to Balfour of Baith," said I, for I was ready for the surgeon now.

"The same, sir," said James More. "And since I have been fellow-soldier with your kinsman, you must suffer me to grasp your hand."

He shook hands with me long and tenderly, beaming on me the while as though he had found a brother.

"Ah!" says he, "these are changed days since your cousin and I heard the balls whistle in our lugs."

"I think he was a very far-away cousin," said I drily, "and I ought to tell you that I never clapped eyes upon the man."

"Well, well," said he, "it makes no change. And you—I do not think you were out yourself, sir—I have no clear mind of your face, which is one not probable to be forgotten."

"In the year you refer to, Mr. Macgregor, I was getting skelped in the parish school," said I.

"So young!" cries he. "Ah, then, you will never be able to think what this meeting is to me. In the hour of my adversity, and here in the house of my enemy, to meet in with the blood of an old brother-in-arms—it heartens me, Mr. Balfour, like the skirling of the Highland pipes! Sir, this is a sad look-back that many of us have to make: some with falling tears. I have lived in my own country like a king; my sword, my mountains, and the faith of my friends and kinsmen sufficed for me. Now I lie in a stinking dungeon; and do you know, Mr. Balfour," he went on, taking my arm and beginning to lead me about, "do you know, sir, that I lack mere nearies? The malice of my foes has quite sequestered my resources. I lie, as you know, sir, on a trumped-up charge, of which I am as innocent as yourself. They dare not bring me to my trial, and in the meanwhile I am held naked in my prison. I could have wished it was your cousin I had met, or his brother Baith himself. Either would, I know, have been rejoiced to help me; while a comparative stranger like yourself——"

I would be ashamed to set down all he poured out to me in this beggarly vein, or the very short and grudging answers that I made to him. There were times when I was tempted to stop his mouth with some small change; but whether it was from shame or pride—whether it was for my own sake or Catriona's—whether it was because I thought him no fit father for his daughter, or because I resented that grossness of immediate falsity that clung about the man himself—the thing was clean beyond me. And I was still being wheedled and preached to, and still being marched to and fro, three steps and a turn, in that small chamber, and had already, by some very short replies, highly incensed, although not finally discouraged, my beggar, when Prestongrange appeared in the doorway and bade me eagerly into his big chamber.

"I have a moment's engagement," said he; "and that you may

not sit empty-handed I am going to present you to my three braw daughters, of whom perhaps you may have heard, for I think they are more famous than papa.—This way."

He led me into another long room above, where a dry old lady sat at a frame of embroidery, and the three handsomest young women (I suppose) in Scotland stood together by a window.

"This is my new friend, Mr. Balfour," said he, presenting me by the arm.—"David, here is my sister, Miss Grant, who is so good as keep my house for me, and will be very pleased if she can help you. And here," says he, turning to the three younger ladies, "here are my . A fair question to ye, Mr. Davie: which of the three is the best favoured? And I wager he will never have the impudence to propound honest Allan Ramsay's answer!"

Hereupon all three, and the old Miss Grant as well, cried out against this sally, which (as I was acquainted with the verses he referred to) brought shame into my own cheek. It seemed to me a citation unpardonable in a father, and I was amazed that these ladies could laugh even while they reproved, or made believe to.

Under cover of this mirth, Prestongrange got forth of the chamber, and I was left, like a fish upon dry land, in that very unsuitable society. I could never deny, in looking back upon what followed, that I was eminently stockish; and I must say the ladies were well drilled to have so long a patience with me. The aunt indeed sat close at her embroidery, only looking now and again and smiling; but the misses, and especially the eldest, who was besides the most handsome, paid me a score of attentions which I was very ill able to repay. It was all in vain to tell myself I was a young fellow of some worth as well as a good estate, and had no call to feel abashed before these lasses, the eldest not so much older than myself, and no one of them by any probability half as learned. Reasoning would not change the fact; and there were times when the colour came into my face to think I was shaved that day for the first time.

The talk going, with all their endeavours, very heavily, the eldest took pity on my awkwardness, sat down to her instrument, of which she was a past mistress, and entertained me for a while with playing and singing, both in the Scots and in the Italian manners; this put me more at my ease, and being reminded of Alan's air that he had taught me in the hole near Carriden, I made so bold as to whistle a bar or two, and ask if she knew that.

She shook her head. "I never heard a note of it," said she. "Whistle it all through. And now once again," she added, after I had done so.

Then she picked it out upon the keyboard, and (to my surprise) instantly enriched the same with well-sounding chords, and sang, as she played, with a very droll expression and broad accent—

"Haena I got just the lilt of it?
Isna this the tune that ye whustled?"

"You see," she says, "I can do the poetry too, only it won't rhyme. And then again:

"I am Miss Grant, sib to the Advocate:
You, I believe, are Dauvit Balfour."

I told her how much astonished I was by her genius.

"And what do you call the name of it?" she asked.

"I do not know the real name," said I. "I just call it 'Alan's air'."

She looked at me directly in the face. "I shall call it 'David's air,'" said she; "though if it's the least like what your namesake of Israel played to Saul I would never wonder that the king got little good by it, for it's but melancholy music. Your other name I do not like; so if you was ever wishing to hear your tune again you are to ask for it by mine."

This was said with a significance that gave my heart a jog.

"Why that, Miss Grant?" I asked.

"Why," says she, "if ever you should come to get hanged, I

51

will set your last dying speech and confession to that tune and sing it."

This put it beyond a doubt that she was partly informed of my story and peril. How, or just how much, it was more difficult to guess. It was plain she knew there was something of danger in the name of Alan, and thus warned me to leave it out of reference; and plain she knew that I stood under some criminal suspicion. I judged besides that the harshness of her last speech (which besides she had followed up immediately with a very noisy piece of music) was to put an end to the present conversation. I stood beside her, affecting to listen and admire, but truly whirled away by my own thoughts. I have always found this young lady to be a lover of the mysterious; and certainly this first interview made a mystery that was beyond my plummet. One thing I learned long after: the hours of Sunday had been well employed, the bank-porter had been found and examined, my visit to Charles Stewart was discovered, and the deduction made that I was pretty deep with James and Alan, and most likely in a continued correspondence with the last. Hence this broad hint that was given me across the harpsichord.

In the midst of the piece of music one of the younger misses, who was at a window over the close, cried on her sisters to come quick, for there was " again." The whole family trooped there at once, and crowded one another for a look. The window whither they ran was in an odd corner of that room, gave above the entrance door, and flanked up the close.

"Come, Mr. Balfour," they cried, "come and see. She is the most beautiful creature! She hangs round the close-head these last days, always with some wretched-like gillies, and yet seems quite a lady."

I had no need to look; neither did I look twice, or long. I was afraid she might have seen me there, looking down upon her from that chamber of music, and she without, and her father in the same house, perhaps begging for his life with tears, and myself come but newly from rejecting his petitions. But even that glance set me in a better conceit of myself, and much less awe of the young ladies. They were beautiful, that was beyond question, but Catriona was beautiful too, and had a kind of brightness in her like a coal of fire. As much as the others cast me down, she lifted me up. I remembered I had talked easily with her. If I could make no hand of it with these fine maids, it was perhaps something their own fault. My embarrassment began to be a little mingled and lightened with a sense of fun; and when the aunt smiled at me from her embroidery, and the three daughters unbent to me like a baby, all with "papa's orders" written on their faces, there were times when I could have found it in my heart to smile myself.

Presently papa returned, the same kind, happy-like, pleasant-spoken man.

"Now, girls," said he, "I must take Mr. Balfour away again; but I hope you have been able to persuade him to return where I shall be always gratified to find him."

So they each made me a little farthing compliment, and I was led away.

If this visit to the family had been meant to soften my resistance, it was the worst of failures. I was no such ass but what I understood how poor a figure I had made, and that the girls would be yawning their jaws off as soon as my stiff back was turned. I felt I had shown how little I had in me of what was soft and graceful; and I longed for a chance to prove that I had something of the other stuff, the stern and dangerous.

Well, I was to be served to my desire, for the scene to which he was conducting me was of a different character.

CHAPTER VI

Umquhile the Master of Lovat

There was a man waiting us in Prestongrange's study, whom I
distasted at the first look, as we distaste a ferret or an earwig.
He was bitter ugly, but seemed very much of a gentleman; had
still manners, but capable of sudden leaps and violences; and
a small voice, which could ring out shrill and dangerous when
he so desired.

The Advocate presented us in a familiar, friendly way.

"Here, Fraser," said he, "here is Mr. Balfour whom we talked
about.—Mr. David, this is Mr. Simon Fraser, whom we used to
call by another title, but that is an old song. Mr. Fraser has an
errand to you."

With that he stepped aside to his bookshelves, and made
believe to consult a quarto volume in the far end.

I was thus left (in a sense) alone with perhaps the last person
in the world I had expected. There was no doubt upon the
terms of introduction; this could be no other than the forfeited
Master of Lovat and chief of the great clan Fraser. I knew he
had led his men in the Rebellion; I knew his father's head—my
old lord's, that grey fox of the mountains—to have fallen on the
block for that offence, the lands of the family to have been
seized, and their nobility attainted. I could not conceive what
he should be doing in Grant's house; I could not conceive that
he had been called to the Bar, had eaten all his principles, and
was now currying favour with the Government, even to the
extent of acting Advocate-Depute in the Appin murder.

"Well, Mr. Balfour," said he, "what is all this I hear of ye?"

"It would not become me to prejudge," said I, "but if the
Advocate was your authority he is fully possessed of my
opinions."

"I may tell you I am engaged in the Appin case," he went on;
"I am to appear under Prestongrange; and from my study of
the precognitions I can assure you your opinions are

erroneous. The guilt of Breck is manifest; and your testimony, in which you admit you saw him on the hill at the very moment, will certify his hanging."

"It will be rather ill to hang him till you catch him," I observed. "And for other matters, I very willingly leave you to your own impressions."

"The Duke has been informed," he went on. "I have just come from his Grace, and he expressed himself before me with an honest freedom, like the great noble man he is. He spoke of you by name, Mr. Balfour, and declared his gratitude beforehand in case you would be led by those who understand your own interests and those of the country so much better than yourself. Gratitude is no empty expression in that mouth: *experto crede.* I daresay you know something of my name and clan, and the damnable example and lamented end of my late father, to say nothing of my own errata. Well, I have made my peace with that good Duke; he has intervened for me with our friend Prestongrange; and here I am with my foot in the stirrup again and some of the responsibility shared into my hand of prosecuting King George's enemies and avenging the late daring and barefaced insult to his Majesty."

"Doubtless a proud position for your father's son," says I.

He wagged his bald eyebrows at me. "You are pleased to make experiments in the ironical, I think," said he. "But I am here upon duty; I am here to discharge my errand in good faith; it is in vain you think to divert me. And let me tell you, for a young fellow of spirit and ambition like yourself, a good shove in the beginning will do more than ten years' drudgery. The shove is now at your command; choose what you will to be advanced in, the Duke will watch upon you with the affectionate disposition of a father."

"I am thinking that I lack the docility of the son," says I.

"And do you really suppose, sir, that the whole policy of this country is to be suffered to trip up and tumble down for an ill-mannered colt of a boy?' he cried. "This has been made a test case, all who would prosper in the future must put a shoulder to the wheel. Look at me! Do you suppose it is for my pleasure that I put myself in the highly invidious position of prosecuting a man that I have drawn the sword alongside of? The choice is not left me."

"But I think, sir, that you forfeited your choice when you mixed in with that unnatural rebellion," I remarked. "My case is happily otherwise: I am a true man, and can look either the Duke or King George in the face without concern."

"Is it so the wind sits?" says he. "I protest you are fallen in the worst sort of error. Prestongrange has been hitherto so civil (he tells me) as not to combat your allegations; but you must not think they are not looked upon with strong suspicion. You say you are innocent. My dear sir, the facts declare you guilty."

"I was waiting for you there," said I.

"The evidence of Mungo Campbell; your flight after the completion of the murder; your long course of secrecy—my good young man!" said Mr. Simon, "here is enough evidence to hang a bullock, let be a David Balfour! I shall be upon that trial; my voice shall be raised; I shall then speak much otherwise from what I do today, and far less to your gratification, little as you like it now! Ah, you look white!" cries he. "I have found the key of your impudent heart. You look pale, your eyes waver, Mr. David! You see the grave and the gallows nearer by than you had fancied."

"I own to a natural weakness," said I. "I think no shame for that. Shame... " I was going on.

"Shame waits for you on the gibbet," he broke in.

"Where I shall but be even'd with my lord your father," said I.

"Aha, but not so!" he cried, "and you do not yet see to the bottom of this business. My father suffered in a great cause, and for dealing in the affairs of kings. You are to hang for a dirty murder about boddle-pieces. Your personal part in it, the treacherous one of holding the poor wretch in talk, your accomplices a pack of ragged Highland gillies. And it can be shown, my great Mr. Balfour—it can be shown, and it *will* be shown, trust *me* that has a finger in the pie—it can be shown, and shall be shown, that you were paid to do it. I think I can see the looks go round the Court when I adduce my evidence, and it shall appear that you, a young man of education, let yourself be corrupted to this shocking act for a suit of cast clothes, a bottle of Highland spirits, and three-and-fivepence-halfpenny in copper money."

There was a touch of the truth in these words that knocked me like a blow: clothes, a bottle of *usquebaugh*, and three-and-fivepence-halfpenny in change, made up, indeed, the most of what Alan and I had carried from Aucharn; and I saw that some of James's people had been blabbing in their dungeons.

"You see I know more than you fancied," he resumed in triumph. "And as for giving it this turn, great Mr. David, you must not suppose the Government of Great Britain and Ireland will ever be stuck for want of evidence. We have men here in prison who will swear out their lives as we direct them; as I direct, if you prefer the phrase. So now you are to guess your part of glory if you choose to die. On the one hand, life, wine, women, and a duke to be your hand-gun: on the other, a rope to your craig, and a gibbet to clatter your bones on, and the lousiest, lowest story to hand down to your namesakes in the future that was ever told about a hired assassin. And see here!" he cried, with a formidable shrill voice, "see this paper that I pull out of my pocket. Look at the name there: it is the name of the great David, I believe, the ink scarce dry yet. Can you guess its nature? It is the warrant for your arrest, which I have but to touch this bell beside me to have executed on the spot. Once in the Tolbooth upon this paper, may God help you, for the die is cast!"

I must never deny that I was greatly horrified by so much baseness, and much unmanned by the immediacy and ugliness of my danger. Mr. Simon had already gloried in the changes of my hue; I make no doubt I was now no ruddier than my shirt; my speech besides trembled.

"There is a gentleman in this room," cried I. "I appeal to him. I put my life and credit in his hands."

Prestongrange shut his book with a snap. "I told you so,

Simon," said he; "you have played your hand for all it was worth, and you have lost.—Mr. David," he went on, "I wish you to believe it was by no choice of mine you were subjected to this proof. I wish you could understand how glad I am you should come forth from it with so much credit. You may not quite see how, but it is a little of a service to myself. For had our friend here been more successful than I was last night, it might have appeared that he was a better judge of men than I; it might have appeared we were altogether in the wrong situations, Mr. Simon and myself. And I know our friend Simon to be ambitious," says he, striking lightly on Fraser's shoulder. "As for this stage-play, it is over; my sentiments are very much engaged in your behalf; and whatever issue we can find to this unfortunate affair, I shall make it my business to see it is adopted with tenderness to you."

These were very good words, and I could see besides that there was little love, and perhaps a spice of genuine ill-will, between those two who were opposed to me. For all that, it was unmistakable this interview had been designed, perhaps rehearsed, with the consent of both; it was plain my adversaries were in earnest to try me by all methods; and now (persuasion, flattery, and menaces having been tried in vain) I could not but wonder what would be their next expedient. My eyes besides were still troubled, and my knees loose under me, with the distress of the late ordeal; and I could do no more than stammer the same form of words: "I put my life and credit in your hands."

"Well, well," says he, "we must try to save them. And in the meanwhile let us return to gentler methods. You must not bear any grudge upon my friend Mr. Simon, who did but speak by his brief. And even if you did conceive some malice against myself, who stood by and seemed rather to hold a candle, I must not let that extend to innocent members of my family. These are greatly engaged to see more of you, and I cannot consent to have my young women-folk disappointed. Tomorrow they will be going to Hope Park, where I think it very proper you should make your bow. Call for me first, when I may possibly have something for your private hearing; then you shall be turned abroad again under the conduct of my misses; and until that time repeat to me your promise of secrecy."

I had done better to have instantly refused, but in truth I was beside the power of reasoning; did as I was bid; took my leave I know not how; and when I was forth again in the close, and the door had shut behind me, was glad to lean on a house-wall and wipe my face. That horrid apparition (as I may call it) of Mr. Simon rang in my memory, as a sudden noise rings after it is over in the ear. Tales of the man's father, of his falseness, of his manifold perpetual treacheries, rose before me from all that I had heard and read, and joined on with what I had just experienced of himself. Each time it occurred to me, the ingenious foulness of that calumny he had proposed to nail upon my character startled me afresh. The case of the man upon the gibbet by Leith Walk appeared scarce distinguishable from that I was now to consider as my own. To rob a child of so little more than nothing was certainly a paltry enterprise for two grown men; but my own tale, as it was to be represented in a court by Simon Fraser, appeared a fair second in every possible point of view of sordidness and cowardice.

The voices of two of Prestongrange's liveried men upon his doorstep recalled me to myself.

"Hae," said the one; "this billet as fast as ye can link to the captain."

"Is that for the cateran back again?" asked the other.

"It would seem sae," returned the first. "Him and Simon are seeking him."

"I think Prestongrange is gane gyte," says the second. "He'll have James More in bed with him next."

"Weel, it's neither your affair nor mine's," says the first.

And they parted, the one upon his errand, and the other back into the house.

This looked as ill as possible. I was scarce gone and they

were sending already for James More, to whom I thought Mr. Simon must have pointed when he spoke of men in prison and ready to redeem their lives by all extremities. My scalp curdled among my hair, and the next moment the blood leaped in me to remember Catriona. Poor lass! her father stood to be hanged for pretty indefensible misconduct. What was yet more unpalatable, it now seemed he was prepared to save his four quarters by the worst of shame and the most foul of cowardly murders—murder by the false oath; and, to complete our misfortunes, it seemed myself was picked out to be the victim.

I began to walk swiftly and at random, conscious only of a desire for movement, air, and the open country.

CHAPTER VII

I Make a Fault in Honour

I came forth, I vow I know not how, on the *Lang Dykes*. This is
a rural road which runs on the north side over-against the city.
Thence I could see the whole black length of it tail down, from
where the castle stands upon its crags above the loch, in a long
line of spires and gable-ends and smoking chimneys, and at
the sight my heart swelled in my bosom. My youth, as I have
told, was already inured to dangers; but such danger as I had
seen the face of but that morning, in the midst of what they call
the safety of a town, shook me beyond experience. Peril of
slavery, peril of shipwreck, peril of sword and shot, I had stood
all of these without discredit; but the peril there was in the
sharp voice and the fat face of Simon, properly Lord Lovat,
daunted me wholly.

I sat by the lakeside in a place where the rushes went down
into the water, and there steeped my wrists and laved my
temples. If I could have done so with any remains of self-
esteem, I would now have fled from my foolhardy enterprise.
But (call it courage or cowardice, and I believe it was both the
one and the other) I decided I was ventured out beyond the
possibility of a retreat. I had outfaced these men, I would
continue to outface them; come what might, I would stand by
the word spoken.

The sense of my own constancy somewhat uplifted my
spirits, but not much. At the best of it there was an icy place
about my heart, and life seemed a black business to be at all
engaged in. For two souls in particular my pity flowed. The one
was myself, to be so friendless and lost among dangers. The
other was the girl, the daughter of James More. I had seen but
little of her; yet my view was taken and my judgment made. I
thought her a lass of a clean honour, like a man's; I thought her
one to die of a disgrace; and now I believed her father to be at
that moment bargaining his vile life for mine. It made a bond in

my thoughts betwixt the girl and me. I had seen her before only as a wayside appearance, though one that pleased me strangely; I saw her now in a sudden nearness of relation, as the daughter of my blood-foe, and, I might say, my murderer. I reflected it was hard I should be so plagued and persecuted all my days for other folk's affairs, and have no manner of pleasure myself. I got meals and a bed to sleep in when my concerns would suffer it; beyond that my wealth was of no help to me.

If I was to hang, my days were like to be short; if I was not to hang, but to escape out of this trouble, they might yet seem long to me ere I was done with them. Of a sudden her face appeared in my memory, the way I had first seen it, with the parted lips; at that, weakness came in my bosom and strength into my legs; and I set resolutely forward on the way to Dean. If I was to hang tomorrow, and it was sure enough I might very likely sleep that night in a dungeon, I determined I should hear and speak once more with Catriona.

The exercise of walking and the thought of my destination braced me yet more, so that I began to pluck up a kind of spirit. In the village of Dean, where it sits in the bottom of a glen beside the river, I inquired my way of a miller's man, who sent me up the hill upon the father side by a plain path, and so to a decent-like small house in a garden of lawns and apple-trees. My heart beat high as I stepped inside the garden hedge, but it fell low indeed when I came face to face with a grim and fierce old lady, walking there in a white mutch with a man's hat strapped upon the top of it.

"What do ye come seeking here?" she asked.

I told her I was after Miss Drummond.

"And what may be your business with Miss Drummond?" says she.

I told her I had met her on Saturday last, had been so fortunate as to render her a trifling service, and was come now on the young lady's invitation.

"O, so you're Saxpence!" she cried, with a very sneering manner. "A braw gift, a bonny gentleman. And hae ye ony ither name and designation, or were ye bapteesed Saxpence?" she asked.

I told my name.

"Preserve me!" she cried. "Has Ebenezer gotten a son?"

"No, ma'am," said I. "I am a son of Alexander's. It's I that am the Laird of Shaws."

"Ye'll find your work cut out for ye to establish that," quoth she.

"I perceive you know my uncle," said I; "and I daresay you may be the better pleased to hear that business is arranged."

"And what brings ye here after Miss Drummond?" she pursued.

"I'm come after my saxpence, mem," said I. "It's to be thought, being my uncle's nephew, I would be found a careful lad."

"So ye have a spark of sleeness in ye?" observed the old lady, with some approval. "I thought ye had just been a cuif—you and your saxpence, and your *lucky day* and your *sake of Balwhidder*"—from which I was gratified to learn that Catriona had not forgotten some of our talk. "But all this is by the purpose," she resumed. "Am I to understand that ye come here keeping company?"

"This is surely rather an early question," said I. "The maid is young, so am I, worse fortune. I have but seen her the once. I'll not deny," I added, making up my mind to try her with some frankness, "I'll not deny but she has run in my head a good deal since I met in with her. That is one thing; but it would be quite another, and I think I would look very like a fool, to commit myself."

"You can speak out of your mouth, I see," said the old lady. "Praise God, and so can I! I was fool enough to take charge of this rogue's daughter: a fine charge I have gotten; but it's mine, and I'll carry it the way I want to. Do ye mean to tell me, Mr. Balfour of Shaws, that you would marry James More's daughter, and him hanged? Well, then, where there's no possible marriage there shall be no manner of carryings-on,

63

and take that for said. Lasses are bruckle things," she added, with a nod; "and though ye would never think it by my wrunkled chafts, I was a lassie mysel', and a bonny one."

"Lady Allardyce," said I, "for that I suppose to be your name, you seem to do the two sides of the talking, which is a very poor manner to come to an agreement. You give me rather a home-thrust when you ask if I would marry, at the gallows' foot, a young lady whom I have seen but the once. I have told you already I would never be so untenty as to commit myself. And yet I'll go some way with you. If I continue to like the lass as well as I have reason to expect, it will be something more than her father, or the gallows either, that keeps the two of us apart. As for my family, I found it by the wayside like a lost bawbee! I owe less than nothing to my uncle; and if ever I marry, it will be to please one person: that's myself."

"I have heard this kind of talk before ye were born," said Mrs. Ogilvy, "which is perhaps the reason that I think of it so little. There's much to be considered. This James More is a kinsman of mine, to my shame be it spoken. But the better the family, the mair men hanged or heided, that's always been poor Scotland's story. And if it was just the hanging! For my part, I think I would be best pleased with James upon the gallows, which would be at least an end to him. Catrine's a good lass enough, and a good-hearted, and lets herself be deaved all day with a runt of an auld wife like me. But, ye see, there's the weak bit. She's daft about that long, false, fleeching beggar of a father of hers, and red-mad about the Gregara, and proscribed names, and King James, and a wheen blethers. And you might think ye could guide her, ye would find yourself sore mista'en. Ye say ye've seen her but the once . . . "

"Spoke with her but the once, I should have said," I interrupted. "I saw her again this morning from a window at Prestongrange's."

This I daresay I put in because it sounded well; but I was properly paid for my ostentation on the return.

"What's this of it?" cries the old lady, with a sudden pucker of her face. "I think it was at the Advocate's door-cheek that ye met her first."

I told her that was so.

"H'm," she said; and then suddenly, upon rather a scolding tone, "I have your bare word for it," she cries, "as to who and what you are. By your way of it, you're Balfour of the Shaws; but for what I ken you may be Balfour of the Deevil's oxter. It's possible ye may come here for what ye say, and it's equally possible ye may come here for deil care what! I'm good enough Whig to sit quiet, and to have keepit all my men-folk's heads upon their shoulders. But I'm not just a good enough Whig to be made a fool of neither. And I tell you fairly, there's too much Advocate's door and Advocate's window here for a man that comes taigling after a Macgregor's daughter. Ye can tell that to the Advocate that sent ye, with my fond love. And I kiss my loof to ye, Mr. Balfour," says she, suiting the action to the word; "and a braw journey to ye back to where ye cam frae."

"If you think me a spy," I broke out, and speech stuck in my throat. I stood and looked murder at the old lady for a space, then bowed and turned away.

"Here! Hoots! The callant's in a creel!" she cried. "Think ye a spy? what else would I think ye—me that kens naething by ye? But I see that I was wrong; and as I cannot fight, I'll have to apologise. A bonny figure I would be with a broadsword. Ay! ay!" she went on, "you're none such a bad lad in your way; I think ye'll have some redeeming vices. But, O! Davit Balfour, ye're damned countryfeed. Ye'll have to win over that, lad; ye'll have to soople your backbone, and think a wee pickle less of your dainty self; and ye'll have to try to find out that womenfolk are nae grenadiers. But that can never be. To your last day you'll ken no more of womenfolk than what I do of sow-gelding."

I had never been used with such expressions from a lady's tongue, the only two ladies I had known, Mrs. Campbell and my mother, being most devout and most particular women;

65

and I suppose my amazement must have been depicted in my countenance, for Mrs. Ogilvy burst forth suddenly in a fit of laughter.

"Keep me!" she cried, struggling with her mirth, "you have the finest timber face—and you to marry the daughter of a Hieland cateran! Davie, my dear, I think we'll have to make a match of it— if it was just to see the weans. And now," she went on, "there's no manner of service in your daidling here, for the young woman is from home, and it's my fear that the old woman is no suitable companion for your father's son. Forbye that I have nobody but myself to look after my reputation, and have been long enough alone with a sedooctive youth. And come back another day for your saxpence!" she cried after me as I left.

My skirmish with this disconcerting lady gave my thoughts a boldness they had otherwise wanted. For two days the image of Catriona had mixed in all my meditations; she made their background, so that I scarce enjoyed my own company without a glint of her in a corner of my mind. But now she came immediately near; I seemed to touch her, whom I had never touched but the once; I let myself flow out to her in a happy weakness, and looking all about, and before and behind, saw the world like an undesirable desert, where men go as soldiers on a march, following their duty with what constancy they have, and Catriona alone there to offer me some pleasure of my days. I wondered at myself that I could dwell on such considerations in that time of my peril and disgrace; and when I remembered my youth I was ashamed. I had my studies to complete; I had to be called into some useful business; I had yet to take my part of service in a place where all must serve; I had yet to learn, and know, and prove myself a man; and I had so much sense as blush that I should be already tempted with these further-on and holier delights and duties. My education spoke home to me sharply; I was never brought up on sugar-biscuits, but on the hard food of the truth. I knew that he was quite unfit to be a husband who was not prepared to be a father also; and for a boy like me to play the father was a mere derision.

When I was in the midst of these thoughts, and about half-way back to town, I saw a figure coming to meet me, and the trouble of my heart was heightened. It seemed I had everything in the world to say to her, but nothing to say first; and remembering how tongue-tied I had been that morning at the Advocate's, I made sure that I would find myself struck dumb. But when she came up my fears fled away; not even the consciousness of what I had been privately thinking disconcerted me the least; and I found I could talk with her as easily and rationally as I might with Alan.

"O!" she cried, "you have been seeking your sixpence: did you get it?"

I told her, no; but now I had met with her, my walk was not in vain. "Though I have seen you today already," said I, and told her where and when.

"I did not see you," she said. "My eyes are big, but there are better than mine at seeing far. Only I heard singing in the house."

"That was Miss Grant," said I, "the eldest and the bonniest."

"They say they are all beautiful," said she.

"They think the same of you, Miss Drummond," I replied, "and were all crowding to the window to observe you."

"It is a pity about my being so blind," said she, "or I might have seen them too.—And you were in the house? You must have been having the fine time with the fine music and the pretty ladies."

"There is just where you are wrong," said I; "for I was as uncouth as a sea-fish upon the brae of a mountain. The truth is that I am better fitted to go about with rudas men than pretty ladies."

"Well, I would think so too, at all events!" said she, at which we both of us laughed.

"It is a strange thing, now," said I. "I am not the least afraid with you, yet I could have run from the Miss Grants. And I was afraid of your cousin too."

"O, I think any man will be afraid of her," she cried. "My father is afraid of her himself."

67

The name of her father brought me to a stop. I looked at her as she walked by my side; I recalled the man, and the little I knew and the much I guessed of him; and, comparing the one with the other, felt like a traitor to be silent.

"Speaking of which," said I, "I met your father no later than this morning."

"Did you?" she cried, with a voice of joy that seemed to mock at me. "You saw James More? You will have spoken with him, then?"

"I did even that," said I.

Then I think things went the worst way for me that was humanly possible. She gave me a look of mere gratitude. "Ah, thank you for that!" says she.

"You thank me for very little," said I, and then stopped. But it seemed when I was holding back so much, something at least had to come out. "I spoke rather ill to him," said I; "I did not like him very much; I spoke him rather ill, and he was angry."

"I think you had little to do then, and less to tell it to his daughter!" she cried out. "But those that do not love and cherish him I will not know."

"I will take the freedom of a word yet," said I, beginning to tremble. "Perhaps neither your father nor I are in the best of good spirits at Prestongrange's. I dare say we both have anxious business there, for it's a dangerous house. I was sorry for him too, and spoke to him the first, if I could but have spoken the wiser. And for one thing, in my opinion, you will soon find that his affairs are mending."

"It will not be through your friendship, I am thinking," said she; "and he is much made up to you for your sorrow."

"Miss Drummond," cried I, "I am alone in this world..."

"And I am not wondering at that," said she.

"O, let me speak!" said I. "I will speak but the once, and then leave you, if you will, for ever. I came this day in the hopes of a kind word that I am sore in want of. I know that what I said must hurt you, and I knew it then. It would have been easy to have spoken smooth, easy to lie to you; can you not think how

I was tempted to the same? Cannot you see the truth of my heart shine out?"

"I think here is a great deal of work, Mr. Balfour," said she. "I think we will have met but the once, and will can part like gentle-folk."

"O, let me have one to believe in me!" I pleaded, "I canna bear it else. The whole world is clanned against me. How am I to go through with my dreadful fate? If there's to be none to believe in me, I cannot do it. The man must just die, for I cannot do it."

She had still looked straight in front of her, head in air; but at my words or the tone of my voice she came to a stop. "What is this you say?" she asked. "What are you talking of?"

"It is my testimony which may save an innocent life," said I, "and they will not suffer me to bear it. What would you do yourself? You know what this is, whose father lies in danger. Would you desert the poor soul? They have tried all ways with me. They have sought to bribe me; they offered me hills and valleys. And today that sleuth-hound told me how I stood, and to what a length he would go to butcher and disgrace me. I am to be brought in a party to the murder; I am to have held Glenure in talk for money and old clothes; I am to be killed and shamed. If this is the way I am to fall, and me scarce a man—if this is the story to be told of me in all Scotland—if you are to believe it too, and my name is to be nothing but a byword— Catriona, how can I go through with it? The thing's not possible; it's more than a man has in his heart."

I poured my words out in a whirl, one upon the other; and when I stopped I found her gazing on me with a startled face.

"Glenure! It is the Appin murder," she said softly, but with a very deep surprise.

I had turned back to bear her company, and we were now come near the head of the brae above Dean village. At this word I stepped in front of her like one suddenly distracted.

"For God's sake!" I cried, "for God's sake, what is this that I have done?" and carried my fists to my temples. "What made me do it? Sure, I am bewitched to say these things!"

"In the name of heaven, what ails you now?" she cried.

"I gave my honour," I groaned, "I gave my honour, and now I have broke it. O Catriona!"

"I am asking you what it is," she said; "was it these things you should not have spoken? And do you think *I* have no honour, then? or that I am one that would betray a friend? I hold up my right hand to you and swear."

"O, I knew you would be true!" said I. "It's me—it's here. I that stood but this morning and outfaced them, that risked rather to die disgraced upon the gallows than do wrong—and a few hours after I throw my honour away by the roadside in common talk! 'There is one thing clear upon our interview,' says he, 'that I can rely on your pledged word.' Where is my word now? Who could believe me now? *You* could not believe me. I am clean fallen down; I had best die!" All this I said with a weeping voice, but I had no tears in my body.

"My heart is sore for you," said she, "but be sure you are too nice. I would not believe you, do you say? I would trust you with anything. And these men? I would not be thinking of them! Men who go about to entrap and to destroy you! Fy! this is no time to crouch. Look up! Do you not think I will be admiring you like a great hero of the good—and you a boy not much older than myself? And because you said a word too much in a friend's ear, that would die ere she betrayed you—to make such a matter! It is one thing that we must both forget."

"Catriona," said I, looking at her, hang-dog, "is this true of it? Would ye trust me yet?"

"Will you not believe the tears upon my face?" she cried. "It is the world I am thinking of you, Mr. David Balfour. Let them hang you; I will never forget, I will grow old and still remember you. I think it is great to die so; I will envy you that gallows."

"And maybe all this while I am but a child frighted with bogles," said I. "Maybe they but make a mock of me."

"It is what I must know," she said. "I must hear the whole. The harm is done, at all events, and I must hear the whole."

I had sat down on the wayside, where she took a place beside me, and I told her all that matter much as I have written it, my thoughts about her father's dealing being alone omitted.

"Well," she said, when I had finished, "you are a hero, surely, and I never would have thought that same! And I think you are in peril, too. O, Simon Fraser! to think upon that man! For his life and the dirty money, to be dealing in such traffic!" And just then she called out aloud with a queer word that was common with her, and belongs, I believe, to her own language. "My torture!" says she, "look at the sun!"

Indeed, it was already dipping towards the mountains.

She bid me come again soon, gave me her hand, and left me in a turmoil of glad spirits. I delayed to go home to my lodging, for I had a terror of immediate arrest; but got some supper at a change-house, and the better part of that night walked by myself in the barley-fields, and had such a sense of Catriona's presence that I seemed to bear her in my arms.

CHAPTER VIII

The Bravo

The next day, August 29th, I kept my appointment at the Advocate's in a coat that I had made to my own measure, and was but newly ready.

"Aha," says Prestongrange, "you are very fine today; my misses are to have a fine cavalier. Come, I take that kind of you. I take that kind of you, Mr. David. O, we shall do very well yet, and I believe your troubles are nearly at an end."

"You have news for me?" cried I.

"Beyond anticipation," he replied. "Your testimony is after all to be received; and you may go, if you will, in my company to the trial, which is to be held at Inverary, Thursday, 21st *proximo*."

I was too much amazed to find words.

"In the meanwhile," he continued, "though I will not ask you to renew your pledge, I must caution you strictly to be reticent. Tomorrow your precognition must be taken; and outside of that, do you know, I think least said will be soonest mended."

"I shall try to go discreetly," said I. "I believe it is yourself that I must thank for this crowning mercy, and I do thank you gratefully. After yesterday, my lord, this is like the doors of heaven. I cannot find it in my heart to get the thing believed."

"Ah, but you must try and manage, you must try and manage to believe it," says he, soothing-like, "and I am very glad to hear your acknowledgment of obligation, for I think you may be able to repay me very shortly"—he coughed—"or even now. The matter is much changed. Your testimony, which I shall not trouble you for today, will doubtless alter the complexion of the case for all concerned, and this makes it less delicate for me to enter with you on a side issue."

"My lord," I interrupted, "excuse me for interrupting you, but how has this been brought about? The obstacles you told me of on Saturday appeared even to me to be quite insurmountable; how has it been contrived?"

"My dear Mr. David," said he, "it would never do for me to divulge (even to you, as you say) the councils of the Government; and you must content yourself, if you please, with the gross fact."

He smiled upon me like a father as he spoke, playing the while with a new pen; methought it was impossible there could be any shadow of deception in the man: yet when he drew to him a sheet of paper, dipped his pen among the ink, and began again to address me, I was somehow not so certain, and fell instinctively into an attitude of guard.

"There is a point I wish to touch upon," he began. "I purposely left it before upon one side, which need be now no longer necessary. This is not, of course, a part of your examination, which is to follow by another hand; this is a private interest of my own.—You say you encountered Alan Breck upon the hill?"

"I did, my lord," said I.

"This was immediately after the murder?"

"It was."

"Did you speak to him?"

"I did."

"You had known him before, I think?" says my lord carelessly.

"I cannot guess your reason for so thinking, my lord," I replied, "but such is the fact."

"And when did you part with him again?" said he.

"I reserve my answer," said I. "The question will be put to me at the assize."

"Mr. Balfour," said he, "will you not understand that all this is without prejudice to yourself? I have promised you life and honour; and, believe me, I can keep my word. You are therefore clear of all anxiety. Alan, it appears, you suppose you can protect; and you talk to me of your gratitude, which I think (if you push me) is not ill-deserved. There are a great many different considerations all pointing the same way; and I will never be persuaded that you could not help us (if you chose) to put salt on Alan's tail."

"My lord," said I, "I give you my word I do not so much as guess where Alan is."

He paused a breath. "Nor how he might be found?" he asked.

I sat before him like a log of wood.

"And so much for your gratitude, Mr. David!" he observed. Again there was a piece of silence. "Well," said he, rising, "I am not fortunate, and we are a couple at cross-purposes. Let us speak of it no more; you will receive notice when, where, and by whom, we are to take your precognition. And in the meantime, my misses must be waiting you. They will never forgive me if I detain their cavalier."

Into the hands of these Graces I was accordingly offered up, and found them dressed beyond what I had thought possible, and looking fair as a posy.

As we went forth from the doors a small circumstance occurred which came afterwards to look extremely big. I heard a whistle sound loud and brief like a signal, and, looking all about, spied for one moment the red head of Neil of the Tom, the son of Duncan. The next moment he was gone again, nor could I see so much as the skirt-tail of Catriona, upon whom I naturally supposed him to be then attending.

My three keepers led me out by Bristo and the Bruntsfield Links; whence a path carried us to Hope Park, a beautiful pleasance, laid with gravel-walks, furnished with seats and summer-sheds, and warded by a keeper. The way there was a little longsome; the two younger misses affected an air of genteel weariness that damped me cruelly, the eldest considered me with something that at times appeared like mirth; and though I thought I did myself more justice than the day before, it was not without some effort. Upon our reaching the park I was launched on a bevy of eight or ten young gentlemen (some of them cockaded officers, the rest chiefly advocates) who crowded to attend upon these beauties; and though I was presented to all of them in very good words, it seemed I was by all immediately forgotten. Young folk in a company are like to savage animals; they fall upon or scorn a stranger without civility, or I may say, humanity; and I am sure, if I had been among baboons, they would have shown me quite as much of both. Some of the advocates set up to be wits, and some of the soldiers to be rattles; and I could not tell which of these extremes annoyed me most. All had a manner of handling their swords and coat-skirts, for the which (in mere black envy) I could have kicked them from that park. I daresay, upon their side, they grudged me extremely the fine company in which I had arrived; and altogether I had soon fallen behind, and stepped stiffly in the rear of all that merriment with my own thoughts.

From these I was recalled by one of the officers, Lieutenant Hector Duncansby, a gawky, leering Highland boy, asking if my name was not "Palfour."

I told him it was, not very kindly, for his manner was scant civil.

"Ha, Palfour," says he, and then, repeating it, "Palfour, Palfour!"

"I am afraid you do not like my name, sir," says I, annoyed with myself to be annoyed with such a rustical fellow.

"No," says he, "but I wass thinking."

"I would not advise you to make a practice of that, sir," says I. "I feel sure you would not find it to agree with you."

"Tit you effer hear where Alan Grigor fand the tangs?" said he.

I asked him what he could possibly mean, and he answered, with a heckling laugh, that he thought I must have found the poker in the same place and swallowed it.

There could be no mistake about this, and my cheek burned.

"Before I went about to put affronts on gentlemen," said I, "I think I would learn the English language first."

He took me by the sleeve with a nod and a wink, and led me quietly outside Hope Park. But no sooner were we beyond the view of the promenaders than the fashion of his countenance changed. "You tam lowland scoon'rel!" cries he, and hit me a buffet on the jaw with his closed fist.

I paid him as good or better on the return; whereupon he stepped a little back and took off his hat to me decorously.

"Enough plows, I think," says he. "I will be the offended shentleman, for who effer heard of such suffeeciency as tell a shentlemans that is the King's officer he canna speak Cot's English? We have swords at our hurdies, and here is the King's Park at hand. Will ye walk first, or let me show ye the way?"

I returned his bow, told him to go first, and followed him. As he went I heard him grumble to himself about *Cot's English* and the *King's coat*, so that I might have supposed him to be seriously offended. But his manner at the beginning of our interview was there to belie him. It was manifest he had come prepared to fasten a quarrel on me, right or wrong; manifest that I was taken in a fresh contrivance of my enemies; and to me (conscious as I was of my deficiencies) manifest enough that I should be the one to fall in our encounter.

As we came into that rough, rocky desert of the King's Park I was tempted half a dozen times to take to my heels and run for it, so loath was I to show my ignorance in fencing, and so much averse to die or even to be wounded. But I considered if their malice went as far as this, it would likely stick at nothing; and that to fall by the sword, however ungracefully, was still an improvement on the gallows. I considered, besides, that by the unguarded pertness of my words and the quickness of my blow, I had put myself quite out of court; and that even if I ran, my adversary would probably pursue and catch me, which would add disgrace to my misfortune. So that, taking all in all, I continued marching behind him, much as a man follows the hangman, and certainly with no more hope.

We went about the end of the long craigs, and came into the Hunter's Bog. Here, on a piece of fair turf, my adversary drew. There was nobody there to see us but some birds; and no resource for me but to follow his example, and stand on guard with the best face I could display. It seems it was not good enough for Mr. Duncansby, who spied some flaw in my manœuvres, paused, looked upon me sharply, and came off and on, and menaced me with his blade in the air. As I had seen no such proceedings from Alan, and was besides a good deal affected with the proximity of death, I grew quite bewildered, stood helpless, and could have longed to run away.

"Fat deil ails her?" cries the lieutenant.

And suddenly engaging, he twitched the sword out of my grasp, and sent it flying far among the rushes.

Twice was this manoeuvure repeated; and the third time, when I brought back my humiliated weapon, I found he had returned his own to the scabbard, and stood awaiting me with a face of some anger, and his hands clasped under his skirt.

"Pe tamned if I touch you!" he cried, and asked me bitterly what right I had to stand up before "shentlemans" when I did not know the back of a sword from the front of it.

I answered that was the fault of my upbringing; and would he do me the justice to say I had given him all the satisfaction it was unfortunately in my power to offer, and had stood up like a man?

"And that is the truth," said he. "I am fery prave myself, and pold as a lions. But to stand up there—and you ken naething of fence!—the way that you did, I declare it was peyond me. And I am sorry for the plow; though I declare I pelief your own was the elder brother, and my heid still sings with it. And I declare if I had kent what way it wass, I would not put a hand to such a piece of pusiness."

"That is handsomely said," I replied, "and I am sure you will not stand up a second time to be the actor for my private enemies."

"Indeed, no, Palfour," said he; "and I think I wass used extremely suffeeiently myself to be set up to fecht with an auld wife, or all the same as a bairn whateffer! And I will tell the Master so, and fecht him, by Cot, himself!"

"And if you knew the nature of Mr. Simon's quarrel with me," said I, "you would be yet the more affronted to be mingled up with such affairs."

He swore he could well believe it; that all the Lovats were made of the same meal and the devil was the miller that ground that; then suddenly shaking me by the hand, he vowed I was a pretty enough fellow after all, that it was a thousand pities I had been neglected, and that if he could find the time he would give an eye himself to have me educated.

"You can do me a better service than even what you propose," said I; and when he had asked its nature—"Come with me to the house of one of my enemies, and testify how I have carried myself this day," I told him. "That will be the true service. For though he has sent me a gallant adversary for the first, the thought in Mr. Simon's mind is merely murder. There will be a second and then a third; and by what you have seen of my cleverness with the cold steel, you can judge for yourself what is like to be the upshot."

"And I would not like it myself, if I wass no more of a man than what you wass!" he cried. "But I will do you right, Palfour. Lead on!"

If I had walked slowly on the way into that accursed park, my heels were light enough on the way out. They kept time to a very good old air, that is as ancient as the Bible, and the words of it are: "*Surely the bitterness of death is past.*" I mind that I was extremely thirsty, and had a drink at St. Margaret's Well on the road down, and the sweetness of that water passed belief. We went through the Sanctuary, up the Canongate, in by the Nether Bow, and straight to Prestongrange's door, talking as we came, and arranging the details of our affair. The footman owned his master was at home, but declared him engaged with other gentlemen on very private business, and his door forbidden.

"My business is but for three minutes, and it cannot wait," said I. "You may say it is by no means private, and I shall be even glad to have some witnesses."

As the man departed unwillingly enough upon this errand, we made so bold as to follow him to the antechamber, whence I could hear for a while the murmuring of several voices in the room within. The truth is, they were three at the one table—Prestongrange, Simon Fraser, and Mr. Erskine, Sheriff of Perth; and as they were met in consultation on the very business of the Appin murder, they were a little disturbed at my appearance, but decided to receive me.

"Well, well, Mr. Balfour, and what brings you here again? and who is this you bring with you?" says Prestongrange.

As for Fraser, he looked before him on the table.

"He is here to bear a little testimony in my favour, my lord, which I think it very needful you should hear," said I, and turned to Duncansby.

"I have only to say this," said the lieutenant, "that I stood up this day with Palfour in the Hunter's Pog, which I am now fery sorry for, and he behaved himself as pretty as a shentlemans could ask it. And I have creat respects for Palfour," he added.

"I thank you for your honest expressions," said I.

Whereupon Duncansby made his bow to the company, and left the chamber, as we had agreed upon before.

"What have I to do with this?" says Prestongrange.

"I will tell your lordship in two words," said I. "I have brought this gentleman, a King's officer, to do me so much justice. Now I think my character is covered, and until a certain date, which your lordship can very well supply, it will be quite in vain to despatch against me any more officers. I will not consent to fight my way through the garrison of the castle."

The veins swelled on Prestongrange's brow, and he regarded me with fury.

"I think the devil uncoupled this dog of a lad between my legs!" he cried; and then, turning fiercely on his neighbour, "This is some of your work, Simon," he said. "I spy your hand in the business, and, let me tell you, I resent it. It is disloyal, when we are agreed upon one expedient, to follow another in the dark. You are disloyal to me. What! you let me send this lad to the place with my very daughters! And because I let drop a word to you. ...Fy, sir, keep your dishonours to yourself!"

Simon was deadly pale. "I will be a kick-ball between you and the Duke no longer," he exclaimed. "Either come to an agreement, or come to a differ, and have it out among yourselves. But I will no longer fetch and carry, and get your contrary instructions, and be blamed by both. For if I were to tell you what I think of all your Hanover business it would make your head sing."

But Sheriff Erskine had preserved his temper, and now intervened smoothly. "And in the meantime," says he, "I think we should tell Mr. Balfour that his character for valour is quite established. He may sleep in peace. Until the date he was so good as to refer to, it shall be put to the proof no more."

His coolness brought the others to their prudence; and they made haste, with a somewhat distracted civility, to pack me from the house.

CHAPTER IX

The Heather on Fire

When I left Prestongrange that afternoon I was for the first time angry. The Advocate had made a mock of me. He had pretended my testimony was to be received and myself respected; and in that very hour, not only was Simon practising against my life by the hands of the Highland soldier, but (as appeared from his own language) Prestongrange himself had some design in operation. I counted my enemies: Prestongrange with all the King's authority behind him; and the Duke with the power of the West Highlands; and the Lovat interest by their side to help them with so great a force in the north, and the whole clan of old Jacobite spies and traffickers. And when I remembered James More, and the red head of Neil the son of Duncan, I thought there was perhaps a fourth in the confederacy, and what remained of Rob Roy's old desperate sept of caterans would be banded against me with the others. One thing was requisite—some strong friend or wise adviser. The country must be full of such, both able and eager to support me, or Lovat and the Duke and Prestongrange had not been nosing for expedients; and it made me rage to think that I might brush against my champions in the street and be no wiser.

And just then (like an answer) a gentleman brushed against me going by, gave me a meaning look, and turned into a close. I knew him with the tail of my eye—it was Stewart the Writer; and, blessing my good fortune, turned in to follow him. As soon as I had entered the close I saw him standing in the mouth of a stair, where he made me a signal and immediately vanished. Seven storeys up, there he was again in a house-door, the which he locked behind us after we had entered. The house was quite dismantled, with not a stick of furniture; indeed, it was one of which Stewart had the letting in his hands.

"We'll have to sit upon the floor," said he, "but we're safe here for the time being, and I've been wearying to see ye, Mr. Balfour."

"How's it with Alan?" I asked.

"Brawly," said he. "Andie picks him up at Gillane Sands tomorrow, Wednesday. He was keen to say good-bye to ye, but, the way that things were going, I was feared the pair of ye was maybe best apart. And that brings me to the essential: how does your business speed?"

"Why," said I, "I was told only this morning that my testimony was accepted, and I was to travel to Inverary with the Advocate, no less."

"Hout awa!" cried Stewart. "I'll never believe that."

"I have maybe a suspicion of my own," says I, "but I would like fine to hear your reasons."

"Well, I tell ye fairly, I'm horn-mad," cries Stewart. "If my one hand could pull their Government down I would pluck it like a rotten apple. I'm doer for Appin and for James of the Glens; and, of course, it's my duty to defend my kinsman for his life. Hear how it goes with me, and I'll leave the judgment of it to yourself. The first thing they have to do is to get rid of Alan. They canna bring in James as art and part until they've brought in Alan first as principal; that's sound law: they could never put the cart before the horse."

"And how are they to bring in Alan till they can catch him?" says I.

"Ah, but there is a way to evite that arrestment," said he. "Sound law, too. It would be a bonny thing if, by the escape of one ill-doer another was to go scatheless, and the remeid is to summon the principal and put him to outlawry for the non-compearance. Now there's four places where a person can be summoned: at his dwelling-house; at a place where he has resided forty days; at the head burgh of the shire where he ordinarily resorts; or lastly (if there be ground to think him furth of Scotland) *at the cross of Edinburgh, and the pier and shore of Leith, for sixty days*. The purpose of which last provision is evident upon its face: being that outgoing ships may have time to carry news of the transaction, and the summoning be something other than a form. Now take the case of Alan. He has no dwelling-house that ever I could hear of; I would be obliged if any one would show me where he has lived forty days together since the 'Forty-five; there is no shire where he resorts, whether ordinarily or extraordinarily; if he has a domicile at all, which I misdoubt, it must be with his regiment in France; and if he is not yet furth of Scotland (as we happen to know and they happen to guess) it must be evident to the most dull it's what he's aiming for. Where, then, and what way should he be summoned? I ask it at yourself, a layman."

"You have given the very words," said I. "Here at the cross, and at the pier and shore of Leith, for sixty days."

"Ye're a sounder Scots lawyer than Prestongrange, then!" cries the Writer. "He has had Alan summoned once; that was on the twenty-fifth, the day that we first met. Once, and done with it. And where? Where, but at the cross of Inverary, the head burgh of the Campbells? A word in your ear, Mr. Balfour—they're not seeking Alan."

"What do you mean?" I cried. "Not seeking him?"

"By the best that I can make of it," said he. "Not wanting to find him, in my poor thought. They think perhaps he might set up a fair defence, upon the back of which James, the man they're really after, might climb out. This is not a case, ye see, it's a conspiracy."

"Yet I can tell you Prestongrange asked after Alan keenly," said I; "though, when I come to think of it, he was something of the easiest put by."

"See that," says he. "But there! I may be right or wrong, that's guesswork at the best, and let me get to my facts again. It comes to my ears that James and the witnesses—the witnesses, Mr. Balfour!—lay in close dungeons, and shackled forbye, in the military prison at Fort William; none allowed in to them, nor they to write. The witnesses, Mr. Balfour; heard ye ever the match of that? I assure ye, no old, crooked Stewart of the gang ever outfaced the law more impudently. It's clean in the two eyes of the Act of Parliament of 1700, anent wrongous imprisonment. No sooner did I get the news than I petitioned the Lord Justice-Clerk. I have his word today. There's law for ye! here's justice!"

He put a paper in my hand, that same mealy-mouthed, false-faced paper that was printed since in the pamphlet "by a bystander," for behoof (as the title says) of James's "poor widow and five children."

"See," said Stewart, "he couldn't dare to refuse me access to my client, so he *recommends the commanding officer to let me in.* Recommends!—the Lord Justice-Clerk of Scotland recommends. Is not the purpose of such language plain? They hope the officer may be so dull, or so very much the reverse, as to refuse the recommendation. I would have to make the journey back again betwixt here and Fort William. Then would follow a fresh delay till I got fresh authority, and they had disavowed the officer—military man, notoriously ignorant of the law, and that—I ken the cant of it. Then the journey a third time; and there we should be on the immediate heels of the trial before I had received my first instruction. Am I not right to call this a conspiracy?"

"It will bear that colour," said I.

"And I'll go on to prove it you outright," said he. "They have the right to hold James in prison, yet they cannot deny me to visit him. They have no right to hold the witnesses; but am I to get a sight of them, that should be as free as the Lord Justice-Clerk himself? See—read: *For the rest, refuses to give any orders to keepers of prisons who are not accused as having done anything contrary to the duties of their office.* Anything contrary! Sirs! And the Act of seventeen hunner? Mr. Balfour, this makes my heart to burst; the heather is on fire inside my wame."

"And the plain English of that phrase," said I, "is that the witnesses are still to lie in prison, and you are not to see them?"

"And I am not to see them until Inverary, when the court is set!" cries he, "and then to hear Prestongrange upon *the anxious responsibilities of his office and the great facilities afforded the defence!* But I'll begowk them there, Mr. David. I have a plan to waylay the witnesses upon the road, and see if I canna get a little harle of justice out of the *military man notoriously ignorant of the law* that shall command the party."

It was actually so—it was actually on the wayside near Tyndrum, and by the connivance of a soldier officer, that Mr. Stewart first saw the witnesses upon the case.

"There is nothing that would surprise me in this business," I remarked.

"I'll surprise you ere I'm done!" cries he. "Do ye see this?"— producing a print still wet from the press. "This is the libel: see, there's Prestongrange's name to the list of witnesses, and I find no word of any Balfour. But here is not the question. Who do ye think paid for the printing of this paper?"

"I suppose it would likely be King George," said I.

"But it happens it was me!" he cried. "Not but it was printed by and for themselves, for the Grants and the Erskines, and yon thief of the black midnight, Simon Fraser. But could *I* win to get a copy? No! I was to go blindfold to my defence; I was to hear the charges for the first time in court alongst the jury."

"Is not this against the law?" I asked.

"I cannot say so much," he replied. "It was a favour so natural and so constantly rendered (till this nonesuch business) that the law has never looked to it. And now admire the hand of Providence! A stranger is in Fleming's printing-house, spies a proof on the floor, picks it up, and carries it to me. Of all things, it was just this libel. Whereupon I had it set again— printed at the expense of the defence: *sumptibus moesti rei:* heard ever man the like of it?—and here it is for anybody, the muckle secret out—all may see it now. But how do you think I would enjoy this, that has the life of my kinsman on my conscience?"

"Troth, I think you would enjoy it ill," said I.

"And now you see how it is," he concluded, "and why, when you tell me your evidence is to be let in, I laugh aloud in your face."

It was now my turn. I laid before him in brief Mr. Simon's threats and offers, and the whole incident of the bravo, with the subsequent scene at Prestongrange's. Of my first talk, according to promise, I said nothing, nor indeed was it necessary. All the time I was talking Stewart nodded his head like a mechanical figure; and no sooner had my voice ceased than he opened his mouth and gave me his opinion in two words, dwelling strong on both of them.

"Disappear yourself," said he.

"I do not take you," said I.

"Then I'll carry you there," said he. "By my view of it you're to disappear whatever. O, that's outside debate. The Advocate, who is not without some spunks of a remainder decency, has wrung your life-safe out of Simon and the Duke. He has refused to put you on your trial, and refused to have you killed; and there is the clue to their ill words together, for Simon and the Duke can keep faith with neither friend nor enemy. Ye're not to be tried then, and ye're not to be murdered; but I'm in bitter error if ye're not to be kidnapped and carried away like the Lady Grange. Bet me what ye please—there was their *expedient!*"

"You make me think," said I, and told him of the whistle and the red-headed retainer, Neil.

"Wherever James More is there's one big rogue, never be deceived on that," said he. "His father was none so ill a man, though a kenning on the wrong side of the law, and no friend to my family, that I should waste my breath to be defending him! But as for James, he's a brock and a blagyard. I like the appearance of this red-headed Neil as little as yourself. It looks uncanny: fiegh! it smells bad. It was old Lovat that managed the Lady Grange affair; if young Lovat is to handle yours, it'll be all in the family. What's James More in prison for? The same offence: abduction. His men have had practice in the business.

86

He'll be to lend them to be Simon's instruments; and the next thing we'll be hearing, James will have made his peace, or else he'll have escaped; and you'll be in Benbecula or Applecross."

"Ye make a strong case," I admitted.

"And what I want," he resumed, "is that you should disappear yourself ere they can get their hands upon ye. Lie quiet until just before the trial, and spring upon them at the last of it when they'll be looking for you least. This is always supposing, Mr. Balfour, that your evidence is worth so very great a measure of both risk and fash."

"I will tell you one thing," said I. "I saw the murderer, and it was not Alan."

"Then, by God, my cousin's saved!" cried Stewart. "You have his life upon your tongue; and there's neither time, risk, nor money to be spared to bring you to the trial." He emptied his pockets on the floor. "Here is all that I have by me," he went on. "Take it, ye'll want it ere ye're through. Go straight down this close, there's a way out by there to the Lang Dykes, and by my will of it! see no more of Edinburgh till the clash is over."

"Where am I to go, then?" I inquired.

"And I wish that I could tell ye!" says he, "but all the places that I could send ye to would be just the places they would seek. No, ye must fend for yourself, and God be your guiding! Five days before the trial, September the sixteen, get word to me at the 'King's Arms' in Stirling; and if ye've managed for yourself as long as that, I'll see that ye reach Inverary."

"One thing more," said I: "Can I no' see Alan?"

He seemed boggled. "Hech, I would rather you wouldna," said he. "But I can never deny that Alan is extremely keen of it, and is to lie this night by Silvermills on purpose. If you're sure that you're not followed, Mr. Balfour—but make sure of that,—lie in a good place and watch your road for a clear hour before ye risk it. It would be a dreadful business if both you and him was to miscarry!"

CHAPTER X

The Red–Headed Man

It was about half-past three when I came forth on the Lang
Dykes. Dean was where I wanted to go. Since Catriona dwelled
there, and her kinsfolk the Glengyle Macgregors appeared
almost certainly to be employed against me, it was just one of
the few places I should have kept away from; and being a very
young man, and beginning to be very much in love, I turned my
face in that direction without pause. As a salve to my conscience
and common sense, however, I took a measure of precaution.
Coming over the crown of a bit of a rise in the road, I clapped
down suddenly among the barley and lay waiting. After a while,
a man went by that looked to be a Highlandman, but I had
never seen him till that hour. Presently after came Neil of the
red head. The next to go past was a miller's cart, and after that
nothing but manifest country people. Here was enough to have
turned the most foolhardy from his purpose, but my inclination
ran too strong the other way. I argued it out that if Neil was on
that road, it was the right road to find him in, leading direct to
his chief's daughter; as for the other Highlandman, if I was to be
startled off by every Highlandman I saw, I would scarce reach
anywhere. And having quite satisfied myself with this
disingenuous debate, I made the better speed of it, and came a
little after four to Mrs. Drummond-Ogilvy's.

Both ladies were within the house; and upon my perceiving
them together by the open door, I plucked off my hat and said,
"Here was a lad come seeking saxpence," which I thought
might please the dowager.

Catriona ran out to greet me heartily, and, to my surprise, the
old lady seemed scarce less forward than herself. I learned
long afterwards that she had despatched a horseman by
daylight to Rankeillor at the Queen's Ferry, whom she knew to
be the doer for Shaws, and had then in her pocket a letter from
that good friend of mine, presenting, in the most favourable

view, my character and prospects. But had I read it I could scarce have seen more clear in her designs. Maybe I was *countryfeed;* at least, I was not so much so as she thought; and it was plain enough, even to my homespun wits, that she was bent to hammer up a match between her cousin and a beardless boy that was something of a laird in Lothian.

"Saxpence had better take his broth with us, Catrine," says she. "Run and tell the lasses."

And for the little while we were alone she was at a good deal of pains to flatter me; always cleverly, always with the appearance of a banter, still calling me Saxpence, but with such a turn that should rather uplift me in my own opinion. When Catriona returned, the design became if possible more obvious; and she showed off the girl's advantages like a horse-couper with a horse. My face flamed that she should think me so obtuse. Now I would fancy the girl was being innocently made a show of, and then I could have beaten the old carline wife with a cudgel; and now, that perhaps these two had set their heads together to entrap me, and at that I sat and gloomed betwixt them like the very image of ill-will. At last the match-maker had a better device, which was to leave the pair of us alone. When my suspicions are anyway roused it is sometimes a little the wrong side of easy to allay them. But though I knew what breed she was of, and that was a breed of thieves, I could never look in Catriona's face and disbelieve her.

"I must not ask?" says she eagerly, the same moment we were left alone.

"Ah, but today I can talk with a free conscience," I replied. "I am lightened of my pledge, and indeed (after what has come and gone since morning) I would not have renewed it were it asked."

"Tell me," she said. "My cousin will not be so long."

So I told her the tale of the lieutenant from the first step to the last of it, making it as mirthful as I could, and, indeed, there was matter of mirth in that absurdity.

"And I think you will be as little fitted for the rudas men as for the pretty ladies, after all!" says she, when I had done. "But what was your father that he could not learn you to draw the sword? It is most ungentle; I have not heard the match of that in any one."

"It is most misconvenient at least," said I; "and I think my father (honest man!) must have been wool-gathering to learn me Latin in the place of it. But you see I do the best I can, and just stand up like Lot's wife and let them hammer at me."

"Do you know what makes me smile?" said she. "Well, it is this. I am made this way, that I should have been a man child. In my own thoughts it is so I am always; and I go on telling myself about this thing that is to befall and that. Then it comes to the place of the fighting, and it comes over me that I am only a girl at all events, and cannot hold a sword or give one good blow; and then I have to twist my story round about, so that the fighting is to stop, and yet me have the best of it, just like you and the lieutenant; and I am the boy that makes the fine speeches all through, like Mr. David Balfour."

"You are a bloodthirsty maid," said I.

"Well, I know it is good to sew and spin, and to make samplers," she said, "but if you were to do nothing else in the great world, I think you will say yourself it is a driech business; and it is not that I want to kill, I think. Did ever you kill any one?"

"That I have, as it chances. Two, no less, and me still a lad that should be at the college," said I. "But yet, in the look-back, I take no shame for it."

"But how did you feel, then—after it?" she asked.

"'Deed, I sat down and grat like a bairn," said I.

"I know that, too," she cried. "I feel where these tears should come from. And at any rate, I would not wish to kill, only to be Catherine Douglas, that put her arm through the staples of the bolt, where it was broken. That is my chief hero. Would you not love to die so—for your king?" she asked.

"Troth," said I, "my affection for my king, God bless the

puggy face of him! is under more control; and I thought I saw death so near to me this day already, that I am rather taken up with the notion of living."

"Right," she said, "the right mind of a man! Only you must learn arms; I would not like to have a friend that cannot strike. But it will not have been with the sword that you killed these two?"

"Indeed, no," said I, "but with a pair of pistols. And a fortunate thing it was the men were so near-hand to me, for I am about as clever with the pistols as I am with the sword."

So then she drew from me the story of our battle in the brig, which I had omitted in my first account of my affairs.

"Yes," said she, "you are brave. And your friend, I admire and love him."

"Well, and I think any one would!" said I. "He has his faults, like other folk; but he is brave and staunch and kind, God bless him! That will be a strange day when I forget Alan." And the thought of him, and that it was within my choice to speak with him that night, had almost overcome me.

"And where will my head be gone that I have not told my news!" she cried, and spoke of a letter from her father, bearing that she might visit him tomorrow in the castle, whither he was now transferred, and that his affairs were mending. "You do not like to hear it," said she. "Will you judge my father and not know him?"

"I am a thousand miles from judging," I replied. "And I give you my word I do rejoice to know your heart is lightened. If my face fell at all, as I suppose it must, you will allow this is rather an ill day for compositions, and the people in power extremely ill persons to be compounding with. I have Simon Fraser extremely heavy on my stomach still."

"Ah!" she cried, "you will not be evening these two; and you should bear in mind that Prestongrange and James More, my father, are of the one blood."

"I never heard tell of that," said I.

"It is rather singular how little you are acquainted with," said she. "One part may call themselves Grant, and one Macgregor, but they are still of the same clan. They are all the sons of Alpin, from whom, I think, our country has its name."

"What country is that?" I asked.

"My country and yours," said she.

"This is my day for discoveries, I think," said I, "for I always thought the name of it was Scotland."

"Scotland is the name of what you call Ireland," she replied. "But the old ancient true name of this place that we have our foot-soles on, and that our bones are made of, will be Alban. It was Alban they called it when our forefathers will be fighting for it against Rome and Alexander; and it is called so still in your own tongue that you forget."

"Troth," said I, "and that I never learned!" For I lacked heart to take her up about the Macedonian.

"But your fathers and mothers talked it, one generation with another," said she. "And it was sung about the cradles before you or me were ever dreamed of; and your name remembers it still. Ah, if you could talk that language you would find me another girl. The heart speaks in that tongue."

I had a meal with the two ladies, all very good, served in fine old plate, and the wine excellent, for it seems that Mrs. Ogilvy was rich. Our talk, too, was pleasant enough; but as soon as I saw the sun decline sharply and the shadows to run out long, I rose to take my leave. For my mind was now made up to say farewell to Alan; and it was needful I should see the trysting wood, and reconnoitre it, by daylight. Catriona came with me as far as to the garden gate.

"It is long till I see you now?" she asked.

"It is beyond my judging," I replied. "It will be long, it may be never."

"It may be so," said she. "And you are sorry?"

I bowed my head, looking upon her.

"So am I, at all events," said she. "I have seen you but a small time, but I put you very high. You are true, you are brave; in time I think you will be more of a man yet. I will be proud to hear of that. If you should speed worse, if it will come to fall as we are afraid—O well! think you have the one friend. Long after you are dead, and me an old wife, I will be telling the bairns about David Balfour, and my tears running. I will be telling how we parted, and what I said to you, and did to you. *God go with you, and guide you, prays your little friend:* so I said—I will be telling them—and here is what I did."

She took up my hand and kissed it. This so surprised my spirits that I cried out like one hurt. The colour came strong in her face, and she looked at me and nodded.

"O yes, Mr. David," said she, "that is what I think of you. The heart goes with the lips."

I could read in her face high spirit, and a chivalry like a brave child's; not anything besides. She kissed my hand, as she had kissed Prince Charlie's, with a higher passion than the common kind of clay has any sense of. Nothing before had taught me how deep I was her lover, nor how far I had yet to climb to make her think of me in such a character. Yet I could tell myself I had advanced some way, and that her heart had beat and her blood flowed at thoughts of me.

After that honour she had done me I could offer no more trivial civility. It was even hard for me to speak; a certain lifting in her voice had knocked directly at the door of my own tears.

"I praise God for your kindness, dear," said I. "Farewell, my little friend!" giving her that name which she had given to herself; with which I bowed and left her.

My way was down the glen of the Leith river, towards Stockbridge and Silvermills. A path led in the foot of it, the water bickered and sang in the midst; the sunbeams overhead struck out of the west among long shadows and (as the valley turned) made like a new scene and a new world of it at every corner. With Catriona behind and Alan before me, I was like one lifted up.

The place, besides, and the hour, and the talking of the water, infinitely pleased me; and I lingered in my steps and looked before and behind me as I went. This was the cause, under Providence, that I spied a little in my rear a red head among some bushes.

Anger sprang in my heart, and I turned straight about and walked at a stiff pace to where I came from. The path lay close by the bushes where I had remarked the head. The cover came to the wayside, and as I passed I was all strung up to meet and to resist an onfall. No such thing befell, I went by unmeddled with; and at that, fear increased upon me. It was still day indeed, but the place exceeding solitary. If my haunters had let slip that fair occasion I could but judge they aimed at something more than David Balfour. The lives of Alan and James weighed upon my spirit with the weight of two grown bullocks.

Catriona was yet in the garden walking by herself.

"Catriona," said I, "you see me back again."

"With a changed face," said she.

"I carry two men's lives besides my own," said I. "It would be a sin and a shame not to walk carefully. I was doubtful whether I did right to come here. I would like it ill, if it was by that means we were brought to harm."

"I could tell you one that would be liking it less, and will like little enough to hear you talking at this very same time," she cried. "What have I done, at all events?"

"O, you! you are not alone," I replied. "But since I went off I have been dogged again, and I can give you the name of him that follows me. It is Neil, son of Duncan, your man or your father's."

"To be sure, you are mistaken there," she said, with a white face. "Neil is in Edinburgh on errands from my father."

"It is what I fear," said I, "the last of it. But for his being in Edinburgh I think I can show you another of that. For sure you have some signal, a signal of need, such as would bring him to your help, if he was anywhere within the reach of ears and legs?"

"Why, how will you know that?" says she.

"By means of a magical talisman God gave to me when I was

94

born, and the name they call it by is Commonsense," said I. "Oblige me so far as make your signal, and I will show you the red head of Neil."

No doubt but I spoke bitter and sharp. My heart was bitter. I blamed myself and the girl and hated both of us: her for the vile crew that she was come of, myself for my wanton folly to have stuck my head in such a byke of wasps.

Catriona set her fingers to her lips and whistled once, with an exceeding clear, strong, mounting note, as full as a ploughman's. A while we stood silent: and I was about to ask her to repeat the same, when I heard the sound of some one bursting through the bushes below on the braeside. I pointed in that direction with a smile, and presently Neil leaped into the garden. His eyes burned, and he had a black knife (as they call it on the Highland side) naked in his hand; but, seeing me beside his mistress, stood like a man struck.

"He has come to your call," said I; "judge how near he was to Edinburgh, or what was the nature of your father's errands. Ask himself. If I am to lose my life, or the lives of those that hang by me, through the means of your clan, let me go where I have to go with my eyes open."

She addressed him tremulously in the Gaelic. Remembering Alan's anxious civility in that particular, I could have laughed out loud for bitterness; here, sure, in the midst of these suspicions, was the hour she should have stuck by English.

Twice or thrice they spoke together, and I could make out that Neil (for all his obsequiousness) was an angry man.

Then she turned to me. "He swears it is not," she said.

"Catriona," said I, "do you believe the man yourself?"

She made a gesture like wringing the hands.

"How will I can know?" she cried.

"But I must find some means to know," said I. "I cannot continue to go dovering round in the black night with two men's lives at my girdle! Catriona, try to put yourself in my place, as I vow to God I try hard to put myself in yours. This is no kind of talk that should ever have fallen between me and

95

you; no kind of talk; my heart is sick with it. See, keep him here till two of the morning, and I care not. Try him with that."

They spoke together once more in the Gaelic.

"He says he has James More my father's errand," said she. She was whiter than ever, and her voice faltered as she said it.

"It is pretty plain now," said I, "and may God forgive the wicked!"

She said never anything to that, but continued gazing at me with the same white face.

"This is a fine business," said I again. "Am I to fall, then, and those two along with me?"

"Oh, what am I to do?" she cried. "Could I go against my father's orders, and him in prison, in the danger of his life?"

"But perhaps we go too fast," said I. "This may be a lie too. He may have no right orders; all may be contrived by Simon, and your father knowing nothing."

She burst out weeping between the pair of us; and my heart smote me hard, for I thought this girl was in a dreadful situation.

"Here," said I, "keep him but the one hour; and I'll chance it, and say God bless you."

She put out her hand to me. "I will be needing one good word," she sobbed.

"The full hour, then?" said I, keeping her hand in mine. "Three lives of it, my lass!"

"The full hour!" she said, and cried aloud on her Redeemer to forgive her.

I thought it no fit place for me, and fled.

CHAPTER XI

The Wood by Silvermills

I lost no time, but down through the valley, and by Stockbridge and Silvermills as hard as I could stave. It was Alan's tryst to lie every night between twelve and two "in a bit scrog of wood by east of Silvermills, and by south the south mill-lade." This I found easy enough, where it grew on a steep brae, with the mill-lade flowing swift and deep along the foot of it: and here I began to walk slower and to reflect more reasonably on my employment. I saw I had made but a fool's bargain with Catriona. It was not to be supposed that Neil was sent alone upon his errand, but perhaps he was the only man belonging to James More; in which case, I should have done all I could to hang Catriona's father, and nothing the least material to help myself. To tell the truth, I fancied neither one of these ideas. Suppose, by holding back Neil, the girl should have helped to hang her father, I thought she would never forgive herself this side of time. And suppose there were others pursuing me that moment, what kind of a gift was I come bringing to Alan? and how would I like that?

I was up with the west end of that wood when these two considerations struck me like a cudgel. My feet stopped of themselves, and my heart along with them. "What wild game is this that I have been playing?" thought I; and turned instantly upon my heels to go elsewhere.

This brought my face to Silvermills; the path came past the village with a crook, but all plainly visible; and, Highland or Lowland, there was nobody stirring. Here was my advantage, here was just such a conjuncture as Stewart had counselled me to profit by, and I ran by the side of the mill-lade, fetched about beyond the east corner of the wood, threaded through the midst of it, and returned to the west selvage, whence I could again command the path, and yet be myself unseen. Again it was all empty, and my heart began to rise.

For more than an hour I sat close in the border of the trees, and no hare or eagle could have kept a more particular watch. When that hour began the sun was already set, but the sky still all golden and the daylight clear: before the hour was done it had fallen to be half mirk, the images and distances of things were mingled, and observation began to be difficult. All that time not a foot of man had come east from Silvermills, and the few that had gone west were honest countryfolk and their wives upon the road to bed. If I were tracked by the most cunning spies in Europe, I judged it was beyond the course of nature they could have any jealousy of where I was; and going a little further home into the wood I lay down to wait for Alan.

The strain of my attention had been great, for I had watched not the path only, but every bush and field within my vision. That was now at an end. The moon, which was in her first quarter, glinted a little in the wood; all round there was a stillness of the country; and as I lay there on my back, the next three or four hours, I had a fine occasion to review my conduct.

Two things became plain to me first: that I had had no right to go that day to Dean, and (having gone there) had now no right to be lying where I was. This (where Alan was to come) was just the one wood in all broad Scotland that was, by every proper feeling, closed against me; I admitted that, and yet stayed on, wondering at myself. I thought of the measure with which I had meted to Catriona that same night; how I had prated of the two lives I carried, and had thus forced her to enjeopardy her father's; and how I was here exposing them again, it seemed in wantonness. A good conscience is eight parts of courage. No sooner had I lost conceit of my behaviour, than I seemed to stand disarmed amidst a throng of terrors. Of a sudden I sat up. How if I went now to Prestongrange, caught him (as I still easily might) before he slept, and made a full submission? Who could blame me? Not Stewart the Writer; I had but to say that I was followed, despaired of getting clear, and so gave in. Not Catriona: here, too, I had my answer ready;

that I could not bear she should expose her father. So, in a moment, I could lay all these troubles by, which were after all and truly none of mine; swim clear of the Appin murder; get forth out of hand-stroke of all the Stewarts and Campbells, all the Whigs and Tories, in the land; and live thenceforth to my own mind, and be able to enjoy and to improve my fortunes, and devote some hours of my youth to courting Catriona, which would be surely a more suitable occupation than to hide and run and be followed like a hunted thief, and begin over again the dreadful miseries of my escape with Alan.

At first I thought no shame of this capitulation; I was only amazed I had not thought upon the thing and done it earlier; and began to inquire into the causes of the change. These I traced to my lowness of spirits, that back to my late reck-lessness, and that again to the common, old, public, disconsidered sin of self-indulgence. Instantly the text came in my head, "*How can Satan cast out Satan?*" What? (I thought) I had, by self-indulgence, and the following of pleasant paths, and the lure of a young maid, cast myself wholly out of conceit with my own character, and jeopardised the lives of James and Alan? And I was to seek the way out by the same road as I had entered in? No; the hurt that had been caused by self-indulgence must be cured by self-denial; the flesh I had pampered must be crucified. I looked about me for that course which I least liked to follow: this was to leave the wood without waiting to see Alan, and go forth again alone, in the dark and in the midst of my perplexed and dangerous fortunes.

I have been the more careful to narrate this passage of my reflections, because I think it is of some utility, and may serve as an example to young men. But there is reason (they say) in planting kale, and, even in ethic and religion, room for common sense. It was already close on Alan's hour, and the moon was down. If I left (as I could not very decently whistle to my spies to follow me) they might miss me in the dark and tack themselves to Alan by mistake. If I stayed, I could at the least of it set my friend upon his guard, which might prove his mere salvation. I had adventured other people's safety in a course of self-indulgence; to have endangered them again, and now on a mere design of penance, would have been scarce rational. Accordingly, I had scarce risen from my place, ere I sat down again, but already in a different frame of spirits, and equally marvelling at my past weakness, and rejoicing in my present composure.

Presently after came a crackling in the thicket. Putting my mouth near down to the ground, I whistled a note or two of Alan's air; an answer came, in the like guarded tone, and soon we had knocked together in the dark.

"Is this you at last, Davie?" he whispered.

"Just myself," said I.

"God, man, but I've been wearying to see ye!" says he. "I've had the longest kind of a time. A' day I've had my dwelling into the inside of a stack of hay, where I couldna see the nebs of my ten fingers; and then two hours of it waiting here for you, and you never coming! Dod, and ye're none too soon the way it is, with me to sail the morn! The morn? what am I saying?—the day, I mean."

"Ay, Alan man, the day, sure enough," said I. "It's past twelve now, surely, and ye sail the day. This'll be a long road you have before you."

"We'll have a long crack of it first," said he.

"Well, indeed, and I have a good deal it will be telling you to hear," said I.

And I told him what behoved, making rather a jumble of it, but clear enough when done. He heard me out with very few questions, laughing here and there like a man delighted: and the sound of his laughing (above all there, in the dark, where neither one of us could see the other) was extraordinary friendly to my heart.

"Ay, Davie, ye're a queer character," says he, when I had done: "a queer bitch after a', and I have no mind of meeting with the like of ye. As for your story, Prestongrange is a Whig like yoursel', so I'll say the less of him; and, dod! I believe he was the best friend ye had, if ye could only trust him. But Simon Fraser and James More are my ain kind of cattle, and I'll give them the name that they deserve. The muckle black deil was father to the Frasers, a'body kens that; and as for the Gregara, I never could abye the reek o' them since I could stotter on two feet. I bloodied the nose of one, I mind, when I was still so wambly on my legs that I cowped upon the top of him. A proud man was my father that day, God rest him! and I think he had the cause. I'll never can deny but what Robin was something of a piper," he added; "but as for James More, the deil guide him for me!"

"One thing we have to consider," said I. "Was Charles Stewart right or wrong? Is it only me they're after, or the pair of us?"

"And what's your ain opinion, you that's a man of so much experience?" said he.

"It passes me," said I.

"And me too," says Alan. "Do ye think this lass would keep her word to ye?" he asked.

"I do that," said I.

"Well, there's nae telling," said he. "And anyway, that's over and done: he'll be joined to the rest of them lang syne."

"How many would ye think there would be of them?" I asked.

"That depends," said Alan. "If it was only you, they would likely send two-three lively, brisk young birkies, and if they thought that I was to appear in the employ, I daresay ten or twelve," said he.

It was no use, I gave a little crack of laughter.

"And I think your own two eyes will have seen me drive that number, or the double of it, nearer hand!" cries he.

"It matters the less," said I, "because I am well rid of them for this time."

"Nae doubt that's your opinion," said he; "but I wouldna be the least surprised if they were hunkering in this wood. Ye see, David man, they'll be Hieland folk. There'll be some Frasers, I'm thinking, and some of the Gregara; and I would never deny but what the both of them, and the Gregara in especial, were clever experienced persons. A man kens little till he's driven a spreagh of neat cattle (say) ten miles through a throng lowland country and the black soldiers maybe at his tail. It's there that I learned a great part of my penetration. And ye needna tell me: it's better than war; which is the next best, however, though generally rather a bauchle of a business. Now the Gregara have had grand practice."

"No doubt that's a branch of education that was left out with me," said I.

"And I can see the marks of it upon ye constantly," said Alan. "But that's the strange thing about you folk of the college learning: ye're ignorant, and ye canna see't. Wae's me for my Greek and Hebrew; but, man, I ken that I dinna ken them— there's the differ of it. Now, here's you. Ye lie on your wame a bittie in the bield of this wood, and ye tell me that ye've cuist off these Frasers and Macgregors. Why! *Because I couldna see them*, says you. Ye blockhead, that's their livelihood."

"Take the worst of it," said I, "and what are we to do?"

"I am thinking of that same," said he. "We might twine. It wouldna be greatly to my taste; and forbye that, I see reasons against it. First, it's now unco dark, and it's just humanly possible we might give them the clean slip. If we keep together, we make but the ae line of it; if we gang separate, we make twae of them: the more likelihood to stave in upon some of these gentry of yours. And then, second, if they keep the track of us, it may come to a fecht for it yet, Davie; and then, I'll confess I would be blithe to have you at my oxter, and I think you would be none the worse of having me at yours. So, by my way of it, we should creep out of this wood no further gone than just the inside of next minute, and hold away east for Gillane, where I'm to find my ship. It'll be like old days while it lasts, Davie; and (come the time) we'll have to think what you should be doing. I'm wae to leave ye here, wanting me."

"Have with ye, then!" says I. "Do ye gang back where you were stopping."

"Deil a fear!" said Alan. "They were good folks to me, but I think they would be a good deal disappointed if they saw my bonny face again. For (the way times go) I amna just what ye could call a Walcome Guest. Which makes me the keener for your company, Mr. David Balfour of the Shaws, and set ye up! For, leave aside twa cracks here in the wood with Charlie Stewart, I have scarce said black or white since the day we parted at Corstorphine."

With which he rose from his place, and we began to move quietly eastward through the wood.

CHAPTER XII

On the March again with Alan

It was likely between one and two; the moon (as I have said) was down; a strongish wind, carrying a heavy wrack of cloud, had set in suddenly from the west; and we began our movement in as black a night as ever a fugitive or a murderer wanted. The whiteness of the path guided us into the sleeping town of Broughton, thence through Picardy, and beside my old acquaintance the gibbet of the two thieves. A little beyond we made a useful beacon, which was a light in an upper window of Lochend. Steering by this, but a good deal at random, and with some trampling of the harvest, and stumbling and falling down upon the bauks, we made our way across country, and won forth at last upon the linky, boggy muirland that they call the Figgate Whins. Here, under a bush of whin, we lay down the remainder of that night and slumbered.

The day called us about five. A beautiful morning it was, the high westerly wind still blowing strong, but the clouds all blown away to Europe. Alan was already sitting up and smiling to himself. It was my first sight of my friend since we were parted, and I looked upon him with enjoyment. He had still the same big great-coat on his back; but (what was new) he had now a pair of knitted boot-hose drawn above the knee. Doubtless these were intended for disguise; but, as the day promised to be warm, he made a most unseasonable figure.

"Well, Davie," said he, "is this no' a bonny morning? Here is a day that looks the way that a day ought to. This is a great change of it from the belly of my haystack; and while you were there sottering and sleeping I have done a thing that maybe I do over seldom."

"And what was that?" said I.

"O, just said my prayers," said he.

"And where are my gentry, as ye call them?" I asked.

"Gude kens," says he; "and the short and the long of it is that we must take our chance of them. Up with your foot-soles, Davie! Forth, Fortune, once again of it! And a bonny walk we are like to have."

So we went east by the beach of the sea, towards where the salt-pans were smoking, in by the Esk mouth. No doubt there was a by-ordinary bonny blink of morning sun on Arthur's Seat and the green Pentlands; and the pleasantness of the day appeared to set Alan among nettles.

"I feel like a gomeril," says he, "to be leaving Scotland on a day like this. It sticks in my head; I would maybe like it better to stay here and hing."

"Ay, but ye wouldna, Alan," said I.

"No' but what France is a good place too," he explained; "but it's some way no' the same. It's brawer, I believe, but it's no' Scotland. I like it fine when I'm there, man; yet I kind of weary for Scots divots and the Scots peat-reek."

"If that's all you have to complain of, Alan, it's no such great affair," said I.

"And it sets me ill to be complaining, whatever," said he, "and me but new out of yon deil's haystack."

"And so you were unco weary of your haystack?" I asked.

"Weary's nae word for it," said he. "I'm not just precisely a man that's easily cast down; but I do better with caller air and the lift above my head. I'm like the auld Black Douglas (wasna't?) that likit better to hear the laverock sing than the mouse cheep. And yon place, ye see, Davie—whilk was a very suitable place to hide in, as I'm free to own—was pit mirk from dawn to gloaming. There were days (or nights, for how would I tell one from other?) that seemed to me as long as a long winter."

"How did you know the hour to bide your tryst?" I asked.

"The goodman brought me my meat and a drop brandy, and a candle-dowp to eat it by, about eleeven," said he. "So, when I had swallowed a bit, it would be time to be getting to the wood. There I lay and wearied for ye sore, Davie," says he, laying his hand on my shoulder, "and guessed when the two hours would be about by—unless Charlie Stewart would come and tell me on his watch—and then back to the dooms haystack. Na, it was a driech employ, and praise the Lord that I have warstled through with it!"

"What did you do with yourself?" I asked.

"Faith," said he, "the best I could! Whiles I played at the knucklebones. I'm an extraordinar good hand at the knucklebones, but it's a poor piece of business playing with naebody to admire ye. And whiles I would make songs."

"What were they about?" says I.

"O, about the deer and the heather," says he, "and about the ancient old chiefs that are all by with it lang syne, and just about what songs are about in general. And then whiles I would make believe I had a set of pipes and I was playing. I played some grand springs, and I thought I played them awful bonny; I vow whiles that I could hear the squeal of them! But the great affair is that it's done with."

With that he carried me again to my adventures, which he heard all over again with more particularity, and extraordinary approval, swearing at intervals that I was "a queer character of a callant."

"So ye were frich'ened of Sim Fraser?" he asked once.

"In troth was I!" cried I.

"So would I have been, Davie," said he. "And that is indeed a dreidful man. But it is only proper to give the deil his due; and I can tell you he is a most respectable person on the field of war."

"Is he so brave?" I asked.

"Brave!" said he. "He is as brave as my steel sword."

The story of my duel set him beside himself.

"To think of that!" he cried. "I showed ye the trick in Corrynakiegh too. And three times—three times disarmed! It's a disgrace upon my character that learned ye! Here, stand up, out with your airn; ye shall walk no step beyond this place upon the road till ye can do yoursel' and me mair credit."

"Alan," said I, "this is midsummer madness. Here is no time for fencing lessons."

"I canna well say no to that," he admitted. "But three times, man! And you standing there like a straw bogle and rinning to fetch your ain sword like a doggie with a pocket-napkin! David, this man Duncansby must be something altogether by-ordinar! He maun be extraordinar skilly. If I had the time, I would gang straight back and try a turn at him mysel'. The man must be a provost."

"You silly fellow," said I, "you forget it was just me."

"Na," said he, "but three times!"

"When ye ken yourself that I am fair incompetent," I cried.

"Well, I never heard tell the equal of it," said he.

"I promise you the one thing, Alan," said I. "The next time that we forgather, I'll be better learned. You shall not continue to bear the disgrace of a friend that cannot strike."

"Ay, the next time!" says he. "And when will that be, I would like to ken?"

"Well, Alan, I have had some thoughts of that, too," said I; "and my plan is this. It's my opinion to be called an advocate."

"That's but a weary trade, Davie," says Alan, "and rather a blagyard one forbye. Ye would be better in a king's coat than that."

"And no doubt that would be the way to have us meet," cried I. "But as you'll be in King Lewie's coat, and I'll be in King Geordie's, we'll have a dainty meeting of it."

"There's some sense in that," he admitted.

"An advocate, then, it'll have to be," I continued, "and I think it a more suitable trade for a gentleman that was *three times* disarmed. But the beauty of the thing is this: that one of the best colleges for that kind of learning—and the one where my kinsman, Pilrig, made his studies—is the college of Leyden in Holland. Now, what say you, Alan? Could not a cadet of *Royal Ecossais* get a furlough, slip over the marches, and call in upon a Leyden student!"

"Well, and I would think he could!" cried he. "Ye see, I stand well in with my colonel, Count Drummond-Melfort; and, what's mair to the purpose, I have a cousin of mine lieutenant-colonel in a regiment of the Scots-Dutch. Naething could be mair proper than what I would get a leave to see Lieutenant-Colonel Stewart of Halkett's. And Lord Melfort, who is a very scienteefic kind of a man, and writes books like Cæsar, would be doubtless very pleased to have the advantage of my observes."

"Is Lord Melfort an author, then?" I asked; for much as Alan thought of soldiers, I thought more of the gentry that write books.

"The very same, Davie," said he. "One would think a colonel would have something better to attend to. But what can I say that make songs?"

"Well, then," said I, "it only remains you should give me an address to write you at in France; and as soon as I am got to Leyden I will send you mine."

"The best will be to write me in the care of my chieftain," said he, "Charles Stewart, of Ardshiel, Esquire, at the town of Melons, in the Isle of France. It might take long, or it might take short, but it would aye get to my hands at the last of it."

We had a haddock to our breakfast in Musselburgh, where it amused me vastly to hear Alan. His great-coat and boot-hose were extremely remarkable this warm morning, and perhaps some hint of an explanation had been wise; but Alan went into that matter like a business, or, I should rather say, like a diversion. He engaged the goodwife of the house with some compliments upon the rizzoring of our haddocks; and the whole of the rest of our stay held her in talk about a cold he had taken on his stomach, gravely relating all manner of symptoms and sufferings, and hearing with a vast show of interest all the old wives' remedies she could supply him with in return.

We left Musselburgh before the first ninepenny coach was due from Edinburgh, for (as Alan said) that was a rencounter we might very well avoid. The wind, although still high, was very mild, the sun shone strong, and Alan began to suffer in proportion. From Prestonpans he had me aside to the field of

108

Gladsmuir, where he exerted himself a great deal more than needful to describe the stages of the battle. Thence, at his old round pace, we travelled to Cockenzie. Though they were building herring-busses there at Mrs. Cadell's, it seemed a desert-like, back-going town, about half full of ruined houses; but the ale-house was clean, and Alan, who was now in a glowing heat, must indulge himself with a bottle of ale, and carry on to the new luckie with the old story of the cold upon his stomach, only now the symptoms were all different.

I sat listening; and it came in my mind that I had scarce ever heard him address three serious words to any woman, but he was always drolling and fleering and making a private mock of them, and yet brought to that business a remarkable degree of energy and interest. Something to this effect I remarked to him, when the goodwife (as chanced) was called away.

"What do ye want?" says he. "A man should aye put his best foot forrit with the women-kind; he should aye give them a bit of a story to divert them, the poor lambs! It's what ye should learn to attend to, David; ye should get the principles, it's like a trade. Now, if this had been a young lassie, or onyways bonny, she would never have heard tell of my stomach, Davie. But aince they're too old to be seeking joes, they a' set up to be apotecaries. Why? What do I ken? They'll be just the way God made them, I suppose. But I think a man would be a gomeril that didna give his attention to the same."

And here, the luckie coming back, he turned from me as if with impatience to renew their former conversation. The lady had branched some while before from Alan's stomach to the case of a good-brother of her own in Aberlady, whose last sickness and demise she was describing at extraordinary length. Sometimes it was merely dull, sometimes both dull and awful, for she talked with unction. The upshot was that I fell in a deep muse, looking forth of the window on the road, and scarce marking what I saw. Presently, had any been looking, they might have seen me to start.

"We pit a fomentation to his feet," the goodwife was saying, "and a het stane to his wame, and we gied him hyssop and water of pennyroyal, and fine clean balsam of sulphur for the hoast..."

"Sir," says I, cutting very quietly in, "there's a friend of mine gone by the house."

"Is that e'en sae?" replies Alan, as though it were a thing of small account. And then, "Ye were saying, mem?" says he; and the wearyful wife went on.

Presently, however, he paid her with a half-crown piece, and she must go forth after the change.

"Was it him with the red head?" asked Alan.

"Ye have it," said I.

"What did I tell you in the wood?" he cried. "And yet it's strange he should be here too. Was he his lane?"

"His lee-lane for what I could see," said I.

"Did he gang by?" he asked.

"Straight by," said I, "and looked neither to the right nor left."

"And that's queerer yet," said Alan. "It sticks in my mind, Davie, that we should be stirring. But where to?—deil hae't! This is like old days fairly," cries he.

"There is one big differ, though," said I, "that now we have money in our pockets."

"And another big differ, Mr. Balfour," says he, "that now we have dogs at our tail. They're on the scent; they're in full cry, David. It's a bad business and be damned to it." And he sat thinking hard with a look of his that I knew well.

"I'm saying, Luckie," says he, when the goodwife returned, "have ye a back road out of this change-house?"

She told him there was, and where it led to.

"Then, sir," says he to me, "I think that will be the shortest road for us. And here's good-bye to ye, my braw woman; and I'll no' forget thon of the cinnamon-water."

We went out by way of the woman's kale-yard, and up a lane among fields. Alan looked sharply to all sides, and seeing we were in a little hollow place of the country, out of view of men, sat down.

"Now for a council of war, Davie," said he. "But first of all, a bit lesson to ye. Suppose that I had been like you, what would yon old wife have minded of the pair of us? Just that we had gone out by the back gate. And what does she mind now? A fine, canty, friendly, cracky man, that suffered with the stomach, poor body! and was rael ta'en up about the good-brother. O man, David, try and learn to have some kind of intelligence!"

"I'll try, Alan," said I.

"And now for him of the red head," says he; "was he gaun fast or slow?"

"Betwixt and between," said I.

"No kind of a hurry about the man?" he asked.

"Never a sign of it," said I.

"Nhm!" said Alan, "it looks queer. We saw nothing of them this morning on the Whins; he's passed us by, he doesna seem to be looking, and yet here he is on our road! Dod, Davie, I begin to take a notion. I think it's no' you they're seeking, I think it's me; and I think they ken fine where they're gaun."

"They ken?" I asked.

"I think Andie Scougal's sold me—him, or his mate, wha kennt some part of the affair—or else Chairlie's clerk callant, which would be a pity too," says Alan; "and if you askit me for just my inward private conviction, I think there'll be heads cracked on Gillane Sands."

"Alan," I cried, "if you're at all right, there'll be folk there and to spare. It'll be small service to crack heads."

"It would aye be a satisfaction, though," says Alan. "But bide a bit, bide a bit; I'm thinking—and thanks to this bonny westland wind, I believe I've still a chance of it. It's this way, Davie. I'm no' trysted with this man Scougal till the gloaming comes. '*But*,' says he, '*if I can get a bit of a wind out of the west I'll be there long or that,*' he says, '*and lie-to for ye behind the Isle of Fidra.*' Now if your gentry kens the place, they ken the time forbye. Do ye see me coming, Davie? Thanks to Johnnie Cope and other red-coat gomerils, I should ken this country like the back of my hand; and if ye're ready for another bit run with Alan Breck, we'll can cast back inshore, and come down to the seaside again by Dirleton. If the ship's there, we'll try and get on board of her. If she's no' there, I'll just have to get back to my weary haystack. But either way of it, I think we will leave your gentry whistling on their thumbs."

"I believe there's some chance in it," said I. "Have on with ye, Alan!"

CHAPTER XIII

Gillane Sands

I did not profit by Alan's pilotage as he had done by his marchings under General Cope; for I can scarce tell what way we went. It is my excuse that we travelled exceeding fast. Some part we ran, some trotted, and the rest walked at a vengeance of a pace. Twice, while we were at top speed, we ran against country-folk; but though we plumped into the first from round a corner, Alan was as ready as a loaded musket.

"Hae ye seen my horse?" he gasped.

"Na, man, I haena seen nae horse the day," replied the countryman.

And Alan spared the time to explain to him that we were travelling "ride and tie"; that our charger had escaped, and it was feared he had gone home to Linton. Not only that, but he expended some breath (of which he had not very much left) to curse his own misfortune and my stupidity, which was said to be its cause.

"Them that canna tell the truth," he observed to myself as we went on again, "should be aye mindfu' to leave an honest, handy lee behind them. If folk dinna ken what ye're doing, Davie, they're terrible taken up with it; but if they think they ken, they care nae mair for it than what I do for pease porridge."

As we had first made inland, so our road came in the end to lie very near due north; the old Kirk of Aberlady for a landmark on the left; on the right, the top of the Berwick Law; and it was thus we struck the shore again, not far from Dirleton. From North Berwick west to Gillane Ness there runs a string of four small islets, Craigleith, the Lamb, Fidra, and Eyebrough, notable by their diversity of size and shape. Fidra is the most particular, being a strange grey islet of two humps, made the more conspicuous by a piece of ruin; and I mind that (as we drew closer to it) by some door or window of these ruins the sea peeped through like a man's eye. Under the lee of Fidra there is a good anchorage in westerly winds, and there, from a far way off, we could see the *Thistle* riding.

The shore in face of these islets is altogether waste. Here is no dwelling of man, and scarce any passage, or at most of vagabond children running at their play. Gillane is a small place on the far side of the Ness, the folk of Dirleton go to their business in the inland fields, and those of North Berwick straight to the sea-fishing from their haven; so that few parts of the coast are lonelier.

But I mind, as we crawled upon our bellies into that multiplicity of heights and hollows, keeping a bright eye upon all sides, and our hearts hammering at our ribs, there was such a shining of the sun and the sea, such a stir of the wind in the bent-grass, and such a bustle of down-popping rabbits and up-flying gulls, that the desert seemed to me like a place alive. No doubt it was in all ways well chosen for a secret embarkation, if the secret had been kept; and even now that it was out, and the place watched, we were able to creep unperceived to the front of the sandhills, where they look down immediately on the beach and sea.

But here Alan came to a full stop.

"Davie," said he, "this is a kittle passage! As long as we lie here we're safe; but I'm nane sae muckle nearer to my ship or the coast of France. And as soon as we stand up and signal the brig, it's another matter. For where will your gentry be, think ye?"

"Maybe they're no' come yet," said I. "And even if they are, there's one clear matter in our favour. They'll be all arranged to take us, that's true. But they'll have arranged for our coming from the east and here we are upon their west."

"Ay," says Alan, "I wish we were in some force, and this was a battle, we would have bonnily outmanœuvred them! But it isna, Davit; and the way it is, is a wee thing less inspiring to Alan Breck. I swither, Davie."

"Time flies, Alan," said I.

"I ken that," said Alan. "I ken naething else, as the French folk say. But this is a dreidful case of heids or tails. O! if I could but ken where your gentry were!"

"Alan," said I, "this is no' like you. It's got to be now or never."

"This is no' me, quo' he,"

sang Alan, with a queer face betwixt shame and drollery,

"Neither you nor me, quo' he, neither you nor me,
Wow, na, Johnnie man! neither you nor me."

And then of a sudden he stood straight up where he was, and with a handkerchief flying in his right hand, marched down upon the beach. I stood up myself, but lingered behind him, scanning the sandhills to the east. His appearance was at first unremarked: Scougal not expecting him so early, and *my gentry* watching on the other side. Then they awoke on board the *Thistle*, and it seemed they had all in readiness, for there was scarce a second's bustle on the deck before we saw a skiff put round her stern and begin to pull lively for the coast. Almost at the same moment of time, and perhaps half a mile away towards Gillane Ness, the figure of a man appeared for a blink upon a sandhill, waving with his arms; and though he was gone again in the same flash, the gulls in that part continued a little longer to fly wild.

Alan had not seen this, looking straight to seaward at the ship and skiff.

"It maun be as it will!" said he, when I had told him. "Weel may yon boatie row, or my craig'll have to thole a raxing."

That part of the beach was long and flat, and excellent walking when the tide was down; a little cressy burn flowed over it in one place to the sea; and the sandhills ran along the head of it like the rampart of a town. No eye of ours could spy what was passing behind there in the bents, no hurry of ours could mend the speed of the boat's coming: time stood still with us through that uncanny period of waiting.

"There is one thing I would like to ken," says Alan. "I would like fine to ken these gentry's orders. We're worth four hunner pound the pair of us: how if they took the guns to us, Davie? They would get a bonny shot from the top of that lang sandy bauk."

"Morally impossible," said I. "The point is that they can have no guns. This thing has been gone about too secret; pistols they may have, but never guns."

"I believe ye'll be in the right," says Alan. "For all which I am wearying a good deal for yon boat."

And he snapped his fingers and whistled to it like a dog.

It was now perhaps a third of the way in, and we ourselves already hard on the margin of the sea, so that the soft sand rose over my shoes.

There was no more to do whatever but to wait, to look as much as we were able at the creeping nearer of the boat, and as little as we could manage at the long impenetrable front of the sandhills, over which the gulls twinkled and behind which our enemies were doubtless marshalling.

"This is a fine, bright, caller place to get shot in," says Alan suddenly; "and, man, I wish that I had your courage!"

"Alan!" I cried, "what kind of talk is this of it? You're just made of courage; it's the character of the man, as I could prove myself if there was nobody else."

"And you would be the more mistaken," said he. "What makes the differ with me is just my great penetration and knowledge of affairs. But for auld, cauld, dour, deidly courage, I am not fit to hold a candle to yourself. Look at us two here upon the sands. Here am I, fair hotching to be off; here's you (for all that I ken) in two minds of it whether you'll no' stop. Do you think that I could do that, or would? No' me! Firstly, because I havena got the courage and wouldna daur; and secondly, because I am a man of so much penetration and would see ye damned first."

"It's there ye're coming, is it?" I cried. "Ah, man Alan, you can wile your old wives, but you never can wile me."

116

Remembrance of my temptation in the wood made me strong as iron.

"I have a tryst to keep," I continued. "I am trysted with your cousin Charlie; I have passed my word."

"Braw trysts that you'll can keep," said Alan. "Ye'll just mistryst aince and for a' with the gentry in the bents. And what for?" he went on with an extreme threatening gravity. "Just tell me that, my mannie! Are ye to be speerited away like Lady Grange? Are they to drive a dirk in your inside and bury ye in the bents? Or is it to be the other way, and are they to bring ye in with James? Are they folk to be trustit? Would ye stick your head in the mouth of Simon Fraser and the ither Whigs?" he added with extraordinary bitterness.

"Alan," cried I, "they're all rogues and liars, and I'm with ye there. The more reason there should be one decent man in such a land of thieves! My word is passed, and I'll stick to it. I said long syne to your kinswoman that I would stumble at no risk. Do ye mind of that?—the night Red Colin fell, it was. No more I will, then. Here I stop. Prestongrange promised me my life; if he's to be man-sworn, here I'll have to die."

"Aweel, aweel," said Alan.

All this time we had seen or heard no more of our pursuers. In truth we had caught them unawares; their whole party (as I was to learn afterwards) had not yet reached the scene; what there was of them was spread among the bents towards Gillane. It was quite an affair to call them in and bring them over, and the boat was making speed. They were, besides, but cowardly fellows; a mere leash of Highland cattle-thieves, of several clans, no gentleman there to be the captain: and the more they looked at Alan and me upon the beach, the less (I must suppose) they liked the looks of us.

Whoever had betrayed Alan it was not the captain: he was in the skiff himself, steering and stirring up his oarsmen, like a man with his heart in his employ. Already he was near in, and the boat scouring—already Alan's face had flamed crimson with the excitement of his deliverance, when our friends in the bents, either in despair to see their prey escape them, or with some hope of scaring Andie, raised suddenly a shrill cry of several voices.

This sound, arising from what appeared to be a quite deserted coast, was really very daunting, and the men in the boat held water instantly.

"What's this of it?" sings out the captain, for he was come within an easy hail.

"Freens o' mine," says Alan, and began immediately to wade forth in the shallow water towards the boat. "Davie," he said, pausing, 'Davie, are ye no' coming? I am sweer to leave ye."

"Not a hair of me," said I.

He stood part of a second where he was to his knees in the salt water, hesitating.

"He that will to Cupar, maun to Cupar," said he, and swashing in deeper than his waist, was hauled into the skiff, which was immediately directed for the ship.

I stood where he had left me, with my hands behind my back; Alan sat with his head turned, watching me; and the boat drew smoothly away. Of a sudden I came the nearest hand to shedding tears, and seemed to myself the most deserted, solitary lad in Scotland. With that I turned my back upon the sea and faced the sandhills. There was no light or sound of man; the sun shone on the wet sand and the dry, the wind blew in the bents, the gulls made a dreary piping. As I passed higher up the beach, the sand-lice were hopping nimbly about the stranded tangles. The devil any other sight or sound in that unchancy place. And yet I knew there were folk there, observing me, upon some secret purpose. They were no soldiers, or they would have fallen on and taken us ere now: doubtless they were some common rogues hired for my undoing, perhaps to kidnap, perhaps to murder me outright. From the position of those engaged, the first was the more likely; from what I knew of their character and ardency in this business, I thought the second very possible; and the blood ran cold about my heart.

I had a mad idea to loosen my sword in the scabbard; for though I was very unfit to stand up like a gentleman blade to blade, I thought I could do some scathe in a random combat. But I perceived in time the folly of resistance. This was no doubt the joint "expedient" on which Prestongrange and Fraser were agreed. The first, I was very sure, had done something to secure my life; the second was pretty likely to have slipped in some contrary hints into the ears of Neil and his companions; and if I were to show bare steel I might play straight into the hands of my worst enemy and seal my own doom.

These thoughts brought me to the head of the beach. I cast a look behind, the boat was nearing the brig, and Alan flew his handkerchief for a farewell, which I replied to with the waving of my hand. But Alan himself was shrunk to a small thing in my view, alongside of this pass that lay in front of me. I set my hat hard on my head, clenched my teeth, and went right before me up the face of the sand-wreath. It made a hard climb, being steep, and the sand like water underfoot. But I caught hold at last by the long bent-grass on the brae-top, and pulled myself to a good footing. The same moment men stirred and stood up here and there, six or seven of them, ragged-like knaves, each with a dagger in his hand. The fair truth is, I shut my eyes and prayed. When I opened them again, the rogues were crept the least thing nearer without speech or hurry. Every eye was upon mine, which struck me with a strange sensation of their brightness, and of the fear with which they continued to approach me. I held out my hands empty: whereupon one asked, with a strong Highland brogue, if I surrendered.

"Under protest," said I, "if ye ken what that means, which I misdoubt."

At that word, they came all in upon me like a flight of birds upon a carrion, seized me, took my sword, and all the money from my pockets, bound me hand and foot with some strong line, and cast me on a tussock of bent. There they sat about their captive in a part of a circle and gazed upon him silently like something dangerous, perhaps a lion or a tiger on the spring. Presently this attention was relaxed. They drew nearer together, fell to speech in the Gaelic, and very cynically divided my property before my eyes. It was my diversion in this time that I could watch from my place the progress of my friend's escape. I saw the boat come to the brig and be hoisted in, the sails fill, and the ship pass out seaward behind the isles and by North Berwick.

In the course of two hours or so, more and more ragged Highlandmen kept collecting, Neil among the first, until the party must have numbered near a score. With each new arrival there was a fresh bout of talk, that sounded like complaints and explanations; but I observed one thing, none of those that came late had any share in the division of my spoils. The last discussion was very violent and eager, so that once I thought they would have quarrelled; on the heels of which their company parted, the bulk of them returning westward in a troop, and only three, Neil and two others, remaining sentries on the prisoner.

"I could name one who would be very ill pleased with your day's work, Neil Duncanson," said I, when the rest had moved away.

He assured me in answer I should be tenderly used, for he knew I was "acquent wi' the leddy."

This was all our talk, nor did any other son of man appear upon that portion of the coast until the sun had gone down among the Highland mountains, and the gloaming was beginning to grow dark. At which hour I was aware of a long, lean, bony-like Lothian man of a very swarthy countenance, that came towards us among the bents on a farm horse.

"Lads," cried he, "hae ye a paper like this?" and held up one in his hand. Neil produced a second, which the newcomer studied through a pair of horn spectacles, and saying all was right and we were the folk he was seeking, immediately dismounted. I was then set in his place, my feet tied under the horse's belly, and we set forth under the guidance of the

Lowlander. His path must have been very well chosen, for we met but one pair—a pair of lovers—the whole way, and these, perhaps taking us to be free-traders, fled on our approach. We were at one time close at the foot of Berwick Law on the south side; at another, as we passed over some open hills, I spied the lights of a clachan and the old tower of a church among some trees not far off, but too far to cry for help, if I had dreamed of it. At last we came again within sound of the sea. There was moonlight, though not much; and by this I could see the three huge towers and broken battlements of Tantallon, that old chief place of the Red Douglases. The horse was picketed in the bottom of the ditch to graze, and I was led within, and forth into the court, and thence into a tumble-down stone hall. Here my conductors built a brisk fire in the midst of the pavement, for there was a chill in the night. My hands were loosed, I was set by the wall in the inner end, and (the Lowlander having produced provisions) I was given oatmeal bread and a pitcher of French brandy. This done, I was left once more alone with my three Highlandmen. They sat close by the fire drinking and talking; the wind blew in by the breaches, cast about the smoke and flames, and sang in the tops of the towers; I could hear the sea under the cliffs, and my mind being reassured as to my life, and my body and spirits wearied with the day's employment, I turned upon one side and slumbered.

I had no means of guessing at what hour I was wakened, only the moon was down and the fire low. My feet were now loosed, and I was carried through the ruins and down the cliff-side by a precipitous path to where I found a fisher's boat in a haven of the rocks. This I was had on board of, and we began to put forth from the shore in a fine starlight.

CHAPTER XIV

The Bass

I had no thought where they were taking me; only looked here and there for the appearance of a ship; and there ran the while in my head a word of Ransome's—the *twenty-pounders*. If I were to be exposed a second time to that same former danger of the plantations, I judged it must turn ill with me; there was no second Alan, and no second shipwreck and spare yard to be expected now; and I saw myself hoe tobacco under the whip's lash. The thought chilled me; the air was sharp upon the water, the stretchers of the boat drenched with a cold dew; and I shivered in my place beside the steersman. This was the dark man whom I have called hitherto the Lowlander; his name was Dale, ordinarily called Black Andie. Feeling the thrill of my shiver, he very kindly handed me a rough jacket full of fish-scales, with which I was glad to cover myself.

"I thank you for this kindness," said I, "and will make so free as to repay it with a warning. You take a high responsibility in this affair. You are not like these ignorant, barbarous Highlanders, but know what the law is, and the risks of those that break it."

"I am no' just exactly what ye would ca' an extremist for the law," says he, "at the best of times; but in this business I act with a good warranty."

"What are you going to do with me?" I asked.

"Nae harm," said he, "nae harm ava'. Ye'll hae strong freens, I'm thinking. Ye'll be richt eneuch yet."

There began to fall a greyness on the face of the sea; little dabs of pink and red, like coals of slow fire, came in the east; and at the same time the geese awakened, and began crying about the top of the Bass. It is just the one crag of rock, as everybody knows, but great enough to carve a city from. The sea was extremely little, but there went a hollow plowter round the base of it. With the growing of the dawn I could see it clearer and clearer; the straight crags painted with sea-birds' droppings like a morning frost, the sloping top of it green with grass, the clan of white geese that cried about the sides, and the black, broken buildings of the prison sitting close on the sea's edge.

At the sight the truth came in upon me in a clap.

"It's there you're taking me!" I cried.

"Just to the Bass, mannie," said he: "whaur the auld sants were afore ye, and I misdoubt if ye have come so fairly by your preeson."

"But none dwells there now," I cried; "the place is long a ruin."

"It'll be the mair pleisand a change for the solan geese, then," quoth Andie drily.

The day coming slowly brighter I observed on the bilge, among the big stones with which fisherfolk ballast their boats, several kegs and baskets, and a provision of fuel. All these were discharged upon the crag. Andie, myself, and my three Highlanders (I call them mine, although it was the other way about), landed along with them. The sun was not yet up when the boat moved away again, the noise of the oars on the thole-pins echoing from the cliffs, and left us in our singular reclusion.

Andie Dale was the Prefect (as I would jocularly call him) of the Bass, being at once the shepherd and the game-keeper of that small and rich estate. He had to mind the dozen or so of sheep that fed and fattened on the grass of the sloping part of it, like beasts grazing the roof of a cathedral. He had charge, besides, of the solan geese that roosted in the crags; and from these an extraordinary income is derived. The young are dainty eating, as much as two shillings apiece being a common price, and paid willingly by epicures; even the grown birds are valuable for their oil and feathers; and a part of the minister's stipend of North Berwick is paid to this day in solan geese, which makes it (in some folk's eyes) a parish to be coveted. To perform these several businesses, as well as to protect the geese from poachers, Andie had frequent occasion to sleep and pass days altogether on the crag; and we found the man at home there like a farmer in his steading. Bidding us all shoulder some of the packages, a matter in which I made haste to bear a hand, he led us in by a locked gate, which was the only admission to the island, and through the ruins of the fortress, to the governor's house. There we saw, by the ashes in the chimney and a standing bed-place in one corner, that he made his usual occupation.

This bed he now offered me to use, saying he supposed I would set up to be gentry.

"My gentrice has nothing to do with where I lie," said I. "I bless God I have laid hard ere now, and can do the same again with thankfulness. While I am here, Mr. Andie, if that be your name, I will do my part and take my place beside the rest of you; and I ask you on the other hand to spare me your mockery, which I own I like ill."

He grumbled a little at this speech, but seemed upon reflection to approve it. Indeed, he was a long-headed, sensible man, and a good Whig and Presbyterian; read daily in a pocket Bible, and was both able and eager to converse seriously on religion, leaning more than a little towards the Cameronian extremes. His morals were of a more doubtful colour. I found he was deep in the free trade, and used the ruins of Tantallon for a magazine of smuggled merchandise. As for a gauger, I do not believe he valued the life of one at half a farthing. But that part of the coast of Lothian is to this day as wild a place, and the commons there as rough a crew, as any in Scotland.

One incident of my imprisonment is made memorable by a consequence it had long after. There was a warship at this time stationed in the Firth, the *Seahorse*, Captain Palliser. It chanced she was cruising in the month of September, plying between Fife and Lothian, and sounding for sunk dangers. Early one fine morning she was seen about two miles to east of us, where she lowered a boat, and seemed to examine the Wildfire Rocks and Satan's Bush, famous dangers of that coast. And presently, after having got her boat again, she came before the wind and was headed directly for the Bass. This was very troublesome to Andie and the Highlanders; the whole business of my sequestration was designed for privacy, and here, with a navy captain perhaps blundering ashore, it looked to become public enough, if it were nothing worse. I was in a minority of one, I am no Alan to fall upon so many, and I was far from sure that a warship was the least likely to improve my condition. All which considered, I gave Andie my parole of good behaviour and obedience, and was had briskly to the summit of the rock, where we all lay down, at the cliff's edge, in different places of observation and concealment. The *Seahorse* came straight on till I thought she would have struck, and we (looking giddily down) could see the ship's company at their quarters and hear the leadsman singing at the lead. Then she suddenly wore and let fly a volley of I know not how many great guns. The rock was shaken with the thunder of the sound, the smoke flowed over our heads, and the geese rose in number beyond computation or belief. To hear their screaming and to see the twinkling of their wings, made a most inimitable curiosity; and I suppose it was after this somewhat childish pleasure that Captain Palliser had come so near the Bass. He was to pay dear for it in time. During his approach I had the opportunity to make a remark upon the rigging of that ship by which I ever after knew it miles away; and this was a means (under Providence) of my averting from a friend a great calamity, and inflicting on Captain Palliser himself a sensible disappointment.

All the time of my stay on the rock we lived well. We had small ale and brandy, and oatmeal of which we made our porridge night and morning. At times a boat came from the Castleton and brought us a quarter of mutton, for the sheep upon the rock we must not touch, these being specially fed to market. The geese were unfortunately out of season, and we let them be. We fished ourselves, and yet more often made the geese to fish for us: observing one when he had made a capture and scaring him from his prey ere he had swallowed it.

The strange nature of this place, and the curiosities with which it abounded, held me busy and amused. Escape being impossible, I was allowed my entire liberty, and continually explored the surface of the isle wherever it might support the foot of man. The old garden of the prison was still to be observed, with flowers and pot-herbs running wild, and some ripe cherries on a bush. A little lower stood a chapel or a hermit's cell; who built or dwelt in it, none may know, and the thought of its age made a ground of many meditations. The prison, too, where I now bivouacked with Highland cattle-thieves, was a place full of history, both human and divine. I thought it strange so many saints and martyrs should have gone by there so recently, and left not so much as a leaf out of their Bibles, or a name carved upon the wall, while the rough soldier-lads that mounted guard upon the battlements had filled the neighbourhood with their mementoes—broken tobacco-pipes for the most part, and that in a surprising plenty, but also metal buttons from their coats. There were times when I thought I could have heard the pious sound of psalms out of the martyrs' dungeons, and see the soldiers tramp the ramparts with their glinting pipes, and the dawn rising behind them out of the North Sea.

No doubt it was a good deal Andie and his tales that put these fancies in my head. He was extraordinary well acquainted with the story of the rock in all particulars, down to the names of private soldiers, his father having served there in that same capacity. He was gifted, besides, with a natural genius for narration, so that the people seemed to speak and the things to be done before your face. This gift of his, and my assiduity to listen, brought us the more close together. I could not honestly deny but what I liked him; I soon saw that he liked me; and indeed, from the first I had set myself out to capture his goodwill. An odd circumstance (to be told presently) effected this beyond my expectation; but even in early days we made a friendly pair to be a prisoner and his gaoler.

I should trifle with my conscience if I pretended my stay

upon the Bass was wholly disagreeable. It seemed to me a safe place, as though I was escaped there out of my troubles. No harm was to be offered me; a material impossibility, rock and the deep sea, prevented me from fresh attempts; I felt I had my life safe and my honour safe, and there were times when I allowed myself to gloat on them like stolen waters. At other times my thoughts were very different. I recalled how strong I had expressed myself both to Rankeillor and to Stewart; I reflected that my captivity upon the Bass, in view of a great part of the coasts of Fife and Lothian, was a thing I should be thought more likely to have invented than endured; and in the eyes of these two gentlemen, at least, I must pass for a boaster and a coward. Now I would take this lightly enough; tell myself that so long as I stood well with Catriona Drummond, the opinion of the rest of man was but moonshine and spilled water; and thence pass off into those meditations of a lover which are so delightful to himself and must always appear so surprisingly idle to a reader.

But anon the fear would take me otherwise; I would be shaken with a perfect panic of self-esteem, and these supposed hard judgments appear an injustice impossible to be supported. With that another train of thought would be presented, and I had scarce begun to be concerned about men's judgments of myself, than I was haunted with the remembrance of James Stewart in his dungeon and the lamentations of his wife. Then, indeed, passion began to work in me; I could not forgive myself to sit there idle; it seemed (if I were a man at all) that I could fly or swim out of my place of safety; and it was in such humours and to amuse my self-reproaches, that I would set the more particularly to win the good side of Andie Dale.

At last, when we two were alone on the summit of the rock on a bright morning, I put in some hint about a bribe. He looked at me, cast back his head, and laughed out loud.

"Ay, you're funny, Mr. Dale," said I, "but perhaps if you'll glance and eye upon that paper you may change your note."

The stupid Highlanders had taken from me at the time of my seizure nothing but hard money, and the paper I now showed Andie was an acknowledgment from the British Linen Company for a considerable sum.

He read it. "Troth, and ye're nane sae ill aff," said he.

"I thought that would maybe vary your opinions," said I.

"Hout!" said he. "It shows me ye can bribe; but I'm no' to be bribit."

"We'll see about that yet a while," says I. "And first, I'll show you that I know what I am talking. You have orders to detain me here till after Thursday, 21st September."

"Ye're no' a'thegether wrong either," says Andie. "I'm to let ye gang, bar orders contrair, on Saturday, the 23rd."

I could not but feel there was something extremely insidious in this arrangement. That I was to reappear precisely in time to be too late would cast the more discredit on my tale, if I were minded to tell one; and this screwed me to fighting point.

"Now then, Andie, you that kens the world, listen to me, and think while ye listen," said I. "I know there are great folks in the business, and I make no doubt you have their names to go upon. I have seen some of them myself since this affair began, and said my say into their faces too.

But what kind of a crime would this be that I had committed? or what kind of a process is this that I am fallen under? To be apprehended by some ragged John-Hieland-men on August 30th, carried to a rickle of old stones that is now neither fort nor gaol (whatever it once was) but just the gamekeeper's lodge of the Bass Rock, and set free again, September 23rd, as secretly as I was first arrested—does that sound like law to you? or does it sound like justice? or does it not sound honestly like a piece of some low, dirty intrigue, of which the very folk that meddle with it are ashamed?"

"I canna gainsay ye, Shaws. It looks unco underhand," says Andie. "And werena the folk guid sound Whigs and true-blue Presbyterians I would hae seen them ayont Jordan and Jeroozlem or I would have set hand to it."

"The Master of Lovat'll be a braw Whig," says I, "and a grand Presbyterian."

"I ken naething by him," said he. "I hae nae trokings wi' Lovats."

"No, it'll be Prestongrange that you'll be dealing with," said I.

"Ah, but I'll no' tell ye that," said Andie.

"Little need when I ken," was my retort.

"There's just the ae thing ye can be fairly sure of, Shaws," says Andie. "And that is that (try as ye please) I'm no' dealing wi' yoursel'; nor yet I amna goin' to," he added.

"Well, Andie, I see I'll have to speak out plain with you," I replied. And I told him so much as I thought needful of the facts.

He heard me out with serious interest, and when I had done, seemed to consider a little with himself.

"Shaws," said he at last, "I'll deal with the naked hand. It's a queer tale, and no' very creditable, the way you tell it; and I'm far frae minting that is other than the way that ye believe it. As for yoursel', ye seem to me rather a dacent-like young man. But me, that's aulder and mair judeecious, see perhaps a wee bit further forrit in the job than what ye can dae. And here is the maitter clear and plain to ye. There'll be nae skaith to yoursel' if I keep ye here; far frae that, I think ye'll be a hantle better by it. There'll be nae skaith to the kintry—just ae mair Hielantman hangit—Gude kens, a guid riddance! On the ither hand, it would be considerable skaith to me if I would let you free. Sae, speakin' as a guid Whig, an honest freen' to you, and an anxious freen' to my ainsel', the plain fact is that I think ye'll just have to bide here wi' Andie an' the solans."

"Andie," said I, laying my hand upon his knee, "this Hielantman's innocent."

"Ay, it's a peety about that," said he. "But ye see, in this warld, the way God made it, we canna just get a'thing that we want."

129

CHAPTER XV

Black Andie's Tale of Tod Lapraik

I have yet said little of the Highlanders. They were all three of the followers of James More, which bound the accusation very tight about their master's neck. All understood a word or two of English; but Neil was the only one who judged he had enough of it for general converse, in which (when once he got embarked) his company was often tempted to the contrary opinion. They were tractable, simple creatures; showed much more courtesy than might have been expected from their raggedness and their uncouth appearance, and fell spontaneously to be like three servants for Andie and myself.

Dwelling in that isolated place, in the old falling ruins of a prison, and among endless strange sounds of the sea and the sea-birds, I thought I perceived in them early the effects of superstitious fear. When there was nothing doing they would either lie and sleep, for which their appetite appeared insatiable, or Neil would entertain the others with stories which seemed always of a terrifying strain. If neither of these delights were within reach—if perhaps two were sleeping and the third could find no means to follow their example—I would see him sit and listen and look about him in a progression of uneasiness, starting, his face blenching, his hands clutched, a man strung like a bow. The nature of these fears I had never an occasion to find out, but the sight of them was catching, and the nature of the place that we were in favourable to alarms. I can find no word for it in the English, but Andie had an expression for it in the Scots from which he never varied.

"Ay," he would say, "*it's an unco place, the Bass.*"

It is so I always think of it. It was an unco place by night, unco by day; and these were unco sounds, of the calling of the solans, and the plash of the sea and the rock echoes, that hung continually in our ears. It was chiefly so in moderate weather. When the waves were any way great they roared about the rock like thunder and the drums of armies, dreadful but merry to hear; and it was in the calm days that a man could daunt himself with listening—not a Highlandman only, as I several times experimented on myself, so many still, hollow noises haunted and reverberated in the porches of the rock.

This brings me to a story I heard, and a scene I took part in, which quite changed our terms of living, and had a great effect on my departure. It chanced one night I fell in a muse beside the fire and (that little air of Alan's coming back to my memory) began to whistle. A hand was laid upon my arm, and the voice of Neil bade me to stop, for it was not "canny musics."

"Not canny?" I asked. "How can that be?"

"Na," said he; "it will be made by a bogle and her wanting ta heid upon his body."

"Well," said I, "there can be no bogles here, Neil; for it's not likely they would fash themselves to frighten solan geese."

"Ay?" says Andie, "is that what ye think of it? But I'll can tell ye there's been waur nor bogles here."

"What's waur than bogles, Andie?" said I.

"Warlocks," said he. "Or a warlock at the least of it. And that's a queer tale, too," he added. "And if ye would like, I'll tell it ye."

To be sure we were all of the one mind, and even the Highlander that had the least English of the three set himself to listen with all his might.

THE TALE OF TOD LAPRAIK

My faither, Tam Dale, peace to his banes, was a wild sploring lad in his young days, wi' little wisdom and less grace. He was fond of a lass and fond of a glass, and fond of a ran-dan; but I could never hear tell that he was muckle use for honest employment. Frae ae thing to anither, he listed at last for a sodger, and was in the garrison of this fort, which was the first way that ony of the Dales cam to set foot upon the Bass. Sorrow upon that service! The governor brewed his ain ale; it seems it was the warst conceivable. The rock was proveesioned frae the shore with vivers, the thing was ill-guided, and there were whiles when they büt to fish and shoot solans for their diet. To crown a', thir was the Days of the Persecution. The perishin' cauld chalmers were a' occupeed wi' sants and martyrs, the saut of the yerd, of which it wasna worthy. And though Tam Dale carried a firelock there, a single sodger, and likit a lass and a glass, as I was sayin', the mind of the man was mair just than set with his position. He had glints of the glory of the kirk; there were whiles when his dander rase to see the Lord's sants misguided, and shame covered him that he should be hauldin' a can'le (or carrying a firelock) in so black a business. There were nights of it when he was here on sentry, the place a' wheesht, the frosts o' winter maybe riving in the wa's, and he would hear ane o' the prisoners strike up a psalm, and the rest join in, and the blessed sounds rising from the different chalmers—or dungeons, I would raither say—so that this auld craig in the sea was like a pairt of Heev'n. Black shame was on his saul; his sins hove up before him muckle as the Bass, and above a', that chief sin, that he should have a hand in hagging and hashing at Christ's Kirk. But the truth is that he resisted the spirit. Day cam, there were the rousing compainions, and his guid resolves depairtit.

In thir days, dwalled upon the Bass a man of God, Peden the Prophet was his name. Ye'll have heard tell of Prophet Peden. There was never the wale of him sinsyne, and it's a question wi' mony if there ever was his like afore. He was wild's a peat-hag, fearsome to look at, fearsome to hear, his face like the day of judgment. The voice of him was like a solan's and dinnled in folk's lugs, and the words of him like coals of fire.

Now there was a lass on the rock, and I think she had little to do, for it was nae place for dacent weemen; but it seems she was bonny, and her and Tam Dale were very well agreed. It befell that Peden was in the gairden his lane at the praying when Tam and the lass cam by; and what should the lassie do but mock with laughter at the sant's devotions? He rose and lookit at the twa o' them, and Tam's knees knoitered thegether at the look of him. But when he spak, it was mair in sorrow than in anger. "Poor thing, poor thing!" says he, and it was the lass he lookit at, "I hear you skirl and laugh," he says, "but the Lord has a deid shot prepared for you, and at that surprising judgment ye shall skirl but the ae time!" Shortly thereafter she was daundering on the craigs wi' twa-three sodgers, and it was a blawy day. There cam a gowst of wind, claught her by the coats, and awa' wi' her, bag and baggage. And it was remarkit by the sodgers that she gied but the ae skirl.

Nae doubt this judgment had some weicht upon Tam Dale; but it passed again, and him nane the better. Ae day he was flyting wi' anither sodger-lad. "Deil hae me!" quo' Tam, for he was a profane swearer. And there was Peden glowering at him, gash an' waefu'; Peden wi' his lang chafts an' luntin' een, the maud haappit about his kist, and the hand of him held out wi' the black nails upon the finger-nebs—for he had nae care of the body. "Fy, fy, poor man!" cries he, "the poor fool man! *Deil hae me*, quo' he; an' I see the deil at his oxter." The conviction of guilt and grace cam in on Tam like the deep sea; he flang doun the pike that was in his hands—"I will nae mair lift arms against the cause o' Christ!" says he, and was as gude's word. There was a sair fyke in the beginning, but the governor, seeing him resolved, gied him his dischairge, and he went and dwallt and married in North Berwick, and had aye a gude name with honest folk frae that day on.

It was in the year seeventeen hunner and sax that the Bass cam in the hands o' the Da'rymples, and there was twa men soucht the chairge of it. Baith were weel qualified, for they had baith been sodgers in the garrison, and kennt the gate to handle solans, and the seasons and values of them. Forbye that they were baith—or they baith seemed—earnest professors and men of comely conversation. The first of them was just Tam Dale, my faither. The second was ane Lapraik, whom the folk ca'd Tod Lapraik maistly, but whether for his name or his nature I could never hear tell. Weel, Tam gaed to see Lapraik upon this business, and took me, that was a toddlin' laddie, by the hand. Tod had his dwallin' in the lang loan benorth the kirkyaird. It's a dark, uncaanny loan, forbye that the kirk has aye had an ill name since the days o' James the Saxt and the deevil's cantrips played therein when the Queen was on the seas; and as for Tod's house, it was in the mirkest end, and was little likit by some that kenned the best. The door was on the sneck that day, and me and my faither gaed straucht in. Tod was a wabster to his trade; his loom stood in the but. There he sat, a muckle fat, white hash of a man like creish, wi' a kind of a holy smile that gart me scunner. The hand of him aye cawed the shuttle, but his een was steekit. We cried to him by his name, we skirled in the deid lug of him, we shook him by the shouther. Nae mainner o' service! There he sat on his dowp, an' cawed the shuttle and smiled like creish.

"God be guid to us," says Tam Dale, "this is no' canny!"

He had jimp said the word, when Tod Lapraik cam to himsel'.

"Is this you, Tam?" says he. "Haith, man! I'm blithe to see ye. I whiles fa' into a bit dwam like this," he says; "it's frae the stamach."

Weel, they began to crack about the Bass, and which of them twa was to get the warding o't, and by little and little cam to very ill words, and twined in anger. I mind weel, that as my faither and me gaed hame again, he came ower and ower the same expression, how little he likit Tod Lapraik and his dwams.

"Dwam!" says he. "I think folk hae brunt for dwams like yon."

Aweel, my faither got the Bass, and Tod had to go wantin'. It was remembered sinsyne what way he had ta'en the thing. "Tam," says he, "ye hae gotten the better o' me aince mair, and I hope," says he, "ye'll find at least a' that ye expeckit at the Bass." Which have since been thought remarkable expressions. At last the time came for Tam Dale to take young solans. This was a business he was weel used wi', he had been a craigsman frae a laddie, and trustit nane but himsel'. So there was he, hingin' by a line an' speldering on the craig face, whaur it's hieest and steighest. Fower tenty lads were on the tap, hauldin' the line and mindin' for his signals. But whaur Tam hung there was naething but the craig, and the sea below, and the solans skirling and flying. It was a braw spring morn, and Tam whustled as he claught in the young geese. Mony's the time I heard him tell of this experience, and aye the swat ran upon the man.

It chanced, ye see, that Tam keekit up, and he was awaur of a muckle solan, and the solan pyking at the line. He thocht this by-ordinar and outside the creature's habits. He minded that ropes was unco saft things, and the solan's neb and the Bass Rock unco hard, and that twa hunner feet were raither mair than he would care to fa'.

"Shoo!" says Tam. "Awa', bird! Shoo, awa' wi' ye!" says he.

The solan keekit doun into Tam's face, and there was something unco in the creature's ee. Just the ae keek it gied, and back to the rope. But now it wroucht and warstl't like a thing dementit. There never was the solan made that wroucht as that solan wroucht; and it seemed to understand its employ brawly, birzing the saft rope between the neb of it and a crunkled jag o' stane.

There gaed a cauld stend o' fear into Tam's heart. "This thing is nae bird," thinks he. His een turnt backward in his heid and the day gaed black about him. "If I get a dwam here," he thocht, "it's by wi' Tam Dale." And he signalled for the lads to pu' him up.

And it seemed the solan understood about signals. For nae sooner was the signal made than he let be the rope, spried his wings, squawked out loud, took a turn flying, and dashed straucht at Tam Dale's een. Tam had a knife, he gart the cauld steel glitter.

And it seemed the solan understood about knives, for nae suner did the steel glint in the sun than he gied the ae squawk, but laigher, like a body disappointit, and flegged aff about the roundness of the craig, and Tam saw him nae mair. And as sune as that thing was gane, Tam's heid drapt upon his shouther, and they pu'd him up like a deid corp, dadding on the craig.

A dram of brandy (which he went never without) broucht him to his mind, or what was left of it. Up he sat.

"Rin, Geordie, rin to the boat, mak' sure of the boat, man—rin!" he cries, "or yon solan'll have it awa'," says he.

The fower lads stared at ither, an' tried to whillywha him to be quiet. But naething would satisfy Tam Dale, till ane o' them had startit on aheid to stand sentry on the boat. The ithers askit if he was for down again.

"Na," says he, "and neither you nor me," says he, "and as sune as I can win to stand on my twa feet we'll be aff frae this craig o' Sawtan."

Sure eneuch, nae time was lost, and that was over muckle; for before they won to North Berwick Tam was in a crying fever. He lay a' the simmer; and wha was sae kind as come speiring for him but Tod Lapraik! Folk thocht afterwards that ilka time Tod cam near the house the fever had worsened. I kenna for that; but what I ken the best, that was the end of it.

It was about this time o' the year; my grandfaither was out at the white fishing; and like a bairn, I büt to gang wi' him. We had a grand take, I mind, and the way that the fish lay broucht us near in by the Bass, whaur we forgathered wi' anither boat that belanged to a man Sandie Fletcher in Castleton. He's no' lang deid neither, or ye could speir at himsel'. Weel, Sandie hailed.

"What's yon on the Bass?" says he.

"On the Bass?" says grandfaither.

"Ay," says Sandie, "on the green side o't."

"Whatten kind of a thing?" says grandfaither. "There canna be naething on the Bass but just the sheep."

"It looks unco like a body," quo' Sandie, who was nearer in.

"A body!" says we, and we nane of us likit that. For there was nae boat that could have broucht a man, and the key o' the prison yett hung ower my faither's heid at hame in the press bed.

We keepit the twa boats closs for company, and crap in nearer hand. Grandfaither had a gless, for he had been a sailor, and the captain of a smack, and had lost her on the sands of Tay.

136

And when we took the gless to it, sure eneuch there was a man. He was in a crunkle o' green brae, a wee below the chaipel, a' by his lee-lane, and lowped and flang and danced like a daft quean at a waddin'.

"It's Tod," says grandfaither, and passed the gless to Sandie.

"Ay, it's him," says Sandie.

"Or ane in the likeness o' him," says grandfaither.

"Sma' is the differ," quo' Sandie. "Deil or warlock, I'll try the gun at him," quo' he, and broucht up a fowling-piece that he aye carried, for Sandie was a notable famous shot in a' that country.

"Haud your hand, Sandie," says grandfaither; "we maun see clearer first," says he, "or this may be a dear day's wark to the baith of us."

"Hout!" says Sandie, "this is the Lord's judgments surely, and be damned to it!" says he.

"Maybe ay, and maybe no," says my grandfaither, worthy man! "But have you a mind of the Procurator Fiscal, that I think ye'll have forgathered wi' before," says he.

This was ower true, and Sandie was a wee thing set ajee. "Aweel, Edie," says he, "and what would be your way of it?"

"Ou, just this," says grandfaither. "Let me that has the fastest boat gang back to North Berwick, and let you bide here and keep an eye on Thon. If I canna find Lapraik, I'll join ye, and the twa of us'll have a crack wi' him. But if Lapraik's at hame, I'll rin up the flag at the harbour, and ye can try Thon Thing wi' the gun."

Aweel, so it was agreed between them twa. I was just a bairn, an' clum in Sandie's boat, whaur I thocht I would see the best of the employ. My grandsire gied Sandie a siller tester to pit in his gun wi' the leid draps, bein' mair deidly again bogles. And then the ae boat set aff for North Berwick, an' the tither lay whaur it was and watched the wanchancy thing on the brae-side.

A' the time we lay there it lowped and flang and capered and span like a teetotum, and whiles we could hear it skelloch as it span. I hae seen lassies, the daft queans, that would lowp and

137

dance a winter's nicht, and still be lowping and dancing when the winter's day cam in. But there would be folk there to hauld them company, and the lads to egg them on; and this thing was its lee-lane. And there would be a fiddler diddling his elbock in the chimney-side; and this thing had nae music but the skirling of the solans. And the lassies were bits o' young things wi' the reid life dinnling and standing in their members; and this was a muckle, fat, creishy man, and him fa'n in the vale o' years. Say what ye like, I maun say what I believe. It was joy was in the creature's heart; the joy o' hell, I daursay: joy whatever. Mony a time I have askit mysel', why witches and warlocks should sell their sauls (whilk are their maist dear possessions) and be auld, duddy, wrunkl't wives, or auld, feckless, doddered men; and then I mind upon Tod Lapraik dancing a' thae hours by his lane in the black glory of his heart. Nae doubt they burn for it in muckle hell, but they have a grand time here of it, whatever!—and the Lord forgie us!

Weel, at the hinder end, we saw the wee flag yirk up to the mast-heid upon the harbour rocks. That was a' Sandie waited for. He up wi' the gun, took a deleeberate aim, an' pu'd the trigger. There cam a bang and then ae waefu' skirl frae the Bass. And there were we, rubbin' our een and lookin' at ither like daft folk. For wi' the bang and the skirl the thing had clean disappeared. The sun glintit, the wund blew, and there was the bare yerd whaur the Wonder had been lowping and flinging but ae second syne.

The hale way hame I roared and grat wi' the terror of that dispensation. The grawn folk were nane sae muckle better; there was little said in Sandie's boat but just the name of God; and when we won in by the pier, the harbour rocks were fair black wi' the folk waitin' us. It seems they had fund Lapraik in ane of his dwams, cawing the shuttle and smiling. Ae lad they sent to hoist the flag, and the rest abode there in the wabster's house. You may be sure they likit it little; but it was a means of grace to severals that stood there praying in to themsel's (for nane cared to pray out loud) and looking on thon awesome

thing as it cawed the shuttle. Syne, upon a suddenty, and wi'
the ae dreidfu' skelloch, Tod sprang up frae his hinderlands
and fell forrit on the wab, a bluidy corp.

When the corp was examined the leid draps hadna played
buff upon the warlock's body; sorrow a leid drap was to be
fund; but there was grandfaither's siller tester in the puddock's
heart of him.

Andie had scarce done when there befell a mighty silly affair
that had its consequence. Neil, as I have said, was himself a
great narrator. I have heard since that he knew all the stories in
the Highlands; and thought much of himself, and was thought
much of by others, on the strength of it. Now Andie's tale
reminded him of one he had already heard.

"She would ken that story afore," he said. "She was the story
of Uistean More M'Gillie Phadrig and the Gavar Vore."

"It is no sic a thing," cried Andie. "It is the story of my faither
(now wi' God) and Tod Lapraik. And the same in your beard,"
says he; "and keep the tongue of ye inside your Hielant chafts!"

In dealing with Highlanders it will be found, and has been
shown in history, how well it goes with Lowland gentlefolk; but
the thing appears scarce feasible for Lowland commons. I had
already remarked that Andie was continually on the point of
quarrelling with our three Macgregors, and now, sure enough,
it was to come.

"Thir will be no words to use to shentlemans," says Neil.

"Shentlemans!" cries Andie. "Shentlemans, ye Hielant stot! If
God would gie ye the grace to see yoursel' the way that ithers
see ye, ye would throw your denner up."

There came some kind of a Gaelic oath from Neil, and the
black knife was in his hand that moment.

There was no time to think; and I caught the Highlander by
the leg, and had him down, and his armed hand pinned out,
before I knew what I was doing. His comrades sprang to
rescue him, Andie and I were without weapons, the Gregara
three to two. It seemed we were beyond salvation, when Neil

screamed in his own tongue, ordering the others back, and made his submission to myself in a manner the most abject, even giving me up his knife, which (upon a repetition of his promises) I returned to him on the morrow.

Two things I saw plain: the first, that I must not build too high on Andie, who had shrunk against the wall and stood there, as pale as death, till the affair was over; the second, the strength of my own position with the Highlanders, who must have received extraordinary charges to be tender of my safety. But if I thought Andie came not very well out in courage, I had no fault to find with him upon the account of gratitude. It was not so much that he troubled me with thanks, as that his whole mind and manner appeared changed; and as he preserved ever after a great timidity of our companions, he and I were yet more constantly together.

CHAPTER XVI

The Missing Witness

On the seventeenth, the day I was trysted with the Writer, I had much rebellion against fate. The thought of him waiting in the "King's Arms," and of what he would think, and what he would say, when next we met, tormented and oppressed me. The truth was unbelievable, so much I had to grant, and it seemed cruel hard I should be posted as a liar and a coward, and have never consciously omitted what it was possible that I should do. I repeated this form of words with a kind of bitter relish, and re-examined in that light the steps of my behaviour. It seemed I had behaved to James Stewart as a brother might; all the past was a picture that I could be proud of, and there was only the present to consider. I could not swim the sea, nor yet fly in the air, but there was always Andie. I had done him a service, he liked me; I had a lever there to work on; if it were just for decency, I must try once more with Andie.

It was late afternoon; there was no sound in all the Bass but the lap and bubble of a very quiet sea; and my four companions were all crept apart, the three Macgregors higher on the rock, and Andie with his Bible to a sunny place among the ruins; there I found him in deep sleep, and, as soon as he was awake, appealed to him with some fervour of manner and a good show of argument.

"If I thocht it was to do guid to ye, Shaws!" said he, staring at me over his spectacles.

"It's to save another," said I, "and to redeem my word. What would be more good than that? Do ye no' mind the scripture, Andie? And you with the Book upon your lap! *What shall it profit a man if he gain the whole world?*"

"Ay," said he, "that's grand for you. But where do I come in? I have my word to redeem the same's yoursel'. And what are ye asking me to do, but just to sell it ye for siller?"

"Andie! have I named the name of siller?" cried I.

141

"Ou, the name's naething," said he; "the thing is there, whatever. It just comes to this: if I am to service ye the way that you
propose, I'll lose my lifelihood. Then it's clear ye'll have to
make it up to me, and a pickle mair, for your ain credit like. And
what's that but just a bribe? And if even I was certain of the
bribe! But by a' that I can learn, it's far frae that; and if *you* were
to hang, where would *I* be? Na: the thing's no' possible. And
just awa' wi' ye like a bonny lad! and let Andie read his chapter."

I remember I was at bottom a good deal gratified with this
result; and the next humour I fell into was one (I had near said)
of gratitude to Prestongrange, who had saved me, in this
violent, illegal manner, out of the midst of my dangers, temptations, and perplexities. But this was both too flimsy and too
cowardly to last me long, and the remembrance of James
began to succeed to the possession of my spirits. The 21st, the
day set for the trial, I passed in such misery of mind as I can
scarce recall to have endured, save perhaps upon Isle Earraid
only. Much of the time I lay on a brae-side betwixt sleep and
waking, my body motionless, my mind full of violent thoughts.
Sometimes I slept indeed; but the court-house of Inverary and
the prisoner glancing on all sides to find his missing witness,
followed me in slumber; and I would wake again with a start to
darkness of spirit and distress of body. I thought Andie seemed
to observe me, but I paid him little heed. Verily, my bread was
bitter to me, and my days a burthen.

Early the next morning (Friday, 22nd) a boat came with
provisions, and Andie placed a packet in my hand. The cover
was without address but sealed with a Government seal. It
enclosed two notes. "Mr. Balfour can now see for himself it is
too late to meddle. His conduct will be observed and his
discretion rewarded." So ran the first, which seemed to be
laboriously writ with the left hand. There was certainly nothing
in these expressions to compromise the writer, even if that
person could be found; the seal, which formidably served
instead of signature, was affixed to a separate sheet on which
there was no scratch of writing; and I had to confess that (so

far) my adversaries knew what they were doing, and to digest as well as I was able the threat that peeped under the promise.

But the second enclosure was by far the more surprising. It was in a lady's hand of writ. *"Maister Dauvit Balfour is informed a friend was speiring for him, and her eyes were of the grey,"* it ran—and seemed so extraordinary a piece to come to my hands at such a moment and under cover of a Government seal, that I stood stupid. Catriona's grey eyes shone in my remembrance. I thought, with a bound of pleasure, she must be the friend. But who should the writer be, to have her billet thus enclosed with Prestongrange's? And of all wonders, why was it thought needful to give me this pleasing but most inconsequential intelligence upon the Bass? For the writer, I could hit upon none possible except Miss Grant. Her family, I remembered, had remarked on Catriona's eyes, and even named her for their colour; and she herself had been much in the habit to address me with a broad pronunciation, by way of a sniff, I supposed, at my rusticity. No doubt, besides, but she lived in the same house as this letter came from. So there remained but one step to be accounted for; and that was how Prestongrange should have permitted her at all in an affair so secret, or let her daft-like billet go in the same cover with his own. But even here I had a glimmering. For, first of all, there was something rather alarming about the young lady, and papa might be more under her domination than I knew. And second, there was the man's continual policy to be remembered, how his conduct had been continually mingled with caresses, and he had scarce ever, in the midst of so much contention, laid aside a mask of friendship. He must conceive that my imprisonment had incensed me. Perhaps this little jesting, friendly message was intended to disarm my rancour?

I will be honest—and I think it did. I felt a sudden warmth towards that beautiful Miss Grant, that she should stoop to so much interest in my affairs. The summoning up of Catriona moved me of itself to milder and more cowardly counsels. If the Advocate knew of her and of our acquaintance—if I should please him by some of that "discretion" at which his letter pointed—to what might not this lead? *In vain is the net spread in the sight of any fowl*, the scripture says. Well, fowls must be wiser than folk! For I thought I perceived the policy, and yet fell in with it.

I was in this frame, my heart beating, the grey eyes plain before me like two stars, when Andie broke in upon my musing.

"I see ye hae gotten guid news," said he.

I found him looking curiously in my face; with that, there came before me like a vision of James Stewart and the court of Inverary; and my mind turned at once like a door upon its hinges. Trials, I reflected, sometimes draw out longer than is looked for. Even if I came to Inverary just too late, something might yet be attempted in the interests of James—and in those of my own character, the best would be accomplished. In a moment, it seemed without thought, I had a plan devised.

"Andie," said I, "is it still to be tomorrow?"

He told me nothing was changed.

"Was anything said about the hour?" I asked.

He told me it was to be two o'clock afternoon.

"And about the place?" I pursued.

"Whatten place?" says Andie.

"The place I'm to be landed at," said I.

He owned there was nothing as to that.

"Very well, then," I said, "this shall be mine to arrange. The wind is in the east, my road lies westward; keep your boat, I hire it; let us work up the Forth all day; and land me at two o'clock tomorrow at the westmost we'll can have reached."

"Ye daft callant!" he cried, "ye would try for Inverary after a'!"

"Just that, Andie," says I.

"Weel, ye're ill to beat!" says he. "And I was kind o' sorry for ye a' day yesterday," he added. "Ye see, I was never entirely sure till then, which way of it ye really wantit."

Here was a spur to a lame horse!

"A word in your ear, Andie," said I. "This plan of mine has another advantage yet. We can leave these Hielandmen behind us on the rock, and one of your boats from the Castleton can bring them off tomorrow. Yon Neil has a queer eye when he regards you; maybe, if I was once out of the gate there might be knives again; these red-shanks are unco grudgeful. And if there should come to be any question, here is your excuse. Our lives were in danger by these savages; being answerable for my safety, you chose the part to bring me from their neighbourhood and detain me the rest of the time on board your boat: and do you know, Andie," says I, with a smile, "I think it was very wisely chosen."

"The truth is, I have nae goo for Neil," says Andie, "nor he for me, I'm thinking; and I would like ill to come to my hands wi' the man. Tam Anster will make a better hand of it with the cattle, onyway." (For this man, Anster, came from Fife, where the Gaelic is still spoken.) "Ay, ay!" says Andie, "Tam'll can deal wi' them the best. And troth! the mair I think of it, the less I see what way we would be required. The place—ay, feggs! they had forgot the place. Eh, Shaws, ye're a lang-heided chield when ye like! Forbye that I'm awing ye my life," he added, with more solemnity, and offered me his hand upon the bargain.

Whereupon, with scarce more words, we stepped suddenly on board the boat, cast off, and set the lug. The Gregara were then busy upon breakfast, for the cookery was their usual part; but, one of them stepping to the battlements, our flight was observed before we were twenty fathoms from the rock; and the three of them ran about the ruins and the landing-shelf, for all the world like ants about a broken nest, hailing and crying on us to return. We were still in both the lee and the shadow of the rock, which last lay broad upon the waters, but presently came forth in almost the same moment into the wind and sunshine; the sail filled, the boat heeled to the gunwale, and we swept immediately beyond sound of the men's voices. To what terrors they endured upon the rock, where they were now deserted without the countenance of any civilised person or

145

so much as the protection of a Bible, no limit can be set, nor had they any brandy left to be their consolation, for even in the haste and secrecy of our departure Andie had managed to remove it.

It was our first care to set Anster ashore in a cove by the Glenteithy Rocks, so that the deliverance of our maroons might be duly seen to the next day. Thence we kept away up Firth. The breeze, which was then so spirited, swiftly declined, but never wholly failed us. All day we kept moving, though often not much more; and it was after dark ere we were up with the Queen's Ferry. To keep the letter of Andie's engagement (or what was left of it) I must remain on board, but I thought no harm to communicate with the shore in writing. On Prestongrange's cover, where the Government seal must have a good deal surprised my correspondent, I writ, by the boat's lantern, a few necessary words, and Andie carried them to Rankeillor. In about an hour he came aboard again, with a purse of money and the assurance that a good horse should be standing saddled for me by two tomorrow at Clackmannan Pool. This done, and the boat riding by her stone anchor, we lay down to sleep under the sail.

We were in the Pool the next day long ere two; and there was nothing left for me but sit and wait. I felt little alacrity upon my errand. I would have been glad of any passable excuse to lay it down; but, none being to be found, my uneasiness was no less great than if I had been running to some desired pleasure. By shortly after one the horse was at the waterside, and I could see a man walking it to and fro till I should land, which vastly swelled my impatience. Andie ran the moment of liberation very fine, showing himself a man of his bare word, but scarce serving his employers with a heaped measure; and by about fifty seconds after two I was in the saddle and on the full stretch for Stirling. In a little more than an hour I had passed that town and was already mounting Allan Water side, when the weather broke in a small tempest. The rain blinded me, the wind had nearly beat me from the saddle, and the first darkness of the night surprised me in a wilderness still some way east of Balwhidder, not very sure of my direction, and mounted on a horse that began already to be weary.

In the press of my hurry, and to be spared the delay and annoyance of a guide, I had followed (so far as it was possible for any horseman) the line of my journey with Alan. This I did with open eyes, foreseeing a great risk in it, which the tempest had now brought to a reality. The last that I knew of where I was, I think it must have been about Uam Var; the hour perhaps six at night. I must still think it great good fortune that I got about eleven to my destination, the house of Duncan Dhu. Where I had wandered in the interval perhaps the horse could tell. I know we were twice down, and once over the saddle and for a moment carried away in a roaring burn. Steed and rider were bemired up to the eyes.

From Duncan I had news of the trial. It was followed in all these Highland regions with religious interest; news of it spread from Inverary as swift as men could travel; and I was rejoiced to learn that, up to a late hour that Saturday, it was not yet concluded: and all men began to suppose it must spread over to the Monday. Under the spur of this intelligence I would not sit to eat; but, Duncan having agreed to be my guide, took the road again on foot, with the piece in my hand and munching as I went. Duncan brought with him a flask of usquebaugh and a hand-lantern; which last enlightened us just so long as we could find houses where to rekindle it, for the thing leaked outrageously and blew out with every gust. The more part of the night we walked blindfold among sheets of rain, and day found us aimless on the mountains. Hard by we struck a hut on a burn-side, where we got a bite and a direction: and, a little before the end of the sermon, came to the kirk-doors of Inverary.

The rain had somewhat washed the upper parts of me, but I was still bogged as high as to the knees; I streamed water; I was so weary I could hardly limp, and my face was like a ghost's. I stood certainly more in need of a change of raiment and a bed to lie on than of all the benefits in Christianity. For all which (being persuaded the chief point for me was to make myself immediately public) I set the door open, entered that church with the dirty Duncan at my tails, and, finding a vacant place hard by, sat down.

"Thirteenthly, my brethren, and in parenthesis, the law itself must be regarded as a means of grace," the minister was saying, in the voice of one delighting to pursue an argument.

The sermon was in English on account of the assize. The judges were present with their armed attendants, the halberts glittered in a corner by the door, and the seats were thronged beyond custom with the array of lawyers. The text was in Romans 5th and 13th—the minister a skilled hand; and the whole of that able churchful—from Argyle, and my Lords Elchies and Kilkerran, down to the halbertmen that came in their attendance—was sunk with gathered brows in a profound critical attention. The minister himself and a sprinkling of those about the door observed our entrance at the moment and immediately forgot the same; the rest either did not hear or would not heed; and I sat there amongst my friends and enemies unremarked.

The first that I singled out was Prestongrange. He sat well forward, like an eager horseman in the saddle, his lips moving with relish, his eyes glued on the minister; the doctrine was clearly to his mind. Charles Stewart, on the other hand, was half-asleep, and looked harassed and pale. As for Simon Fraser, he appeared like a blot, and almost a scandal, in the midst of that attentive congregation, digging his hands in his pockets, shifting his legs, clearing his throat, rolling up his bald eyebrows and shooting out his eyes to right and left, now with a yawn, now with a secret smile. At times too, he would take the Bible in front of him, run it through, seem to read a bit, run it through again, and stop and yawn prodigiously: the whole as if for exercise.

In the course of this restlessness his eye alighted on myself. He sat a second stupefied, then tore a half leaf out of the Bible, scrawled upon it with a pencil, and passed it with a whispered word to his next neighbour. The note came to Prestongrange, who gave me but the one look; thence it voyaged to the hands of Mr. Erskine; thence again to Argyle, where he sat between the other two lords of session, and his Grace turned and fixed me with an arrogant eye. The last of those interested to observe my presence was Charlie Stewart, and he too began to pencil and hand about despatches, none of which I was able to trace to their destination in the crowd.

But the passage of these notes had aroused notice; all who were in the secret (or supposed themselves to be so) were whispering information—the rest questions; and the minister himself seemed quite discountenanced by the flutter in the church and sudden stir and whispering. His voice changed, he plainly faltered, nor did he again recover the easy conviction and full tones of his delivery. It would be a puzzle to him till his dying day, why a sermon that had gone with triumph through four parts, should thus miscarry in the fifth.

As for me, I continued to sit there, very wet and weary, and a good deal anxious as to what should happen next, but greatly exulting in my success.

CHAPTER XVII

The Memorial

The last word of the blessing was scarce out of the minister's mouth before Stewart had me by the arm. We were the first to be forth of the church, and he made such extraordinary expedition that we were safe within the four walls of a house before the street had begun to be thronged with the home-going congregation.

"Am I yet in time?" I asked.

"Ay and no," said he. "The case is over; the jury is enclosed, and will be so kind as let us ken their view of it tomorrow in the morning, the same as I could have told it my own self three days ago before the play began. The thing has been public from the start. The panel kennt it, '*Ye may do what ye will for me*,' whispers he two days ago. '*I ken my fate by what the Duke of Argyle has just said to Mr. Macintosh.*' O, it's been a scandal!

"The great Argyle he gaed before,
He gart the cannons and guns to rear,

and the very macer cried 'Cruachan!' But now that I have got you again I'll never despair. The oak shall go over the myrtle yet; we'll ding the Campbells yet in their own town. Praise God that I should see the day!"

He was leaping with excitement, emptied out his mails upon the floor that I might have a change of clothes, and incommoded me with his assistance as I changed. What remained to be done, or how I was to do it, was what he never told me, nor, I believe, so much as thought of. "We'll ding the Campbells yet!" that was still his owercome. And it was forced home upon my mind how this, that had the externals of a sober process of law, was in its essence a clan battle between savage clans. I thought my friend the Writer none of the least savage. Who, that had only seen him at a counsel's back before

150

the Lord Ordinary, or following a golf-ball and laying down his clubs on Bruntsfield links, could have recognised for the same person this voluble and violent clansman?

James Stewart's counsel were four in number—Sheriffs Brown of Colstoun and Miller, Mr. Robert Macintosh and Mr. Stewart, younger of Stewart Hall. These were covenanted to dine with the Writer after sermon, and I was very obligingly included of the party. No sooner the cloth lifted, and the first bowl very artfully compounded by Sheriff Miller, than we fell to the subject in hand. I made a short narration of my seizure and captivity, and was then examined and re-examined upon the circumstances of the murder. It will be remembered this was the first time I had had my say out, or the matter at all handled, among lawyers; and the consequence was very dispiriting to the others and (I must own) disappointing to myself.

"To sum up," said Colstoun, "you prove that Alan was on the spot; you have heard him proffer menaces against Glenure; and though you assure us he was not the man who fired, you leave a strong impression that he was in league with him, and consenting, perhaps immediately assisting, in the act. You show him besides, at the risk of his own liberty, actively furthering the criminal's escape. And the rest of your testimony (so far as the least material) depends on the bare word of Alan or of James, the two accused. In short, you do not at all break, but only lengthen by one personage, the chain that binds our client to the murderer; and I need scarcely say that the introduction of a third accomplice rather aggravates that appearance of a conspiracy which has been our stumbling-block from the beginning."

"I am of the same opinion," said Sheriff Miller. "I think we may all be very much obliged to Prestongrange for taking a most uncomfortable witness out of our way. And chiefly, I think, Mr. Balfour himself might be obliged. For you talk of a third accomplice, but Mr. Balfour (in my view) has very much the appearance of a fourth."

"Allow me, sirs!" interposed Stewart the Writer. "There is another view. Here we have a witness—never fash whether material or not—a witness in this cause, kidnapped by that old, lawless, bandit crew of the Glengyle Macgregors, and sequestered for near upon a month in a bourock of old cold ruins on the Bass. Move that and see what dirt you fling on the proceedings! Sirs, this is a tale to make the world ring with! It would be strange, with such a grip as this, if we couldna squeeze out a pardon for my client."

"And suppose we took up Mr. Balfour's cause tomorrow?" said Stewart Hall. "I am much deceived or we should find so many impediments thrown in our path, as that James should have been hanged before we had found a court to hear us. This is a great scandal, but I suppose we have none of us forgot a greater still, I mean the matter of the Lady Grange. The woman was still in durance; my friend Mr. Hope of Rankeillor did what was humanly possible; and how did he speed? He never got a warrant! Well, it'll be the same now; the same weapons will be used. This is a scene, gentlemen, of clan animosity. The hatred of the name which I have the honour to bear rages in high quarters. There is nothing here to be viewed but naked Campbell spite and scurvy Campbell intrigue."

You may be sure this was to touch a welcome topic, and I sat for some time in the midst of my learned counsel, almost deaved with their talk, but extremely little the wiser for its purport. The Writer was led into some hot expressions; Colstoun must take him up and set him right; the rest joined in on different sides, but all pretty noisy; the Duke of Argyle was beaten like a blanket; King George came in for a few digs in the by-going and a great deal of rather elaborate defence: and there was only one person that seemed to be forgotten, and that was James of the Glens.

Through all this Mr. Miller sat quiet. He was a slip of an oldish gentleman, ruddy and twinkling; he spoke in a smooth rich voice, with an infinite effect of pawkiness, dealing out each word the way an actor does, to give the most expression possible; and even now, when he was silent, and sat there with his wig laid aside, his glass in both hands, his mouth funnily pursed, and his chin out, he seemed the mere picture of a merry slyness. It was plain he had a word to say, and waited for the fit occasion.

It came presently. Colstoun had wound up one of his speeches with some expression of their duty to their client. His brother sheriff was pleased, I suppose, with the transition. He took the table in his confidence with a gesture and a look.

"That suggests to me a consideration which seems overlooked," said he. "The interest of our client goes certainly before all, but the world does not come to an end with James Stewart." Whereas he cocked his eye. "I might condescend, *exempli gratia*, upon a Mr. George Brown, a Mr. Thomas Miller, and a Mr. David Balfour. Mr. David Balfour has a very good ground of complaint, and I think, gentlemen—if his story was properly redd out—I think there would be a number of wigs on the green."

The whole table turned to him with a common movement.

"Properly handled and carefully redd out, his is a story that could scarcely fail to have some consequence," he continued. "The whole administration of justice, from its highest officer downward, would be totally discredited; and it looks to me as if they would need to be replaced." He seemed to shine with cunning as he said it. "And I need not point out to ye that this of Mr. Balfour's would be a remarkable bonny cause to appear in," he added.

Well, there they all were started on another hare; Mr. Balfour's cause, and what kind of speeches could be there delivered, and what officials could be thus turned out, and who would succeed to their positions. I shall give but the two specimens. It was proposed to approach Simon Fraser, whose testimony, if it could be obtained, would prove certainly fatal to Argyle and Prestongrange. Miller highly approved of the attempt. "We have here before us a dreeping roast," said he, "here is cut-and-come-again for all." And methought all licked their lips. The other was already near the end. Stewart the Writer was out of the body with delight, smelling vengeance on his chief enemy, the Duke.

"Gentlemen," cried he, charging his glass, "here is to Sheriff Miller. His legal abilities are known to all. His culinary, this bowl in front of us is here to speak for. But when it comes to the poleetical!"—cries he, and drains the glass.

"Ay, but it will hardly prove politics in your meaning, my friend," said the gratified Miller. "A revolution, if you like, and I think I can promise you that historical writers shall date from Mr. Balfour's cause. But, properly guided, Mr. Stewart, tenderly guided, it shall prove a peaceful revolution."

"And if the damned Campbells get their ears rubbed, what care I?" cries Stewart, smiting down his fist.

It will be thought I was not very well pleased with all this, though I could scarce forbear smiling at a kind of innocency in these old intriguers. But it was not my view to have undergone so many sorrows for the advancement of Sheriff Miller or to make a revolution in the Parliament House: and I interposed accordingly with as much simplicity of manner as I could assume.

"I have to thank you, gentlemen, for your advice," said I. "And now I would like, by your leave, to set you two or three questions. There is one thing that has fallen rather on one side,—for instance: Will this cause do any good to our friend James of the Glens?"

They seemed all a hair set back, and gave various answers, but concurring practically in one point, that James had now no hope but in the King's mercy.

"To proceed, then," said I, "will it do any good to Scotland? We have a saying that it is an ill bird that fouls his own nest. I remember hearing we had a riot in Edinburgh when I was an infant child, which gave occasion to the late Queen to call this country barbarous; and I always understood that we had rather lost than gained by that. Then came the year 'Forty-five, which made Scotland to be talked of everywhere; but I never heard it said we had anyway gained by the 'Forty-five. And now we come to this cause of Mr. Balfour's, as you call it. Sheriff Miller tells us historical writers are to date from it, and I would not wonder. It is only my fear they would date from it as a period of calamity and public reproach."

The nimble-witted Miller had already smelt where I was travelling to, and made haste to get on the same road. "Forcibly put, Mr. Balfour," says he. "A weighty observe, sir."

"We have next to ask ourselves if it will be good for King George," I pursued. "Sheriff Miller appears pretty easy upon this; but I doubt you will scarce be able to pull down the house from under him, without his Majesty coming by a knock or two, one of which might easily prove fatal."

I gave them a chance to answer, but none volunteered.

"Of those for whom the case was to be profitable," I went on, "Sheriff Miller gave us the names of several, among the which he was good enough to mention mine. I hope he will pardon me if I think otherwise. I believe I hung not the least back in this affair while there was life to be saved; but I own I thought myself extremely hazarded, and I own I think it would be a pity for a young man, with some idea of coming to the Bar, to ingrain upon himself the character of a turbulent, factious fellow before he was yet twenty. As for James, it seems—at this date of the proceedings, with the sentence as good as pronounced—he has no hope but in the King's mercy. May not his Majesty, then, be more pointedly addressed, the characters of these high officers sheltered from the public, and myself kept out of a position which I think spells ruin for me?"

They all sat and gazed into their glasses, and I could see they found my attitude on the affair unpalatable. But Miller was ready at all events.

"If I may be allowed to put our young friend's notion in more formal shape," says he, "I understand him to propose that we should embody the fact of his sequestration, and perhaps some heads of the testimony he was prepared to offer, in a memorial to the Crown. This plan has elements of success. It is as likely as any other (and perhaps likelier) to help our client. Perhaps his Majesty would have the goodness to feel a certain gratitude to all concerned in such a memorial, which might be construed into an expression of a very delicate loyalty; and I think, in the drafting of the same, this view might be brought forward."

They all nodded to each other, not without sighs, for the former alternative was doubtless more after their inclination.

"Paper then, Mr. Stewart, if you please," pursued Miller; "and I think it might very fittingly be signed by the five of us here present, as procurators for the 'condemned man.'"

"It can do none of us any harm at least," says Colstoun, heaving another sigh, for he had seen himself Lord Advocate the last ten minutes.

Thereupon they set themselves, not very enthusiastically, to draft the memorial—a process in the course of which they soon caught fire; and I had no more ado but to sit looking on and answer an occasional question. The paper was very well expressed; beginning with a recitation of the facts about myself, the reward offered for my apprehension, my surrender, the pressure brought to bear upon me; my sequestration; and my arrival at Inverary in time to be too late; going on to explain the reasons of loyalty and public interest for which it was agreed to waive any right of action; and winding up with a forcible appeal to the King's mercy on behalf of James.

Methought I was a good deal sacrificed, and rather represented in the light of a firebrand of a fellow whom my cloud of lawyers had restrained with difficulty from extremes. But I let it pass, and made but the one suggestion, that I should be described as ready to deliver my own evidence and adduce that of others before any commission of inquiry—and the one demand, that I should be immediately furnished with a copy.

Colstoun hummed and hawed. "This is a very confidential document," said he.

"And my position towards Prestongrange is highly peculiar," I replied. "No question but I must have touched his heart at our first interview, so that he has since stood my friend consistently. But for him, gentlemen, I must now be lying dead, or awaiting my sentence alongside poor James. For which reason I choose to communicate to him the fact of this memorial as soon as it is copied. You are to consider also that this step will make for my protection. I have enemies here accustomed to drive hard; his Grace is in his own country, Lovat by his side; and if there should hang any ambiguity over our proceedings I think I might very well awake in gaol."

Not finding any very ready answer to these considerations, my company of advisers were at the last persuaded to consent, and made only this condition, that I was to lay the paper before Prestongrange with the express compliments of all concerned.

The Advocate was at the castle dining with his Grace. By the hand of one of Colstoun's servants I sent him a billet asking for an interview, and received a summons to meet him at once in a private house of the town. Here I found him alone in a chamber; from his face there was nothing to be gleaned; yet I was not so unobservant but what I spied some halberts in the hall, and not so stupid but what I could gather he was prepared to arrest me there and then, should it appear advisable.

"So, Mr. David, this is you?" said he.

"Where I fear I am not overly welcome, my lord," said I. "And I would like before I go further to express my sense of your lordship's continued good offices, even should they now cease."

"I have heard of your gratitude before," he replied drily, "and I think this can scarce be the matter you called me from my wine to listen to. I would remember also, if I were you, that you still stand on a very boggy foundation."

"Not now, my lord, I think," said I; "and if your lordship will but glance an eye along this, you will perhaps think as I do."

He read it sedulously through, frowning heavily; then turned back to one part and another which he seemed to weigh and compare the effect of. His face a little lightened.

"This is not so bad but what it might be worse," said he;

"though I am still likely to pay dear for my acquaintance with Mr. David Balfour."

"Rather for your indulgence to that unlucky young man, my lord," said I.

He still skimmed the paper, and all the while his spirits seemed to mend.

"And to whom am I indebted for this?" he asked presently. "Other counsels must have been discussed, I think. Who was it proposed this private method? Was it Miller?"

"My lord, it was myself," said I. "These gentlemen have shown me no such consideration, as that I should deny myself any credit I can fairly claim, or spare them any responsibility they should properly bear. And the mere truth is, that they were all in favour of a process which should have remarkable consequences in the Parliament House, and prove for them (in one of their own expressions) a dripping roast. Before I intervened, I think they were on the point of sharing out the different law appointments. Our friend Mr. Simon was to be taken in upon some composition."

Prestongrange smiled. "These are our friends!" said he. "And what were your reasons for dissenting, Mr. David?"

I told them without concealment, expressing, however, with more force and volume those which regarded Prestongrange himself.

"You do me no more than justice," said he. "I have fought as hard in your interest as you have fought against mine. And how came you here today?" he asked. "As the case drew out, I began to grow uneasy that I had clipped the period so fine, and I was even expecting you tomorrow. But today—I never dreamed of it."

I was not, of course, going to betray Andie.

"I suspect there is some very weary cattle by the road," said I.

"If I had known you were such a moss-trooper you should have tasted longer of the Bass," says he.

"Speaking of which, my lord, I return your letter." And I gave him the enclosure in the counterfeit hand.

"There was the cover also with the seal," said he.

"I have it not," said I. "It bore not even an address, and could not compromise a cat. The second enclosure I have, and with your permission, I desire to keep it."

I thought he winced a little, but he said nothing to the point. "Tomorrow," he resumed, "our business here is to be finished, and I proceed by Glasgow. I would be very glad to have you of my party, Mr. David."

"My lord..." I began.

"I do not deny it will be of service to me," he interrupted. "I desire even that, when we shall come to Edinburgh, you should alight at my house. You have very warm friends in the Miss Grants, who will be overjoyed to have you to themselves. If you think I have been of use to you, you can thus easily repay me, and so far from losing, may reap some advantage by the way. It is not every strange young man who is presented in society by the King's Advocate."

Often enough already (in our brief relations) this gentleman had caused my head to spin; no doubt but what for a moment he did so again now. Here was the old fiction still maintained of my particular favour with his daughters, one of whom had been so good as laugh at me, while the other two had scarce deigned to remark the fact of my existence. And now I was to ride with my lord to Glasgow; I was to dwell with him in Edinburgh; I was to be brought into society under his protection! That he should have so much good-nature as to forgive me was surprising enough; that he could wish to take me up and serve me seemed impossible; and I began to seek for some ulterior meaning. One was plain. If I became his guest, repentance was excluded; I could never think better of my present design and bring any action. And besides, would not my presence in his house draw out the whole pungency of the memorial? For that complaint could not be very seriously regarded, if the person chiefly injured was the guest of the official most incriminated. As I thought upon this, I could not quite refrain from smiling.

"This is in the nature of a countercheck to the memorial?" said I.

"You are cunning, Mr. David," said he, "and you do not wholly guess wrong; the fact will be of use to me in my defence. Perhaps, however, you underrate my friendly sentiments, which are perfectly genuine. I have a respect for you, Mr. David, mingled with awe," says he, smiling.

"I am more than willing, I am earnestly desirous to meet your wishes," said I. "It is my design to be called to the Bar, where your lordship's countenance would be invaluable; and I am besides sincerely grateful to yourself and family for different marks of interest and of indulgence. The difficulty is here. There is one point in which we pull two ways. You are trying to hang James Stewart, I am trying to save him. In so far as my riding with you would better your lordship's defence, I am at your lordship's orders; but in so far as it would help to hang James Stewart, you see me at a stick."

I thought he swore to himself. "You should certainly be called; the Bar is the true scene for your talents," says he bitterly, and then fell a while silent. "I will tell you," he presently resumed, "there is no question of James Stewart, for or against. James is a dead man; his life is given and taken—bought (if you like it better) and sold; no memorial can help—no defalcation of a faithful Mr. David hurt him. Blow high, blow low, there will be no pardon for James Stewart: and take that for said! The question is now of myself: am I to stand or fall? and I do not deny to you that I am in some danger. But will Mr. David Balfour consider why? It is not because I have pushed the case unduly against James; for that, I am sure of condonation. And it is not because I have sequestered Mr. David on a rock, though it will pass under that colour; but because I did not take the ready and plain path, to which I was pressed repeatedly, and send Mr. David to his grave or to the gallows. Hence the scandal—hence this damned memorial," striking the paper on his leg. "My tenderness for you has brought me in this difficulty. I wish to know if your tenderness to your own conscience is too great to let you help me out of it?"

No doubt but there was much of the truth in what he said; if James was past helping, whom was it more natural that I should turn to help than just the man before me, who had helped myself so often, and was even now setting me a pattern of patience? I was besides not only weary, but beginning to be ashamed of my perpetual attitude of suspicion and refusal.

"If you will name the time and place, I will be punctually ready to attend your lordship," said I.

He shook hands with me. "And I think my misses have some news for you," says he, dismissing me.

I came away, vastly pleased to have my peace made, yet a little concerned in conscience; nor could I help wondering, as I went back, whether, perhaps, I had not been a scruple too good-natured. But there was the fact, that this was a man that might have been my father, an able man, a great dignitary, and one that, in the hour of my need, had reached a hand to my assistance. I was in the better humour to enjoy the remainder of that evening, which I passed with the advocates, in excellent company no doubt, but perhaps with rather more than a sufficiency of punch: for though I went early to bed I have no clear mind of how I got there.

CHAPTER XVIII

The Tee'd Ball

On the morrow, from the justices' private room, where none could see me, I heard the verdict given in and judgment rendered upon James. The Duke's words I am quite sure I have correctly; and since that famous passage has been made a subject of dispute, I may as well commemorate my version. Having referred to the year 'Forty-five, the chief of the Campbells, sitting as Justice General upon the Bench, thus addressed the unfortunate Stewart before him: "If you had been successful in that rebellion, you might have been giving the law where you have now received the judgment of it; we, who are this day your judges, might have been tried before one of your mock courts of judicature; and then you might have been satiated with the blood of any name or clan to which you had an aversion."

"This is to let the cat out of the bag indeed," thought I. And that was the general impression. It was extraordinary how the young advocate lads took hold and made a mock of this speech, and how scarce a meal passed but what some one would get in the words: "And then you might have been satiated." Many songs were made in that time for the hour's diversion, and are near all forgot. I remember one began:

> "What do ye want the bluid of, bluid of?
>   Is it a name, or is it a clan,
>   Or is it an aefauld Hielandman,
> That ye want the bluid of, bluid of?"

Another went to my old favourite air, "The House of Airlie," and began thus:

> "It fell on a day when Argyle was on the bench,
>   That they served him a Stewart for his denner."

162

And one of the verses ran:

> "Then up and spak the Duke, and flyted on his cook,
>   I regaird it as a sensible aspersion,
> That I would sup ava', an' satiate my maw
>   With the bluid of ony clan of my aversion."

James was as fairly murdered as though the Duke had got a fowling-piece and stalked him. So much of course I knew: but others knew not so much, and were more affected by the items of scandal that came to light in the progress of the cause. One of the chief was certainly this sally of the Justice's. It was run hard by another of a juryman, who had struck into the midst of Colstoun's speech for the defence with a "Pray, sir, cut short, we are quite weary," which seemed the very excess of impudence and simplicity. But some of my new lawyer friends were still more staggered with an innovation that had disgraced and even vitiated the proceedings. One witness was never called. His name, indeed, was printed, where it may still be seen on the fourth page of the list: "James Drummond, *alias* Macgregor, *alias* James More, late tenant in Inveronachile"; and his precognition had been taken, as the manner is, in writing. He had remembered or invented (God help him) matter which was lead in James Stewart's shoes, and I saw was like to prove wings to his own. This testimony it was highly desirable to bring to the notice of the jury, without exposing the man himself to the perils of cross-examination, and the way it was brought about was a matter of surprise to all. For the paper was handed round (like a curiosity) in court; passed through the jury-box, where it did its work; and disappeared again (as though by accident) before it reached the counsel for the prisoner. This was counted a most insidious device; and that the name of James More should be mingled up with it filled me with shame for Catriona and concern for myself.

The following day, Prestongrange and I, with a considerable company, set out for Glasgow, where (to my impatience) we continued to linger some time in a mixture of pleasure and affairs. I lodged with my lord, with whom I was encouraged to familiarity; had my place at entertainments; was presented to the chief guests; and altogether made more of than I thought accorded either with my parts or station; so that, on strangers being present, I would often blush for Prestongrange. It must be owned the view I had taken of the world in these last months was fit to cast a gloom upon my character. I had met many men, some of them leaders in Israel, whether by their birth or talents; and who among them all had shown clean hands? As for the Browns and Millers, I had seen their self-seeking, I could never again respect them. Prestongrange was the best yet; he had saved me, had spared me rather, when others had it in their minds to murder me outright; but the blood of James lay at his door; and I thought his present dissimulation with myself a thing below pardon. That he should affect to find a pleasure in my discourse almost surprised me out of my patience. I would sit and watch him with a kind of a slow fire of anger in my bowels. "Ah, friend, friend," I would think to myself, "if you were but through with this affair of the memorial, would you not kick me in the streets?" Here I did him, as events have proved, the most grave injustice; and I think he was at once far more sincere, and a far more artful performer, than I supposed.

But I had some warrant for my incredulity in the behaviour of that court of young advocates that hung about him in the hope of patronage. The sudden favour of a lad not previously heard of troubled them at first out of measure, but two days were not gone by before I found myself surrounded with flattery and attention. I was the same young man, and neither better nor bonnier, that they had rejected a month before; and now there was no civility too fine for me! The same, do I say? It was not so; and the by-name by which I went behind my back confirmed it. Seeing me so firm with the Advocate, and persuaded that I was to fly high and far, they had taken a word from the golfing green, and called me *the Tee'd Ball*. I was told

I was now "one of themselves"; I was to taste of their soft lining, who had already made my own experience of the roughness of the outer husk; and one, to whom I had been presented in Hope Park, was so assured as even to remind me of that meeting. I told him I had not the pleasure of remembering it.

"Why," says he, "it was Miss Grant herself presented me! My name is So-and-so."

"It may very well be, sir," said I; "but I have kept no mind of it."

At which he desisted; and in the midst of the disgust that commonly overflowed my spirits I had a glisk of pleasure.

But I have not patience to dwell upon that time at length. When I was in company with these young politics I was borne down with shame for myself and my own plain ways, and scorn for them and their duplicity. Of the two evils, I thought Prestongrange to be the least; and while I was always as stiff as buckram to the young bloods, I made rather a dissimulation of my hard feelings towards the Advocate, and was (in old Mr. Campbell's word) "soople to the laird." Himself commented on the difference, and bid me be more of my age, and make friends with my young comrades.

I told him I was slow of making friends.

"I will take the word back," said he. "But there is such a thing as *Fair gude-e'en and fair gude-day*, Mr. David. These are the same young men with whom you are to pass your days and get through life: your backwardness has a look of arrogance; and unless you can assume a little more lightness of manner, I fear you will meet difficulties in the path."

"It will be an ill job to make a silk purse of a sow's ear," said I.

On the morning of October 1st I was awakened by the clattering in of an express; and getting to my window almost before he had dismounted, I saw the messenger had ridden hard. Somewhile after I was called to Prestongrange, where he was sitting in his bedgown and nightcap, with his letters round him.

"Mr. David," said he, "I have a piece of news for you. It concerns some friends of yours, of whom I sometimes think you are a little ashamed, for you have never referred to their existence."

I suppose I blushed.

"I see you understand, since you make the answering signal," said he. "And I must compliment you on your excellent taste in beauty. But do you know, Mr. David, this seems to me a very enterprising lass? She crops up from every side. The Government of Scotland appears unable to proceed for Mistress Katrine Drummond, which was somewhat the case (no great while back) with a certain Mr. David Balfour. Should not these make a good match? Her first intromission in politics—but I must not tell you that story, the authorities have decided you are to hear it otherwise and from a livelier narrator. This new example is more serious, however; and I am afraid I must alarm you with the intelligence that she is now in prison."

I cried out.

"Yes," said he, "the little lady is in prison. But I would not have you to despair. Unless you (with your friends and memorials) shall procure my downfall, she is to suffer nothing."

"But what has she done? What is her offence?" I cried.

"It might be almost construed a high treason," he returned, "for she has broke the King's Castle of Edinburgh."

"The lady is much my friend," I said. "I know you would not mock me if the thing were serious."

"And yet it is serious in a sense," said he; "for this rogue of a Katrine—or Cateran, as we may call her—has set adrift again upon the world that very doubtful character, her papa."

Here was one of my previsions justified: James More was once again at liberty. He had lent his men to keep me a prisoner; he had volunteered his testimony in the Appin case, and the same (no matter by what subterfuge) had been employed to influence the jury. Now came his reward, and he was free. It might please the authorities to give to it the colour of an escape; but I knew better—I knew it must be the fulfilment of a bargain. The same course of thought relieved me of the least alarm for Catriona. She might be thought to have broke prison for her father; she might have believed so herself. But the chief hand in the whole business was that of Prestongrange; and I was sure, so far from letting her come to punishment, he would not suffer her to be even tried. Whereupon thus came out of me the not very politic ejaculation:

"Ah! I was expecting that!"

"You have at times a great deal of discretion too!" says Prestongrange.

"And what is my lord pleased to mean by that?" I asked.

"I was just marvelling," he replied, "that being so clever as to draw these inferences, you should not be clever enough to keep them to yourself. But I think you would like to hear the details of the affair. I have received two versions: and the least official is the more full and far the more entertaining, being from the lively pen of my eldest daughter. 'Here is all the town bizzing with a fine piece of work,' she writes, 'and what would make the thing more noted (if it were only known) the malefactor is a *protégée* of his lordship my papa. I am sure your heart is too much in your duty (if it were nothing else) to have forgotten Grey Eyes. What does she do, but get a broad hat with the flaps open, a long hairy-like man's great-coat, and a big gravatt; kilt her coats up to *Gude kens whaur*, clap two pair of boot-hose upon her legs, take a pair of *clouted brogues* in her hand, and off to the Castle! Here she gives herself out to be a soutar in the employ of James More, and gets admitted to his cell, the lieutenant (who seems to have been full of pleasantry) making sport among his soldiers of the soutar's great-coat. Presently they hear disputation and the sound of blows inside. Out flies the cobbler, his coat flying, the flaps of his hat beat about his face, and the lieutenant and his soldiers mock at him as he runs off. They laugh not so hearty the next time they had occasion to visit the cell, and found nobody but a tall, pretty, grey-eyed lass in the female habit! As for the cobbler, he was "over the hills ayont Dumblane," and it's thought that poor Scotland will have to console herself without him. I drank Catriona's health this night in public. Indeed, the whole town admires her; and I think the beaux would wear bits of her garters in their button-holes if they could only get them. I would have gone to visit her in prison too, only I remembered in time I was papa's daughter; so I wrote her a billet instead, which I entrusted to the faithful Doig, and I hope you will admit I can be political when I please. The same faithful gomeril is to despatch this letter by the express along with those of the wiseacres, so that you may hear Tom Fool in company with Solomon. Talking of *gomerils*, do tell *Dauvit Balfour* I would I could see the face of him at the thought of a long-legged lass in such a predicament! to say nothing of the levities of your affectionate daughter, and his respectful friend.' So my rascal signs herself!" continued Prestongrange. "And you see, Mr. David, it is quite true what I tell you, that my daughters regard you with the most affectionate playfulness."

"The gomeril is much obliged," said I.

"And was not this prettily done?" he went on. "Is not this Highland maid a piece of a heroine?"

"I was always sure she had a great heart," said I. "And I wager she guessed nothing. . . . But I beg your pardon, this is to tread upon forbidden subjects."

"I will go bail she did not," he returned, quite openly. "I will go bail she thought she was flying straight into King George's face."

Remembrance of Catriona, and the thought of her lying in captivity, moved me strangely. I could see that even Prestongrange admired, and could not withhold his lips from smiling when he considered her behaviour. As for Miss Grant, for all her ill habit of mockery, her admiration shone out plain. A kind of a heat came on me.

"I am not your lordship's daughter..." I began.

"That I know of!" he put in, smiling.

"I speak like a fool," said I; "or rather I began wrong. It would doubtless be unwise in Mistress Grant to go to her in prison;

but for me, I think I would look like a half-hearted friend if I did not fly there instantly."

"So-ho, Mr. David," says he; "I thought that you and I were in a bargain?"

"My lord," I said, "when I made that bargain I was a good deal affected by your goodness, but I'll never can deny that I was moved besides by my own interest. There was self-seeking in my heart, and I think shame of it now. It may be for your lordship's safety to say this fashious Davie Balfour is your friend and housemate. Say it then; I'll never contradict you. But as for your patronage, I give it all back. I ask but one thing—let me go, and give me a pass to see her in her prison."

He looked at me with a hard eye. "You put the cart before the horse, I think," says he. "That which I had given was a portion of my liking, which your thankless nature does not seem to have remarked. But for my patronage, it is not given, nor (to be exact) is it yet offered." He paused a bit. "And I warn you, you do not know yourself," he added. "Youth is a hasty season; you will think better of all this before a year."

"Well, and I would like to be that kind of youth!" I cried. "I have seen too much of the other party in these young advocates that fawn upon your lordship, and are even at the pains to fawn on me. And I have seen it in the old ones also. They are all for by-ends, the whole clan of them! It's this that makes me seem to misdoubt your lordship's liking. Why would I think that you would like me? But ye told me yourself ye had an interest!"

I stopped at this, confounded that I had run so far; he was observing me with an unfathomable face.

"My lord, I ask your pardon," I resumed. "I have nothing in my chafts but a rough country tongue. I think it would be only decent-like if I would go to see my friend in her captivity; but I'm owing you my life—I'll never forget that; and if it's for your lordship's good, here I'll stay. That's barely gratitude."

"This might have been reached in fewer words," says Prestongrange grimly. "It is easy, and it is at times gracious, to say a plain Scots 'ay'."

"Ah, but, my lord, I think ye take me not yet entirely!" cried I. "For *your* sake, for my life-safe, and the kindness that ye say ye bear to me—for these I'll consent; but not for any good that might be coming to myself. If I stand aside when this young maid is in her trial, it's a thing I will be noways advantaged by; I will lose by it, I will never gain. I would rather make a shipwreck wholly than to build on that foundation."

He was a minute serious, then smiled. "You mind me of the man with the long nose," said he; "was you to look at the moon by a telescope, you would see David Balfour there! But you shall have your way of it. I will ask at you one service, and then set you free. My clerks are over-driven; be so good as copy me these few pages," says he, visibly swithering among some huge rolls of manuscripts, "and when that is done, I shall bid you God-speed! I would never charge myself with Mr. David's conscience; and if you could cast some part of it (as you went by) in a moss-hag, you would find yourself to ride much easier without it."

"Perhaps not just entirely in the same direction though, my lord!" says I.

"And you shall have the last word too!" cries he gaily.

Indeed he had some cause for gaiety, having now found the means to gain his purpose. To lessen the weight of the memorial, or to have a readier answer at his hand, he desired I should appear publicly in the character of his intimate. But if I were to appear with the same publicity as a visitor to Catriona in her prison the world would scarce stint to draw conclusions, and the true nature of James More's escape must become evident to all. This was the little problem I had set him of a sudden, and to which he had so briskly found an answer. I was to be tethered in Glasgow by that job of copying, which in mere outward decency I could not well refuse; and during these hours of my employment Catriona was to be privately got rid of. I think shame to write of this man that loaded me with so many goodnesses. He was kind to me as any father, yet I ever thought him as false as a cracked bell.

CHAPTER XIX

I am much in the Hands of the Ladies

The copying was a weary business, the more so as I perceived very early there was no sort of urgency in the matters treated, and began very early to consider my employment a pretext. I had no sooner finished than I got to horse, used what remained of daylight to the best purpose, and being at last fairly benighted, slept in a house by Almond Waterside. I was in the saddle again before the day, and the Edinburgh booths were just opening when I clattered in by the West Bow, and drew up a smoking horse at my Lord Advocate's door. I had a written word for Doig, my lord's private hand that was thought to be in all his secrets—a worthy, little plain man, all fat and snuff and self-sufficiency. Him I found already at his desk, and already bedabbled with maccabaw, in the same anteroom where I rencountered with James More. He read the note scrupulously through like a chapter in his Bible.

"H'm," says he; "ye come a wee thing ahint-hand, Mr. Balfour. The bird's flown—we hae letten her out."

"Miss Drummond is set free?" I cried.

"Achy!" said he. "What would we keep her for, ye ken? To hae made a steer about the bairn would hae pleased naebody."

"And where'll she be now?" says I.

"Gude kens!" says Doig, with a shrug.

"She'll have gone home to Lady Allardyce, I'm thinking," said I.

"That'll be it," said he.

"Then I'll gang there straight," says I.

"But ye'll be for a bite or ye go?" said he.

"Neither bite nor sup," said I. "I had a good wauch of milk in by Ratho."

"Aweel, aweel," says Doig. "But ye'll can leave your horse here and your bags, for it seems we're to have your up-put."

"Na, na," said I. "Tamson's mear would never be the thing for me this day of all days."

Doig speaking somewhat broad, I had been led by imitation into an accent much more countrified than I was usually careful to affect—a good deal broader indeed than I have written it down; and I was the more ashamed when another voice joined in behind me with a scrap of a ballad:

> "Gae saddle me the bonny black,
> Gae saddle sune, and mak' him ready,
> For I will down the Gatehope-slack,
> An' a' to see my bonny leddy."

The young lady, when I turned to her, stood in a morning gown, and her hands muffled in the same, as if to hold me at a distance. Yet I could not but think there was kindness in the eye with which she saw me.

"My best respects to you, Mistress Grant," said I, bowing.

"The like to yourself, Mr. David," she replied, with a deep curtsy. "And I beg to remind you of an old musty saw, that meat and mass never hindered man. The mass I cannot afford you, for we are all good Protestants. But the meat I press on your attention. And I would not wonder but I could find something for your private ear that would be worth the stopping for."

"Mistress Grant," said I, "I believe I am already your debtor for some merry words—and I think they were kind too—on a piece of unsigned paper."

"Unsigned paper?" says she, and made a droll face, which was likewise wondrous beautiful, as of one trying to remember.

"Or else I am the more deceived," I went on. "But to be sure, we shall have the time to speak of these, since your father is so good as to make me for a while your inmate; and the *gomeril* begs you at this time only for the favour of his liberty."

"You give yourself hard names," said she.

"Mr. Doig and I would be blithe to take harder at your clever pen," says I.

"Once more I have to admire the discretion of all menfolk,"

172

she replied. "But if you will not eat, off with you at once; you will be back the sooner, for you go on a fool's errand. Off with you, Mr. David," she continued, opening the door.

> "He has lowpen on his bonny grey,
>   He rade the richt gate and the ready;
>   I trow he would neither stint nor stay,
>   For he was seeking his bonny leddy."

I did not wait to be twice bidden, and did justice to Miss Grant's citation on the way to Dean.

Old Lady Allardyce walked there alone in the garden, in her hat and mutch, and having a silver-mounted staff of some black wood to lean upon. As I alighted from my horse, and drew near to her with *congees*, I could see the blood come in her face, and her head fling into the air like what I had conceived of empresses.

"What brings you to my poor door?" she cried, speaking high through her nose. "I cannot bar it. The males of my house are dead and buried; I have neither son nor husband to stand in the gate for me; any beggar can pluck me by the baird—and a baird there is, and that's the worst of it yet!" she added, partly to herself.

I was extremely put out at this reception, and the last remark, which seemed like a daft wife's, left me near-hand speechless.

"I see I have fallen under your displeasure, ma'am," said I. "Yet I will still be so bold as to ask after Mistress Drummond."

She considered me with a burning eye, her lips pressed close together into twenty creases, her hand shaking on her staff. "This cowes all!" she cried. "Ye come to me to speir for her? Would God I knew!"

"She is not here?" I cried.

She threw up her chin and made a step and a cry at me, so that I fell back incontinent.

"Out upon your leeing throat!" she cried. "What! ye come and speir at me! She's in jyle, whaur ye took her to—that's all

173

there is to it. And of a' the beings ever I beheld in breeks, to
think it should be you! Ye timmer scoun'rel, if I had a male left
to my name I would have your jaicket dustit till ye raired."

I thought it not good to delay longer in that place, because I
remarked her passion to be rising. As I turned to the horse-post
she even followed me; and I make no shame to confess that I
rode away with the one stirrup on and scrambling for the other.

As I knew no other quarter where I could push my inquiries,
there was nothing left me but to return to the Advocate's. I was
well received by the four ladies, who were now in company
together, and must give the news of Prestongrange and what
word went in the west country, at the most inordinate length
and with great weariness to myself; while all the time that
young lady, with whom I so much desired to be alone again,
observed me quizzically, and seemed to find pleasure in the
sight of my impatience. At last, after I had endured a meal with
them, and was come very near the point of appealing for an
interview before her aunt, she went and stood by the music-
case, and picking out a tune, sang to it on a high key—"He that
will not when he may, When he will he shall have nay." But this
was the end of her rigours, and presently, after making some
excuse of which I have no mind, she carried me away in private
to her father's library. I should not fail to say that she was
dressed to the nines, and appeared extraordinary handsome.

"Now, Mr. David, sit ye down here, and let us have a two-
handed crack," said she. "For I have much to tell you, and it
appears besides that I have been grossly unjust to your good
taste."

"In what manner, Mistress Grant?" I asked. "I trust I have
never seemed to fail in due respect."

"I will be your surety, Mr. David," said she. "Your respect,
whether to yourself or your poor neighbours, has been always
and most fortunately beyond imitation. But that is by the
question.—You got a note from me?" she asked.

"I was so bold as to suppose so upon inference," said I, "and
it was kindly thought upon."

"It must have prodigiously surprised you," said she. "But let us begin with the beginning. You have not perhaps forgot a day when you were so kind as to escort three very tedious misses to Hope Park? I have the less cause to forget it myself, because you were so particular obliging as to introduce me to some of the principles of the Latin grammar, a thing which wrote itself profoundly on my gratitude."

"I fear I was sadly pedantical," said I, overcome with confusion at the memory. "You are only to consider I am quite unused with the society of ladies."

"I will say the less about the grammar then," she replied. "But how came you to desert your charge? 'He has thrown her out, overboard, his ain, dear Annie!'" she hummed; "and his ain dear Annie and her two sisters had to taigle home by theirselves like a string of green geese! It seems you returned to my papa's, where you showed yourself excessively martial, and then on to realms unknown, with an eye (it appears) to the Bass Rock; solan geese being perhaps more to your mind than bonny lasses."

Through all this raillery there was something indulgent in the lady's eye which made me suppose there might be better coming.

"You take a pleasure to torment me," said I, "and I make a very feckless plaything; but let me ask you to be more merciful. At this time there is but the one thing that I care to hear of, and that will be news of Catriona."

"Do you call her by that name to her face, Mr. Balfour?" she asked.

"In troth, and I am not very sure," I stammered.

"I would not do so in any case to strangers," said Miss Grant.—"And why are you so much immersed in the affairs of this young lady?"

"I heard she was in prison," said I.

"Well, and now you hear that she is out of it," she replied, "and what more would you have? She has no need of any further champion."

"I may have the greater need of her, ma'am," said I.

"Come, this is better!" says Miss Grant. "But look me fairly in the face; am I not bonnier than she?"

"I would be the last to be denying it," said I. "There is not your marrow in all Scotland."

"Well, here you have the pick of the two at your hand, and must needs speak of the other," said she. "This is never the way to please the ladies, Mr. Balfour."

"But, mistress," said I, "there are surely other things besides mere beauty."

"By which I am to understand that I am no better than I should be, perhaps?" she asked.

"By which you will please understand that I am like the cock in the midden in the fable-book," said I. "I see the braw jewel—and I like fine to see it too—but I have more need of the pickle corn."

"Bravissimo!" she cried. "There is a word well said at last, and I will reward you for it with my story. That same night of your desertion I came late from a friend's house—where I was excessively admired, whatever you may think of it—and what should I hear but that a lass in a tartan screen desired to speak with me? She had been there an hour or better, said the servant-lass, and she grat in to herself as she sat waiting. I went to her direct; she rose as I came in, and I knew her at a look. (*'Grey Eyes!'* says I to myself, but was more wise than to let on.) *You will be Miss Grant at last?* she says, rising and looking at me hard and pitiful. *Ay, it was true he said, you are bonny, at all events.—The way God made me, my dear*, I said, *but I would be geyan obliged if ye could tell me what brought you here at such a time of the night.—Lady*, she said, *we are kinsfolk, we are both come of the blood of the sons of Alpin.—My dear*, I replied, *I think no more of Alpin or his sons than what I do of a kale-stock. You have a better argument in these tears upon your bonny face.* And at that I was so weak-minded as to kiss her, which is what you would like to do dearly, and I wager will never find the courage of. I say it was weak-minded of me, for

I knew no more of her than the outside; but it was the wisest stroke I could have hit upon. She is a very staunch, brave nature, but I think she has been little used with tenderness; and at that caress (though to say the truth, it was but lightly given) her heart went out to me. I will never betray the secrets of my sex, Mr. Davie; I will never tell you the way she turned me round her thumb, because it is the same she will use to twist yourself. Ay, it is a fine lass! She is as clean as hill well-water."

"She is e'en 't!" I cried.

"Well, then, she told me her concerns," pursued Miss Grant, "and in what a swither she was in about her papa, and what a taking about yourself, with very little cause, and in what a perplexity she had found herself after you was gone away. *And then I minded at long last, says she, that we were kinswomen, and that Mr. David should have given you the name of the bonniest of the bonny, and I was thinking to myself, 'If she is so bonny she will be good, at all events'; and I took up my foot-soles out of that.* That was when I forgave yourself, Mr. Davie. When you was in my society, you seemed upon hot iron: by all marks, if ever I saw a young man that wanted to be gone, it was yourself, and I and my two sisters were the ladies you were so desirous to be gone from; and now it appeared you had given me some notice in the bygoing, and was so kind as to comment on my attractions! From that hour you may date our friendship, and I began to think with tenderness upon the Latin grammar."

"You will have many hours to rally me in," said I; "and I think besides you do yourself injustice. I think it was Catriona turned your heart in my direction. She is too simple to perceive as you do the stiffness of her friend."

"I would not like to wager upon that, Mr. David," said she. "The lasses have clear eyes. But at least she is your friend entirely, as I was to see. I carried her in to his lordship, my papa; and his Advocacy, being in a favourable stage of claret, was so good as to receive the pair of us. *Here is Grey Eyes that you have been deaved with these days past*, said I; *she is come to prove that we spoke true, and I lay the prettiest lass in the three Lothians at your feet*—making a papistical reservation of myself. She suited her action to my words: down she went upon her knees to him—I would not like to swear but he saw two of her, which doubtless made her appeal the more irresistible, for you are all a pack of Mahomedans—told him what had passed that night, and how she had withheld her father's man from following of you, and what a case she was in about her father, and what a flutter for yourself; and begged with weeping for the lives of both of you (neither of which was in the slightest danger), till I vow I was proud of my sex because it was done so pretty, and ashamed for it because of the smallness of the occasion. She had not gone far, I assure you, before the Advocate was wholly sober, to see his inmost politics ravelled out by a young lass and discovered to the most unruly of his daughters. But we took him in hand, the pair of us, and brought that matter straight. Properly managed—and that means managed by me—there is no one to compare with my papa."

"He has been a good man to me," said I.

"Well, he was a good man to Katrine, and I was there to see to it," said she.

"And she pled for me!" says I.

"She did that, and very movingly," said Miss Grant. "I would not like to tell you what she said—I find you vain enough already."

"God reward her for it!" cried I.

"With Mr. David Balfour, I suppose?" says she.

"You do me too much injustice at the last!" I cried. "I would tremble to think of her in such hard hands. Do you think I would presume, because she begged my life? She would do that for a new-whelped puppy! I have had more than that to set me up, if you but kenned. She kissed that hand of mine. Ay, but she did. And why? because she thought I was playing a brave part, and might be going to my death. It was not for my sake—but I need not be telling that to you, that cannot look at me without laughter. It was for the love of what she thought was bravery. I believe there is none but me and poor Prince Charlie had that honour done them. Was this not to make a god of me? and do you not think my heart would quake when I remember it?"

"I do laugh at you a good deal, and a good deal more than is quite civil," said she; "but I will tell you one thing: if you speak to her like that, you have some glimmerings of a chance."

"Me?" I cried, "I would never dare. I can speak to you, Miss Grant, because it's a matter of indifference what ye think of me. But her? no fear!" said I.

"I think you have the largest feet in all broad Scotland," says she.

"Troth, they are no' very small," said I, looking down.

"Ah, poor Catriona!" cries Miss Grant.

And I could but stare upon her; for though I now see very well what she was driving at (and perhaps some justification for the same), I was never swift at the uptake in such flimsy talk.

"Ah well, Mr. David," she said, "it goes sore against my conscience, but I see I shall have to be your speaking-board. She shall know you came to her straight upon the news of her imprisonment; she shall know you would not pause to eat; and of our conversation she shall hear just so much as I think convenient for a maid of her age and inexperience. Believe me, you will be in that way much better served than you could serve yourself, for I will keep the big feet out of the platter."

"You know where she is, then?" I exclaimed.

"That I do, Mr. David, and will never tell," said she.

"Why that?" I asked.

"Well," she said, "I am a good friend, as you will soon discover; and the chief of those that I am friend to is my papa. I assure you, you will never heat nor melt me out of that, so you may spare me your sheep's eyes; and adieu to your David-Balfourship for the now."

"But there is yet one thing more," I cried. "There is one thing that must be stopped, being mere ruin to herself, and to me too."

"Well," she said, "be brief; I have spent half the day on you already."

"My Lady Allardyce believes," I began—"she supposes—she thinks that I abducted her."

The colour came into Miss Grant's face, so that at first I was quite abashed to find her ear so delicate, till I bethought me she was struggling rather with mirth, a notion in which I was altogether confirmed by the shaking of her voice as she replied—

"I will take up the defence of your reputation," said she. "You may leave it in my hands."

And with that she withdrew out of the library.

CHAPTER XX

I Continue to Move in Good Society

For about exactly two months I remained a guest in Prestongrange's family, where I bettered my acquaintance with the Bench, the Bar, and the flower of Edinburgh company. You are not to suppose my education was neglected; on the contrary, I was kept extremely busy. I studied the French, so as to be more prepared to go to Leyden; I set myself to the fencing, and wrought hard, sometimes three hours in the day, with notable advancement; at the suggestion of my cousin Pilrig, who was an apt musician, I was put to a singing-class; and by the orders of my Miss Grant, to one for the dancing, at which I must say I proved far from ornamental. However, all were good enough to say it gave me an address a little more genteel; and there is no question but I learned to manage my coat-skirts and sword with more dexterity, and to stand in a room as though the same belonged to me. My clothes themselves were all earnestly re-ordered; and the most trifling circumstance, such as where I should tie my hair, or the colour of my ribbon, debated among the three misses like a thing of weight. One way with another, no doubt I was a good deal improved to look at, and acquired a bit of a modish air that would have surprised the good folks at Essendean.

The two younger misses were very willing to discuss a point of my habiliment, because that was in the line of their chief thoughts. I cannot say that they appeared any other way conscious of my presence; and though always more than civil, with a kind of heartless cordiality, could not hide how much I wearied them. As for the aunt, she was a wonderful still woman; and I think she gave me much the same attention as she gave the rest of the family, which was little enough. The eldest daughter and the Advocate himself were thus my principal friends, and our familiarity was much increased by a pleasure that we took in common. Before the court met we spent a day or two at the house of Grange, living very nobly with an open table, and here it was that we three began to ride out together in the fields, a practice afterwards maintained in Edinburgh, so far as the Advocate's continual affairs permitted. When we were put in a good frame by the briskness of the exercise, the difficulties of the way, or the accidents of bad weather, my shyness wore entirely off; we forgot that we were strangers, and speech not being required, it flowed the more naturally on. Then it was that they had my story from me, bit by bit, from the time that I left Essendean, with my voyage and battle in the *Covenant*, wanderings in the heather, etc.; and from the interest they found in my adventures sprung the circumstance of a jaunt we made a little later on, on a day when the courts were not sitting, and of which I will tell a trifle more at length.

We took horse early, and passed first by the house of Shaws, where it stood smokeless in a great field of white frost, for it was yet early in the day. Here Prestongrange alighted down, gave me his horse, and proceeded alone to visit my uncle. My heart, I remember, swelled up bitter within me at the sight of that bare house and the thought of the old miser sitting chittering within in the cold kitchen.

"There is my home," said I; "and my family."

"Poor David Balfour!" said Miss Grant.

What passed during the visit I have never heard; but it would doubtless not be very agreeable to Ebenezer, for when the Advocate came forth again his face was dark.

"I think you will soon be the laird indeed, Mr. Davie," says he, turning half about with the one foot in the stirrup.

"I will never pretend sorrow," said I; and, to say the truth, during his absence Miss Grant and I had been embellishing the place in fancy with plantations, parterres, and a terrace—much as I have since carried out in fact.

Thence we pushed to the Queen's Ferry, where Rankeillor gave us a good welcome, being indeed out of the body to receive so great a visitor. Here the Advocate was so unaffectedly good as to go quite fully over my affairs, sitting perhaps two hours with the Writer in his study, and expressing (I was told) a great esteem for myself and concern for my fortunes. To while this time, Miss Grant and I and young Rankeillor took boat and passed the Hope to Limekilns. Rankeillor made himself very ridiculous (and, I thought, offensive) with his admiration for the young lady, and to my wonder (only it is so common a weakness of her sex) she seemed, if anything, to be a little gratified. One use it had: for when we were come to the other side, she laid her commands on him to mind the boat, while she and I passed a little farther to the alehouse. This was her own thought, for she had been taken with my account of Alison Hastie, and desired to see the lass herself. We found her once more alone—indeed, I believe her father wrought all day in the fields—and she curtsied dutifully to the gentry-folk and the beautiful young lady in the riding-coat.

"Is this all the welcome I am to get?" said I, holding out my hand. "And have you no more memory of old friends?"

"Keep me! wha's this of it?" she cried, and then, "God's truth, it's the tautit laddie!"

"The very same," says I.

"Mony's the time I've thocht upon you and your freen, and blithe am I to see you in your braws," she cried; "though I kennt ye were come to your ain folk by the grand present that ye sent me, and that I thank ye for with a' my heart."

"There," said Miss Grant to me, "run out by with ye, like a good bairn. I didna come here to stand and haud a candle; it's her and me that are to crack."

I suppose she stayed ten minutes in the house, but when she came forth I observed two things—that her eyes were reddened, and a silver brooch was gone out of her bosom. This very much affected me.

"I never saw you so well adorned," said I.

"O, Davie man, dinna be a pompous gowk!" said she, and was more than usually sharp to me the remainder of the day.

About candlelight we came home from this excursion.

For a good while I heard nothing further of Catriona—my Miss Grant remaining quite impenetrable, and stopping my mouth with pleasantries. At last, one day that she returned from walking, and found me alone in the parlour over my French, I thought there was something unusual in her looks; the colour heightened, the eyes sparkling high, and a bit of a smile continually bitten in as she regarded me. She seemed indeed like the very spirit of mischief, and, walking briskly in the room, had soon involved me in a kind of quarrel over nothing and (at the least) with nothing intended on my side. I was like Christian in the slough—the more I tried to clamber out upon the side, the deeper I became involved; until at last I heard her declare, with a great deal of passion, that she would take that answer at the hands of none, and I must down upon my knees for pardon.

The causelessness of all this fuff stirred my own bile. "I have said nothing you can properly object to," said I, "and as for my knees, that is an attitude I keep for God."

"And as a goddess I am to be served!" she cried, shaking her brown locks at me and with a bright colour. "Every man that comes within waft of my petticoats shall use me so!"

"I will go so far as ask your pardon for the fashion's sake, although I vow I know not why," I replied. "But for these play-acting postures, you can go to others."

"O Davie!" she said. "Not if I was to beg you?"

I bethought me I was fighting with a woman, which is the same as to say a child, and that upon a point entirely formal.

"I think it a bairnly thing," I said, "not worthy in you to ask, or me to render. Yet I will not refuse you, neither," said I; "and the stain, if there be any, rests with yourself." And at that I kneeled fairly down.

"There!" she cried. "There is the proper station, there is where I have been manœuvring to bring you." And then, suddenly, "Kep," said she, flung me a folded billet, and ran from the apartment laughing.

The billet had neither place nor date. "Dear Mr. David," it began, "I get your news continually by my cousin, Miss Grant, and it is a pleisand hearing. I am very well, in a good place, among good folk, but necessitated to be quite private, though I am hoping that at long last we may meet again. All your friendships have been told me by my loving cousin, who loves us both. She bids me to send you this writing, and oversees the same. I will be asking you to do all her commands, and rest your affectionate friend, Catriona Macgregor-Drummond. *P.S.*—Will you not see my cousin, Allardyce?"

I think it not the least brave of my campaigns (as the soldiers say) that I should have done as I was here bidden and gone forthright to the house by Dean. But the old lady was now entirely changed, and supple as a glove. By what means Miss Grant had brought this round I could never guess; I am sure, at least, she dared not to appear openly in the affair, for her papa was compromised in it pretty deep. It was he, indeed, who had persuaded Catriona to leave, or rather, not to return to, her cousin's, placing her instead with a family of Gregorys—decent people, quite at the Advocate's disposition, and in whom she might have the more confidence because they were of her own clan and family. These kept her private till all was ripe, heated and helped her to attempt her father's rescue, and after she was discharged from prison received her again into the same secrecy. Thus Prestongrange obtained and used his instrument; nor did there leak out the smallest word of his acquaintance with the daughter of James More. There was some whispering, of course, upon the escape of that discredited person; but the Government replied by a show of rigour, one of the cell-porters was flogged, the lieutenant of the guard (my poor friend, Duncansby) was broken of his rank, and as for Catriona, all men were well enough pleased that her fault should be passed by in silence.

I could never induce Miss Grant to carry back an answer. "No," she would say, when I persisted, "I am going to keep the big feet out of the platter." This was the more hard to bear, as I was aware she saw my little friend many times in the week, and carried her my news whenever (as she said) I "had behaved myself." At last she treated me to what she called an indulgence, and I thought rather more of a banter. She was certainly a strong, almost a violent, friend to all she liked, chief among whom was a certain frail old gentlewoman, very blind and very witty, who dwelt in the top of a tall land on a strait close, with a nest of linnets in a cage, and thronged all day with visitors. Miss Grant was very fond to carry me there and put me to entertain her friend with the narrative of my misfortunes; and Miss Tibbie Ramsay (that was her name) was particular kind, and told me a great deal that was worth knowledge of old folks and past affairs in Scotland. I should say that from her chamber window, and not three feet away, such is the straitness of that close, it was possible to look into a barred loophole lighting the stairway of the opposite house.

Here, upon some pretext, Miss Grant left me one day alone with Miss Ramsay. I mind I thought that lady inattentive and like one preoccupied. It was besides very uncomfortable, for the window, contrary to custom, was left open, and the day was cold. All at once the voice of Miss Grant sounded in my ears as from a distance.

"Here, Shaws!" she cried, "keek out of the window and see what I have broughten you."

I think it was the prettiest sight that ever I beheld. The well of the close was all in clear shadow where a man could see distinctly, the walls very black and dingy; and there from the barred loophole I saw two faces smiling across at me—Miss Grant's and Catriona's.

"There!" says Miss Grant, "I wanted her to see you in your braws, like the lass of Limekilns. I wanted her to see what I could make of you, when I buckled to the job in earnest!"

It came in my mind she had been more than common particular that day upon my dress: and I think that some of the same care had been bestowed upon Catriona. For so merry and sensible a lady, Miss Grant was certainly wonderful taken up with duds.

186

"Catriona!" was all I could get out.

As for her, she said nothing in the world, but only waved her hand and smiled to me, and was suddenly carried away again from before the loophole.

That vision was no sooner lost than I ran to the house door, where I found I was locked in; thence back to Miss Ramsay, crying for the key, but might as well have cried upon the Castle rock. She had passed her word, she said, and I must be a good lad. It was impossible to burst the door, even if it had been mannerly; it was impossible I should leap from the window, being seven storeys above ground. All I could do was to crane over the close and watch for their reappearance from the stair. It was little to see, being no more than the tops of their two heads, each on a ridiculous bobbin of skirts, like to a pair of pincushions. Nor did Catriona so much as look up for a farewell; being prevented (as I heard afterwards) by Miss Grant, who told her folk were never seen to less advantage than from above downward.

On the way home, as soon as I was free, I upbraided Miss Grant for her cruelty.

"I am sorry you was disappointed," says she demurely. "For my part I was very pleased. You looked better than I dreaded; you looked—if it will not make you vain—a mighty pretty young man when you appeared in the window. You are to remember that she could not see your feet," says she, with the manner of one reassuring me.

"O!" cried I, "leave my feet be—they are no bigger than my neighbours'."

"They are even smaller than some," said she, "but I speak in parables, like a Hebrew prophet."

"I marvel little they were sometimes stoned!" says I. "But, you miserable girl, how could you do it? Why should you care to tantalise me with a moment?"

"Love is like folk," says she; "it needs some kind of vivers."

"O, Barbara, let me see her properly!" I pleaded. "*You* can—you see her when you please; let me have half an hour."

"Who is it that is managing this love-affair? You? Or me?" she asked, and, as I continued to press her with my instances, fell back upon a deadly expedient: that of imitating the tones of my voice when I called on Catriona by name; with which, indeed, she held me in subjection for some days to follow.

There was never the least word heard of the memorial, or none by me. Prestongrange and his Grace the Lord President may have heard of it (for what I know) on the deafest sides of their heads; they kept it to themselves at least—the public was none the wiser; and in course of time, on November 8th, and in the midst of a prodigious storm of wind and rain, poor James of the Glens was duly hanged at Lettermore by Balachulish.

So there was the final upshot of my politics! Innocent men have perished before James, and are like to keep on perishing (in spite of all our wisdom) till the end of time. And till the end of time young folk (who are not yet used with the duplicity of life and men) will struggle as I did, and make heroical resolves, and take long risks; and the course of events will push them upon the one side and go on like a marching army. James was hanged; and here was I, dwelling in the house of Prestongrange, and grateful to him for his fatherly attention. He was hanged; and behold! when I met Mr. Simon in the causeway, I was fain to pull off my beaver to him like a good little boy before his dominie. He had been hanged by fraud and violence, and the world wagged along, and there was not a pennyweight of difference; and the villains of that horrid plot were decent, kind, respectable fathers of families, who went to kirk and took the sacrament!

But I had had my view of that detestable business they call politics—I had seen it from behind, when it is all bones and blackness; and I was cured for life of any temptations to take part in it again. A plain, quiet, private path was that which I was ambitious to walk in, where I might keep my head out of the way of dangers and my conscience out of the road of temptation. For, upon a retrospect, it appeared I had not done so grandly, after all; but, with the greatest possible amount of big speech and preparation, had accomplished nothing.

The 25th of the same month a ship was advertised to sail from Leith; and I was suddenly recommended to make up my mails for Leyden. To Prestongrange I could, of course, say nothing; for I had already been a long while sorning on his house and table. But with his daughter I was more open, bewailing my fate that I should be sent out of the country, and assuring her, unless she should bring me to farewell with Catriona, I would refuse at the last hour.

"Have I not given you my advice?" she asked.

"I know you have," said I, "and I know how much I am beholden to you already, and that I am bidden to obey your orders. But you must confess you are something too merry a lass at times to lippen to entirely."

"I will tell you, then," said she. "Be you on board by nine o'clock forenoon; the ship does not sail before one; keep your boat alongside; and if you are not pleased with my farewells when I shall send them, you can come ashore again and seek Katrine for yourself."

Since I could make no more of her, I was fain to be content with this.

The day came round at last when she and I were to separate. We had been extremely intimate and familiar; I was much in her debt; and what way we were to part was a thing that put me from my sleep, like the vails I was to give to the domestic servants. I knew she considered me too backward, and rather desired to rise in her opinion on that head. Besides which, after so much affection shown and (I believe) felt upon both sides, it would have looked cold-like to be anyways stiff. Accordingly, I got my courage up and my words ready, and the last chance we were like to be alone, asked pretty boldly to be allowed to salute her in farewell.

"You forget yourself strangely, Mr. Balfour," said she. "I cannot call to mind that I have given you any right to presume on our acquaintancy."

I stood before her like a stopped clock, and knew not what to think, far less to say, when of a sudden she cast her arms about my neck and kissed me with the best will in the world.

"You inimitable bairn!" she cried. "Did you think that I would let us part like strangers? Because I can never keep my gravity at you five minutes on end, you must not dream I do not love you very well: I am all love and laughter, every time I cast an eye on you! And now I will give you an advice to conclude your education, which you will have need of before it's very long. Never *ask* womenfolk. They are bound to answer 'No'; God never made the lass that could resist the temptation. It's supposed by divines to be the curse of Eve: because she did not say it when the devil offered her the apple, her daughters can say nothing else."

"Since I am so soon to lose my bonny professor," I began.

"This is gallant, indeed," says she, curtsying.

"—I would put the one question," I went on: "May I ask a lass to marry me?"

"You think you could not marry her without?" she asked. "Or else get her to offer?"

"You see you cannot be serious," said I.

"I shall be very serious in one thing, David," said she: "I shall always be your friend."

As I got to my horse the next morning, the four ladies were all at the same window whence we had once looked down on Catriona, and all cried farewell and waved their pocket-napkins as I rode away. One out of the four I knew was truly sorry; and at the thought of that, and how I had come to the door three months ago for the first time, sorrow and gratitude made a confusion in my mind.

PART II

FATHER AND DAUGHTER

CHAPTER XXI

The Voyage into Holland

The ship lay at a single anchor, well outside the pier of Leith, so that all we passengers must come to it by the means of skiffs. This was very little troublesome, for the reason that the day was a flat calm, very frosty and cloudy, and with a low shifting fog upon the water. The body of the vessel was thus quite hid as I drew near, but the tall spars of her stood high and bright in a sunshine like the flickering of a fire. She proved to be a very roomy, commodious merchant, but somewhat blunt in the bows, and loaden extraordinary deep with salt, salted salmon, and fine white linen stockings for the Dutch. Upon my coming on board, the captain welcomed me—one Sang (out of Lesmahago, I believe), a very hearty, friendly tarpaulin of a man, but at the moment in rather of a bustle. There had no other of the passengers yet appeared, so that I was left to walk about upon the deck, viewing the prospect and wondering a good deal what these farewells should be which I was promised.

All Edinburgh and the Pentland Hills glinted above me in a kind of smuisty brightness, now and again overcome with blots of cloud; of Leith there was no more than the tops of chimneys visible, and on the face of the water, where the haar lay, nothing at all. Out of this I was presently aware of a sound of oars pulling, and a little after (as if out of the smoke of a fire) a boat issued. There sat a grave man in the stern-sheets, well muffled from the cold, and by his side a tall, pretty, tender figure of a maid that brought my heart to a stand. I had scarce the time to catch my breath in, and be ready to meet her, as she stepped upon the deck, smiling, and making my best bow, which was now vastly finer than some months before, when first I made it to her ladyship. No doubt we were both a good deal changed: she seemed to have shot up taller, like a young, comely tree. She had now a kind of pretty backwardness that became her well, as of one that regarded herself more highly, and was fairly woman; and for another thing, the hand of the same magician had been at work upon the pair of us, and Miss Grant had made us both *braw*, if she could make but the one *bonny*.

The same cry, in words not very different, came from both of us, that the other was come in compliment to say farewell, and then we perceived in a flash we were to ship together.

"O, why will not Baby have been telling me!" she cried; and then remembered a letter she had been given, on the condition of not opening it till she was well on board. Within was an enclosure for myself, and ran thus:—

"Dear Davie,—What do you think of my farewell? and what do you say to your fellow-passenger? Did you kiss, or did you ask? I was about to have signed here, but that would leave the purport of my question doubtful; and in my own case *I ken the answer*. So fill up here with good advice. Do not be too blate,1 and for God's sake do not try to be too forward; nothing sets you worse.—I am

"Your affectionate friend and governess,
"Barbara Grant."

I wrote a word of answer and compliment on a leaf out of my pocket-book, put it in with another scratch from Catriona, sealed the whole with my new signet of the Balfour arms, and despatched it by the hand of Prestongrange's servant, that still waited in my boat.

Then we had time to look upon each other more at leisure, which we had not done for a piece of a minute before (upon a common impulse) we shook hands again.

"Catriona!" said I. It seemed that was the first and last word of my eloquence.

"You will be glad to see me again?" says she.

"And I think that is an idle word," said I. "We are too deep friends to make speech upon such trifles."

"Is she not the girl of all the world?" she cried again. "I was never knowing such a girl, so honest and so beautiful."

"And yet she cared no more for Alpin than what she did for a kale-stock," said I.

"Ah, she will say so indeed!" cries Catriona. "Yet it was for the name and the gentle kind blood that she took me up and was so good to me."

"Well, I will tell you why it was," said I. "There are all sorts of people's faces in this world. There is Barbara's face, that every one must look at and admire, and think her a fine, brave, merry girl. And then there is your face, which is quite different—I never knew how different till today. You cannot see yourself, and that is why you do not understand; but it was for the love of your face that she took you up and was so good to you. And everybody in the world would do the same."

"Everybody?" says she.

"Every living soul!" said I.

"Ah, then, that will be why the soldiers at the Castle took me up!" she cried.

"Barbara has been teaching you to catch me," said I.

"She will have taught me more than that, at all events. She will have taught me a great deal about Mr. David—all the ill of him, and a little that was not so ill either, now and then," she said, smiling. "She will have told me all there was of Mr. David, only just that he would sail upon this very same ship. And why it is you go?"

I told her.

"Ah, well," said she, "we will be some days in company, and then (I suppose) good-bye for altogether! I go to meet my father at a place of the name of Helvoetsluys, and from there to France, to be exiles by the side of our chieftain."

I could say no more than just "O!" the name of James More always drying up my very voice.

She was quick to perceive it, and to guess some portion of my thought.

"There is one thing I must be saying first of all, Mr. David," said she. "I think two of my kinsfolk have not behaved to you altogether very well. And the one of them two is James More, my father, and the other is the Laird of Prestongrange. Prestongrange will have spoken by himself, or his daughter in the place of him. But for James More, my father, I have this much to say: he lay shackled in a prison; he is a plain honest soldier and a plain Highland gentleman; what they would be after he would never be guessing; but if he had understood it was to be some prejudice to a young gentleman like yourself, he would have died first. And for the sake of all your friendships, I will be asking you to pardon my father and family for that same mistake."

"Catriona," said I, "what that mistake was I do not care to know. I know but the one thing—that you went to Preston-grange and begged my life upon your knees. O, I ken well it was for your father that you went, but when you were there you pleaded for me also. It is a thing I cannot speak of. There are two things I cannot think of in to myself: and the one is your good words when you called yourself my little friend, and the other that you pleaded for my life. Let us never speak more, we two, of pardon or offence."

We stood after that silent, Catriona looking on the deck and I on her; and before there was more speech, a little wind having sprung up in the nor'-west, they began to shake out the sails and heave in upon the anchor.

There were six passengers besides our two selves, which made of it a full cabin. Three were solid merchants out of Leith, Kirkcaldy, and Dundee, all engaged in the same adventure into High Germany. One was a Hollander returning; the rest worthy merchants' wives, to the charge of one of whom Catriona was recommended. Mrs. Gebbie (for that was her name) was by great good fortune heavily incommoded by the sea, and lay day and night on the broad of her back. We were besides the only creatures at all young on board the *Rose*, except a white-faced boy that did my old duty to attend upon the table; and it came about that Catriona and I were left almost entirely to ourselves. We had the next seats together at the table, where I waited on her with extraordinary pleasure. On deck, I made her a soft place with my cloak; and the weather being singularly fine for that season, with bright frosty days and nights, a steady, gentle wind, and scarce a sheet started all the way through the North Sea, we sat there (only now and again walking to and fro for warmth) from the first blink of the sun till eight or nine at night under the clear stars. The merchants or Captain Sang would sometimes glance and smile upon us, or pass a merry word or two and give us the go-by again; but the most part of the time they were deep in herring and chintzes and linen, or in computations of the slowness of the passage, and left us to our own concerns, which were very little important to any but ourselves.

At the first we had a great deal to say, and thought ourselves pretty witty; and I was at a little pains to be the *beau*, and she (I believe) to play the young lady of experience. But soon we grew plainer with each other. I laid aside my high, clipped English (what little there was of it) and forgot to make my Edinburgh bows and scrapes; she, upon her side, fell into a sort of kind familiarity; and we dwelt together like those of the same household, only (upon my side) with a more deep emotion. About the same time, the bottom seemed to fall out of our conversation, and neither one of us the less pleased. Whiles she would tell me old wives' tales, of which she had a wonderful variety, many of them from my friend red-headed Neil. She told them very pretty, and they were pretty enough childish tales; but the pleasure to myself was in the sound of her voice, and the thought that she was telling and I was listening. Whiles, again, we would sit entirely silent, not communicating even with a look, and tasting pleasure enough in the sweetness of that neighbourhood. I speak here only for myself. Of what was in the maid's mind I am not very sure that ever I asked myself; and what was in my own I was afraid to consider. I need make no secret of it now, either to myself or to the reader: I was fallen totally in love. She came between me and the sun. She had grown suddenly taller, as I say, but with a wholesome growth; she seemed all health, and lightness, and brave spirits; and I thought she walked like a young deer, and stood like a birch upon the mountains. It was enough for me to sit near by her on the deck; and I declare I scarce spent two thoughts upon the future, and was so well content with what I then enjoyed that I was never at the pains to imagine any further step; unless perhaps that I would be sometimes tempted to take her hand in mine and hold it there. But I was too like a miser of what joys I had, and would venture nothing on a hazard.

What we spoke was usually of ourselves or of each other, so that if any one had been at so much pains as overhear us, he must have supposed us the most egotistical persons in the world. It befell one day when we were at this practice, that we came on a discourse of friends and friendship, and I think now that we were sailing near the wind. We said what a fine thing friendship was, and how little we had guessed of it, and how it made life a new thing, and a thousand covered things of the same kind that will have been said, since the foundation of the world, by young folk in the same predicament. Then we remarked upon the strangeness of that circumstance, that friends came together in the beginning as if they were there for the first time, and yet each had been alive a good while, losing time with other people.

"It is not much that I have done," said she, "and I could be telling you the five-fifths of it in two-three words. It is only a girl I am, and what can befall a girl, at all events? But I went with the clan in the year 'Forty-five. The men marched with swords and firelocks, and some of them in brigades in the same set of tartan; they were not backward at the marching, I can tell you. And there were gentlemen from the Low Country, with their tenants mounted and trumpets to sound, and there was a grand skirling of war-pipes. I rode on a little Highland horse on the right hand of my father, James More, and of Glengyle himself. And here is one fine thing that I remember, that Glengyle kissed me in the face, because (says he) 'my kinswoman, you are the only lady of the clan that has come out,' and me a little maid of maybe twelve years old! I saw Prince Charlie too, and the blue eyes of him; he was pretty indeed! I had his hand to kiss in the front of the army. O, well, these were the good days, but it is all like a dream that I have seen and then awakened. It went what way you very well know; and these were the worst days of all, when the red-coat soldiers were out, and my father and my uncles lay in the hill, and I was to be carrying them their meat in the middle night, or at the short side of day when the cocks crow. Yes, I have walked in the night, many's the time, and my heart great in me for terror of the darkness. It is a strange thing I will never have been meddled with a bogle; but they say a maid goes safe. Next there was my uncle's marriage, and that was a dreadful affair beyond all. Jean Kay was that woman's name; and she had me in the room with her that night at Inversnaid, the night we took her from her friends in the old, ancient manner. She would and she wouldn't; she was for marrying Rob the one minute, and the next she would be for none of him. I will never have seen such a feckless creature of a woman; surely all there was of her would tell her ay or no. Well, she was a widow, and I can never be thinking a widow a good woman."

"Catriona!" says I, "how do you make out that?"

"I do not know," said she; "I am only telling you the seeming in my heart. And then to marry a new man! Fy! But that was her; and she was married again upon my uncle Robin, and went with him a while to kirk and market; and then wearied, or else her friends got claught of her and talked her round, or maybe she turned ashamed; at the least of it, she ran away, and went back to her own folk, and said we had held her in the lake, and I will never tell you all what. I have never thought much of any females since that day. And so, in the end, my father, James More, came to be cast in prison, and you know the rest of it as well as me."

"And through all you had no friends?" said I.

"No," said she; "I have been pretty chief with two-three lasses on the braes, but not to call it friends."

"Well, mine is a plain tale," said I. "I never had a friend to my name till I met in with you."

"And that brave Mr. Stewart?" she asked.

"O, yes, I was forgetting him," I said. "But he is a man, and that is very different."

"I would think so," said she. "O, yes, it is quite different."

"And then there was one other," said I. "I once thought I had a friend, but it proved a disappointment."

She asked me who she was.

"It was a he, then," said I. "We were the two best lads at my father's school, and we thought we loved each other dearly. Well, the time came when he went to Glasgow, to a merchant's house, that was his second cousin once removed; and wrote me two-three times by the carrier; and then he found new friends, and I might write till I was tired, he took no notice. Eh, Catriona, it took me a long while to forgive the world. There is not anything more bitter than to lose a fancied friend."

Then she began to question me close upon his looks and character, for we were each a great deal concerned in all that touched the other; till at last, in a very evil hour, I minded of his letters and went and fetched the bundle from the cabin.

"Here are his letters," said I, "and all the letters that ever I got. That will be the last I'll can tell of myself; you know the lave as well as I do."

"Will you let me read them, then?" says she.

I told her, *if she would be at the pains;* and she bade me go away and she would read them from the one end to the other. Now, in this bundle that I gave her there were packed together not only all the letters of my false friend, but one or two of Mr. Campbell's when he was in town at the Assembly, and to make a complete roll of all that ever was written to me, Catriona's little word, and the two I had received from Miss Grant, one when I was on the Bass, and one on board that ship. But of these last I had no particular mind at the moment.

I was in that state of subjection to the thought of my friend that it mattered not what I did, nor scarce whether I was in her presence or out of it; I had caught her like some kind of a noble fever that lived continually in my bosom, by night and by day, and whether I was waking or asleep. So it befell that after I was come into the fore-part of the ship, where the broad bows splashed into the billows, I was in no such hurry to return, as you might fancy; rather prolonged my absence like a variety in pleasure. I do not think I am by nature much of an Epicurean; and there had come till then so small a share of pleasure in my way that I might be excused, perhaps, to dwell on it unduly.

When I returned to her again, I had a faint, painful impression as of a buckle slipped, so coldly she returned the packet.

"You have read them?" said I; and I thought my voice sounded not wholly natural, for I was turning in my mind for what could ail her.

"Did you mean me to read all?" she asked.

I told her "Yes," with a drooping voice.

"The last of them as well?" said she.

I knew where we were now; yet I would not lie to her either. "I gave them all without afterthought," I said, "as I supposed that you would read them. I see no harm in any."

"I will be differently made," said she. "I thank God I am differently made. It was not a fit letter to be shown me. It was not fit to be written."

"I think you are speaking of your own friend, Barbara Grant?" said I.

"There will not be anything as bitter as to lose a fancied friend," said she, quoting my own expression.

"I think it is sometimes the friendship that was fancied!" I cried. "What kind of justice do you call this, to blame me for some words that a tomfool of a madcap lass has written down upon a piece of paper? You know yourself with what respect I have behaved—and would do always."

"Yet you would show me that same letter!" says she. "I want

no such friends. I can be doing very well, Mr. Balfour, without her—or you."

"This is your fine gratitude!" says I.

"I am very much obliged to you," said she. "I will be asking you to take away your—letters." She seemed to choke upon the word, so that it sounded like an oath.

"You shall never ask twice," said I; picked up that bundle, walked a little way forward and cast them as far as possible into the sea. For a very little more I could have cast myself after them.

The rest of the day I walked up and down raging. There were few names so ill but what I gave her them in my own mind before the sun went down. All that I had ever heard of Highland pride seemed quite outdone; that a girl (scarce grown) should resent so trifling an allusion, and that from her next friend, that she had near wearied me with praising of! I had bitter, sharp, hard thoughts of her, like an angry boy's. If I had kissed her indeed (I thought), perhaps she would have taken it pretty well; and only because it had been written down, and with a spice of jocularity, up she must fuff in this ridiculous passion. It seemed to me there was a want of penetration in the female sex, to make angels weep over the case of the poor men.

We were side by side again at supper, and what a change was there! She was like curdled milk to me; her face was like a wooden doll's; I could have indifferently smitten her or grovelled at her feet, but she gave me not the least occasion to do either. No sooner the meal done than she betook herself to attend on Mrs. Gebbie, which I think she had a little neglected heretofore. But she was to make up for lost time, and in what remained of the passage was extraordinary assiduous with the old lady, and on deck began to make a great deal more than I thought wise of Captain Sang. Not but what the captain seemed a worthy, fatherly man; but I hated to behold her in the least familiarity with any one except myself.

Altogether, she was so quick to avoid me, and so constant to keep herself surrounded with others, that I must watch a long while before I could find my opportunity; and after it was found, I made not much of it, as you are now to hear.

"I have no guess how I have offended," said I; "it should scarce be beyond pardon, then. O, try if you can pardon me."

"I have no pardon to give," said she; and the words seemed to come out of her throat like marbles. "I will be very much obliged for all your friendships." And she made me an eighth part of a curtsy.

But I had schooled myself beforehand to say more, and I was going to say it too.

"There is one thing," said I. "If I have shocked your particularity by the showing of that letter, it cannot touch Miss Grant. She wrote not to you, but to a poor, common, ordinary lad, who might have had more sense than show it. If you are to blame me——"

"I will advise you to say no more about that girl, at all events!" said Catriona. "It is her I will never look the road of, not if she lay dying." She turned away from me, and suddenly back. "Will you swear you will have no more to deal with her?" she cried.

"Indeed, and I will never be so unjust then," said I; "nor yet so ungrateful."

And now it was I that turned away.

CHAPTER XXII

Helvoetsluys

The weather in the end considerably worsened; the wind sang in the shrouds, the sea swelled higher, and the ship began to labour and cry out among the billows. The song of the leadsman in the chains was now scarce ceasing, for we thrid all the way among shoals. About nine in the morning, in a burst of wintry sun between two squalls of hail, I had my first look of Holland—a line of windmills birling in the breeze. It was besides my first knowledge of these daft-like contrivances, which gave me a near sense of foreign travel and a new world and life. We came to an anchor about half-past eleven, outside the harbour of Helvoetsluys, in a place where the sea sometimes broke and the ship pitched outrageously. You may be sure we were all on deck, save Mrs. Gebbie, some of us in cloaks, others mantled in the ship's tarpaulins, all clinging on by ropes, and jesting the most like old sailor-folk that we could imitate.

Presently a boat, that was backed like a partan-crab, came gingerly alongside, and the skipper of it hailed our master in the Dutch. Thence Captain Sang turned, very troubled-like, to Catriona; and, the rest of us crowding about, the nature of the difficulty was made plain to all. The *Rose* was bound to the port of Rotterdam, whither the other passengers were in a great impatience to arrive, in view of a conveyance due to leave that very evening in the direction of the Upper Germany. This, with the present half-gale of wind, the captain (if no time were lost) declared himself still capable to save. Now James More had trysted in Helvoet with his daughter, and the captain had engaged to call before the port and place her (according to the custom) in a shore boat. There was the boat, to be sure, and here was Catriona ready: but both our master and the patroon of the boat scrupled at the risk, and the first was in no humour to delay.

"Your father," said he, "would be geyan little pleased if we was to break a leg to ye, Miss Drummond, let-a-be drowning of you. Take my way of it," says he, "and come on-by with the rest of us here to Rotterdam. Ye can get a passage down the Maes in a sailing scoot as far as to the Brill, and thence on again, by a place in a rattel-waggon, back to Helvoet."

But Catriona would hear of no change. She looked white-like as she beheld the bursting of the sprays, the green seas that sometimes poured upon the forecastle, and the perpetual bounding and swooping of the boat among the billows; but she stood firmly by her father's orders. "My father, James More, will have arranged it so," was her first word and her last. I thought it very idle, and indeed wanton, in the girl to be so literal and stand opposite to so much kind advice; but the fact is she had a very good reason, if she would have told us. Sailing scoots and rattel-waggons are excellent things; only the use of them must first be paid for, and all she was possessed of in the world was just two shillings and a penny-halfpenny sterling. So it fell out that captain and passengers, not knowing of her destitution—and she being too proud to tell them—spoke in vain.

"But you ken nae French and nae Dutch neither," said one.

"It is very true," says she, "but since the year 'Forty-six there are so many of the honest Scots abroad that I will be doing very well, I thank you."

There was a pretty country simplicity in this that made some laugh, others looked the more sorry, and Mr. Gebbie fell outright in a passion. I believe he knew it was his duty (his wife having accepted charge of the girl) to have gone ashore with her and seen her safe: nothing would have induced him to have done so, since it must have involved the loss of his conveyance; and I think he made it up to his conscience by the loudness of his voice. At least he broke out upon Captain Sang, raging and saying the thing was a disgrace; that it was mere death to try to leave the ship, and at any event we could not cast down an innocent maid in a boatful of nasty Holland fishers, and leave her to her fate. I was thinking something of the same; took the mate upon one side, arranged with him to send on my chests by track-scoot to an address I had in Leyden, and stood up and signalled to the fishers.

"I will go ashore with the young lady, Captain Sang," said I. "It is all one what way I go to Leyden"; and leaped at the same time into the boat, which I managed not so elegantly but what I fell with two of the fishers in the bilge.

From the boat the business appeared yet more precarious than from the ship, she stood so high over us, swung down so swift, and menaced us so perpetually with her plunging and passaging upon the anchor cable. I began to think I had made a fool's bargain, that it was merely impossible Catriona should be got on board to me, and that I stood to be set ashore at Helvoet all by myself and with no hope of any reward but the pleasure of embracing James More, if I should want to. But this was to reckon without the lass's courage. She had seen me leap with very little appearance (however much reality) of hesitation; to be sure, she was not to be beat by her discarded friend. Up she stood on the bulwarks and held by a stay, the wind blowing in her petticoats, which made the enterprise more dangerous, and gave us rather more of a view of her stockings than would be thought genteel in cities. There was no minute lost, and scarce time given for any to interfere, if they had wished the same. I stood up on the other side and spread my arms; the ship swung down on us, the patroon humoured his boat nearer in than was perhaps wholly safe, and Catriona leaped into the air. I was so happy as to catch her, and the fishers readily supporting us, escaped a fall. She held to me a moment very tight, breathing quick and deep; thence (she still clinging to me with both hands) we were passed aft to our places by the steersman; and, Captain Sang and all the crew and passengers cheering and crying farewell, the boat was put about for shore.

As soon as Catriona came a little to herself she unhanded me suddenly, but said no word. No more did I; and indeed the whistling of the wind and the breaching of the sprays made it no time for speech; and our crew not only toiled excessively but made extremely little way, so that the *Rose* had got her anchor and was off again before we had approached the harbour mouth.

We were no sooner in smooth water than the patroon, according to their beastly Hollands custom, stopped his boat and required of us our fares. Two guilders was the man's demand—between three and four shillings English money—for each passenger. But at this Catriona began to cry out with a vast deal of agitation. She had asked of Captain Sang, she said, and the fare was but an English shilling. "Do you think I will have come on board and not ask first?" cries she. The patroon scolded back upon her in a lingo where the oaths were English and the rest right Hollands; till at last (seeing her near tears) I privately slipped in the rogue's hand six shillings, whereupon he was obliging enough to receive from her the other shilling without more complaint. No doubt I was a good deal nettled and ashamed. I like to see folk thrifty, but not with so much passion; and I daresay it would be rather coldly that I asked her, as the boat moved on again for shore, where it was that she was trysted with her father.

"He is to be inquired of at the house of one Sprott, an honest Scots merchant," says she; and then with the same breath, "I am wishing to thank you very much—you are a brave friend to me."

"It will be time enough when I get you to your father," said I, little thinking that I spoke so true. "I can tell him a fine tale of a loyal daughter."

"O, I do not think I will be a loyal girl, at all events," she cried, with a great deal of painfulness in the expression. "I do not think my heart is true."

"Yet there are very few that would have made that leap, and all to obey a father's orders," I observed.

"I cannot have you to be thinking of me so," she cried again. "When you had done that same, how would I stop behind? And at all events that was not all the reasons." Whereupon, with a burning face, she told me the plain truth upon her poverty.

"Good guide us!" cried I, "what kind of daft-like proceeding is this, to let yourself be launched on the continent of Europe with an empty purse; I count it hardly decent—scant decent!" I cried.

"You forget James More, my father, is a poor gentleman," said she. "He is a hunted exile."

"But I think not all your friends are hunted exiles," I exclaimed. "And was this fair to them that care for you? Was it fair to me? was it fair to Miss Grant, that counselled you to go, and would be driven fair horn-mad if she could hear of it? Was it even fair to these Gregory folk that you were living with, and used you lovingly? It's a blessing you have fallen in my hands! Suppose your father hindered by an accident, what would become of you here, and you your lee-lone in a strange place? The thought of the thing frightens me," I said.

"I will have lied to all of them," she replied. "I will have told them all that I had plenty. I told *her* too. I could not be lowering James More to them."

I found out later on that she must have lowered him in the very dust, for the lie was originally the father's, not the daughter's, and she thus obliged to persevere in it for the man's reputation. But at the time I was ignorant of this, and the mere thought of her destitution and the perils in which she must have fallen, had ruffled me almost beyond reason.

"Well, well, well," said I, "you will have to learn more sense."

I left her mails for the moment in an inn upon the shore, where I got a direction for Sprott's house in my new French, and we walked there—it was some little way—beholding the place with wonder as we went. Indeed, there was much for Scots folk to admire: canals and trees being intermingled with the houses; the houses, each within itself, of a brave red brick, the colour of a rose, with steps and benches of blue marble at the cheek of every door, and the whole town so clean you might have dined upon the causeway. Sprott was within, upon his ledgers, in a low parlour, very neat and clean, and set out with china and pictures and a globe of the earth in a brass frame. He was a big-chafted, ruddy, lusty man, with a crooked hard look to him; and he made us not that much civility as offer us a seat.

"Is James More Macgregor now in Helvoet, sir?" says I.

"I ken nobody by such a name," says he, impatient-like.

"Since you are so particular," says I, "I will amend my question, and ask you where we are to find in Helvoet one James Drummond, *alias* Macgregor, *alias* James More, late tenant in Inveronachile?"

"Sir," says he, "he may be in Hell for what I ken, and for my part I wish he was."

"The young lady is that gentleman's daughter, sir," said I, "before whom, I think you will agree with me, it is not very becoming to discuss his character."

"I have nothing to make either with him, or her, or you!" cries he in his gross voice.

"Under your favour, Mr. Sprott," said I, "this young lady is come from Scotland seeking him, and, by whatever mistake, was given the name of your house for a direction. An error it seems to have been, but I think this places both you and me— who am but her fellow-traveller by accident—under a strong obligation to help our countrywoman."

"Will you ding me daft?" he cries. "I tell ye I ken naething and care less either for him or his breed. I tell ye the man owes me money."

"That may very well be, sir," said I, who was now rather more angry than himself. "At least, I owe you nothing; the young lady is under my protection; and I am neither at all used with these manners, nor in the least content with them."

As I said this, and without particularly thinking what I did, I drew a step or two nearer to his table; thus striking, by mere good fortune, on the only argument that could at all affect the man. The blood left his lusty countenance.

"For the Lord's sake dinna be hasty, sir!" he cried. "I am truly wishfu' no' to be offensive. But ye ken, sir, I'm like a wheen guid-natured, honest, canty auld fallows—my bark is waur nor my bite. To hear me, ye micht whiles fancy I was a wee thing

209

dour; but na, na! it's a kind auld fallow at heart, Sandie Sprott! And ye could never imagine the fyke and fash this man has been to me."

"Very good, sir," said I. "Then I will make that much freedom with your kindness as trouble you for your last news of Mr. Drummond."

"You're welcome, sir!" said he. "As for the young leddy (my respec's to her!), he'll just have clean forgotten her. I ken the man, ye see; I have lost siller by him ere now. He thinks of naebody but just himsel'; clan, king, or dauchter, if he can get his wameful, he would give them a' the go-by! ay, or his correspondent either. For there is a sense in whilk I may be nearly almost said to be his correspondent. The fact is, we are employed thegither in a business affair, and I think it's like to turn out a dear affair for Sandie Sprott. The man's as guid's my pairtner, and I give ye my mere word I ken naething by where he is. He micht be coming here to Helvoet; he micht come here the morn, he michtna come for a twalmonth; I would wonder at naething—or just at the ae thing, and that's if he was to pay me my siller. Ye see what way I stand with it; and it's clear I'm no' very likely to meddle up with the young leddy, as ye ca' her. She canna stop here, that's ae thing certain sure. Dod, sir, I'm a lone man! If I was to tak' her in, it's highly possible the hellicat would try and gar me marry her when he turned up."

"Enough of this talk," said I. "I will take the young lady among better friends. Give me pen, ink, and paper, and I will leave here for James More the address of my correspondent in Leyden. He can inquire from me where he is to seek his daughter."

This word I wrote and sealed; which while I was doing, Sprott of his own motion made a welcome offer, to charge himself with Miss Drummond's mails, and even send a porter for them to the inn. I advanced him to that effect a dollar or two to be a cover, and he gave me an acknowledgment in writing of the sum.

Whereupon (I giving my arm to Catriona) we left the house

of this unpalatable rascal. She had said no word throughout, leaving me to judge and speak in her place; I, upon my side, had been careful not to embarrass her by a glance; and even now, although my heart still glowed inside of me with shame and anger, I made it my affair to seem quite easy.

"Now," said I, "let us get back to yon same inn where they can speak the French, have a piece of dinner, and inquire for conveyances to Rotterdam. I will never be easy till I have you safe again in the hands of Mrs. Gebbie."

"I suppose it will have to be," said Catriona, "though, whoever will be pleased, I do not think it will be her. And I will remind you this once again, that I have but one shilling and three bawbees."

"And just this once again," said I, "I will remind you it was a blessing that I came alongst with you."

"What else would I be thinking all this time?" says she, and I thought weighed a little on my arm. "It is you that are the good friend to me."

CHAPTER XXIII

Travels in Holland

The rattel-waggon, which is a kind of a long waggon set with benches, carried us in four hours of travel to the great city of Rotterdam. It was long past dark by then, but the streets pretty brightly lighted and thronged with wild-like, outlandish characters—bearded Hebrews, black men, and the hordes of courtesans, most indecently adorned with finery, and stopping seamen by their very sleeves; the clash of talk about us made our heads to whirl; and, what was the most unexpected of all, we appeared to be no more struck with all these foreigners than they with us. I made the best face I could, for the lass's sake and my own credit; but the truth is, I felt like a lost sheep, and my heart beat in my bosom with anxiety. Once or twice I inquired after the harbour or the berth of the ship *Rose;* but either fell on some who spoke only Hollands, or my own French failed me. Trying a street at a venture, I came upon a lane of lighted houses, the doors and windows thronged with wauf-like painted women; these jostled and mocked upon us as we passed, and I was thankful we had nothing of their language. A little after we issued forth upon an open place along the harbour.

"We shall be doing now," cries I, as soon as I spied masts. "Let us walk here by the harbour. We are sure to meet some that has the English, and at the best of it we may light upon that very ship."

We did the next best, as happened; for, about nine of the evening, whom should we walk into the arms of but Captain Sang? He told us they had made their run in the most incredible brief time, the wind holding strong till they reached port; by which means his passengers were all gone already on their further travels. It was impossible to chase after the Gebbies into the High Germany, and we had no other acquaintance to fall back upon but Captain Sang himself. It was the more gratifying to find the man friendly and wishful to assist. He made it a small affair to find some good plain family of merchants, where Catriona might harbour till the *Rose* was loaden; declared he would then blithely carry her back to Leith for nothing and see her safe in the hands of Mr. Gregory; and in the meanwhile carried us to a late ordinary for the meal we stood in need of. He seemed extremely friendly, as I say, but, what surprised me a good deal, rather boisterous in the bargain; and the cause of this was soon to appear. For at the ordinary, calling for Rhenish wine and drinking of it deep, he soon became unutterably tipsy. In this case, as too common with all men, but especially with those of his rough trade, what little sense or manners he possessed deserted him; and he behaved himself so scandalous to the young lady, jesting most ill-favouredly at the figure she had made on the ship's rail, that I had no resource but carry her suddenly away.

She came out of that ordinary clinging to me close. "Take me away, David," she said. "*You* keep me. I am not afraid with you."

"And have no cause, my little friend!" cried I, and could have found it in my heart to weep.

"Where will you be taking me?" she said again. "Don't leave me, at all events—never leave me."

"Where am I taking you indeed?" says I, stopping, for I had been staving on ahead in mere blindness. "I must stop and think. But I'll not leave you, Catriona; the Lord do so to me, and more also, if I should fail or fash you."

She crept closer in to me by way of a reply.

"Here," I said, "is the stillest place that we have hit on yet in this busy byke of a city. Let us sit down here under yon tree and consider of our course."

That tree (which I am little like to forget) stood hard by the harbourside. It was a black night, but lights were in the houses, and nearer hand in the quiet ships; there was a shining of the city on the one hand, and a buzz hung over it of many thousands walking and talking; on the other, it was dark, and the water bubbled on the sides. I spread my cloak upon a builder's stone, and made her sit there; she would have kept her hold upon me, for she still shook with the late affronts; but I wanted to think clear, disengaged myself, and paced to and fro before her, in the manner of what we call a smuggler's walk, belabouring my brains for any remedy. By the course of these scattering thoughts I was brought suddenly face to face with a remembrance that, in the heat and haste of our departure, I had left Captain Sang to pay the ordinary. At this I began to laugh out loud, for I thought the man well served; and at the same time, by an instinctive movement, carried my hand to the pocket where my money was. I suppose it was in the lane where the women jostled us; but there is only the one thing certain, that my purse was gone.

"You will have thought of something good," said she, observing me to pause.

At the pinch we were in, my mind became suddenly clear as a perspective-glass, and I saw there was no choice of methods. I had not one doit of coin, but in my pocket-book I had still my letter on the Leyden merchant; and there was now but the one way to get to Leyden, and that was to walk on our two feet.

"Catriona," said I, "I know you're brave, and I believe you're strong—do you think you could walk thirty miles on a plain road?" We found it, I believe, scarce the two-thirds of that, but such was my notion of the distance.

"David," she said, "if you will just keep near, I will go anywhere and do anything. The courage of my heart, it is all broken. Do not be leaving me in this horrible country by myself, and I will do all else."

"Can you start now and march all night?" said I.

"I will do all that you can ask of me," she said, "and never ask you why. I have been a bad, ungrateful girl to you; and do what you please with me now! And I think Miss Barbara Grant is the best lady in the world," she added, "and I do not see what she would deny you for at all events."

This was Greek and Hebrew to me; but I had other matters to consider, and the first of these was to get clear of that city on the Leyden road. It proved a cruel problem; and it may have been one or two at night ere we had solved it. Once beyond the houses, there was neither moon nor stars to guide us; only the whiteness of the way in the midst, and a blackness of an alley on both hands. The walking was besides made most extraordinary difficult by a plain black frost that fell suddenly in the small hours and turned that highway into one long slide.

"Well, Catriona," said I, "here we are, like the king's sons and the old wives' daughters in your daft-like Highland tales. Soon we'll be going over the *'seven Bens, the seven glens, and the seven mountain moors'*"—which was a common byword or overcome in those tales of hers that had stuck in my memory. ●$

"Ah," says she, "but here are no glens or mountains! Though I will never be denying but what the trees and some of the plain places hereabouts are very pretty. But our country is the best yet."

"I wish we could say as much for our own folk," says I, recalling Sprott and Sang, and perhaps James More himself.

"I will never complain of the country of my friend," said she, and spoke it out with an accent so particular that I seemed to see the look upon her face.

I caught in my breath sharp and came near falling (for my pains) on the black ice.

"I do not know what *you* think, Catriona," said I, when I was a little recovered, "but this has been the best day yet! I think shame to say it, when you have met in with such misfortunes and disfavours; but for me, it has been the best day yet."

"It was a good day when you showed me so much love," said she.

"And yet I think shame to be happy too," I went on, "and you here on the road in the black night."

"Where in the great world would I be else?" she cried. "I am thinking I am safest where I am with you."

"I am quite forgiven, then?" I asked.

"Will you not forgive me that time so much as not to take it in your mouth again?" she cried. "There is nothing in this heart to you but thanks. But I will be honest too," she added, with a

215

kind of suddenness, "and I'll never can forgive that girl."

"Is this Miss Grant again?" said I. "You said yourself she was the best lady in the world."

"So she will be, indeed!" says Catriona. "But I will never forgive her for all that. I will never, never forgive her, and let me hear tell of her no more."

"Well," said I, "this beats all that ever came to my knowledge; and I wonder that you can indulge yourself in such bairnly whims. Here is a young lady that was the best friend in the world to the both of us, that learned us how to dress ourselves, and in a great manner how to behave, as any one can see that knew us both before and after."

But Catriona stopped square in the midst of the highway.

"It is this way of it," said she. "Either you will go on to speak of her, and I will go back to yon town, and let come of it what God pleases! Or else you will do me that politeness to talk of other things."

I was the most nonplussed person in this world; but I bethought me that she depended altogether on my help, that she was of the frail sex, and not so much beyond a child, and it was for me to be wise for the pair of us.

"My dear girl," said I, "I can make neither head nor tails of this; but God forbid that I should do anything to set you on the jee. As for talking of Miss Grant, I have no such a mind to it, and I believe it was yourself began it. My only design (if I took you up at all) was for your own improvement, for I hate the very look of injustice. Not that I do not wish you to have a good pride and a nice female delicacy; they become you well; but here you show them to excess."

"Well, then, have you done?" said she.

"I have done," said I.

"A very good thing," said she, and we went on again, but now in silence.

It was an eerie employment to walk in the gross night, beholding only shadows, and hearing nought but our own steps. At first, I believe our hearts burned against each other with a deal of enmity; but the darkness and the cold, and the silence, which only the cocks sometimes interrupted, or sometimes the farmyard dogs, had pretty soon brought down our pride to the dust; and for my own particular, I would have jumped at any decent opening for speech.

Before the day peeped, came on a warmish rain, and the frost was all wiped away from among our feet. I took my cloak to her and sought to hap her in the same; she bade me, rather impatiently, to keep it.

"Indeed and I will do no such thing," said I. "Here am I, a great, ugly lad that has seen all kinds of weather, and here are you, a tender, pretty maid! My dear, you would not put me to a shame?"

Without more words she let me cover her; which as I was doing in the darkness, I let my hand rest a moment on her shoulder, almost like an embrace.

"You must try to be more patient of your friend," said I.

I thought she seemed to lean the least thing in the world against my bosom, or perhaps it was but fancy.

"There will be no end to your goodness," said she.

And we went on again in silence; but now all was changed; and the happiness that was in my heart was like a fire in a great chimney.

The rain passed ere day; it was but a sloppy morning as we came into the town of Delft. The red gabled houses made a handsome show on either hand of a canal; the servant lasses were out slaistering and scrubbing at the very stones upon the public highway; smoke rose from a hundred kitchens; and it came in upon me strongly it was time to break our fasts.

"Catriona," said I. "I believe you have yet a shilling and three bawbees?"

"Are you wanting it?" said she, and passed me her purse. "I am wishing it was five pounds! What will you want it for?"

"And what have we been walking for all night, like a pair of waif Egyptians?" says I. "Just because I was robbed of my purse and all I possessed in that unchancy town of Rotterdam. I will tell you of it now, because I think the worst is over, but we have still a good tramp before us till we get to where my money is, and if you would not buy me a piece of bread, I were like to go fasting."

She looked at me with open eyes. By the light of the new day she was all black and pale for weariness, so that my heart smote me for her. But as for her, she broke out laughing.

"My torture! are we beggars then?" she cried. "You too? O, I could have wished for this same thing! And I am glad to buy your breakfast to you.

But it would be pleisand if I would have had to dance to get a meal to you! For I believe they are not very well acquainted with our manner of dancing over here, and might be paying for the curiosity of that sight."

I could have kissed her for that word, not with a lover's mind, but in a heat of admiration. For it always warms a man to see a woman brave.

We got a drink of milk from a country wife but new come to the town, and, in a baker's, a piece of excellent, hot, sweet-smelling bread, which we ate upon the road as we went on. That road from Delft to the Hague is just five miles of a fine avenue shaded with trees, a canal on the one hand, on the other excellent pastures of cattle. It was pleasant here indeed.

"And now, Davie," said she, "what will you do with me at all events?"

"It is what we have to speak of," said I, "and the sooner yet the better. I can come by money in Leyden; that will be all well. But the trouble is how to dispose of you until your father come. I thought last night you seemed a little sweer to part from me!"

"It will be more than seeming then," said she.

"You are a very young maid," said I, "and I am but a very young callant. This is a great piece of difficulty. What way are we to manage? Unless, indeed, you could pass to be my sister?"

"And what for no?" said she, "if you would let me!"

"I wish you were so, indeed!" I cried. "I would be a fine man if I had such a sister. But the rub is that you are Catriona Drummond."

"And now I will be Catrine Balfour," she said. "And who is to ken? They are all strange folk here."

"If you think that it would do," says I. "I own it troubles me. I would like it very ill, if I advised you at all wrong."

"David, I have no friend here but you," she said.

"The mere truth is, I am too young to be your friend," said I. "I am too young to advise you, or you to be advised. I see not what else we are to do, and yet I ought to warn you."

"I will have no choice left," said she. "My father James More has not used me very well, and it is not the first time. I am cast upon your hands like a sack of barley-meal, and have nothing else to think of but your pleasure. If you will have me, good and well. If you will not"—she turned and touched her hand upon my arm—"David, I am afraid," said she.

"No, but I ought to warn you," I began; and then bethought me that I was the bearer of the purse, and it would never do to seem too churlish. "Catriona," said I, "don't misunderstand me: I am just trying to do my duty by you, girl! Here am I, going alone to this strange city, to be a solitary student there; and here is this chance arisen that you might dwell with me a bit, and be like my sister: you can surely understand this much, my dear, that I would just love to have you?"

"Well, and here I am," said she. "So that's soon settled."

I know I was in duty bounden to have spoke more plain. I know this was a great blot upon my character, for which I was lucky that I did not pay more dear. But I minded how easy her delicacy had been startled with a word of kissing her in Barbara's letter; now that she depended on me, how was I to be more bold? Besides, the truth is, I could see no other feasible method to dispose of her. And I daresay inclination pulled me very strong.

A little beyond the Hague she fell very lame, and made the rest of the distance heavily enough. Twice she must rest by the wayside, which she did with pretty apologies, calling herself a shame to the Highlands and the race she came of, and nothing but a hindrance to myself. It was her excuse, she said, that she was not much used with walking shod. I would have had her strip off her shoes and stockings and go barefoot. But she pointed out to me that the women of that country, even in the landward roads, appeared to be all shod.

"I must not be disgracing my brother," said she, and was very merry with it all, although her face told tales of her.

There is a garden in that city we were bound to, sanded below with clean sand, the trees meeting overhead, some of them trimmed, some pleached, and the whole place beautified with alleys and arbours. Here I left Catriona, and went forward by myself to find my correspondent. There I drew on my credit, and asked to be recommended to some decent, retired lodging. My baggage not being yet arrived, I told him I supposed I should require his caution with the people of the house; and explained that, my sister being come for a while to keep house with me, I should be wanting two chambers. This was all very well; but the trouble was that Mr. Balfour in his letter of recommendation had condescended on a great deal of particulars, and never a word of any sister in the case. I could see my Dutchman was extremely suspicious; and viewing me over the rims of a great pair of spectacles—he was a poor, frail body, and reminded me of an infirm rabbit—he began to question me close.

Here I fell in a panic. Suppose he accept my tale (thinks I), suppose he invite my sister to his house, and that I bring her. I shall have a fine ravelled pirn to unwind, and may end by disgracing both the lassie and myself. Thereupon I began hastily to expound to him my sister's character. She was of a bashful disposition, it appeared, and so extremely fearful of meeting strangers that I had left her at that moment sitting in a public place alone. And then, being launched upon the stream of falsehood, I must do like all the rest of the world in the same circumstance, and plunge in deeper than was any service; adding some altogether needless particulars of Miss Balfour's ill-health and retirement during childhood. In the midst of which I awoke to a sense of my behaviour, and was turned to one blush.

The old gentleman was not so much deceived but what he discovered a willingness to be quit of me. But he was first of all a man of business; and knowing that my money was good enough, however it might be with my conduct, he was so far obliging as to send his son to be my guide and caution in the matter of a lodging. This implied my presenting of the young man to Catriona. The poor, pretty child was much recovered with resting, looked and behaved to perfection, and took my arm and gave me the name of brother more easily than I could answer her. But there was one misfortune: thinking to help, she was rather towardly than otherwise to my Dutchman. And I could not but reflect that Miss Balfour had rather suddenly outgrown her bashfulness. And there was another thing, the difference of our speech. I had the Low-Country tongue and dwelled upon my words; she had a hill voice, spoke with something of an English accent, only far more delightful, and was scarce quite fit to be called a deacon in the craft of talking English grammar; so that, for a brother and sister, we made a most uneven pair. But the young Hollander was a heavy dog, without so much spirit in his belly as to remark her prettiness, for which I scorned him. And as soon as he had found a cover to our heads, he left us alone, which was the greater service of the two.

CHAPTER XXIV

Full Story of a Copy of Heineccius

The place found was in the upper part of a house backed on a canal. We had two rooms, the second entering from the first; each had a chimney built out into the floor in the Dutch manner; and being alongside, each had the same prospect from the window of the top of a tree below us in a little court, of a piece of the canal, and of houses in the Hollands architecture and a church spire upon the farther side. A full set of bells hung in that spire, and made delightful music; and when there was any sun at all, it shone direct in our two chambers. From a tavern hard by we had good meals sent in.

The first night we were both pretty weary, and she extremely so. There was little talk between us, and I packed her off to her bed as soon as she had eaten. The first thing in the morning I wrote word to Sprott to have her mails sent on, together with a line to Alan at his chief's; and had the same despatched, and her breakfast ready, ere I waked her. I was a little abashed when she came forth in her one habit, and the mud of the way upon her stockings. By what inquiries I had made, it seemed a good few days must pass before her mails could come to hand in Leyden, and it was plainly needful she must have a shift of things. She was unwilling at first that I should go to that expense; but I reminded her she was now a rich man's sister, and must appear suitably in the part, and we had not got to the second merchant's before she was entirely charmed into the spirit of the thing, and her eyes shining. It pleased me to see her so innocent and thorough in this pleasure. What was more extraordinary was the passion into which I fell on it myself; being never satisfied that I had bought her enough or fine enough, and never weary of beholding her in different attires. Indeed, I began to understand some little of Miss Grant's immersion in that interest of clothes; for the truth is, when you have the ground of a beautiful person to adorn, the whole business becomes beautiful. The Dutch chintzes I should say were extraordinary cheap and fine; but I would be ashamed to set down what I paid for stockings to her. Altogether I spent so great a sum upon this pleasuring (as I may call it) that I was ashamed for a great while to spend more; and, by way of a set-off, I left our chambers pretty bare. If we had beds, if Catriona was a little braw, and I had light to see her by, we were richly enough lodged for me.

By the end of this merchandising I was glad to leave her at the door with all our purchases, and go for a long walk alone in which to read myself a lecture. Here had I taken under my roof, and as good as to my bosom, a young lass extremely beautiful, and whose innocence was her peril. My talk with the old Dutchman, and the lies to which I was constrained, had already given me a sense of how my conduct must appear to others; and now, after the strong admiration I had just experienced and the immoderacy with which I had continued my vain purchases, I began to think of it myself as very hazarded. I bethought me, if I had a sister indeed, whether I would so expose her; then, judging the case too problematical, I varied my question into this, whether I would so trust Catriona in the hands of any other Christian being: the answer to which made my face to burn. The more cause, since I had been entrapped, and had entrapped the girl into an undue situation, that I should behave in it with scrupulous nicety. She depended on me wholly for her bread and shelter; in case I should alarm her delicacy, she had no retreat. Besides, I was her host and her protector; and the more irregularly I had fallen in these positions, the less excuse for me if I should profit by the same to forward even the most honest suit; for with the opportunities that I enjoyed, and which no wise parent would have suffered for a moment, even the most honest suit would be unfair. I saw I must be extremely hold-off in my relations; and yet not too much so neither; for if I had no right to appear at all in the character of a suitor, I must yet appear continually, and if possible agreeably, in that of host. It was plain I should require a great deal of tact and conduct, perhaps more than my years afforded. But I had rushed in where angels might have feared to tread, and there was no way out of that position save by behaving right while I was in it. I made a set of rules for my guidance; prayed for strength to be enabled to observe them, and as a more human aid to the same end purchased a study-book in law. This being all that I could think of, I relaxed from these grave considerations; whereupon my mind bubbled at once into an effervescency of pleasing spirits, and it was like one treading on air that I turned homeward. As I thought that name of home, and recalled the image of that figure awaiting me between four walls, my heart beat upon my bosom.

My troubles began with my return. She ran to greet me with an obvious and affecting pleasure. She was clad, besides, entirely in the new clothes that I had bought for her; looked in them beyond expression well; and must walk about and drop me curtsies to display them and to be admired. I am sure I did it with an ill grace, for I thought to have choked upon the words.

"Well," she said, "if you will not be caring for my pretty clothes, see what I have done with our two chambers." And she showed me the place all very finely swept, and the fires glowing in the two chimneys.

I was glad of a chance to seem a little more severe than I quite felt. "Catriona," said I, "I am very much displeased with you, and you must never again lay a hand upon my room. One of us two must have the rule while we are here together; it is most fit it should be I, who am both the man and the elder; and I give you that for my command."

She dropped me one of her curtsies, which were extraordinary taking. "If you will be cross," said she, "I must be making pretty manners at you, Davie. I will be very obedient, as I should be when every stitch upon all there is of me belongs to you. But you will not be very cross either, because now I have not anyone else."

This struck me hard, and I made haste, in a kind of penitence, to blot out all the good effect of my last speech. In this direction progress was more easy, being down hill; she led me forward, smiling; at the sight of her, in the brightness of the fire and with her pretty becks and looks, my heart was altogether melted. We made our meal with infinite mirth and tenderness; and the two seemed to be commingled into one, so that our very laughter sounded like a kindness.

In the midst of which I awoke to better recollections, made a lame word of excuse, and set myself boorishly to my studies. It was a substantial, instructive book that I had bought, by the late Dr. Heineccius, in which I was to do a great deal of reading these next days, and often very glad that I had no one to question me of what I read. Methought she bit her lip at me a little, and that cut me. Indeed, it left her wholly solitary, the more as she was very little of a reader, and had never a book. But what was I to do?

So the rest of the evening flowed by almost without speech.

I could have beat myself. I could not lie in my bed that night for rage and repentance, but walked to and fro on my bare feet till I was nearly perished, for the chimney was gone out and the frost keen. The thought of her in the next room, the thought that she might even hear me as I walked, the remembrance of my churlishness and that I must continue to practise the same ungrateful course or be dishonoured, put me beside my reason. I stood like a man between Scylla and Charybdis: *What must she think of me?* was my one thought that softened me continually into weakness. *What is to become of us?* the other which steeled me again to resolution. This was my first night of wakefulness and divided counsels, of which I was now to pass many, pacing like a madman, sometimes weeping like a childish boy, sometimes praying (I would fain hope) like a Christian.

But prayer is not very difficult, and the hitch comes in practice. In her presence, and above all if I allowed any beginning of familiarity, I found I had very little command of what should follow. But to sit all day in the same room with her, and feign to be engaged upon Heineccius, surpassed my strength. So that I fell instead upon the expedient of absenting myself so much as I was able; taking out classes and sitting there regularly, often with small attention, the test of which I found the other day in a notebook of that period, where I had left off to follow an edifying lecture, and actually scribbled in my book some very ill verses, though the Latinity is rather better than I thought I could ever have compassed. The evil of this course was unhappily near as great as its advantage. I had the less time of trial, but I believe, while that time lasted, I was tried the more extremely. For she being so much left to solitude, she came to greet my return with an increasing fervour that came nigh to overmaster me. These friendly offers I must barbarously cast back; and my rejection sometimes wounded her so cruelly that I must unbend and seek to make it up to her in kindness. So that our time passed in ups and downs, tiffs and disappointments, upon the which I could almost say (if it may be said with reverence) that I was crucified.

The base of my trouble was Catriona's extraordinary innocence, at which I was not so much surprised as filled with pity and admiration. She seemed to have no thought of our position, no sense of my struggles; welcomed any mark of my weakness with responsive joy; and, when I was drove again to my retrenchments, did not always dissemble her chagrin. There were times when I have thought to myself, "If she were over head in love, and set her cap to catch me, she would scarce behave much otherwise"; and then I would fall again into wonder at the simplicity of woman, from whom I felt (in these moments) that I was not worthy to be descended.

There was one point in particular on which our warfare turned, and of all things, this was the question of her clothes. My baggage had soon followed me from Rotterdam, and hers from Helvoet. She had now, as it were, two wardrobes; and it grew to be understood between us (I could never tell how) that when she was friendly she would wear my clothes, and when otherwise her own. It was meant for a buffet, and (as it were) the renunciation of her gratitude; and I felt it so in my bosom, but was generally more wise than to appear to have observed the circumstance.

Once, indeed, I was betrayed into a childishness greater than her own; it fell in this way. On my return from classes, thinking upon her devoutly with a great deal of love and a good deal of annoyance in the bargain, the annoyance began to fade away out of my mind; and spying in a window one of those forced flowers, of which the Hollanders are so skilled in the artifice, I gave way to an impulse and bought it for Catriona. I do not know the name of that flower, but it was of the pink colour, and I thought she would admire the same, and carried it home to her with a wonderful soft heart. I had left her in my clothes, and when I returned to find her all changed, and a face to match, I cast but the one look at her from head to foot, ground my teeth together, flung the window open, and my flower into the court, and then (between rage and prudence) myself out of that room again, of which I slammed the door as I went out.

On the steep stair I came near falling, and this brought me to myself, so that I began at once to see the folly of my conduct. I went, not into the street as I had purposed, but to the house court, which was always a solitary place, and where I saw my flower (that had cost me vastly more than it was worth) hanging in the leafless tree. I stood by the side of the canal, and looked upon the ice. Country people went by on their skates, and I envied them. I could see no way out of the pickle I was in: no way so much as to return to the room I had just left. No doubt was in my mind but I had now betrayed the secret of my feelings; and, to make things worse, I had shown at the same time (and that with wretched boyishness) incivility to my helpless guest.

I suppose she must have seen me from the open window. It did not seem to me that I had stood there very long before I heard the crunching of footsteps on the frozen snow, and turning somewhat angrily (for I was in no spirit to be interrupted) saw Catriona drawing near. She was all changed again, to the clocked stockings.

"Are we not to have our walk today?" she said.

I was looking at her in a maze. "Where is your brooch?" says I.

She carried her hand to her bosom and coloured high. "I will have forgotten it," said she. "I will run upstairs for it quick, and then surely we'll can have our walk?"

There was a note of pleading in that last that staggered me; I had neither words nor voice to utter them; I could do no more than nod by way of answer; and the moment she had left me, climbed into the tree and recovered my flower, which on her return I offered her.

"I bought it for you, Catriona," said I.

She fixed it in the midst of her bosom with the brooch, I could have thought tenderly.

"It is none the better of my handling," said I again, and blushed.

"I will be liking it none the worse, you may be sure, of that," said she.

We did not speak so much that day; she seemed a thought on the reserve, though not unkindly. As for me, all the time of our walking, and after we came home, and I had seen her put my flower into a pot of water, I was thinking to myself what puzzles women were. I was thinking, the one moment, it was the most stupid thing on earth she should not have perceived my love; and the next, that she had certainly perceived it long ago, and (being a wise girl, with the fine female instinct of propriety) concealed her knowledge.

We had our walk daily. Out in the streets I felt more safe; I relaxed a little in my guardedness; and for one thing, there was no Heineccius. This made these periods not only a relief to myself, but a particular pleasure to my poor child. When I came back about the hour appointed, I would generally find her ready dressed and glowing with anticipation. She would prolong their duration to the extreme, seeming to dread (as I did myself) the hour of the return; and there is scarce a field or waterside near Leyden, scarce a street or lane there, where we have not lingered. Outside of these, I bade her confine herself entirely to our lodgings; this in the fear of her encountering any acquaintance, which would have rendered our position very difficult. From the same apprehension I would never suffer her to attend church, nor even go myself; but made some kind of shift to hold worship privately in our own chamber—I hope with an honest, but I am quite sure with a very much divided mind. Indeed, there was scarce anything that more affected me than thus to kneel down alone with her before God like man and wife.

One day it was snowing downright hard. I had thought it not possible that we should venture forth, and was surprised to find her waiting for me ready dressed.

"I will not be doing without my walk," she cried. "You are never a good boy, Davie, in the house; I will never be caring for you only in the open air. I think we two will better turn Egyptian and dwell by the roadside."

That was the best walk yet of all of them; she clung near to me in the falling snow; it beat about and melted on us, and the drops stood upon her bright cheeks like tears and ran into her smiling mouth. Strength seemed to come upon me with the sight like a giant's; I thought I could have caught her up and run with her into the uttermost places in the earth; and we spoke together all that time beyond belief for freedom and sweetness.

It was the dark night when we came to the house-door. She pressed my arm upon her bosom. "Thank you kindly for these same good hours," said she, on a deep note of her voice.

The concern in which I fell instantly on this address put me with the same swiftness on my guard; and we were no sooner in the chamber, and the light made, than she beheld the old, dour, stubborn countenance of the student of Heineccius. Doubtless she was more than usually hurt; and I know for myself I found it more than usually difficult to maintain my strangeness.

Even at the meal I durst scarce unbuckle and scarce lift my eyes to her; and it was no sooner over than I fell again to my civilian, with more seeming abstraction and less understanding than before. Methought, as I read, I could hear my heart strike like an eight-day clock. Hard as I feigned to study, there was still some of my eyesight that spilled beyond the book upon Catriona. She sat on the floor by the side of my great mail, and the chimney lighted her up, and shone and blinked upon her, and made her glow and darken through a wonder of fine hues. Now she would be gazing in the fire, and then again at me: and at that I would be plunged in a terror of myself, and turn the pages of Heineccius like a man looking for the text in church.

Suddenly she called out aloud. "O, why does not my father come?" she cried, and fell at once into a storm of tears.

I leapt up, flung Heineccius fairly in the fire, ran to her side, and cast an arm round her sobbing body.

She put me from her sharply. "You do not love your friend," says she. "I could be so happy too, if you would let me!" And then, "O, what will I have done that you should hate me so?"

"Hate you!" cries I, and held her firm. "You blind lass, can you not see a little in my wretched heart? Do you think when I sit there, reading in that fool-book that I have just burned, and be damned to it, I take ever the least thought of any stricken thing but just yourself? Night after night I could have grat to see you sitting there your lone. And what was I to do? You are here under my honour; would you punish me for that? Is it for that that you would spurn a loving servant?"

At the word, with a small, sudden motion, she clung near to me. I raised her face to mine, I kissed it, and she bowed her brow upon my bosom, clasping me tight. I sat in a mere whirl, like a man drunken. Then I heard her voice sound very small and muffled in my clothes.

"Did you kiss her truly?" she asked.

There went through me so great a heave of surprise that I was all shook with it.

230

"Miss Grant!" I cried, all in a disorder. "Yes, I asked her to kiss me good-bye, the which she did."

"Ah, well!" said she, "you have kissed me too, at all events."

At the strangeness and sweetness of that word I saw where we had fallen; rose, and set her on her feet.

"This will never do," said I. "This will never, never do. O, Catrine, Catrine!" Then there came a pause in which I was debarred from any speaking. And then, "Go away to your bed," said I. "Go away to your bed and leave me."

She turned to obey me like a little child, and the next I knew of it had stopped in the very doorway.

"Good-night, Davie!" said she.

"And O, good-night, my love!" I cried, with a great outbreak of my soul, and caught her to me again, so that it seemed I must have broken her. The next moment I had thrust her from the room, shut-to the door even with violence, and stood alone.

The milk was spilt now, the word was out and the truth told. I had crept like an untrusty man into the poor maid's affections; she was in my hand like any frail, innocent thing to make or mar; and what weapon of defence was left me? It seemed like a symbol that Heineccius, my old protection, was now burned. I repented, yet could not find it in my heart to blame myself for that great failure. It seemed not possible to have resisted the boldness of her innocence or that last temptation of her weeping. And all that I had to excuse me did but make my sin appear the greater—it was upon a nature so defenceless, and with such advantages of the position, that I seemed to have practised.

What was to become of us now? It seemed we could no longer dwell in the one place. But where was I to go? or where she? Without either choice or fault of ours, life had conspired to wall us together in that narrow place. I had a wild thought of marrying out of hand; and the next moment put it from me with revolt. She was a child, she could not tell her own heart; I had surprised her weakness, I must never go on to build on that surprisal; I must keep her not only clear of reproach, but free as she had come to me.

Down I sat before the fire, and reflected, and repented, and beat my brains in vain for any means of escape. About two of the morning, there were three red embers left, and the house and all the city was asleep, when I was aware of a small sound of weeping in the next room. She thought that I slept, the poor soul; she regretted her weakness—and what perhaps (God help her!) she called her forwardness—and in the dead of the night solaced herself with tears. Tender and bitter feelings, love and penitence and pity, struggled in my soul; it seemed I was under bond to heal that weeping.

"O, try to forgive me!" I cried out, "try, try to forgive me. Let us forget it all, let us try if we'll no' can forget it."

There came no answer, but the sobbing ceased. I stood a long while with my hands still clasped as I had spoken; then the cold of the night laid hold upon me with a shudder, and I think my reason reawakened.

"You can make no hand of this, Davie," thinks I. "To bed with you, like a wise lad, and try if you can sleep. Tomorrow you may see your way."

CHAPTER XXV

The Return of James More

I was called on the morrow out of a late and troubled slumber by a knocking on my door, ran to open it, and had almost swooned with the contrariety of my feelings, mostly painful; for on the threshold, in a rough wrap-rascal and an extraordinary big laced hat, there stood James More.

I ought to have been glad perhaps without admixture, for there was a sense in which the man came like an answer to prayer. I had been saying till my head was weary that Catriona and I must separate, and looking till my head ached for any possible means of separation.

Here were the means come to me upon two legs, and joy was the hindmost of my thoughts. It is to be considered, however, that even if the weight of the future were lifted off me by the man's arrival, the present heaved up the more black and menacing; so that, as I first stood before him in my shirt and breeches, I believe I took a leaping step backward like a person shot.

"Ah," said he, "I have found you, Mr. Balfour," and offered me his large, fine hand, the which (recovering at the same time my post in the doorway, as if with some thought of resistance) I took him by doubtfully. "It is a remarkable circumstance how our affairs appear to intermingle," he continued. "I am owing you an apology for an unfortunate intrusion upon yours, which I suffered myself to be entrapped into by my confidence in that false-face, Prestongrange; I think shame to own to you that I was ever trusting to a lawyer."

He shrugged his shoulders with a very French air. "But indeed the man is very plausible," says he. "And now it seems that you have busied yourself handsomely in the matter of my daughter, for whose direction I was remitted to yourself."

"I think, sir," said I, with a very painful air, "that it will be necessary we two should have an explanation."

"There is nothing amiss?" he asked. "My agent, Mr. Sprott——"

"For God's sake moderate your voice!" I cried. "She must not hear till we have had an explanation."

"She is in this place?" cries he.

"That is her chamber-door," said I.

"You are here with her alone?" he asked.

"And who else would I have got to stay with us?" cries I.

I will do him the justice to admit that he turned pale.

"This is very unusual," said he. "This is a very unusual circumstance. You are right, we must hold an explanation."

So saying, he passed me by, and I must own the tall old rogue appeared at that moment extraordinary dignified. He had now, for the first time, the view of my chamber, which I scanned (I may say) with his eyes. A bit of morning sun glinted in by the window-pane, and showed it off; my bed, my mails, and washing-dish, with some disorder of my clothes, and the unlighted chimney, made the only plenishing; no mistake but it looked bare and cold, and the most unsuitable, beggarly place conceivable to harbour a young lady. At the same time came in on my mind the recollection of the clothes that I had bought for her; and I thought this contrast of poverty and prodigality bore an ill appearance.

He looked all about the chamber for a seat, and finding nothing else to his purpose except my bed, took a place upon the side of it; where, after I had closed the door, I could not very well avoid joining him. For however this extraordinary interview might end, it must pass, if possible, without waking Catriona; and the one thing needful was that we should sit close and talk low. But I can scarce picture what a pair we made; he in his great-coat, which the coldness of my chamber made extremely suitable; I shivering in my shirt and breeks; he with very much the air of a judge; and I (whatever I looked) with very much the feelings of a man who has heard the last trumpet.

"Well?" says he.

And "Well," I began, but found myself unable to go further.

"You tell me she is here?" said he again, but now with a spice of impatience that seemed to brace me up.

"She is in this house," said I, "and I knew the circumstance would be called unusual. But you are to consider how very unusual the whole business was from the beginning. Here is a young lady landed on the coast of Europe with two shillings and a penny-halfpenny. She is directed to yon man Sprott in Helvoet. I hear you call him your agent. All I can say is he could do nothing but damn and swear at the mere mention of your name, and I must fee him out of my own pocket even to receive the custody of her effects. You speak of unusual circumstances, Mr. Drummond, if that be the name you prefer. Here was a circumstance, if you like, to which it was barbarity to have exposed her."

"But this is what I cannot understand the least," said James. "My daughter was placed into the charge of some responsible persons, whose names I have forgot."

"Gebbie was the name," said I; "and there is no doubt that Mr. Gebbie should have gone ashore with her at Helvoet. But he did not, Mr. Drummond; and I think you might praise God that I was there to offer in his place."

"I shall have a word to say to Mr. Gebbie before long," said he. "As for yourself, I think it might have occurred that you were somewhat young for such a post."

"But the choice was not between me and somebody else, it was between me and nobody," I cried. "Nobody offered in my place, and I must say I think you show a very small degree of gratitude to me that did."

"I shall wait until I understand my obligation a little more in the particular," says he.

"Indeed, and I think it stares you in the face, then," said I. "Your child was deserted, she was clean flung away in the midst of Europe, with scarce two shillings, and not two words of any language spoken there: I must say, a bonny business! I brought her to this place. I gave her the name and the tenderness due to a sister. All this has not gone without expense, but that I scarce need to hint at. They were services

235

due to the young lady's character which I respect; and I think it would be a bonny business too, if I was to be singing her praises to her father."

"You are a young man," he began.

"So I hear you tell me," said I, with a good deal of heat.

"You are a very young man," he repeated, "or you would have understood the significancy of the step."

"I think you speak very much at your ease," cried I. "What else was I to do? It is a fact I might have hired some decent, poor woman to be a third to us, and I declare I never thought of it until this moment! But where was I to find her, that am a foreigner myself? And let me point out to your observation, Mr. Drummond, that it would have cost me money out of my pocket. For here is just what it comes to, that I had to pay through the nose for your neglect; and there is only the one story to it, just that you were so unloving and so careless as to have lost your daughter."

"He that lives in a glass house should not be casting stones," says he; "and we will finish inquiring into the behaviour of Miss Drummond before we go on to sit in judgment on her father."

"But I will be entrapped into no such attitude," said I. "The character of Miss Drummond is far above inquiry, as her father ought to know. So is mine, and I am telling you that. There are but the two ways of it open. The one is to express your thanks to me as one gentleman to another, and to say no more. The other (if you are so difficult as to be still dissatisfied) is to pay me that which I have expended and be done."

He seemed to soothe me with a hand in the air. "There, there," said he. "You go too fast, you go too fast, Mr. Balfour. It is a good thing that I have learned to be more patient. And I believe you forget that I have yet to see my daughter."

I began to be a little relieved upon this speech and a change in the man's manner that I spied in him as soon as the name of money fell between us.

"I was thinking it would be more fit—if you will excuse the

plainness of my dressing in your presence—that I should go forth and leave you to encounter her alone?" said I.

"What I would have looked for at your hands!" says he; and there was no mistake but what he said it civilly.

I thought this better and better still, and as I began to pull on my hose, recalling the man's impudent mendicancy at Prestongrange's, I determined to pursue what seemed to be my victory.

"If you have any mind to stay some while in Leyden," said I, "this room is very much at your disposal, and I can easy find another for myself: in which way we shall have the least amount of flitting possible, there being only one to change."

"Why, sir," said he, making his bosom big, "I think no shame of a poverty I have come by in the service of my king; I make no secret that my affairs are quite involved: and, for the moment, it would be even impossible for me to undertake a journey."

"Until you have occasion to communicate with your friends," said I, "perhaps it might be convenient for you (as of course it would be honourable to myself) if you were to regard yourself in the light of my guest?"

"Sir," said he, "when an offer is frankly made, I think I honour myself most to imitate that frankness. Your hand, Mr. David; you have the character that I respect the most; you are one of those from whom a gentleman can take a favour and no more words about it. I am an old soldier," he went on, looking rather disgusted-like around my chamber, "and you need not fear I shall prove burthensome. I have ate too often at a dyke-side, drank of the ditch, and had no roof but the rain."

"I should be telling you," said I, "that our breakfasts are sent customarily in about this time of morning. I propose I should go now to the tavern, and bid them add a cover for yourself, and delay the meal the matter of an hour, which will give you an interval to meet your daughter in."

Methought his nostrils wagged at this. "O, an hour?" says he. "That is perhaps superfluous. Half an hour, Mr. David, or say twenty minutes; I shall do very well in that. And by the way," he adds, detaining me by the coat, "what is it you drink in the morning, whether ale or wine?"

"To be frank with you, sir," says I, "I drink nothing else but spare, cold water."

"Tut-tut," says he, "that is fair destruction to the stomach, take an old campaigner's word for it. Our country spirit at home is perhaps the most entirely wholesome; but as that is not come-at-able, Rhenish or a white wine of Burgundy will be next best."

"I shall make it my business to see you are supplied," said I.

"Why, very good," said he, "and we shall make a man of you yet, Mr. David."

By this time I can hardly say that I was minding him at all, beyond an odd thought of the kind of father-in-law that he was like to prove; and all my cares centred about the lass his daughter, to whom I determined to convey some warning of her visitor. I stepped to the door accordingly, and cried through the panels, knocking thereon at the same time: "Miss Drummond, here is your father come at last."

With that I went forth upon my errand, having (by two words) extraordinarily damaged my affairs.

CHAPTER XXVI

The Threesome

Whether or not I was to be so much blamed, or rather perhaps pitied, I must leave others to judge. My shrewdness (of which I have a good deal too) seems not so great with the ladies. No doubt, at the moment when I awakened her, I was thinking a good deal of the effect upon James More; and similarly when I returned and we were all sat down to breakfast, I continued to behave to the young lady with deference and distance; as I still think to have been most wise. Her father had cast doubts upon the innocence of my friendship; and these, it was my first business to allay. But there is a kind of an excuse for Catriona also. We had shared in a scene of some tenderness and passion, and given and received caresses; I had thrust her from me with violence; I had called aloud upon her in the night from the one room to the other: she had passed hours of wakefulness and weeping; and it is not to be supposed I had been absent from her pillow thoughts. Upon the back of this, to be awaked with unaccustomed formality, under the name of Miss Drummond, and to be thenceforth used with a great deal of distance and respect, led her entirely in error on my private sentiments; and she was indeed so incredibly abused as to imagine me repentant and trying to draw off!

The trouble betwixt us seems to have been this: that whereas I (since I had first set eyes on his great hat) thought singly of James More, his return and suspicions, she made so little of these that I may say she scarce remarked them, and all her troubles and doings regarded what had passed between us in the night before. This is partly to be explained by the innocence and boldness of her character; and partly because James More, having sped so ill in his interview with me, or had his mouth closed by my invitation, said no word to her upon the subject. At the breakfast, accordingly, it soon appeared we were at cross-purposes. I had looked to find her in clothes of her own: I found her (as if her father were forgotten) wearing some of the best that I had bought for her, and which she knew (or thought) that I admired her in. I had looked to find her imitate my affectation of distance, and be most precise and formal; instead, I found her flushed and wild-like, with eyes extraordinary bright, and a painful and varying expression, calling me by name with a sort of appeal of tenderness, and referring and deferring to my thoughts and wishes like an anxious or a suspected wife.

But this was not for long. As I beheld her so regardless of her own interests, which I had jeopardised and was now endeavouring to recover, I redoubled my own coldness in the manner of a lesson to the girl. The more she came forward, and further I drew back; the more she betrayed the closeness of our intimacy, the more pointedly civil I became, until even her father (if he had not been so engrossed with eating) might have observed the opposition. In the midst of which, of a sudden, she became wholly changed, and I told myself, with a good deal of relief, that she had took the hint at last.

All day I was at my classes or in quest of my new lodging; and though the hour of our customary walk hung miserably on my hands, I cannot say but I was happy on the whole to find my way cleared, the girl again in proper keeping, the father satisfied, or at least acquiescent, and myself free to prosecute my love with honour. At supper, as at all our meals, it was James More that did the talking. No doubt but he talked well, if any one could have believed him. But I will speak of him presently more at large. The meal at an end, he rose, got his great-coat, and looking (as I thought) at me, observed he had affairs abroad. I took this for a hint that I was to be going also, and got up; whereupon the girl, who had scarce given me greeting at my entrance, turned her eyes on me wide open, with a look that bade me stay. I stood between them like a fish out of water, turning from one to the other; neither seemed to observe me, she gazing on the floor, he buttoning his coat: which vastly swelled my embarrassment. This appearance of indifference argued, upon her side, a good deal of anger very near to burst out. Upon his, I thought it horribly alarming; I made sure there was a tempest brewing there; and considering that to be the chief peril, turned towards him and put myself (so to speak) in the man's hands.

"Can I do anything for *you*, Mr. Drummond?" says I.

He stifled a yawn, which again I thought to be duplicity. "Why, Mr. David," said he, "since you are so obliging as to propose it, you might show me the way to a certain tavern" (of which he gave the name) "where I hope to fall in with some old companions in arms."

There was no more to say, and I got my hat and cloak to bear him company.

"And as for you," says he to his daughter, "you had best go to your bed. I shall be late home, and *Early to bed and early to rise, gars bonny lasses have bright eyes.*"

Whereupon he kissed her with a good deal of tenderness, and ushered me before him from the door. This was so done (I thought on purpose) that it was scarce possible there should be any parting salutation; but I observed she did not look at me, and set it down to terror of James More.

It was some distance to that tavern. He talked all the way of matters which did not interest me the smallest, and at the door dismissed me with empty manners. Thence I walked to my new lodging, where I had not so much as a chimney to hold me warm, and no society but my own thoughts. These were still bright enough; I did not so much as dream that Catriona was turned against me; I thought we were like folk pledged; I thought we had been too near and spoke too warmly to be severed, least of all by what were only steps in a most needful policy. And the chief of my concern was only the kind of father-in-law that I was getting, which was not at all the kind I would have chosen; and the matter of how soon I ought to speak to him, which was a delicate point on several sides. In the first place, when I thought how young I was, I blushed all over, and could almost have found it in my heart to have desisted; only that if once I let them go from Leyden without explanation, I might lose her altogether. And in the second place, there was our very irregular situation to be kept in view, and the rather scant measure of satisfaction I had given James More that morning. I concluded, on the whole, that delay would not hurt anything, yet I could not delay too long neither; and got to my cold bed with a full heart.

The next day, as James More seemed a little on the complaining hand in the matter of my chamber, I offered to have in more furniture; and coming in the afternoon, with porters bringing chairs and tables, found the girl once more left to herself. She greeted me on my admission civilly, but withdrew at once to her own room, of which she shut the door. I made my disposition, and paid and dismissed the men so that she might hear them go, when I supposed she would at once come forth again to speak to me. I waited yet a while, then knocked upon her door.

"Catriona!" said I.

The door was opened so quickly, even before I had the word out, that I thought she must have stood behind it listening. She remained there in the interval quite still; but she had a look that I cannot put a name on, as of one in a bitter trouble.

"Are we not to have our walk today either?" so I faltered.

"I am thanking you," said she. "I will not be caring much to walk now that my father is come home."

"But I think he has gone out himself and left you here alone," said I.

"And do you think that was very kindly said?" she asked.

"It was not unkindly meant," I replied.—"What ails you, Catriona? What have I done to you that you should turn from me like this?"

"I do not turn from you at all," she said, speaking very carefully. "I will ever be grateful to my friend that was good to me; I will ever be his friend in all that I am able. But now that my father James More is come again, there is a difference to be made, and I think there are some things said and done that would be better to be forgotten. But I will ever be your friend in all that I am able, and if that is not all that... if it is not so much ... Not that you will be caring! But I would not have you think of me too hard. It was true what you said to me, that I was too young to be advised, and I am hoping you will remember I was just a child. I would not like to lose your friendship, at all events."

She began this very pale; but before she was done the blood was in her face like scarlet, so that not her words only, but her face and the trembling of her very hands, besought me to be gentle. I saw, for the first time, how very wrong I had done to place the child in that position, where she had been entrapped into a moment's weakness, and now stood before me like a person shamed.

"Miss Drummond," I said, and stuck, and made the same beginning once again, "I wish you could see into my heart," I cried. "You would read there that my respect is undiminished. If that were possible, I should say it was increased. This is but the result of the mistake we made; and had to come; and the less said of it now the better. Of all of our life here, I promise you it shall never pass my lips; I would like to promise you too that I would never think of it, but it's a memory that will be always dear to me. And as for a friend, you have one here that would die for you."

"I am thanking you," said she.

We stood a while silent, and my sorrow for myself began to get the upper hand; for here were all my dreams come to a sad tumble, and my love lost, and myself alone again in the world, as at the beginning.

"Well," said I, "we shall be friends always, that's a certain thing. But this is a kind of a farewell too: it's a kind of a farewell after all; I shall always ken Miss Drummond, but this is a farewell to my Catriona."

I looked at her; I could hardly say I saw her, but she seemed to grow great and brighten in my eyes; and with that I suppose I must have lost my head, for I called out her name again and made a step at her with my hands reached forth.

She shrank back like a person struck, her face flamed; but the blood sprang no faster up into her cheeks than what it flowed back upon my own heart, at sight of it, with penitence and concern. I found no words to excuse myself, but bowed before her very deep, and went my ways out of the house with death in my bosom.

I think it was about five days that followed without any change. I saw her scarce ever but at meals, and then of course in the company of James More. If we were alone, even for a moment, I made it my devoir to behave the more distantly and to multiply respectful attentions, having always in my mind's eye that picture of the girl shrinking and flaming in a blush, and in my heart more pity for her than I could depict in words. I was sorry enough of myself, I need not dwell on that, having fallen all my length and more than all my height in a few seconds; but, indeed, I was near as sorry for the girl, and sorry enough to be scarce angry with her save by fits and starts. Her plea was good: she was but a child; she had been placed in an unfair position; if she had deceived herself and me, it was no more than was to have been looked for.

And, for another thing, she was now very much alone. Her father, when he was by, was rather a caressing parent; but he was very easy led away by his affairs and pleasures, neglected her without compunction or remark, spent his nights in taverns when he had the money, which was more often than I could at all account for; and even in the course of these few days, failed once to come to a meal, which Catriona and I were at last compelled to partake of without him. It was the evening meal, and I left immediately that I had eaten, observing I supposed she would prefer to be alone; to which she agreed, and (strange as it may seem) I quite believed her. Indeed, I thought myself but an eyesore to the girl, and a reminder of a moment's weakness that she now abhorred to think of. So she must sit alone in that room where she and I had been so merry, and in the blink of that chimney whose light had shone upon our many difficult and tender moments. There she must sit alone, and think of herself as of a maid who had most unmaidenly proffered her affections and had the same rejected. And in the meanwhile I would be alone in some other place, and reading myself (whenever I was tempted to be angry) lessons upon human frailty and female delicacy. And altogether I suppose there were never two poor fools made themselves more unhappy in a greater misconception.

As for James, he paid not so much heed to us, or to anything in nature but his pocket, and his belly, and his own prating talk. Before twelve hours were gone he had raised a small loan of me; before thirty, he had asked for a second, and been refused. Money and refusal he took with the same kind of high good-nature. Indeed, he had an outside air of magnanimity that was very well fitted to impose upon a daughter; and the light in which he was constantly presented in his talk, and the man's fine presence and great ways, went together pretty harmoniously. So that a man that had no business with him, and either very little penetration or a furious deal of prejudice, might almost have been taken in. To me, after my first two interviews, he was as plain as print; I saw him to be perfectly selfish, with a perfect innocency in the same; and I would hearken to his swaggering talk (of arms, and "an old soldier," and "a poor Highland gentleman," and "the strength of my country and my friends") as I might to the babbling of a parrot.

The odd thing was that I fancy he believed some part of it himself, or did at times; I think he was so false all through that he scarce knew when he was lying; and for one thing, his moments of dejection must have been wholly genuine. There were times when he would be the most silent, affectionate, clinging creature possible, holding Catriona's hand like a big baby, and begging of me not to leave if I had any love to him; of which, indeed, I had none, but all the more to his daughter. He would press, and indeed beseech us to entertain him with our talk—a thing very difficult in the state of our relations; and again break forth in pitiable regrets for his own land and friends, or into Gaelic singing.

"This is one of the melancholy airs of my native land," he would say. "You may think it strange to see a soldier weep, and indeed it is to make a near friend of you," says he. "But the notes of this singing are in my blood, and the words come out of my heart. And when I mind upon my red mountains, and the wild birds calling there, and the brave streams of water running down, I would scarce think shame to weep before my enemies." Then he would sing again, and translate to me pieces of the song, with a great deal of boggling and much expressed contempt against the English language. "It says here," he would says, "that the sun is gone down, and the battle is at an end, and the brave chiefs are defeated. And it tells here how the stars see them fleeing into strange countries or lying dead on the red mountain; and they will never more shout the call of battle or wash their feet in the streams of the valley. But if you had only some of this language, you would weep also, because the words of it are beyond all expression, and it is mere mockery to tell you it in English."

Well, I thought there was a good deal of mockery in the business, one way and another; and yet, there was some feeling too, for which I hated him, I think, the worst of all. And it used to cut me to the quick to see Catriona so much concerned for the old rogue, and weeping herself to see him weep, when I was sure one half of his distress flowed from his last night's drinking in some tavern. There were times when I was tempted to lend him a round sum, and see the last of him for good; but this would have been to see the last of Catriona as well, for which I was scarcely so prepared; and besides, it went against my conscience to squander my good money on one who was so little of a husband.

CHAPTER XXVII

A Twosome

I believe it was about the fifth day, and I know at least that James was in one of his fits of gloom, when I received three letters. The first was from Alan, offering to visit me in Leyden; the other two were out of Scotland and prompted by the same affair, which was the death of my uncle and my own complete accession to my rights. Rankeillor's was, of course, wholly in the business view; Miss Grant's was like herself, a little more witty than wise, full of blame to me for not having written (though how was I to write with such intelligence?), and of rallying talk about Catriona, which it cut me to the quick to read in her very presence.

For it was of course in my own rooms that I found them, when I came to dinner, so that I was surprised out of my news in the very first moment of reading it. This made a welcome diversion for all three of us, nor could any have foreseen the ill consequences that ensued. It was accident that brought the three letters the same day, and that gave them into my hand in the same room with James More; and of all the events that flowed from that accident, and which I might have prevented if I had held my tongue, the truth is that they were preordained before Agricola came into Scotland or Abraham set out upon his travels.

The first that I opened was naturally Alan's: and what more natural than that I should comment on his design to visit me? but I observed James to sit up with an air of immediate attention.

"Is that not Alan Breck that was suspected of the Appin accident?" he inquired.

I told him, "Ay," it was the same; and he withheld me some time from my other letters, asking of our acquaintance, of Alan's manner of life in France, of which I knew very little, and further of his visit as now proposed.

"All we forfeited folk hang a little together," he explained, "and besides, I know the gentleman: and though his descent is not the thing, and indeed he has no true right to use the name of Stewart, he was very much admired in the day of Drummossie. He did there like a soldier; if some that need not be named had done as well, the upshot need not have been so melancholy to remember. There were two that did their best that day, and it makes a bond between the pair of us," says he.

I could scarce refrain from shooting out my tongue at him, and could almost have wished that Alan had been there to have inquired a little further into that mention of his birth. Though, they tell me, the same was indeed not wholly regular.

Meanwhile, I had opened Miss Grant's, and could not withhold an exclamation.

"Catriona," I cried, forgetting, the first time since her father was arrived, to address her by a handle, "I am come into my kingdom fairly, I am the laird of Shaws indeed—my uncle is dead at last."

She clapped her hands together, leaping from her seat. The next moment it must have come over both of us at once what little cause of joy was left to either, and we stood opposite, staring on each other sadly.

But James showed himself a ready hypocrite. "My daughter," says he, "is this how my cousin learned you to behave? Mr. David has lost a near friend, and we should first condole with him on his bereavement."

"Troth, sir," said I, turning to him in a kind of anger, "I can make no such faces. His death is as blithe news as ever I got."

"It's a good soldier's philosophy," says James. "'Tis the way of flesh, we must all go, all go. And if the gentleman was so far from your favour, why, very well! But we may at least congratulate you on your accession to your estates."

"Nor can I say that either," I replied, with the same heat. "It is a good estate; what matters that to a lone man that has enough already? I had a good revenue before in my frugality; and but for the man's death—which gratifies me, shame to me that must confess it!—I see not how any one is to be bettered by this change."

"Come, come," said he, "you are more affected than you let on, or you would never make yourself out so lonely. Here are three letters; that means three that wish you well; and I could name two more here in this very chamber. I have known you not so very long, but Catriona, when we are alone, is never done with the singing of your praises."

She looked up at him, a little wild at that; and he slid off at once into another matter, the extent of my estate, which (during the most of the dinner time) he continued to dwell upon with interest. But it was to no purpose he dissembled; he had touched the matter with too gross a hand: and I knew what to expect. Dinner was scarce ate when he plainly discovered his designs. He reminded Catriona of an errand, and bid her attend to it. "I do not see you should be gone beyond the hour," he added, "and friend David will be good enough to bear me company till you return." She made haste to obey him without words. I do not know if she understood,—I believe not; but I was completely satisfied, and sat strengthening my mind for what should follow.

The door had scarce closed behind her departure, when the man leaned back in his chair and addressed me with a good affectation of easiness. Only the one thing betrayed him, and that was his face, which suddenly shone all over with fine points of sweat.

"I am rather glad to have a word alone with you," says he, "because in our first interview there was some expressions you misapprehended, and I have long meant to set you right upon. My daughter stands beyond doubt. So do you, and I would make that good with my sword against all gainsayers. But, my dear David, this world is a censorious place—as who should know it better than myself, who have lived ever since the days of my late departed father, God sain him! in a perfect spate of calumnies? We have to face to that; you and me have to consider of that; we have to consider of that." And he wagged his head like a minister in a pulpit.

"To what effect, Mr. Drummond?" said I. "I would be obliged to you if you would approach your point."

"Ay, ay," says he, laughing, "like your character indeed! and what I most admire in it. But the point, my worthy fellow, is sometimes in a kittle bit." He filled a glass of wine. "Though between you and me, that are such fast friends, it need not bother us long. The point, I need scarcely tell you, is my daughter. And the first thing is that I have no thought in my mind of blaming you. In the unfortunate circumstances, what could you do else? 'Deed, and I cannot tell."

"I thank you for that," said I, pretty close upon my guard.

"I have besides studied your character," he went on; "your talents are fair; you seem to have a moderate competence, which does no harm; and, one thing with another, I am very happy to have to announce to you that I have decided on the latter of the two ways open."

"I am afraid I am dull," said I. "What ways are these?"

He bent his brows upon me formidably and uncrossed his legs. "Why, sir," says he, "I think I need scarce describe them to a gentleman of your condition: either that I should cut your throat or that you should marry my daughter."

"You are pleased to be quite plain at last," said I.

"And I believe I have been plain from the beginning!" cries he robustiously. "I am a careful parent, Mr. Balfour; but, I thank God, a patient and deleeberate man. There is many a father, sir, that would have hirsled you at once either to the altar or the field. My esteem for your character——"

"Mr. Drummond," I interrupted, "if you have any esteem for me at all, I will beg of you to moderate your voice. It is quite needless to rowt at a gentleman in the same chamber with yourself, and lending you his best attention."

"Why, very true," says he, with an immediate change. "And you must excuse the agitations of a parent."

"I understand you then," I continued—"for I will take no note of your other alternative, which perhaps it was a pity you let fall—I understand you rather to offer me encouragement in

250

case I should desire to apply for your daughter's hand?"

"It is not possible to express my meaning better," said he, "and I see we shall do well together."

"That remains to be yet seen," said I. "But so much I need make no secret of, that I bear the lady you refer to the most tender affection, and I could not fancy, even in a dream, a better fortune than to get her."

"I was sure of it, I felt certain of you, David," he cried, and reached out his hand to me.

I put it by. "You go too fast, Mr. Drummond," said I. "There are conditions to be made; and there is a difficulty in the path, which I see not entirely how we shall come over. I have told you that, upon my side, there is no objection to the marriage, but I have good reason to believe there will be much on the young lady's."

"This is all beside the mark," says he. "I will engage for her acceptance."

"I think you forget, Mr. Drummond," said I, "that, even in dealing with myself, you have been betrayed into two-three unpalatable expressions. I will have none such employed to the young lady. I am here to speak and think for the two of us; and I give you to understand that I would no more let a wife be forced upon myself than what I would let a husband be forced on the young lady."

He sat and glowered at me like one in doubt and a good deal of temper.

"So that this is to be the way of it," I concluded. "I will marry Miss Drummond, and that blithely, if she is entirely willing. But if there be the least unwillingness, as I have reason to fear— marry her will I never."

"Well, well," said he, "this is a small affair. As soon as she returns I will sound her a bit, and hope to reassure you——"

But I cut in again. "Not a finger of you, Mr. Drummond, or I cry off, and you can seek a husband to your daughter some- where else," said I. "It is I that am to be the only dealer and the only judge. I shall satisfy myself exactly; and none else shall anyways meddle—you the least of all."

"Upon my word, sir!" he exclaimed, "and who are you to be the judge?"

"The bridegroom, I believe," said I.

"This is to quibble," he cried. "You turn your back upon the facts. The girl, my daughter, has no choice left to exercise. Her character is gone."

"And I ask your pardon," said I, "but while this matter lies between her and you and me, that is not so."

"What security have I?" he cried. "Am I to let my daughter's reputation depend upon a chance?"

"You should have thought of all this long ago," said I, "before you were so misguided as to lose her; and not afterwards, when it is quite too late. I refuse to regard myself as any way accountable for your neglect, and I will be browbeat by no man living. My mind is quite made up, and, come what may, I will not depart from it a hair's-breadth. You and me are to sit here in company till her return; upon which, without either word or look from you, she and I are to go forth again to hold our talk. If she can satisfy me that she is willing to this step, I will then make it; and if she cannot, I will not."

He leaped out of his seat like a man stung. "I can spy your manœuvre," he cried; "you would work upon her to refuse!"

"Maybe ay, and maybe no," said I. "That is the way it is to be, whatever."

"And if I refuse?" cries he.

"Then, Mr. Drummond, it will have to come to the throat-cutting," said I.

What with the size of the man, his great length of arm, in which he came near rivalling his father, and his reputed skill at weapons, I did not use this word without some trepidation, to say nothing at all of the circumstance that he was Catriona's father. But I might have spared myself alarms. From the poorness of my lodging—he does not seem to have remarked his daughter's dresses, which were indeed all equally new to him,—and from the face that I had shown myself averse to lend, he had embraced a strong idea of my poverty. The sudden news of my estate convinced him of his error, and he had made but the one bound of it on this fresh venture, to which he was now so wedded, that I believe he would have suffered anything rather than fall to the alternative of fighting.

A little while longer he continued to dispute with me, until I hit upon a word that silenced him.

"If I find you so averse to let me see the lady by herself," said I, "I must suppose you have very good grounds to think me in the right about her unwillingness."

He gabbled some kind of an excuse.

"But all this is very exhausting to both of our tempers," I added, "and I think we would do better to preserve a judicious silence."

The which we did until the girl returned, and I must suppose would have cut a very ridiculous figure had there been any there to view us.

CHAPTER XXVIII

In which I am Left Alone

I opened the door to Catriona and stopped her on the threshold.

"Your father wishes us to take our walk," said I.

She looked at James More, who nodded, and at that, like a trained soldier, she turned to go with me.

We took one of our old ways, where we had gone often together, and been more happy than I can tell of in the past. I came a half a step behind, so that I could watch her unobserved. The knocking of her little shoes upon the way sounded extraordinary pretty and sad; and I thought it a strange moment that I should be so near both ends of it at once, and walk in the midst between two destinies, and could not tell whether I was hearing these steps for the last time, or whether the sound of them was to go in and out with me till death should part us.

She avoided even to look at me, only walked before her, like one who had a guess of what was coming. I saw I must speak soon before my courage was run out, but where to begin I knew not. In this painful situation, when the girl was as good as forced into my arms, and had already besought my forbearance, any excess of pressure must have seemed indecent; yet to avoid it wholly would have a very cold-like appearance. Between these extremes I stood helpless, and could have bit my fingers; so that, when at last I managed to speak at all, it may be said I spoke at random.

"Catriona," said I, "I am in a very painful situation; or rather, so we are both; and I would be a good deal obliged to you if you would promise to let me speak through first of all, and not to interrupt till I have done."

She promised me that simply.

"Well," said I, "this that I have got to say is very difficult, and I know very well I have no right to be saying it. After what passed between the two of us last Friday, I have no manner of right. We have got so ravelled up (and all by my fault) that I know very well the least I could do is just to hold my tongue, which was what I intended fully, and there was nothing further from my thoughts than to have troubled you again. But, my dear, it has become merely necessary, and no way by it. You see, this estate of mine has fallen in, which makes of me rather a better match; and the— the business would not have quite the same ridiculous-like appearance that it would before. Besides which, it's supposed that our affairs have got so much ravelled up (as I was saying) that it would be better to let them be the way they are. In my view, this part of the thing is vastly exaggerate, and if I were you I would not ware two thoughts on it. Only it's right I should mention the same, because there's no doubt it has some influence on James More. Then I think we were none so unhappy when we dwelt together in this town before. I think we did pretty well together. If you would look back, my dear——"

"I will look neither back nor forward," she interrupted. "Tell me the one thing: this is my father's doing?"

"He approves of it," said I. "He approved that I should ask your hand in marriage," and was going on again with somewhat more of an appeal upon her feelings; but she marked me not, and struck into the midst.

"He told you to!" she cried. "It is no sense denying it, you said yourself that there was nothing further from your thoughts. He told you to."

"He spoke of it the first, if that is what you mean," I began.

She was walking ever the faster, and looking fair in front of her; but at this she made a little noise in her head, and I thought she would have run.

"Without which," I went on, "after what you said last Friday, I would never have been so troublesome as make the offer. But when he as good as asked me, what was I to do?"

She stopped and turned round upon me.

"Well, it is refused, at all events," she cried, "and there will be an end of that."

And she began again to walk forward.

"I suppose I could expect no better," said I, "but I think you might try to be a little kind to me for the last end of it. I see not why you should be harsh. I have loved you very well, Catriona— no harm that I should call you so for the last time. I have done the best that I could manage, I am trying the same still, and only vexed that I can do no better. It is a strange thing to me that you can take any pleasure to be hard to me."

"I am not thinking of you," she said, "I am thinking of that man, my father."

"Well, and that way too!" said I. "I can be of use to you that way too; I will have to be. It is very needful, my dear, that we should consult about your father; for the way this talk has gone, an angry man will be James More."

She stopped again. "It is because I am disgraced?" she asked.

"That is what he is thinking," I replied, "but I have told you already to make naught of it."

"It will be all one to me," she cried. "I prefer to be disgraced!"

I did not know very well what to answer, and stood silent.

There seemed to be something working in her bosom after that last cry; presently she broke out, "And what is the meaning of all this? Why is all this shame loundered on my head? How could you dare it, David Balfour?"

"My dear," said I, "what else was I to do?"

"I am not your dear," she said, "and I defy you to be calling me these words."

"I am not thinking of my words," said I. "My heart bleeds for you, Miss Drummond. Whatever I may say, be sure you have my pity in your difficult position. But there is just the one thing that I wish you would bear in view, if it was only long enough to discuss it quietly; for there is going to be a collieshangie when we two get home. Take my word for it, it will need the two of us to make this matter end in peace."

"Ay," said she. There sprang a patch of red in either of her cheeks. "Was he for fighting you?" said she.

"Well, he was that," said I.

She gave a dreadful kind of laugh. "At all events, it is complete!" she cried. And then turning on me: "My father and I are a fine pair," said she, "but I am thanking the good God there will be somebody worse than what we are. I am thanking the good God that he has let me see you so. There will never be the girl made that would not scorn you."

I had borne a good deal pretty patiently, but this was over the mark.

"You have no right to speak to me like that," said I. "What have I done but to be good to you, or try to be? And here is my repayment! O, it is too much."

She kept looking at me with a hateful smile. "Coward!" said she.

"The word in your throat and in your father's!" I cried. "I have dared him this day already in your interest. I will dare him again, the nasty pole-cat; little I care which of us should fall! Come," said I, "back to the house with us; let us be done with it, let me be done with the whole Hieland crew of you! You will see what you think when I am dead."

She shook her head at me with that same smile I could have struck her for.

"O, smile away!" I cried. "I have seen your bonny father smile on the wrong side this day. Not that I mean he was afraid, of course," I added hastily, "but he preferred the other way of it."

"What is this?" she asked.

"When I offered to draw with him," said I.

"You offered to draw upon James More?" she cried.

"And I did so," said I, "and found him backward enough, or how would we be here?"

"There is a meaning upon this," said she. "What is it you are meaning?"

"He was to make you take me," I replied, "and I would not have it. I said you should be free, and I must speak with you alone; little I supposed it would be such a speaking! *And what if I refuse?* says he.—*Then it must come to the throat-cutting,* says I, *for I will no more have a husband forced on that young lady than what I would have a wife forced upon myself.* These were my words, they were a friend's words; bonnily have I been paid for them! Now you have refused me of your own clear free will, and there lives no father in the Highlands, or out of them, that can force on this marriage. I will see that your wishes are respected; I will make the same my business, as I have all through. But I think you might have that decency as to affect some gratitude. 'Deed, and I thought you knew me better! I have not behaved quite well to you, but that was weakness. And to think me a coward, and such a coward as that—O my lass, there was a stab for the last of it!"

"Davie, how would I guess?" she cried. "O, this is a dreadful business! Me and mine"—she gave a kind of wretched cry at the word,—"me and mine are not fit to speak to you. O, I could be kneeling down to you in the street, I could be kissing your hands for your forgiveness!"

"I will keep the kisses I have got from you already," cried I. "I will keep the ones I wanted and that were something worth; I will not be kissed in penitence."

"What can you be thinking of this miserable girl?" says she.

"What I am trying to tell you all this while!" said I, "that you had best leave me alone, whom you can make no more unhappy if you tried, and turn your attention to James More, your father, with whom you are like to have a queer pirn to wind."

"O, that I must be going out into the world alone with such a man!" she cried, and seemed to catch herself in with a great effort. "But trouble yourself no more for that," said she. "He does not know what kind of nature is in my heart. He will pay me dear for this day of it; dear, dear will he pay."

She turned, and began to go home, and I to accompany her. At which she stopped.

"I will be going alone," she said. "It is alone I must be seeing him."

Some little while I raged about the streets, and told myself I was the worst-used lad in Christendom. Anger choked me; it was all very well for me to breathe deep; it seemed there was not air enough about Leyden to supply me, and I thought I would have burst like a man at the bottom of the sea. I stopped and laughed at myself at a street-corner a minute together, laughing out loud, so that a passenger looked at me, which brought me to myself.

"Well," I thought, "I have been a gull and a ninny and a soft Tommy long enough. Time it was done. Here is a good lesson to have nothing to do with that accursed sex, that was the ruin of the man in the beginning, and will be so to the end. God knows I was happy enough before ever I saw her; God knows I can be happy enough again when I have seen the last of her."

That seemed to me the chief affair: to see them go. I dwelled upon the idea fiercely; and presently slipped on, in a kind of malevolence, to consider how very poorly they were like to fare when David Balfour was no longer by to be their milk-cow; at which, to my own very great surprise, the disposition of my mind turned bottom up. I was still angry; I still hated her; and yet I thought I owed it to myself that she should suffer nothing.

This carried me home again at once, where I found the mails drawn out and ready fastened by the door, and the father and daughter with every mark upon them of a recent disagreement. Catriona was like a wooden doll; James More breathed hard, his face was dotted with white spots, and his nose upon one side. As soon as I came in, the girl looked at him with a steady, clear, dark look that might very well have been followed by a blow. It was a hint that was more contemptuous than a command, and I was surprised to see James More accept it. It was plain he had had a master talking-to; and I could see there must be more of the devil in the girl than I had guessed, and more good-humour about the man than I had given him the credit of.

He began, at least, calling me Mr. Balfour, and plainly speaking from a lesson; but he got not very far, for at the first pompous swell of his voice Catriona cut in.

"I will tell you what James More is meaning," said she. "He

means we have come to you, beggar-folk, and have not behaved to you very well, and we are ashamed of our ingratitude and ill-behaviour. Now we are wanting to go away and be forgotten; and my father will have guided his gear so ill, that we cannot even do that unless you will give us some more alms. For that is what we are, at all events, beggar-folk and sorners."

"By your leave, Miss Drummond," said I, "I must speak to your father by myself."

She went into her own room and shut the door, without a word or a look.

"You must excuse her, Mr. Balfour," says James More. "She has no delicacy."

"I am not here to discuss that with you," said I, "but to be quit of you. And to that end I must talk of your position. Now, Mr. Drummond, I have kept the run of your affairs more closely than you bargained for. I know you had money of your own when you were borrowing mine. I know you have had more since you were here in Leyden, though you concealed it even from your daughter."

"I bid you beware. I will stand no more baiting," he broke out. "I am sick of her and you. What kind of a damned trade is this to be a parent! I have had expressions used to me——" There he broke off. "Sir, this is the heart of a soldier and a parent," he went on again, laying his hand on his bosom, "outraged in both characters—and I bid you beware."

"If you would have let me finish," says I, "you would have found I spoke for your advantage."

"My dear friend," he cried, "I know I might have relied upon the generosity of your character."

"Man! will you let me speak?" said I. "The fact is that I cannot win to find out if you are rich or poor. But it is my idea that your means, as they are mysterious in their source, so they are something insufficient in amount; and I do not choose your daughter to be lacking. If I durst speak to herself, you may be certain I would never dream of trusting it to you; because I know you like the back of my hand, and all your blustering talk is that much wind to me. However, I believe in your way you do still care something for your daughter after all; and I must just be doing with that ground of confidence, such as it is."

Whereupon I arranged with him that he was to communicate with me, as to his whereabouts and Catriona's welfare, in consideration of which I was to serve him a small stipend.

He heard the business out with a great deal of eagerness; and when it was done, "My dear fellow, my dear son," he cried out, "this is more like yourself than any of it yet! I will serve you with a soldier's faithfulness——"

"Let me hear no more of it!" says I. "You have got me to that pitch that the bare name of soldier rises on my stomach. Our traffic is settled; I am now going forth and will return in one half-hour, when I expect to find my chambers purged of you."

I gave them good measure of time; it was my one fear that I might see Catriona again, because tears and weakness were ready in my heart, and I cherished my anger like a piece of dignity. Perhaps an hour went by; the sun had gone down, a little wisp of a new moon was following it across a scarlet sunset; already there were stars in the east, and in my chambers, when at last I entered them, the night lay blue. I lit a taper and reviewed the rooms; in the first there remained nothing so much as to awake a memory of those who were gone; but in the second, in a corner of the floor, I spied a little heap that brought my heart into my mouth. She had left behind at her departure all that ever she had of me. It was the blow that I felt sorest, perhaps because it was the last; and I fell upon that pile of clothing and behaved myself more foolish than I care to tell of.

Late in the night, in a strict frost, and my teeth chattering, I came again by some portion of my manhood and considered with myself. The sight of these poor frocks and ribbons, and her shifts, and the clocked stockings, was not to be endured; and if I were to recover any constancy of mind, I saw I must be

261

rid of them ere the morning. It was my first thought to have made a fire and burned them; but my disposition has always been opposed to wastery, for one thing; and for another, to have burned these things that she had worn so close upon her body seemed in the nature of a cruelty. There was a corner cupboard in that chamber; there I determined to bestow them. The which I did, and made it a long business, folding them with very little skill indeed, but the more care; and sometimes dropping them with my tears. All the heart was gone out of me, I was weary as though I had run miles, and sore like one beaten; when, as I was folding a kerchief that she wore often at her neck, I observed there was a corner neatly cut from it. It was a kerchief of a very pretty hue, on which I had frequently remarked; and once that she had it on I remembered telling her (by way of a banter) that she wore my colours. There came a glow of hope and like a tide of sweetness in my bosom; and the next moment I was plunged back in a fresh despair. For there was the corner crumpled in a knot, and cast down by itself in another part of the floor.

But when I argued with myself I grew more hopeful. She had cut that corner off in some childish freak that was manifestly tender; that she had cast it away again was little to be wondered at; and I was inclined to dwell more upon the first than upon the second, and to be more pleased that she had ever conceived the idea of that keepsake, than concerned because she had flung it from her in an hour of natural resentment.

CHAPTER XXIX

We Meet in Dunkirk

Altogether, then, I was scarce so miserable the next days but what I had many hopeful and happy snatches; threw myself with a good deal of constancy upon my studies; and made out to endure the time till Alan should arrive, or I might hear word of Catriona by the means of James More. I had altogether three letters in the time of our separation. One was to announce their arrival in the town of Dunkirk in France, from which place James shortly after started alone upon a private mission. This was to England and to see Lord Holderness; and it has always been a bitter thought that my good money helped to pay the charges of the same. But he has need of a long spoon who sups with the deil, or James More either. During this absence, the time was to fall due for another letter; and as the letter was the condition of his stipend, he had been so careful as to prepare it beforehand and leave it with Catriona to be despatched. The fact of our correspondence aroused her suspicions, and he was no sooner gone than she had burst the seal. What I received began accordingly in the writing of James More:—

"My dear Sir,—Your esteemed favour came to hand duly, and I have to acknowledge the enclosure according to agreement. It shall be all faithfully expended on my daughter, who is well, and desires to be remembered to her dear friend. I find her in rather a melancholy disposition, but trust in the mercy of God to see her re-established. Our manner of life is very much alone, but we solace ourselves with the melancholy tunes of our native mountains, and by walking upon the margin of the sea that lies next to Scotland. It was better days with me when I lay with five wounds upon my body on the field of Gladsmuir. I have found employment here in the *haras* of a French nobleman, where my experience is valued. But, my dear Sir, the wages are so exceedingly unsuitable that I would be ashamed to mention them, which makes your remittances the more necessary to my daughter's comfort, though I daresay the sight of old friends would be still better.

"My dear Sir,
"Your affectionate, obedient servant,
"James Macgregor Drummond."

Below it began again in the hand of Catriona:—

"Do not be believing him, it is all lies together.
"C. M. D."

Not only did she add this postscript, but I think she must have come near suppressing the letter; for it came long after date, and was closely followed by the third.

In the time betwixt them Alan had arrived, and made another life to me with his merry conversation; I had been presented to his cousin of the Scots-Dutch, a man that drank more than I could have thought possible, and was not otherwise of interest; I had been entertained to many jovial dinners, and given some myself, all with no great change upon my sorrow; and we two (by which I mean Alan and myself, and not at all the cousin) had discussed a good deal the nature of my relations with James More and his daughter. I was naturally diffident to give particulars; and this disposition was not anyway lessened by the nature of Alan's commentary upon those I gave.

"I canna make head nor tail of it," he would say, "but it sticks in my mind ye've made a gowk of yourself. There's few people that has had more experience than Alan Breck; and I can never call to mind to have heard tell of a lassie like this one of yours. The way that you tell it, the thing's fair impossible. Ye must have made a terrible hash of the business, David."

"There are whiles that I am of the same mind," said I.

"The strange thing is that ye seem to have a kind of a fancy for her too!" said Alan.

"The biggest kind, Alan," said I, "and I think I'll take it to my grave with me."

"Well, ye beat me, whatever!" he would conclude.

I showed him the letter with Catriona's postscript. "And here again!" he cried. "Impossible to deny a kind of decency to this Catriona, and sense forbye! As for James More, the man's as boss as a drum; he's just a wame and a wheen words; though I'll can never deny that he fought reasonably well at Gladsmuir, and it's true what he says here about the five wounds. But the loss of him is that the man's boss."

"Ye see, Alan," said I, "it goes against the grain with me to leave the maid in such poor hands."

"Ye couldna weel find poorer," he admitted. "But what are ye to do with it? It's this way about a man and a woman, ye see, Davie: the weemenfolk have got no kind of reason to them. Either they like the man, and then a' goes fine; or else they just detest him, and ye may spare your breath—ye can do naething. There's just the two sets of them—them that would sell their coats for ye, and them that never look the road ye're on. That's a' that there is to women; and you seem to be such a gomeril that ye canna tell the tane frae the tither."

"Well, and I'm afraid that's true for me," said I.

"And yet there's naething easier!" cried Alan. "I could easy learn ye the science of the thing; but ye seem to me to be born blind, and there's where the deefficulty comes in!"

"And can *you* no' help me?" I asked, "you that's so clever at the trade?"

"Ye see, David, I wasna here," said he. "I'm like a field officer that has naebody but blind men for scouts and *éclaireurs;* and what would he ken? But it sticks in my mind that ye'll have made some kind of bauchle; and if I was you, I would have a try at her again."

"Would ye so, man Alan?" said I.

"I would e'en't," says he.

The third letter came to my hand while we were deep in some such talk; and it will be seen how pat it fell to the occasion. James professed to be in some concern upon his daughter's health, which I believe was never better; abounded in kind expressions to myself; and finally proposed that I should visit them at Dunkirk.

"You will now be enjoying the society of my old comrade, Mr. Stewart," he wrote. "Why not accompany him so far in his return to France? I have something very particular for Mr. Stewart's ear; and, at any rate, I would be pleased to meet in with an old fellow-soldier and one so mettle as himself. As for you, my dear sir, my daughter and I would be proud to receive our benefactor, whom we regard as a brother and a son. The French nobleman has proved a person of the most filthy avarice of character, and I have been necessitate to leave the *haras*. You will find us, in consequence, a little poorly lodged in the *auberge* of a man Bazin on the dunes; but the situation is caller, and I make no doubt but we might spend some very pleasant days, when Mr. Stewart and I could recall our services, and you and my daughter divert yourselves in a manner more befitting your age.

I beg at least that Mr. Stewart would come here; my business with him opens a very wide door."

"What does the man want with me?" cried Alan when he had read. "What he wants with you is clear enough—it's siller. But what can he want with Alan Breck?"

"O, it'll be just an excuse," said I. "He is still after this marriage, which I wish from my heart that we could bring about. And he asks you because he thinks I would be less likely to come wanting you."

"Well, I wish that I kennt," says Alan. "Him and me were never onyways pack; we used to girn at ither like a pair of pipers. 'Something for my ear,' quo' he! I'll maybe have something for his hinder-end before we're through with it. Dod, I'm thinking it would be a kind of a divertisement to gang and see what he'll be after! Forbye that I could see your lassie then. What say ye, Davie? Will ye ride with Alan?"

You may be sure I was not backward, and, Alan's furlough

running towards an end, we set forth presently upon this joint adventure.

It was near dark of a January day when we rode at last into the town of Dunkirk. We left our horses at the post, and found a guide to Bazin's inn, which lay beyond the walls. Night was quite fallen, so that we were the last to leave that fortress, and heard the doors of it close behind us as we passed the bridge. On the other side there lay a lighted suburb, which we thridded for a while, then turned into a dark lane, and presently found ourselves wading in the night among deep sand where we could hear a bullering of the sea. We travelled in this fashion for some while, following our conductor mostly by the sound of his voice; and I had begun to think he was perhaps misleading us, when we came to the top of a small brae, and there appeared out of the darkness a dim light in a window.

"*Voilà l'auberge à Bazin*," says the guide.

Alan smacked his lips. "An unco lonely bit," said he, and I thought by his tone he was not wholly pleased.

A little after, and we stood in the lower story of that house, which was all in the one apartment, with a stair leading to the chambers at the side, benches and tables by the wall, the cooking fire at the one end of it, and shelves of bottles and the cellar-trap at the other. Here Bazin, who was an ill-looking, big man, told us the Scottish gentleman was gone abroad he knew not where, but the young lady was above, and he would call her down to us.

I took from my breast that kerchief wanting the corner, and knotted it about my throat. I could hear my heart go; and, Alan patting me on the shoulder with some of his laughable expressions, I could scarce refrain from a sharp word. But the time was not long to wait. I heard her step pass overhead, and saw her on the stair. This she descended very quietly, and greeted me with a pale face and a certain seeming of earnestness, or uneasiness, in her manner that extremely dashed me.

"My father, James More, will be here soon. He will be very pleased to see you," she said. And then of a sudden her face flamed, her eyes lightened, the speech stopped upon her lips; and I made sure she had observed the kerchief. It was only for a breath that she was discomposed; but methought it was with a new animation that she turned to welcome Alan. "And you will be his friend Alan Breck?" she cried. "Many is the dozen times I will have heard him tell of you; and I love you already for all your bravery and goodness."

"Well, well," says Alan, holding her hand in his and viewing, "and so this is the young lady at the last of it! David, you're an awful poor hand of a description."

I do not know that ever I heard him speak so straight to people's hearts; the sound of his voice was like song.

"What? will he have been describing me?" she cried.

"Little else of it since I ever came out of France!" says he, "forbye a bit of a speciment one night in Scotland in a shaw of wood by Silvermills. But cheer up, my dear! ye're bonnier than what he said. And now there's one thing sure: you and me are to be a pair of friends. I'm a kind of a henchman to Davie here; I'm like a tyke at his heels: and whatever he cares for, I've got to care for too—and by the holy airn! they've got to care for me! So now you can see what way you stand with Alan Breck, and ye'll find ye'll hardly lose on the transaction. He's no' very bonny, my dear, but he's leal to them he loves."

"I thank you with my heart for your good words," said she. "I have that honour for a brave, honest man that I cannot find any to be answering with."

Using travellers' freedom, we spared to wait for James More, and sat down to meat, we threesome. Alan had Catriona sit by him and wait upon his wants: he made her drink first out of his glass, he surrounded her with continual kind gallantries, and yet never gave me the most small occasion to be jealous; and he kept the talk so much in his own hand, and that in so merry a note, that neither she nor I remembered to be embarrassed. If any had seen us there, it must have been supposed that Alan was the old friend and I the stranger. Indeed, I had often cause to love and to admire the man, but I never loved or admired him better than that night; and I could not help remarking to myself (what I was sometimes rather in danger of forgetting) that he had not only much experience of life, but in his own way a great deal of natural ability besides. As for Catriona, she seemed quite carried away; her laugh was like a peal of bells, her face gay as a May morning; and I own, although I was very well pleased, yet I was a little sad also, and thought myself a dull, stockish character in comparison of my friend, and very unfit to come into a young maid's life, and perhaps ding down her gaiety.

But if that was like to be my part, I found at least that I was not alone in it; for, James More returning suddenly, the girl was changed into a piece of stone. Through the rest of that evening, until she made an excuse and slipped to bed, I kept an eye upon her without cease: and I can bear testimony that she never smiled, scarce spoke, and looked mostly on the board in front of her. So that I really marvelled to see so much devotion (as it used to be) changed into the very sickness of hate.

Of James More it is unnecessary to say much; you know the man already, what there was to know of him; and I am weary of writing out his lies. Enough that he drank a great deal, and told us very little that was to any possible purpose. As for the business with Alan, that was to be reserved for the morrow and his private hearing.

It was the more easy to be put off, because Alan and I were pretty weary with our day's ride, and sat not very late after Catriona.

We were soon alone in a chamber where we were to make shift with a single bed. Alan looked on me with a queer smile.

"Ye muckle ass!" said he.

"What do ye mean by that?" I cried.

"Mean? What do I mean? It's extraordinar, David man," says he, "that you should be so mortal stupit."

Again I begged him to speak out.

"Well, it's this of it," said he. "I told ye there were the two kinds of women—them that would sell their shifts for ye, and the others. Just you try for yoursel', my bonny man.—But what's that neepkin at your craig?"

I told him.

"I thocht it was something thereabout," said he.

Nor would he say another word, though I besieged him long with importunities.

CHAPTER XXX

The Letter from the Ship

Daylight showed us how solitary the inn stood. It was plainly hard upon the sea, yet out of all view of it, and beset on every side with scabbit hills of sand. There was, indeed, only one thing in the nature of a prospect, where there stood out over a brae the two sails of a windmill, like an ass's ears, but with the ass quite hidden. It was strange (after the wind rose, for at first it was dead calm) to see the turning and following of each other of these great sails behind the hillock. Scarce any road came by there; but a number of footways travelled among the bents in all directions up to Mr. Bazin's door. The truth is, he was a man of many trades, not any one of them honest, and the position of his inn was the best of his livelihood. Smugglers frequented it; political agents and forfeited persons bound across the water came there to await their passages; and I daresay there was worse behind, for a whole family might have been butchered in that house and nobody the wiser.

I slept little and ill. Long ere it was day, I had slipped from beside my bedfellow, and was warming myself at the fire or walking to and fro before the door. Dawn broke mighty sullen; but a little after sprang up a wind out of the west, which burst the clouds, let through the sun, and set the mill to the turning. There was something of spring in the sunshine, or else it was in my heart; and the appearing of the great sails one after another from behind the hill diverted me extremely. At times I could hear a creak of the machinery; and by half-past eight of the day Catriona began to sing in the house. At this I would have cast my hat in the air; and I thought this dreary, desert place was like a paradise.

For all which, as the day drew on and nobody came near, I began to be aware of an uneasiness that I could scarce explain. It seemed there was trouble afoot; the sails of the windmill, as they came up and went down over the hill, were like persons

271

spying; and, outside of all fancy, it was surely a strange neighbourhood and house for a young lady to be brought to dwell in.

At breakfast, which we took late, it was manifest that James More was in some danger or perplexity; manifest that Alan was alive to the same, and watched him close; and this appearance of duplicity upon the one side, and vigilance upon the other, held me on live coals. The meal was no sooner over than James seemed to come to a resolve, and began to make apologies. He had an appointment of a private nature in the town (it was with the French nobleman, he told me), and we would please excuse him till about noon. Meanwhile, he carried his daughter aside to the far end of the room, where he seemed to speak rather earnestly and she to listen without much inclination.

"I am caring less and less about this man James," said Alan. "There's something no' right with the man James, and I wouldna wonder but what Alan Breck would give an eye to him this day. I would like fine to see yon French nobleman, Davie; and I daresay you could find an employ to yoursel', and that would be to speir at the lassie for some news of your affair. Just tell it to her plainly—tell her ye're a muckle ass at the off-set; and then, if I were you, and ye could do it naitural, I would just mint to her I was in some kind of a danger; a' weemenfolk likes that."

"I canna lee, Alan, I canna do it naitural," says I, mocking him.

"The more fool you!" says he. "Then ye'll can tell her that I recommended it; that'll set her to the laughing; and I wouldna wonder but what that was the next best. But see to the pair of them! If I didna feel just sure of the lassie, and that she was awful pleased and chief with Alan, I would think there was some kind of hocus-pocus about yon."

"And is she so pleased with ye, then, Alan?" I asked.

"She thinks a heap of me," says he. "And I'm no' like you: I'm one that can tell. That she does—she thinks a heap of Alan. And troth! I'm thinking a good deal of him mysel'; and with your permission, Shaws, I'll be getting a wee yont amang the bents, so that I can see what way James goes."

One after another went, till I was left alone beside the breakfast-table; James to Dunkirk, Alan dogging him, Catriona up the stairs to her own chamber. I could very well understand how she should avoid to be alone with me; yet was none the better pleased with it for that, and bent my mind to entrap her to an interview before the men returned. Upon the whole, the best appeared to me to do like Alan. If I was out of view among the sandhills, the fine morning would decoy her forth; and once I had her in the open, I could please myself.

No sooner said than done; nor was I long under the bield of a hillock before she appeared at the inn-door, looked here and there, and (seeing nobody) set out by a path that led directly seaward, and by which I followed her. I was in no haste to make my presence known; the farther she went I made sure of the longer hearing to my suit; and the ground being all sandy it was easy to follow her unheard. The path rose and came at last to the head of a knowe. Thence I had a picture for the first time of what a desolate wilderness that inn stood hidden in; where was no man to be seen, nor any house of man, except just Bazin's and the windmill. Only a little farther on, the sea appeared and two or three ships upon it, pretty as a drawing. One of these was extremely close in to be so great a vessel; and I was aware of a shock of new suspicion, when I recognised the trim of the *Seahorse*. What should an English ship be doing so near in to France? Why was Alan brought into her neighbourhood, and that in a place so far from any hope of rescue? and was it by accident, or by design, that the daughter of James More should walk that day to the seaside?

Presently I came forth behind her in the front of the sandhills and above the beach. It was here long and solitary; with a man-o'-war's boat drawn up about the middle of the prospect, and an officer in charge and pacing the sands like one who waited. I sat immediately down where the rough grass a good deal covered me, and looked for what should follow. Catriona went straight to the boat; the officer met her with civilities; they had ten words together; I saw a letter changing hands; and there was Catriona returning. At the same time, as if this were all her business on the Continent, the boat shoved off and was headed for the *Seahorse*. But I observed the officer to remain behind and disappear among the bents.

I liked the business little; and, the more I considered of it, liked it less. Was it Alan the officer was seeking? or Catriona? She drew near with her head down, looking constantly on the sand, and made so tender a picture that I could not bear to doubt her innocence. The next, she raised her face and recognised me; seemed to hesitate, and then came on again, but more slowly, and I thought with a changed colour. And at that thought, all else that was upon my bosom—fears, suspicions, the care of my friend's life—was clean swallowed up; and I rose to my feet and stood waiting her in a drunkenness of hope.

I gave her "good-morning" as she came up, which she returned with a good deal of composure.

"Will you forgive my having followed you?" said I.

"I know you are always meaning kindly," she replied; and then, with a little outburst, "but why will you be sending money to that man? It must not be."

"I never sent it for him," said I, "but for you, as you know well."

"And you have no right to be sending it to either one of us," said she. "David, it is not right."

"It is not, it is all wrong," said I; "and I pray God He will help this dull fellow (if it be at all possible) to make it better. Catriona, this is no kind of life for you to lead; and I ask your pardon for the word, but yon man is no fit father to take care of you."

"Do not be speaking of him, even!" was her cry.

"And I need speak of him no more; it is not of him that I am thinking—O, be sure of that!" says I. "I think of the one thing. I have been alone now this long time in Leyden; and when I was by way of at my studies, still I was thinking of that. Next Alan came, and I went among soldier-men to their big dinners; and still I had the same thought. And it was the same before, when I had her there beside me. Catriona, do you see this napkin at my throat? You cut a corner from it once and then cast it from you. They're *your* colours now; I wear them in my heart. My dear, I cannot be wanting you. O, try to put up with me!"

I stepped before her so as to intercept her walking on.

"Try to put up with me," I was saying, "try and bear with me a little."

Still she had never the word, and a fear began to rise in me like a fear of death.

"Catriona," I cried, gazing on her hard, "is it a mistake again? Am I quite lost?"

She raised her face to me, breathless.

"Do you want me, Davie, truly?" said she, and I scarce could hear her say it.

"I do that," said I. "O, sure you know it—I do that."

"I have nothing left to give or to keep back," said she. "I was all yours from the first day, if you would have had a gift of me!" she said.

This was on the summit of a brae; the place was windy and conspicuous, we were to be seen there even from the English ship; but I kneeled down before her in the sand, and embraced her knees, and burst into that storm of weeping that I thought it must have broken me. All thought was wholly beaten from my mind by the vehemency of my discomposure. I knew not where I was, I had forgot why I was happy; only I knew she stooped, and I felt her cherish me to her face and bosom, and heard her words out of a whirl.

"Davie," she was saying, "O, Davie, is this what you think of me? Is it so that you were caring for poor me? O, Davie, Davie!"

With that she wept also, and our tears were commingled in a perfect gladness.

It might have been ten in the day before I came to a clear sense of what a mercy had befallen me; and sitting over against her, with her hands in mine, gazed in her face, and laughed out loud for pleasure like a child, and called her foolish and kind names. I have never seen the place that looked so pretty as these bents by Dunkirk; and the windmill sails, as they bobbed over the knowe, were like a tune of music.

I know not how much longer we might have continued to forget all else besides ourselves, had I not chanced upon a reference to her father, which brought us to reality.

"My little friend," I was calling her again and again, rejoicing to summon up the past by the sound of it, and to gaze across on her, and to be a little distant—"My little friend, now you are mine altogether; mine for good, my little friend; and that man's no longer at all."

There came a sudden whiteness in her face, she plucked her hands from mine.

"Davie, take me away from him!" she cried. "There's something wrong; he's not true. There will be something wrong; I have a dreadful terror here at my heart. What will he be wanting at all events with that King's ship? What will this word be saying?" And she held the letter forth. "My mind misgives me, it will be some ill to Alan. Open it, Davie—open it and see."

I took it, and looked at it, and shook my head.

"No," said I, "it goes against me, I cannot open a man's letter."

"Not to save your friend?" she cried.

"I canna tell," said I. "I think not. If I was only sure!"

"And you have but to break the seal!" said she.

"I know it," said I, "but the thing goes against me."

"Give it here," said she, "and I will open it myself."

"Nor you neither," said I. "You least of all. It concerns your father, and his honour, dear, which we are both misdoubting. No question but the place is dangerous-like, and the English ship being here, and your father having word from it, and yon officer that stayed ashore! He would not be alone either; there must be more along with him; I daresay we are spied upon this minute. Ay, no doubt, the letter should be opened; but somehow, not by you nor me."

I was about thus far with it, and my spirit very much

overcome with a sense of danger and hidden enemies, when I spied Alan, come back again from following James, and walking by himself among the sandhills. He was in his soldier's coat, of course, and mighty fine; but I could not avoid to shudder when I thought how little that jacket would avail him, if he were once caught and flung in a skiff, and carried on board of the *Seahorse*, a deserter, a rebel, and now a condemned murderer.

"There," said I, "there is the man that has the best right to open it: or not, as he thinks fit."

With which I called upon his name, and we both stood up to be a mark for him.

"If it is so—if it be more disgrace—will you can bear it?" she asked, looking upon me with a burning eye.

"I was asked something of the same question when I had seen you but the once," said I. "What do you think I answered? That if I liked you as I thought I did—and O, but I like you better!—I would marry you at his gallows' foot."

The blood rose in her face; she came close up and pressed upon me, holding my hand: and it was so that we awaited Alan.

He came with one of his queer smiles. "What was I telling ye, David?" says he.

"There is a time for all things, Alan," said I, "and this time is serious. How have you sped? You can speak out plain before this friend of ours."

"I have been upon a fool's errand," said he.

"I doubt we have done better than you, then," said I; "and, at least, here is a great deal of matter that you must judge of. Do you see that?" I went on, pointing to the ship. "That is the *Seahorse*, Captain Palliser."

"I should ken her, too," says Alan. "I had fyke enough with her when she was stationed in the Forth. But what ails the man to come so close?"

"I will tell you why he came there first," said I. "It was to bring this letter to James More. Why he stops here now that it's delivered, what it's likely to be about, why there's an officer hiding in the bents, and whether or not it's probable that he's alone—I would rather you considered for yourself."

"A letter to James More?" said he.

"The same," said I.

"Well, and I can tell ye more than that," said Alan. "For last night, when you were fast asleep, I heard the man colloguing with some one in the French, and then the door of that inn to be opened and shut."

"Alan!" cried I, "you slept all night, and I am here to prove it."

"Ay, but I would never trust Alan whether he was asleep or waking!" says he. "But the business looks bad. Let's see the letter."

I gave it him.

"Catriona," said he, "ye'll have to excuse me, my dear; but there's nothing less than my fine bones upon the cast of it, and I'll have to break this seal."

"It is my wish," said Catriona.

He opened it, glanced it through, and flung his hand in the air.

"The stinking brock!" says he, and crammed the paper in his pocket. "Here, let's get our things thegither. This place is fair death to me." And he began to walk towards the inn.

It was Catriona that spoke first. "He has sold you?" she asked.

"Sold me, my dear," said Alan. "But thanks to you and Davie, I'll can jink him yet. Just let me win upon my horse!" he added.

"Catriona must come with us," said I. "She can have no more traffic with that man. She and I are to be married." At which she pressed my hand to her side.

"Are ye there with it?" says Alan, looking back. "The best day's work that ever either of ye did yet! And I'm bound to say, my dawtie, ye make a real bonny couple."

The way that he was following brought us close in by the windmill, where I was aware of a man in seaman's trousers, who seemed to be spying from behind it. Only, of course, we took him in the rear.

"See, Alan!" said I.

"Wheesht!" said he, "this is my affairs."

The man was, no doubt, a little deafened by the clattering of the mill, and we got up close before he noticed. Then he turned, and we saw he was a big fellow with a mahogany face.

"I think, sir," says Alan, "that you speak the English?"

"*Non, monsieur,*" says he, with an incredible bad accent.

"*Non, monsieur,*" cries Alan, mocking him. "Is that how they learn you French on the *Seahorse?* Ye muckle, gutsey hash, here's a Scots boot to your English hurdies!"

And bounding on him before he could escape, he dealt the man a kick that laid him on his nose. Then he stood, with a savage smile, and watched him scramble to his feet and scamper off into the sandhills.

"But it's high time I was clear of these empty bents!" said Alan; and continued his way at top speed, and we still following, to the back-door of Bazin's inn.

It chanced that as we entered by the one door we came face to face with James More entering by the other.

"Here!" said I to Catriona, "quick! upstairs with you and make your packets; this is no fit scene for you."

In the meanwhile James and Alan had met in the midst of the long room. She passed them close by to reach the stairs; and after she was some way up I saw her turn and glance at them again, though without pausing. Indeed, they were worth looking at. Alan wore as they met one of his best appearances of courtesy and friendliness, yet with something eminently warlike, so that James smelled danger off the man, as folk smell fire in a house, and stood prepared for accidents.

Time pressed. Alan's situation in that solitary place, and his enemies about him, might have daunted Cæsar. It made no change in him; and it was in his old spirit of mockery and daffing that he began the interview.

"A braw good day to ye again, Mr. Drummond," said he. "What'll yon business of yours be just about?"

"Why, the thing being private, and rather of a long story," says James, "I think it will keep very well till we have eaten."

"I'm none so sure of that," said Alan. "It sticks in my mind it's either now or never; for the fact is me and Mr. Balfour here have gotten a line, and we're thinking of the road."

I saw a little surprise in James's eye; but he held himself stoutly.

"I have but the one word to say to cure you of that," said he, "and that is the name of my business."

"Say it, then," says Alan. "Hout! wha minds for Davie?"

"It is a matter that would make us both rich men," said James.

"Do ye tell me that?" cries Alan.

"I do, sir," said James. "The plain fact is that it is Cluny's Treasure."

"No!" cried Alan. "Have ye got word of it?"

"I ken the place, Mr. Stewart, and can take you there," said James.

"This crowns all!" says Alan. "Well, and I'm glad I came to Dunkirk. And so this was your business, was it? Halvers, I'm thinking?"

"That is the business, sir," says James.

"Well, well," says Alan; and then in the same tone of childlike interest, "it has naething to do with the *Seahorse*, then?" he asked.

"With what?" says James.

"Or the lad that I have just kicked the bottom of behind yon windmill?" pursued Alan. "Hut, man! have done with your lees! I have Palliser's letter here in my pouch.—You're by with it, James More. You can never show your face again with dacent folk."

James was taken all aback with it. He stood a second, motionless and white, then swelled with the living anger.

"Do you talk to me, you bastard?" he roared out.

"Ye glee'd swine!" cried Alan, and hit him a sounding buffet in the mouth, and the next wink of time their blades clashed together.

At the first sound of the bare steel I instinctively leaped back from the collision. The next I saw, James parried a thrust so

nearly that I thought him killed; and it lowed up in my mind
that this was the girl's father, and in a manner almost my own,
and I drew and ran in to sever them.

"Keep back, Davie! Are ye daft? Damn ye, keep back!" roared
Alan. "Your blood be on your ain heid then!"

I beat their blades down twice. I was knocked reeling against
the wall; I was back again betwixt them. They took no heed of
me, thrusting at each other like two furies. I can never think
how I avoided being stabbed myself or stabbing one of these
two Rodomonts, and the whole business turned about me like
a piece of a dream; in the midst of which I heard a great cry
from the stair, and Catriona sprang before her father. In the
same moment the point of my sword encountered something
yielding. It came back to me reddened. I saw the blood flow on
the girl's kerchief, and stood sick.

"Will you be killing him before my eyes, and me his daughter
after all?" she cried.

"My dear, I have done with him," said Alan, and went and sat
on a table, with his arms crossed and the sword naked in his
hand.

A while she stood before the man, panting, with big eyes,
then swung suddenly about and faced him.

"Begone!" was her word, "take your shame out of my sight;
leave me with clean folk. I am a daughter of Alpin! Shame of
the sons of Alpin, begone!"

It was said with so much passion as awoke me from the
horror of my own bloodied sword. The two stood facing, she
with the red stain on her kerchief, he white as a rag. I knew him
well enough—I knew it must have pierced him in the quick
place of his soul; but he betook himself to a bravado air.

"Why," says he, sheathing his sword, though still with a bright
eye on Alan, "if this brawl is over I will but get my
portmanteau——"

"There goes no pockmantie out of this place except with
me!" says Alan.

"Sir!" cries James.

281

"James More," says Alan, "this lady daughter of yours is to marry my friend Davie, upon the which account I let you pack with a hale carcase. But take you my advice of it and get that carcase out of harm's way or ower late. Little as you suppose it, there are leemits to my temper."

"Be damned, sir, but my money's there!" said James.

"I'm vexed about that too," says Alan, with his funny face, "but now, ye see, it's mine's." And then with more gravity, "Be you advised, James More, you leave this house."

James seemed to cast about for a moment in his mind; but it's to be thought he had enough of Alan's swordsmanship, for he suddenly put off his hat to us and (with a face like one of the damned) bade us farewell in a series.

With which he was gone.

At the same time a spell was lifted from me.

"Catriona," I cried, "it was me—it was my sword. O, are ye much hurt?"

"I know it, Davie, I am loving you for the pain of it; it was done defending that bad man, my father. See!" she said, and showed me a bleeding scratch, "see, you have made a man of me now. I will carry a wound like an old soldier."

Joy that she should be so little hurt, and the love of her brave nature, transported me. I embraced her, I kissed the wound.

"And am I to be out of the kissing, me that never lost a chance?" says Alan; and putting me aside and taking Catriona by either shoulder,

"My dear," he said, "you're a true daughter of Alpin. By all accounts, he was a very fine man, and he may weel be proud of you. If ever I was to get married, it's the marrow of you I would be seeking for a mother to my sons. And I bear a king's name and speak the truth."

He said it with a serious heat of admiration that was honey to the girl, and, through her, to me.

It seemed to wipe us clean of all James More's disgraces. And the next moment he was just himself again.

"And now by your leave, my dawties," said he, "this is a' very bonny; but Alan Breck'll be a wee thing nearer to the gallows than he's caring for; and, Dod! I think this is a grand place to be leaving."

The word recalled us to some wisdom. Alan ran upstairs and returned with our saddle-bags and James More's portmanteau; I picked up Catriona's bundle where she had dropped it on the stair; and we were setting forth out of that dangerous house, when Bazin stopped the way with cries and gesticulations.

He had whipped under a table when the swords were drawn, but now he was as bold as a lion. There was his bill to be settled, there was a chair broken, Alan had sat among his dinner things, James More had fled.

"Here," I cried, "pay yourself," and flung him down some Lewie d'ors; for I thought it was no time to be accounting.

He sprang upon that money, and we passed him by, and ran forth into the open.

Upon three sides of the house were seamen hasting and closing in; a little nearer to us James More waved his hat as if to hurry them; and right behind him, like some foolish person holding up its hands, were the sails of the windmill turning.

Alan gave but the lone glance, and laid himself down to run. He carried a great weight in James More's portmanteau; but I think he would as soon have lost his life as cast away that booty which was his revenge; and he ran so that I was distressed to follow him, and marvelled and exulted to see the girl bounding at my side.

As soon as we appeared, they cast off all disguise upon the other side; and the seamen pursued us with shouts and view-hullohs.

We had a start of some two hundred yards, and they were but bandy-legged tarpaulins after all, that could not hope to better us at such an exercise. I suppose they were armed, but did not care to use their pistols on French ground.

And as soon as I perceived that we not only held our advantage, but drew a little away, I began to feel quite easy of the issue. For all which, it was a hot, brisk bit of work, so long as it lasted; Dunkirk was still far off; and when we popped over a knowe, and found a company of the garrison marching on the other side on some manœuvre, I could very well understand the word that Alan had.

He stopped running at once; and mopping at his brow, "They're a real bonny folk, the French nation," says he.

CONCLUSION

No sooner were we safe within the walls of Dunkirk than we held a very necessary council of war on our position. We had taken a daughter from her father at the sword's point; any judge would give her back to him at once, and by all likelihood clap me and Alan into gaol; and though we had an argument upon our side in Captain Palliser's letter, neither Catriona nor I were very keen to be using it in public. Upon all accounts it seemed the most prudent to carry the girl to Paris, to the hands of her own chieftain, Macgregor of Bohaldie, who would be very willing to help his kinswoman on the one hand, and not at all anxious to dishonour James upon the other.

We made but a slow journey of it up, for Catriona was not so good at the riding as the running, and had scarce sat in a saddle since the 'Forty-five. But we made it out at last, reached Paris early of a Sabbath morning, and made all speed, under Alan's guidance, to find Bohaldie. He was finely lodged, and lived in a good style, having a pension on the Scots Fund, as well as private means; greeted Catriona like one of his own house, and seemed altogether very civil and discreet, but not particularly open. We asked of the news of James More. "Poor James!" said he, and shook his head and smiled, so that I thought he knew further than he meant to tell. Then we showed him Palliser's letter, and he drew a long face at that.

"Poor James!" said he again. "Well, there are worse folk than James More too. But this is dreadful bad. Tut, tut, he must have forgot himself entirely! This is a most undesirable letter. But, for all that, gentlemen, I cannot see what we would want to make it public for. It's an ill bird that fouls his own nest, and we are all Scots folk, and all Hieland."

Upon this we were all agreed, save perhaps Alan; and still more upon the question of our marriage, which Bohaldie took in his own hands, as though there had been no such person as James More, and gave Catriona away with very pretty manners and agreeable compliments in French. It was not till all was over, and our healths drunk, that he told us James was in that city, whither he had preceded us some days, and where he now lay sick, and like to die. I thought I saw by my wife's face what way her inclination pointed.

"And let us go see him, then," said I.

"If it is your pleasure," said Catriona. These were early days.

He was lodged in the same quarter of the city with his chief, in a great house upon a corner; and we were guided up to the garret where he lay by the sound of Highland piping. It seemed he had just borrowed a set of them from Bohaldie to amuse his sickness; though he was no such hand as was his brother Rob, he made good music of the kind; and it was strange to observe the French folk crowding on the stairs, and some of them laughing. He lay propped in a pallet. The first look of him I saw he was upon his last business; and, doubtless, this was a strange place for him to die in. But even now I find I can scarce dwell upon his end with patience. Doubtless, Bohaldie had prepared him; he seemed to know we were married, complimented us on the event, and gave us a benediction like a patriarch.

"I have been never understood," said he. "I forgive you both without an afterthought"; after which he spoke for all the world in his old manner, was so obliging as to play us a tune or two upon his pipes, and borrowed a small sum before I left. I could not trace even a hint of shame in any part of his behaviour; but he was great upon forgiveness; it seemed always fresh to him. I think he forgave me every time we met; and when after some four days he passed away in a kind of odour of affectionate sanctity, I could have torn my hair out for exasperation. I had him buried; but what to put upon his tomb was quite beyond me, till at last I considered the date would look best alone.

I thought it wiser to resign all thoughts of Leyden, where we had appeared once as brother and sister, and it would certainly look strange to return in a new character. Scotland would be doing for us; and thither, after I had recovered that which I had left behind, we sailed in a Low Country ship.

And now, Miss Barbara Balfour (to set the ladies first), and Mr. Alan Balfour, younger of Shaws, here is the story brought fairly to an end. A great many of the folk that took a part in it you will find (if you think well) that you have seen and spoken with. Alison Hastie in Limekilns was the lass that rocked your cradle when you were too small to know of it, and walked abroad with you in the policy when you were bigger. That very fine great lady that is Miss Barbara's name-mamma is no other than the same Miss Grant that made so much a fool of David Balfour in the house of the Lord Advocate. And I wonder whether you remember a little, lean, lively gentleman in a scratch-wig and a wrap-rascal, that came to Shaws very late of a dark night, and whom ye were awakened out of your beds and brought down to the dining-hall to be presented to, by the name of Mr. Jamieson? Or has Alan forgotten what he did at Mr. Jamieson's request—a most disloyal act—for which, by the letter of the law, he might be hanged—no less than drinking the king's health *across the water?* These were strange doings in a good Whig house! But Mr. Jamieson is a man privileged, and might set fire to my corn-barn; and the name they know him by now in France is the Chevalier Stewart.

As for Davie and Catriona, I shall watch you pretty close in the next days, and see if you are so bold as to be laughing at papa and mamma. It is true we were not so wise as we might have been, and made a great deal of sorrow out of nothing; but you will find as you grow up that even the artful Miss Barbara, and even the valiant Mr. Alan, will be not so very much wiser than their parents. For the life of man upon this world of ours is a funny business. They talk of the angels weeping; but I think they must more often be holding their sides, as they look on; and there was one thing I determined to do when I began this long story, and that was to tell out everything as it befell.

When *Kidnapped* went to press in the spring of 1886 Stevenson was far from happy to part with David Balfour, the novel's narrator hero. Illness had prevented him bringing the story to a satisfactory conclusion, while lack of funds had made it imperative the manuscript reach its publisher without further ado. Under these circumstances, the author could only hope that the novel's success would justify his inclination to return at some later date to that Whiggish Lowlander, David Balfour of Shaws, and his flamboyant Highland companion, the Jacobite Alan Breck Stewart. He therefore decided to "leave the door open for a sequel", a measure, as he explained to his father, which would save him "butchering a lot of good material to no purpose" (*Letters*, XXIV, p. 190).

In the event, Stevenson's adventure story, set in the Highlands five years after the devastating defeat of the Jacobites at Culloden in 1746, proved immensely popular. By 1887, he had agreed to write a sequel for his publisher, Cassell, though it was another three years before he put pen to paper, and two more before *David Balfour*, the title under which *Catriona* was serialized in the British girls' magazine *Atlanta*, reached its first readers. The plot takes up the thread precisely where *Kidnapped*, according to Henry James, "stops without ending": with David still pledged to save "James of the Glens" from hanging for a murder he did not commit, Alan still in hiding, dependant on David's good offices to help him flee the country, and both heroes still suspected of the assassination in Appin of Colin Campbell of Glenure.

Reactions to the new novel were mixed, and it is hardly being unfair to Stevenson to say that they have remained so ever since. Sidney Colvin and Henry James were enthusiastic, but Stevenson's old friend Frances Sitwell thought he could do better. At the same time, the author's own feelings towards the book appear to have been no less ambivalent than those of his critics. On the one hand he wrote to George Meredith that

Catriona was among his "best work" (*Letters*, XXV. p. 344), and to Frances Sitwell: "I shall never do a better book than Catriona, that is my high-water mark" (*Letters*, XXV, p. 393). To W.H. Low, however, Stevenson revealed himself much less confident of the book's excellence: "for the top flower of a man's life", he wrote, "it seems to me inadequate" (*Letters*, XXV, pp. 378f.).

If *Catriona* has sometimes been found less convincing than *Kidnapped*, its detractors have usually concentrated on two main problems. The first concerns the questionable nature of continuity between the two volumes. There was a small "hitch" here, as Stevenson was the first to acknowledge, for "instead of three hours between the two parts, I fear there have passed three years over David's character" (*Letters*, XXV, p. 351). A similar problem emerged in Catriona itself, for the "early part of it, about D.'s evidence in the Appin case, is more of a story than anything in *Kidnapped*, but there is no doubt there comes a break in the middle, and the tale is practically in two divisions. In the first James More and the M'Gregors, and Catriona, only show; in the second, the Appin case being disposed of, and James Stewart hung, they rule the roast and usurp the interest – should there be any left" (*Letters*, XXV, pp. 160f.).

Secondly, critics have felt consistently uneasy about the portrayal of the novel's two main female characters: Catriona MacGregor Drummond and Barbara Grant. Catriona, according to Stevenson's biographer James Pope-Hennessy, "never gains the reader's sympathy, and very quickly forewent that of her author" (*Robert Louis Stevenson*, London, 1978). Again, Stevenson was quick to recognize the difficulty, writing on 3 June 1892 to Sidney Colvin: "For the duration of the two chapters in which I dealt with Miss Grant, I totally forgot my heroine, and even – but this is a flat secret – tried to win away David" (*Letters*, XXV, p. 202). Barbara Grant is sketched as a figure of tantalising depth and sophistication, one who might have presented Stevenson with a more ambitious project, had she, rather than Catriona, won David's heart.

Though *Kidnapped* is frequently considered the more successful novel, *Catriona*, a love story set against a background of political intrigue, is undoubtedly the more complex work of the two. Stevenson thought it "nearer what I mean than anything I have ever done; nearer what I mean by fiction" (*Letters*, XXV, p. 250), a conviction vindicated by the important role the novel plays in the development of Stevenson's fiction as a whole. In the period between the writing of the two novels, Stevenson's life had changed dramatically: his health had continued to deteriorate; his father had died; he had seen the last of Scotland and his native Edinburgh and travelled to America and the South Seas, finally settling on the island of Samoa. His ambitions in fiction were transformed, too, and it seems doubtful whether he could ever have returned to that exterior, intensely visual landscape which he had once used to such vivid effect in *Kidnapped*. Henry James, while responding with "jubilation" to *Catriona*, remarked on the "starving of the visual sense in that book", a feature Stevenson had begun to recognize as increasingly typical of his literary sensibility: "I *hear* people talking, and I *feel* them acting, and that seems to me to be fiction. My two aims may be described as – 1*st*. War to the adjective. 2*nd*. Death to the optic nerve" (*Letters*, XXV, p. 367).

Certainly, the regions explored in *Catriona* are darker, or less obviously visual, than the colourful, outwardly topographical focus of the earlier book. *Catriona* is a novel of inward antagonisms: Stevenson's old topic of "the war in the members". At the same time, its auditive and lexical range is quite extraordinary, with Black Andie's 'Tale of Tod Lapraik', in Stevenson's own words, "a piece of living Scots" (*Letters*, XXV, p. 295). If the moral and psychological terrain is no less formidable than that of *Kidnapped*, its dangers are less likely to be found lurking at Glencoe or Rannoch Moor than between the Scylla and Charybdis of moral compromise and political corruption, or, in the second part of the book, stifling conventionality and vertiginous sexual passion.

On the horns of the latter dilemma especially, Stevenson, like David, had discovered himself embarrassingly ill-equipped, as he admitted in May 1892 to Sidney Colvin: "with all my romance, I am a realist and prosaist, and a most fanatical lover of plain physical sensations plainly and expressly rendered; hence my perils. To do love in the same spirit as I did (for instance) D. Balfour's fatigue in the heather; my dear sir, there were grossness – ready made! And hence, how to sugar?" (*Letters*, XXV, pp. 189f.) To its author, *Catriona* thus represented something of an excursion into unknown territory; it was, as Jenni Calder has suggested, "a transitional novel", and a necessary step towards "the bolder, more exploratory writing of the fragments he left behind him" (*R.L.S. A Life Study*, Glasgow, 1980, p. 323). In the course of that expedition, Stevenson achieved a study in character that has continued to win the sympathy of generations of readers, not least for the memorable justice it does to the contradictory nature of human personality: "Davie, with his shrewdness and simplicity, and stockishness and charm" (*Letters*, XXV, p. 296). It is for this that the novel will always be read and cherished.

The text used here is that of the Swanston Edition of Stevenson's works (published 1911-12). Minor alterations have been made in a few cases where it has seemed appropriate to bring hyphenation into line with contemporary usage (*to-day*, *river-side*, etc.). Where Stevenson's works have been cited in the notes, Roman numerals indicate the volumes of the Swanston Edition. Words or phrases requiring clarification are explained at their first occurrence in the text, and Scottish words which lie beyond the scope of a good English dictionary are, unless otherwise stated, glossed with the help of the Compact Edition of the *Scottish National Dictionary* (ed. William Grant and David D. Murison, Aberdeen, 1986), and the *Concise Scots Dictionary* (ed. Mairi Robinson, Aberdeen, 1985). Words originally glossed by Stevenson in the text are indicated in the notes by an asterisk*.

p. 7   *Charles Baxter*: Stevenson's close friend since their student days in Edinburgh, Baxter had proved invaluable in managing the author's complicated financial affairs. Baxter was a Writer to the Signet: a member of an ancient society of legal paracititioners in Scotland who were formally clerks to the office of the crown secretary and held the exclusive right to prepare all warrants or charters for sealing with the crown signet.

p. 7   *these ultimate islands*: Stevenson's first voyage to the South Seas was undertaken in 1888 after Scribners, his American publishers, commissioned him to write a travel book. A year later he bought an estate near Apia, Samoa, where his house "Vailima" was later built. In 1890, the Stevenson household took up residence on Samoa, where Stevenson died four years later.

p. 11   *David Balfour*: the title originally given to *Catriona*. Stevenson's own full name was Robert Louis Balfour Stevenson, after his maternal grandfather Lewis Balfour.

p. 11   *crime*: David is referring here to the Appin Murder, the assassination of Colin Campbell of Glenure (1708-52). In *Kidnapped* David is present when Campbell, one of the factors appointed in the aftermath of the 1745 Jacobite Rising to manage the forfeited estates of the Stewarts of Ardshiel, is shot dead. David, together with his companion, Alan Breck Stewart, also nearby at the time, are suspected of the killing and are forced to flee for their lives. The historical murder took place on 14th May 1752. "There has been much writing on the subject, which, if anything, has still further confused the issue. Among the culprits is Robert Louis Stevenson with *Kidnapped* which has been responsible for the nickname of 'The Red Fox' for Glenure, a sobriquet he never bore in real life" (*Collins Encyclopaedia of Scotland*, ed. John and Julia Keay, London, 1994, p. 32).

p. 12   *kenspeckle*: conspicuous*.

293

p. 12 *waired my siller better gates*: spent my silver in a better way.

p. 12 *for all the world like a rabbit-warren*: the backdrop of *Catriona*, especially in the first part of the novel, is almost consistently urban, an appropriate setting, according to Emma Letley, for political intrigue (*Kidnapped and Catriona*, Oxford, 1986, p. xxi). David's description of Edinburgh as a "tall, black city" full of complicated "passages and holes" is reminiscent – though the comparison may be thought anachronistic – of Stevenson's portrait in *Edinburgh: Picturesque Notes* (London, 1879): "In one house, perhaps two-score families herd together; and, perhaps, not one of them is wholly out of reach of want ... In the first room there is a birth, in another a death, in a third a sordid drinking bout, and the detective and the Bible-reader cross upon the stairs." In fact, the *Picturesque Notes* show a period in which the descendents of figures like Prestongrange had already moved to more generous quarters in the New Town, where Stevenson's own childhood was spent. Daniel Defoe's description of the Old Town, published some thirty years before the events of *Catriona*, seems to confirm David's eighteenth century view: "tho' many Cities have more People in them, yet I believe, this may be said with Truth, that in no City in the World so many People live in so little Room as at *Edinburgh*" (*A Tour thro' the Whole Island of Great Britain*, Vol. 2, London, 1927).

p. 12 *Mr. Balfour of Pilrig*: Stevenson's great-great grandfather on his mother's side. The fictional Mr Balfour, a highly respected lawyer, is to provide David with an introductory letter to the Lord Advocate.

p. 12 *William Grant*: the first law-officer of the crown and public prosecutor of crimes for Scotland; William Grant Esquire of Prestongrange (1701–64) was appointed Lord Advocate in 1746.

p. 13   *pend*: arch.

p. 14   *screen*: shawl, headscarf.

p. 15   *landward*: country*.

p. 15   *the line*: David is referring to the Highland line, an imaginary boundary, generally seen as following that of the great fault between Dumbarton and Stonehaven, between the Highlands and Lowlands, or between the Gaelic-speaking regions and the English and Scots-speaking Lowlands.

p. 16   *Folk of Peace*: the Fairies*. According to Ronald Macdonald Douglas, the fairies, in Gaelic, "are spoken of as *Daoine Sithe*, which may be translated, strangely enough, as 'Men of Peace'" (*Scottish Lore and Folklore*, New York, 1982, pp. 109f.). In fact, *sìth* is the Gaelic word for peace; its homonym means "a fairy".

p. 16   *the Macgregors*: After defeating the Luss Colquhouns at the Battle of Glenfruin in 1603, the entire clan MacGregor was proscribed, and it became a capital offence to bear the name. The proscription was lifted briefly after 1660, but was not fully revoked by Act of Parliament until 1774. The most famous member of the clan was the Jacobite Rob Roy, who mobilised Clan Gregor for the Jacobite cause in 1715. Rob Roy's exploits were legendary, and he was made the hero of a novel by Walter Scott and at least two major films. Receiving a King's pardon in 1725, he ended his days peacefully, dying in 1734 at Inverlochlarig Beag at the head of the Glen of Balquidder.

p. 16   *Robin Oig*: (1715–54), the fifth and youngest son of Rob Roy. In 1750, with the help of his brother James Mor MacGregor, he abducted Jean Key, a rich widow, from Edinbellie farm, near Balfron. They were married at Rowardennan, but she died the following year. Robin was arrested and carried before the High Court of Justiciary at Edinburgh, accused of abduction and forcible marriage. He was found guilty and hanged in 1754.

p. 16 *a daughter of James More's*: James Mor[e] MacGregor, Rob Roy's eldest son. The name MacGregor being proscribed, he took the name Drummond. He fought for the Jacobite cause in 1745, and, as a Captain in the MacGregor Regiment, was wounded in the thigh at the Battle of Prestonpans. Together with his brother he was convicted in 1752 for the abduction of Jean Key (see above) and imprisoned in Edinburgh Castle. With the help of his daughter, who disguised herself as a cobbler, he escaped to Paris. There is reliable evidence to show that he tried to capture Alan Breck Stewart in order to obtain a pardon from the British Government. However, the attempt failed and he died penniless in France, leaving a widow and fourteen children in Scotland.

p. 17 *ta sneeshin*: the pinch of snuff. Several of the characters, including Neil and Catriona herself ("I am loving the smell of that place", p. 16), use pseudo-Highland features in their speech. Even David, presumably as a result of the attraction he feels for Catriona, begins to imitate her use of continuous tenses: "I could be wishing I had brought you a sprig of that heather" (p. 18. See also note to p. 172, on his being "attracted" to Doig's accent). Stevenson, in a letter to Sidney Colvin, admitted that his use of this pseudo-dialect was often problematic: "This is an old puzzle of mine. You see C.'s dialect is not wholly a bed of roses. If only I knew the Gaelic" (*Letters*, XXV, p. 295). As evidence that Stevenson's readers were not always convinced by his attempts to find a credible Gaelic-English crossover, Emma Letley (*Kidnapped and Catriona*, Oxford, 1986, p. 488) cites a review in *The Saturday Review*, LXXVI, 333, 16 September 1893: "Her [Catriona's] forms of speech remind us, rather irritatingly, of those which Mr. Black has put into the mouth of so many young men and maidens that, pleasantly exotic at first, they have at last become wofully hackneyed". For further discussion see Mairi Robinson, 'Modern Literary Scots: Ferguson and After', in: A. J. Aitken (ed.), *Lowland Scots: Papers Presented to an Edinburgh Conference*, Edinburgh, 1973.

p. 18   *gate*: way.

p. 18   *shune*: soon; *callant*: youth.

p. 18   *Cleikin' up wi' baubee-joes!*: linking arms with street-walkers.

p. 19   *capuchin*: hood, bonnet.

p. 19   *gaun ajee*: leaving the straight and narrow.

p. 21   *to lightly*: in reply to a query by Sidney Colvin, Stevenson replied: "to lightly" is a good regular Scots verb" (*Letters*, XXV, p. 249). In fact, the word is more frequent as "lichtlie": to make light of, scorn; *grue*: shudder.

p. 21   *silver button*: a token of trust given to David by Alan Breck. *Kidnapped*, serialized in the magazine *Young Folks* (1 May to 31 July 1886), bore the subtitle *The Lad with the Silver Button*.

p. 21   *buckie*: "A perverse or refractory person is thus denominated by an epithet conjoined; as, a *thrawn buckie*, and sometimes, in still harsher language, a *Deil's buckie*" (John Jamieson, *An Etymylogical Dictionary of the Scottish Language*, Edinburgh, 1808).

p. 21   *tow*: noose.

p. 21   *dod*: God (euphemistic).

p. 21   *Whig*: Stevenson glosses this term in *Kidnapped*: "Whig or Whigamore was the cant name for those who were loyal to King George".

p. 21   *black-foot*: go-between.

p. 21   *forfeited rebel*: After the defeat of Prince Charles Edward and the rout of the Jacobite clans at Culloden on 16th April 1746, the lands of the rebel chiefs, including those of Stewarts of Appin and Ardsheal, fell under the administration of a Committee of Forfeited Estates.

p. 21   *James*: James Stewart, or "James of the Glens", was a half-brother of the forfeited Stewart chief. Taken into custody on the charge of being "art and part of", or accessory to, the assassination of of Colin Campbell of Glenure, in the so-called Appin Murder (see note to p. 13 above), James was tried at Inverary before a practically all-Campbell jury presided over by the Duke of Argyll, the Campbell chief. He was found guilty and hanged on a gibbet overlooking the straits of Ballachulish where his bones, wired together, dangled as a warning for many years afterwards. The evidence leading to James Stewart's conviction, published in the *Precognitions* of the case, was later destroyed by order of the authorities, but a copy survives in the National Library of Scotland. For further information, see F. W. C. Hersey (ed.), *Robert Louis Stevenson's 'Kidnapped'. Followed by 'Who killed the Red Fox?'* (Boston, 1938), and David N. Mackay, *The Trial of James Stewart* (Edinburgh, 1907).

p. 22　*Cluny*: Ewen MacPherson of Cluny played a significant part in the Jacobite Rising of 1745. When his lands were forfeited in the aftermath of Culloden, Cluny lived in hiding for nine years, supported by his clansmen, despite a huge reward offered for his head. He finally escaped to France in 1755, only to die a year later. David and Alan Breck were guests at Cluny's "Cage" during their "flight through the heather".

p. 22　*Henderland*: in *Kidnapped*, an amicable catechist David meets in Morven, with whom he stays during the night before the Appin Murder. On that occasion, Henderland asks David for snuff, which he is unable to give him.

p. 24　*muckle*: big, great.

p. 24　*clanjamfry*: rabble

p. 25　*dooms*: extremely, "dashed".

p. 25　*laigh*: quietly.

p. 25　*willywhas*: flatteries*.

p. 26   *across the water*: the "King James" of the day was James Edward Stewart (1688–1766), son of James VII and II. Exiled in France, he was toasted as "the King over the water".

p. 26   *yadvocate*: there is but one entry for this word in the Scottish National Dictionary: "Nonce form of advocate (Sc. 1893 Stevenson *Catriona* ii)".

p. 26   *hurdies*: buttocks; *kye*: cows, kine.

p. 26   *Act of 1736: recruiting for King Lewie*: Act forbidding the recruiting of men for the French Jacobite regiments.

p. 27   *forbye*: besides.

p. 27   *Thristle*: since the first book edition (Cassell, London, 1893) editors have repeatedly left this unchanged, though the ship is later referred to as the "Thistle". There is some justification for this: though "thrissel", but not "thristle", is a common enough word for "thistle" in Scots, "thristle" or "throstle" can be a song-thrush. Birds' names – "Lark", "Swallow" etc. – are no less frequently lent to ships than heraldic symbols.

p. 27   *gey*: very, rather.

p. 27   *lippen to*: trust to*; *Chevalier*: James Edward Stewart was known as the "Old Chevalier".

p. 28   *Eli kennt of that!*: This must have reference to Dr. Cameron on his first visit. – D.B.*

p. 30   *Mungo Campbell or the sheriff's officer*: both present, according to *Kidnapped*, at the scene of the Appin Murder.

p. 31   *clachan*: hamlet.

p. 31   *bummed*: hummed.

p. 31   *joes*: sweethearts*.

p. 31   *spaed*: foretold.

p. 31   *pickle*: bit.

p. 31   *wean*: child*.

p. 31   *limmer*: old woman, hussy.

p. 31   *loof*: palm*.

p. 31   *weird*: fortune.

p. 31   *unco*: uncanny.

p. 31   *bree*: brow, face.

p. 31   *een*: eyes.

p. 31   *wuddy*: gallows*.

p. 33   *Questions*: my Catechism*.

p. 33   *warrandice*: a guarantee.

p. 39   *change-house*: a small inn.

p. 40   *Aucharn*: where James of the Glens held tenant rights.

p. 42   *Salus populi suprema lex*: The welfare of the people is the supreme legal principle (Cicero, *De Legibus*, II, 3, 8).

p. 42   *might be your father*: the relationship between David and Prestongrange is a mysterious one, with the latter's interest apparently alternating between paternal care and political foresight. Stevenson commented on the peculiar nature of the Lord Advocate's attentions in a letter to Sidney Colvin in April 1893: "'Tis a most curious thing to render that kind, insignificant mask. To make anything precise is to risk my effect. And till the day he died, Davie was never sure of what P. was after. Not only so; very often P. didn't know himself. There was an element of mere liking for Davie; there was an element of being determined, in case of accidents, to keep well of him. He hoped his Barbara would bring him to her feet, besides, and make him manageable. That was why he sent him to Hope Park with them. But Davie cannot *know*; I give you the inside of Davie, and my method condemns me to give only the outside of Prestongrange and his policy" (*Letters*, XXV, p. 294).

p. 44   *Cumberland came upon Drummossie*: William Augustus, Duke of Cumberland (1721-65), 2nd son of George II and Commander of The King's Army in Scotland. It was under Cumberland's command that the Jacobite army was defeated at Drummossie Moor, Culloden, in 1746.

p. 44   *Lord President Culloden*: Duncan Forbes, Laird of Culloden, Lord President of the Court of Session, used his considerable influence to dissuade many of the clans from rallying to Prince Charles' standard in 1745, yet went unrewarded by George II.

p. 44 *the Duke and the great clan of Campbell*: Archibald Campbell, 3rd Duke of Argyll (1682–1761), played such an important part in public affairs, especially through his support for the Hanoverian cause during the Jacobite Rising of 1745, that he became known as "King of Scotland".

p. 44 *disarming is a farce*: the third Disarming Act (there having been previous, even less effective Acts in 1716 and 1725), introduced by Lord Hardwicke in 1746, was one of several measures, including the Act of Proscription (1747), aimed at crushing the threat to Hanoverian rule in Scotland, destroying the clan system and undermining the social cohesion of "these barbarous and disloyal savages". The Act imposed severe penalties not only for possessing arms, but for wearing the kilt or playing the bagpipes, "both the dress and the music being considered too barbarous and martial for good citizenship" (T.C. Smout, *A History of the Scottish People 1560–1830*, Glasgow, 1960, p. 208).

p. 48 *ready for the surgeon now*: here David recalls a meeting at Balquidder with James More's brother, Robin Oig. At that time Robin had told David that "the surgeon that marched with our clan and cured my brother's leg when it was broken in the brush at Prestonpans, was a gentleman of the same name precisely as yourself" (*Kidnapped*, ed. Iain Galbraith, Cologne, 1996, p. 186).

p. 49 *skelped*: slapped, smacked.

p. 50 *Allan Ramsay's answer*: Allan Ramsay (1686–1758), a Scottish poet, best known for the pastoral comedy *The Gentle Shepherd* (1725), his anthology of Middle Scots verse *The Ever Green* (1724), the five volumes of his *Tea Table Miscellany* (1724–37), which collected many of the traditional songs and ballads of Scotland, and for collections of his own verse which he published in 1721 and 1728. David's allusion is to Ramsay's poem 'Spoken to Three Young Ladies, who would have me determine which of them was the bonniest'. The "honest" poet's answer was:

> Shaw, a' your charms, and then ha'e wi' ye,
> > Faith I shall be your Paris
> > > (*Poems*, Glasgow, 1797, I, 173).

p. 54   *distasted at the first look*: David's reaction to the two-faced Simon Lovat recalls reactions to another of Stevenson's characters: Edward Hyde inspires "loathing ... at first sight" in all whom he meets (*Strange Case of Dr. Jekyll and Mr. Hyde*, ed. Michael Hulse, Cologne, 1995, p. 9).

p. 54   *Master of Lovat and chief of the great clan Fraser*: son of Simon Fraser, the 11th Lord Lovat, a noted Jacobite, of whom legend had it that he was captured in Morar "hiding in a hollow tree ... but without the wit to cover his legs" (John Prebble, *Culloden*, London, 1961). He was executed in 1747. During the 1745 Jacobite Rising he sent his first son, the nineteen-year-old Simon Fraser, Master of Lovat, to command his Fraser clansmen at Culloden. According to records, the young Simon Fraser was probably not on the field, but he was taken prisoner and pardoned in 1750. In 1752 he acted as advocate for the widow of Colin Campbell of Glenure. His family estates were restored in 1771.

p. 55   *experto crede*: or *credite* (Virgil, *Aeneid*, XI, 283): trust one who has had experience.

p. 57   *usquebaugh*: *uisge beatha* (Gael.), the water of life, commonly known as whisky.

p. 57   *craig*: neck.

p. 59   *link*: hurry.

p. 59   *cateran*: probably from the Gaelic *ceatharn*, a troop,

302

usually of soldiers. The term "cateran" was first used in the 16th century to denote Highland cattle-thieves, or Highland marauders into the Lowlands.

p. 59   *gyte*: mad.

p. 61   *Lang Dykes*: now Princes Street*.

p. 62   *mutch*: a kind of hood, or coif, chiefly of linen; a close-fitting cap worn by married women.

p. 63   *cuif*: idiot, simpleton.

p. 63   *keeping company*: courting.

p. 64   *bruckle*: fragile, delicate.

p. 64   *wrunkled chafts*: wrinkled cheeks.

p. 64   *untenty*: careless.

p. 64   *deaved*: plagued.

p. 64   *fleeching*: flattering.

p. 64   *a wheen blethers*: a bunch of nonsense.

p. 65   *oxter*: armpit.

p. 65   *taigling*: dallying.

p. 65   *creel*: confusion.

p. 67   *rudas*: wild.

p. 70   *bogles*: ghosts.

p. 75   *Palfour*: see note to p. 17.

p. 76   *craigs*: rocks.

p. 78   *mind*: remember.

p. 82   *horn-mad*: thoroughly mad.

p. 82   *doer*: agent.

p. 82   *remeid*: remedy.

p. 82   *non-compearance*: failing to appear before a court (Sc. law).

p. 84   *the Act of Parliament of 1700*: in Scotland, the Act Anent Wrongous Imprisonment, the equivalent of the English Habeas Corpus, was passed in 1701.

p. 85   *begowk*: make a fool of.

p. 85   *harle*: small amount of something obtained with difficulty.

p. 85   *sumptibus moesti rei*: at the expense of the unhappy defendant.

p. 86 *Lady Grange*: Rachel Grange, the wife of James Erskine, brother of the Earl of Mar and Justice-Clerk from 1710. Erskine kept his wife imprisoned on the remote island of St. Kilda for many years for fear she would disclose his Jacobite activities.

p. 86 *kenning*: trifle.

p. 87 *fash*: trouble.

p. 89 *carline*: witchlike.

p. 90 *Lot's wife*: in *Genesis*, 19. She looked back at Sodom and Gomorrah and was turned into a pillar of salt.

p. 90 *driech*: or dreich, tedious, dull.

p. 90 *grat*: wept.

p. 90 *Catherine Douglas*: according to legend Katherine Douglas, sometimes known as Katherine "Barlass", is said to have barred the door of the royal appartment at Perth's Blackfriars by using her arm as a bar, in a courageous but unsuccessful attempt to help King James I escape when his murderers, led by Sir Robert Graham, came for him on the night of 21 February 1437.

p. 91 *our battle in the brig*: see Chapter X of *Kidnapped*.

p. 92 *all the sons of Alpin*: In Gaelic tradition, the Grants are descended from *Sìol Ailpein*, the descendants of the Dalraidic king Alpin (died c. 840). This involves kindred with the MacGregors: it was believed that Clan Grant descended from the 12th-century Gregor More Mac-Gregor. The Gaelic word for Scotland is *Alba*, but the word pre-dates King Alpin, while "Albion" was the term used for Britain before Roman times. When Kenneth I, son of King Alpin, defeated the Picts in 850, he created a kingdom of Picts and Scots called Alba. However, there is no question of the Gaels of Alba ever having fought against Alexander the Great. The slip is not without realism, since Gaelic oral history frequently flows into myth, but its function here is to show David's respect for the fragility of Catriona's romantic self-esteem.

p. 95 *byke*: nest.

p. 95   *black knife*: (Gael.) *sgian dhu*.

p. 95   *dovering*: wandering.

p. 97   *stave*: stagger.

p. 97   *mill-lade*: mill-race.

p. 97   *selvage*: border.

p. 101 *wambly*: shaky.

p. 101 *cowped*: fell.

p. 101 *birkies*: lively fellows.

p. 101 *hunkering*: huddling.

p. 102 *spreagh*: herd of cattle stolen and driven off in a raid, especially by Highlanders from the Lowlands.

p. 102 *black soldiers*: the Black Watch, or Am Freiceadan Dubh, a military police force or 'watch' set up in 1725 to keep order and uphold the Hanoverian interests in the Highlands after the 1715 Jacobite Rebellion.

p. 102 *bauchle*: muddle.

p. 102 *bield*: shelter.

p. 102 *twine*: part.

p. 102 *ae*: one.

p. 104 *bauks*: ridges.

p. 104 *linky*: sandy.

p. 105 *gomeril*: fool.

p. 105 *divots*: sods, peat used for fuel.

p. 105 *caller*: fresh; *lift*: sky.

p. 105 *laverock*: lark.

p. 105 *pit mirk*: dark as the pit.

p. 105 *dowp*: end.

p. 106 *warstled*: struggled.

p. 107 *by-ordinar*: extraordinary.

p. 107 *blagyard*: scurrilous.

p. 108 *rizzoring*: "Rizzard haddocks are prepared in much the same manner (i.e. hung up with their skin on, and broiled without being rubbed in flour, *Ed.*), but are usually sprinkled with salt inside and outside, and allowed to lie thus for twelve hours before being hung up in the open air, preferably in the wind and always out of the sun" (F. Marian McNeill, *The Scots Kitchen*, Edinburgh, 1929, p. 118).

p. 108 *Prestonpans*: the scene of a Jacobite victory during the Rising of 1745. Sir John Cope, the English Commander-in-Chief, had landed his troops at Dunbar and marched on Edinburgh which, by that time, was firmly in the hands of Prince Charles Edward Stewart. Cope was determined to crush the rebellion before it gathered strength. However, at Gladsmuir, on 21 September 1745, Cope, awaiting reinforcements from Berwick, encountered the Prince's army under the command of Lord George Murray and suffered an inglorious defeat.

p. 109 *luckie*: landlady.

p. 109 *fleering*: sneering.

p. 110 *het*: hot.

p. 110 *hoast*: cough.

p. 110 *his lane*: on his own.

p. 110 *kale-yard*: cabbage patch.

p. 111 *canty*: cheerful; *cracky*: talkative, friendly.

p. 111 *Johnnie Cope*: see note to p. 108.

p. 114 *kittle*: delicate.

p. 114 *swither*: hesitate.

p. 115 *thole a raxing*: suffer a stretching.

p. 116 *hotching*: itching.

p. 118 *unchancy*: unlucky.

p. 121 *Tantallon*: Tantallon Castle, near North Berwick, dating from the mid-14th century, was probably built by William, 1st Earl of Douglas. It was besieged on several occasions to little effect and was thought impregnable. A popular saying went: "Ding doon Tantallon, mak a brig' to the Bass" (knock down Tantallon, build a bridge to the Bass Rock), a putdown of anyone suggesting the impossible. But in 1651 it was successfully stormed by General Monk who laid siege to a troop of Covenanters. The ruin has remained ever since in much the same state as General Monk left it.

p. 122 *The Bass*: a volcanic plug at the entrance to the Firth of Forth. Famous as a bird sanctuary and home to a colony of gannets, or solan geese. The rock has a 16th century chapel on the site of the hermitage of St. Baldred, a 7th or 8th century monk, and the ruins of an earlier fortress.

p. 122 *ava'*: at all.

p. 122 *plowter*: splashing.

p. 124 *Cameronian extremes*: Richard Cameron, one of the most zealous of the Covenanters (see note to p. 134), known as the "Lion of the Covenant". Cameron, returning from exile in Holland, where he had been sent in 1678 to "learn to hold in check the ardencies of his heart and tongue", raised an extremist "army" – the Cameronians – and published the Declaration of Sanquar in 1680. He went into hiding and was eventually killed near Auchinleck.

p. 124 *gauger*: exciseman.

p. 126 *martyrs*: the Bass Rock was bought by the government from the Lauder family in 1651 and used as a prison for the confinement of Covenanters and, later, Jacobites, a group of whom captured the rock in June 1691 and held it until April 1694, when they were granted an amnesty.

p. 129 *trokings*: dealings.

p. 129 *minting*: insinuating.

p. 129 *forrit*: forward.

p. 129 *nae skaith*: no harm.

p. 129 *hantle*: lot.

p. 129 *kintry*: country.

p. 131 *upon his body*: A learned folklorist of my acquaintance hereby identifies Alan's air. It has been printed (it seems) in Campbell's "Tales of the West Highlands," vol. ii., p. 91. Upon examination it would really seem as if Miss Grant's unrhymed doggerel (see Chapter v.) would fit, with a little humouring, to the notes in question. – R.L.S.*

p. 131 *The Tale of Tod Lapraik*: In a letter to Sidney Colvin in

1893 Stevenson rejects the suggestion that he should include notes on the Scots words in this tale: "I'd have to put a note to every word; and he who can't read Scots can *never* enjoy Tod Lapraik. ... *Tod Lapraik* is a piece of living Scots: if I had never writ anything but that and *Thrawn Janet*, still I'd have been a writer" (*Letters*, XXV, pp. 294f.).

p. 131 *sploring*: wildly behaved.

p. 131 *ran-dan*: drinking-match.

p. 132 *vivers*: food.

p. 132 *büt to*: had to.

p. 132 *the Days of the Persecution*: Black Andie is referring to the persecution of the Covenanters. The National Covenant of 1638 was a public petition presuming a direct relationship with God and rejecting interference by the king and "all kinds of Papistry". After the Civil War and the defeat of the Covenanters by Cromwell at the Battle of Dunbar (1650) and Charles II's restoration of episcopacy in 1660, the Covenanters resisted and defected from the church, forming military groups that were fiercely persecuted by the civil and episcopal powers. However, "a military 'solution' was ineffective against fanatics or informed believers. Some 18,000 are estimated to have died in persecutions and encounters between 1661-88, leaving a bitter memory that has tainted and distorted Church and civil history. The harsh line taken by Archbishop Sharp of St. Andrews led to his murder in 1679 on Magus Moor and to the 'Killing Time' retaliation ruthlessly performed by John Graham of Claverhouse, later Viscount Dundee. The violence carried out in the name of religion degenerated into civil disorder creating martyrs of innocent victims and subversive terrorists alike" (*Collins Encyclopaedia of Scotland*, ed. John and Julia Keay, London, 1994, p. 190).

p. 132 *perishin' cauld chalmers*: the cold prison cells.

p. 132 *saut of the yerd*: salt of the earth.

p. 132 *riving*: rending.

p. 132 *Peden the Prophet*: Alexander Peden (c. 1626–86), one of the most charismatic and inspirational of Covenanting preachers. He was ordained a minister in 1660 but was deprived of his post two years later. He then preached at Conventicles, i.e. unauthorised and outlawed gatherings which usually took place outdoors. In June 1673 he was seized at a Conventicle near Ballantrae and sentenced to four years' imprisonment on the Bass Rock.

p. 133 *flyting*: arguing.

p. 133 *gash an' waefu'*: ghastly and sorrowful; *wi' his lang chafts an' luntin een, the maud haappit about his kist*: with his drooping cheeks and glaring eyes, and his plaid wrapped round his chest.

p. 133 *fyke*: commotion.

p. 133 *whether for his name or his nature*: tod, a fox; applied to a person, a sly, cunning, untrustworthy character.

p. 134 *loan*: roadway.

p. 134 *cantrips*: magic, mischief; *when the Queen was on the seas*: Andie is presumably referring to the practices of Stewart of Bothwell, a bastard of James V and a warlock whose coven was alleged to have raised the storm that delayed the return of James VI with his bride Anne of Denmark in 1590.

p. 134 *sneck*: latch.

p. 134 *but*: outer room.

p. 134 *hash*: mess, slovenly person; *creish*: fat.

p. 134 *gart me scunner*: disgusted me.

p. 134 *cawed the shuttle*: moved the shuttle to and fro; *steekit*: closed.

p. 134 *dowp*: bottom.

p. 134 *jimp*: just.

p. 134 *dwam*: swoon, trance, daydream.

p. 134 *speldering*: sprawling.

p. 134 *steighest*: steepest; *tenty*: careful.

p. 135 *pyking*: picking.

p. 134 *wroucht*: wrought.

p. 135 *birzing*: fraying.

p. 135 *stend*: sudden feeling.

p. 135 *gart*: made.

p. 135 *laigher*: lower.

p. 135 *dadding*: falling heavily.

p. 136 *whillywha*: persuade.

p. 136 *speiring*: asking.

p. 136 *ilka*: every

p. 136 *press bed*: a bed built into a recess with wooden doors.

p. 136 *crap*: crept.

p. 137 *crunkle*: wrinkle, fold.

p. 137 *clum*: climbed.

p. 137 *tester*: sixpence.

p. 137 *wanchancy*: uncanny, ill-fated.

p. 137 *lowped and flang*: leaped and capered.

p. 137 *skelloch*: scream.

p. 138 *diddling his elbock*: the arm movements of a fiddler.

p. 138 *dinnling*: trembling.

p. 138 *duddy*: ragged; *feckless*: spiritless; *doddered*: withered.

p. 139 *hadna played buff*: had made no impression.

p. 139 sorrow a: not a.

p. 139 *puddock*: frog.

p. 139 *stot*: bullock, clumsy person.

p. 139 *denner*: dinner.

p. 142 *Isle Earraid*: the isthmus of Erraid, or Earraid, off the south coast of Mull, where David is shipwrecked in Chapter XIV of *Kidnapped*. As a young man, Stevenson had stayed for three weeks on Erraid where his father was supervising the construction of the Dhu Hearteach lighthouse. He recalled his experiences in 'Memoirs of an Islet' (*Memories and Portraits*, IX, p. 68). His story 'The Merry Men' is also set on Erraid.

p. 144 *In vain is the net spread in the sight of any fowl*: Proverbs I, 17.

p. 145 *goo*: liking.

p. 145 *feggs!*: faith!

p. 145 *lang-heided*: shrewd.

p. 148 *Romans 5th and 13th*: these texts are concerned with the law of God; here they act as an ironic commentary on man's law, so easily corrupted in the trial of "James of the Glens".

p. 150 *macer*: an official who keeps order in a court of law (Sc. law); *'Cruachan'*: Cruachan: the rallying-cry of the Campbells. After the peaks of Cruachan Beann, above Loch Awe and Innis Chonaill, the original island stronghold of the Campbells of Argyll.

p. 150 *oak shall go over the myrtle yet*: the Stewart oak shall beat the Campbell myrtle. Stewart is referring to the clan badges.

p. 150 *ding*: beat.

p. 151 *Lord Ordinary*: a judge of the Outer House of the Court of Session (Sc. law).

p. 152 *bourock*: mound.

p. 153 *redd out*: arranged.

p. 154 *a riot in Edinburgh*: the reference is to the Porteous Affair. In 1736, a certain Captain Porteous, who had been sentenced to death for firing on an angry crowd protesting at the public execution of a smuggler, but was subsequently reprieved by Queen Caroline, acting as Regent for George II, was taken from prison and lynched by an angry crowd. The Queen took this as a personal insult and announced her intention of "making Scotland a hunting ground". The incident is described at the beginning of Walter Scott's novel *Heart of Midlothian* (1818).

p. 162 *aefauld*: honest.

p. 162 *"The House of Airlie"*: a Scots ballad about the destruction of the House of Airlie by the Earl of Argyll in 1640. Emma Letley refers astutely to Stevenson's use of songs and ballads at this point in the text "to stress ...

the misconduct of James's trial, and to make a further contrast with the anglicized, legal voice. The fact that a darker commentary, found both in the narrative and in the songs, follows on from the tale of the diabolic makes a strong imaginative link between the dualistic elements dramatized in 'Tod Lapraik' and the double-dealing and duplicity so strongly present in James's trial" (*Kidnapped and Catriona*, Oxford, 1986, p. xxv).

p. 164 *the Tee'd Ball*: a ball placed upon a little mound for convenience of striking* (in golf).

p. 165 *glisk*: gleam, moment.

p. 165 *old Mr. Campbell's word*: Mr. Campbell, the minister of David's home village Essendean, who, in *Kidnapped*, gave David some friendly advice on the day when he "took the key for the last time out of the door of my father's house" and set out to find his fortune.

p. 167 *gravatt*: scarf, muffler.

p. 167 *clouted brogues*: patched shoes*.

p. 167 *soutar*: shoemaker*.

p. 168 *ayont*: beyond.

p. 169 *fashious*: troublesome.

p. 169 *misdoubt your lordship's liking*: see note to p. 42.

p. 169 *nothing in my chafts*: nothing between my cheeks.

p. 171 *ahint-hand*: late.

p. 171 *steer*: stir.

p. 171 *wauch*: drink.

p. 171 *Tamson's mear*: Tamson's mare – to go afoot*.

p. 172 *an accent much more countrified than I was usually careful to affect*: Stevenson commented on this tendency in a letter to Sidney Colvin: "Davie would be attracted into a similar dialect, as he is later – e.g. with Doig, chapter xix. This is truly Scottish" (*Letters*, XXV, p. 294). See also note to p. 15 above. For a useful discussion of the "truly Scottish" tendency to affect an English accent see Robert Crawford, *Devolving English Literature*, Oxford, 1992, especially pp. 22-33).

p. 173 *baird*: beard*.

p. 174 *timmer*: stupid.

p. 174 *raired*: roared.

p. 183 *tautit*: ragged*.

p. 183 *braws*: fine things*.

p. 183 *gowk*: fool.

p. 184 *kep*: catch*.

p. 186 *duds*: clothes.

p. 187 *vivers*: victuals*.

p. 189 *sorning*: scrounging.

p. 189 *lippen*: trust*.

p. 189 *vails*: tips.

p. 193 *smuisty*: smoky.

p. 193 *haar*: sea-fog.

p. 194 *blate*: bashful*.

p. 199 *Jean Kay*: see notes to p. 16. Rob Roy had acquired the lands of Inversnaid on the east shore of Loch Lomond in 1701. Robin Oig MacGregor and Jean Kay (or Key) were married at Rowardennan, further south and also on the east shore.

p. 199 *got claught of*: got hold of.

p. 200 *lave*: rest*.

p. 203 *look the road of*: take notice of, recognize.

p. 204 *thrid*: threaded.

p. 204 *geyan*: very.

p. 209 *wheen*: few.

p. 209 *fallows*: fellows.

p. 210 *hellicat*: good-for-nothing.

p. 212 *wauf-like*: disreputable.

p. 215 *overcome*: refrain, recurring theme.

p. 216 *set you on the jee*: disturb you.

p. 217 *hap*: wrap.

p. 217 *slaistering*: washing down.

p. 218 *sweer*: reluctant.

p. 220 *pleached*: intertwined.

p. 220 *pirn*: weaver's spool.

p. 222 *Heineccius*: Johann Gottlieb Heineccius (1681–1741), a German rationalist and jurist. He became Professor of Philosophy at Halle University in 1713 and Professor of Jurisprudence in 1718.

p. 248 *Drummossie*: see note to p. 42.

p. 248 *friend*: relation.

p. 250 *hirsled*: dragged.

p. 250 *rowt*: roar.

p. 256 *loundered*: aimed.

p. 256 *collieshangie*: uproar.

p. 263 *Lord Holderness*: an English politician (c. 1718–78), Secretary of State from 1751 to 1761. James More probably corresponded with Holderness in his attempt to obtain a pardon from the English Government (see note to p. 16).

p. 263 *Gladsmuir*: see note to p. 108.

p. 265 *wame*: belly.

p. 266 *caller*: refreshing.

p. 266 *girn*: grin.

p. 267 *bullering*: gurgling.

p. 268 *tyke*: dog.

p. 268 *airn*: iron.

p. 273 *knowe*: knoll.

p. 278 *jink*: dodge.

p. 278 *dawtie*: darling.

p. 279 *gutsey*: greedy.

p. 280 *glee'd*: crooked.

p. 281 *Rodomonts*: braggers. After the blustering figure of Rodomonte in Ariosto's *Orlando Furioso*.

p. 281 *pockmantie*: portmanteau. According to Stevenson, "the rape of the pockmantie is historic" (*Letters*, XXV, p. 295).